TAKEN ALIVE

AND OTHER STORIES

WITH AN AUTOBIOGRAPHY

E. P. Roe

1st WORLD
LIBRARY
Literary Society

Taken Alive and Other Stories

E. P. Roe

© 1st World Library – Literary Society, 2004
PO Box 2211
Fairfield, IA 52556
www.1stworldlibrary.org
First Edition

LCCN: 2004091180

Softcover ISBN: 1-59540-626-3
eBook ISBN: 1-59540-726-X

Purchase *"Taken Alive"*
as a traditional bound book at:
www.1stWorldLibrary.org/purchase.asp?ISBN=1-59540-626-3

1st World Library Literary Society is a nonprofit organization dedicated to promoting literacy by:

- Creating a free internet library accessible from any computer worldwide.
- Hosting writing competitions and offering book publishing scholarships.

Readers interested in supporting literacy through sponsorship, donations or membership please contact:
literacy@1stworldlibrary.org
Check us out at: www.1stworldlibrary.org

Taken Alive
contributed by the Charles Family
in support of
1st World Library Literary Society

CONTENTS

"A NATIVE AUTHOR CALLED ROE"

An Autobiography

Two or three years ago the editor of "Lippincott's Magazine" asked me, with many others, to take part in the very interesting "experience meeting" begun in the pages of that enterprising periodical. I gave my consent without much thought of the effort involved, but as time passed, felt slight inclination to comply with the request. There seemed little to say of interest to the general public, and I was distinctly conscious of a certain sense of awkwardness in writing about myself at all. The question, Why should I? always confronted me.

When this request was again repeated early in the current year, I resolved at least to keep my promise. This is done with less reluctance now, for the reason that floating through the press I meet with paragraphs concerning myself that are incorrect, and often absurdly untrue. These literary and personal notes, together with many questioning letters, indicate a certain amount of public interest, and I have concluded that it may be well to give the facts to those who care to know them.

It has been made more clear to me that there are many who honestly do care. One of the most prized rewards of my literary work is the ever-present consciousness that my writings have drawn around me a circle of unknown yet stanch friends, who have stood by me unfalteringly for a number of years. I should indeed be lacking if my heart did not go out to them in responsive friendliness and goodwill. If I looked upon them merely as an aggregation of customers, they would find me out speedily. A popular mood is a very different thing from an abiding popular interest. If one could address this circle of friends only, the embarrassment attendant on a certain amount of egotism would be banished by the assurance of sympathetic regard. Since, from the nature of circumstances, this is impossible, it seems to me in better taste to consider the "author called Roe" in an objective, rather than in a friendly and subjective sense. In other words, I shall try to look at him from the public point of view, and free myself from some predisposition in his favor shared by his friends. I suppose I shall not succeed in giving a colorless statement of fact, but I may avoid much special pleading in his behalf.

Like so many other people, I came from a very old family, one from which there is good proof of an unbroken line through the Dark Ages, and all ages, to the first man. I have never given any time to tracing ancestry, but have a sort of quiet satisfaction that mine is certainly American as far as it well can be. My forefathers (not "rude," to my knowledge) were among the first settlers on the Atlantic seaboard. My paternal and maternal grandfathers were stanch Whigs during the Revolution, and had the courage of their convictions. My grandmother escaped with her children from the village of Kingston almost as the British entered it, and her home was soon in ashes. Her husband, James Roe, was away in the army. My mother died some years before I attained my majority, and I cannot remember when she was not an invalid. Such literary tendencies as I have are derived from her, but I do not possess a tithe of her intellectual power. Her story-books in her youth were the classics; and when she was but twelve years of age she knew "Paradise Lost" by heart. In my recollections of her, the Bible and all works tending to elucidate its prophecies were her favorite themes of study. The retentiveness of her memory was very remarkable. If any one repeated a verse of the New Testament, she could go on and finish the chapter. Indeed, she could quote the greater part of the Bible with the ease and accuracy of one reading from the printed page. The works of Hugh Miller and the Arctic Explorations of Dr. Kane afforded her much pleasure. Confined usually to her room, she took unfailing delight in wandering about the world with the great travellers of that day, her strong fancy reproducing the scenes they described. A stirring bit of history moved her deeply. Well do I remember, when a boy, of reading to her a chapter from Motley's "Dutch Republic," and of witnessing in her flushed cheeks and sparkling black eyes proof of an excitement all too great for one in her frail health. She had the unusual gift of relating in an easy, simple way what she read; and many a book far too abstruse and dull for my boyish taste became an absorbing story from her lips. One of her chief characteristics was the love of flowers. I can scarcely recall her when a flower of some kind, usually a rose, was not within her reach; and only periods of great feebleness kept her from their daily care, winter and summer. Many descendants of her floral pets are now blooming in my garden.

My father, on the other hand, was a sturdy man of action. His love for the country was so strong that he retired from business in New York as soon as he had won a modest competence. For forty-odd years he never wearied in the cultivation of his little valley farm, and the square, flower-bordered garden, at one side of which ran an unfailing brook. In this garden and under his tuition I acquired my love of horticulture - acquired it with many a backache - heartache too, on days good for fishing or hunting; but, taking the bitter with the sweet, the sweet predominated. I find now that I think only of the old-fashioned roses in the borders, and not of my hands bleeding from the thorns. If I groaned over the culture of many vegetables, it was much compensation to a boy that the dinner-table groaned also under the succulent dishes thus provided. I observed that my father's interest in his garden and farm never flagged, thus proving that in them is to be found a pleasure which does not pall with age. During the last summer of his life, when in his eighty-seventh year, he had the delight of a child in driving over to my home in the early morning, long before I was up, and in leaving a basket of sweet corn or some other vegetable which he knew would prove his garden to be ahead of mine.

My father was very simple and positive in his beliefs, always openly foremost in the reform movements of his day and in his neighborhood, yet never, to my knowledge, seeking or taking any office. His house often became a station of the "underground railroad" in slavery times, and on one night in the depth of winter he took a hotly-pursued fugitive in his sleigh and drove him five miles on the ice, diagonally across the Hudson, to Fishkill, thence putting the brave aspirant for freedom on the way to other friends. He incurred several risks in this act. It is rarely safe to drive on the river off the beaten tracks at night, for there are usually air-holes, and the strong tides are continually making changes in the ice. When told that he might be sent to jail for his defiance of the Fugitive Slave Law, he quietly answered, "I can go to jail." The thing he could not do was to deny the man's appeal to him for help. Before the war he was known as an Abolitionist - after it, as a Conservative, his sympathy with and for the South being very strong. During the draft riots in 1863 the spirit of lawlessness was on the point of breaking out in the river towns. I happened to be home from Virginia, and learned that my father's house was among those marked for burning on a certain night. During this night the horde gathered; but one of their leaders had received such empathetic warning of what would happen the following day should outrages be perpetrated, that he persuaded his associates to desist. I sat up that night at my father's door with a double-barrelled gun, more impressed with a sense of danger than at any other time in my experience; he, on the contrary, slept as quietly as a child.

He often practiced close economy in order to give his sons a good education. The one act of my life which I remember with unalloyed pride and pleasure occured while I was at boarding-school in Vermont, preparing for college. I learned through my mother that my father had denied himself his daily newspaper; and I knew well how much he would miss it. We burned wood in the large stone seminary building. Every autumn great ranks of hard maple were piled up, and students who wished to earn a little money were paid a dollar a cord for sawing it into three lengths. I applied for nine cords, and went at the unaccustomed task after study hours. My back aches yet as I recall the experiences of subsequent weeks, for the wood was heavy, thick, and hard as bone. I eventually had the pleasure of sending to my father the subscription price of his paper for a year. If a boy reads these lines, let me assure him that he will never know a sweeter moment in his life than when he receives the thanks of his parents for some such effort in their behalf. No investment can ever pay him better.

In one of my books, "Nature's Serial Story," my father and mother appear, slightly idealized.

Toward the close of my first year in Williams College a misfortune occurred which threatened to be very serious. Studying by defective light injured my eyes. They quickly became so sensitive that I could scarcely endure lamplight or the heat of a stove, only the cold out-door air relieving the pain; so I spent much time in wandering about in the boisterous weather of early spring in Williamstown. At last I became so discouraged that I went to President Hopkins and told him that I feared I must give up the purpose of acquiring an education. Never can I forget how that grand old man met the disheartened boy. Speaking in the wise, friendly way which subdued the heart and strengthened the will, he made the half-hour spent with him the turning-point of my life. In conclusion, he advised me to enter the Senior class the following fall, thus taking a partial course of study. How many men are living to-day who owe much of the best in their lives to that divinely inspired guide and teacher of youth!

I next went to another man great in his sphere of life - Dr. Agnew, the oculist. He gave my eyes a thorough examination, told me that he could do nothing for them; that rest and the vigor acquired from out-door life would restore them. He was as kind and sympathetic in his way as the college president, and charged but a trifle, to relieve me from the sense of taking charity. Dr. Agnew's words proved correct; and the following autumn I entered the class of '61, and spent a happy year. Some of my classmates were very kind in reading aloud to me, while Dr. Hopkins's instruction was invaluable. By the time I entered Auburn Theological Seminary, my eyes were quite restored, and I was able to go through the first year's course of study without difficulty. In the summer of 1862 I could no longer resist the call for men in the army. Learning that the Second New York (Harris's Light) Cavalry was without a chaplain, I obtained the appointment to that position. General Kilpatrick was then lieutenant-colonel, and in command of the regiment. In December, 1862, I witnessed the bloody and disastrous battle of Fredericksburg, and can never forget the experiences of that useless tragedy. I was conscious of a sensation which struck me as too profound to be merely awe. Early in the morning we crossed the Rappahannock on a pontoon bridge and marched up the hill to an open plain. The roar of the battle was simply terrific, shading off from the sharp continuous thunder immediately about us to dull, heavy mutterings far to the right and left. A few hundred yards before us, where the ground began to slope up to the fatal heights crowned with Confederate works and ordnance, were long lines of Union batteries. From their iron mouths puffs of smoke issued incessantly, followed by tremendous reverberations. Back of these batteries the ground was covered with men lying on their arms, that they might present a less obvious target. Then a little further to the rear, on the level ground above the bluff, stood our cavalry. Heavy guns on both sides of the river were sending their great shrieking shells back and forth over our heads, and we often "ducked" instinctively when the missile was at least forty feet above us. Even our horses shuddered at the sound.

I resolved to learn if the men were sharing in my emotions - in brief, what effect the situation had upon them - and rode slowly down our regimental line. So vivid was the impression of that long array of awed, pallid faces that at this moment I can recall them distinctly. There were strange little touches of mingled pathos and humor. Meadow-larks were hemmed in on every side, too frightened to fly far beyond the rude alarms. They would flutter up into the sulphurous air with plaintive cries, then drop again into the open spaces between the troops. At one time, while we were standing at our horses' heads, a startled rabbit ran to us for cover. The poor little creature meant a dinner to the fortunate captor on a day when a dinner was extremely problematical. We engaged in a sharp scramble, the prize being won by the regimental surgeon, who kindly shared his game with me.

General Bayard, commanding our brigade, was mortally wounded, and died like a hero. He was carried to a fine mansion near which he had received his injury. Many other desperately wounded men were brought to the spacious rooms of this abode of Southern luxury, and the surgeons were kept busy all throught the day and night. It was here I gained my first experience in hospital work. This extemporized hospital on the field was so exposed as to be speedily abandoned. In the morning I recrossed the Rappahannock with my regiment, which had been ordered down the river on picket duty. Soon after we

E. P. Roe

went into winter quarters in a muddy cornfield. In February I resigned, with the purpose of completing my studies, and spent the remainder of the term at the Union Theological Seminary of New York. My regiment would not get another chaplain, so I again returned to it. In November I received a month's leave of absence, and was married to Miss Anna P. Sands, of New York City. Our winter quarters in 1864 were at Stevensburg, between the town of Culpeper and the Rapidan River. During the pleasant days of late February several of the officers were enjoying the society of their wives. Mrs. Roe having expressed a willingness to rough it with me for a week, I sent for her, and one Saturday afternoon went to the nearest railroad station to meet her. The train came, but not my wife; and, much disappointed, I found the return ride of five miles a dreary one in the winter twilight. I stopped at our colonel's tent to say to him and his wife that Mrs. Roe had not come, then learned for the first time very startling tidings.

"Chaplain," said the colonel, "we are going to Richmond to-morrow. We are going to wade right through and past everything in a neck-or-nothing ride, and who will come out is a question."

His wife was weeping in her private tent, and I saw that for the first time in my acquaintance with him he was downcast. He was one of the bravest of men, yet now a foreboding of evil oppressed him. The result justified it, for he was captured during the raid, and never fully rallied after the war from the physical depression caused by his captivity. He told me that on the morrow General Kilpatrick would lead four thousand picked cavalry men in a raid on Richmond, having as its special object the release of our prisoners.

I rode to the headquarters of the general, who confirmed the tidings, adding, "You need not go. Non-combatants are not expected to go."

It was most fortunate that my wife had not come. I had recently been appointed chaplain of Hampton Hospital, Virginia, by President Lincoln, and was daily expecting my confirmation by the Senate. I had fully expected to give my wife a glimpse of army life in the field, and then to enter on my new duties. To go or not to go was a question with me that night. The raid certainly offered a sharp contrast with the anticipated week's outing with my bride. I did not possess by nature that kind of courage which is indifferent to danger; and life had never offered more attractions than at that time. I have since enjoyed Southern hospitality abundantly, and hope to again, but then its prospect was not alluring. Before morning, however, I reached the decision that I would go, and during the Sunday forenoon held my last service in the regiment. I had disposed of my horse, and so had to take a sorry beast at the last moment, the only one I could obtain.

In the dusk of Sunday evening four thousand men were masked in the woods on the banks of the Rapidan. Our scouts opened the way by wading the stream and pouncing upon the unsuspecting picket of twenty Confederates opposite. Then away we went across a cold, rapid river, marching all that night through the dim woods and openings in a country that was emphatically the enemy's. Lee's entire army was on our right, the main Confederate cavalry force on our left. The strength of our column and its objective point could not remain long unknown.

In some unimportant ways I acted as aid for Kilpatrick.

E. P. Roe

A few hundred yards in advance of the main body rode a vanguard of two hundred men, thrown forward to warn us should we strike any considerable number of the enemy's cavalry. As is ever the case, the horses of a small force will walk away from a much larger body, and it was necessary from time to time to send word to the vanguard, ordering it to "slow up." This order was occasionally intrusted to me. I was to gallop over the interval between the two columns, then draw up by the roadside and sit motionless on my horse till the general with his staff came up. The slightest irregularity of action would bring a shot from our own men, while the prospect of an interview with the Johnnies while thus isolated was always good. I saw one of our officers shot that night. He had ridden carelessly into the woods, and rode out again just before the head of the column, without instantly accounting for himself. As it was of vital importance to keep the movement secret as long as possible, the poor fellow was silenced in sad error as to his identity.

On we rode, night and day, with the briefest possible halts. At one point we nearly captured a railroad train, and might easily have succeeded had not the station and warehouses been in flames. As it was, the train approached us closely, then backed, the shrieking engine itself giving the impression of being startled to the last degree.

On a dreary, drizzling, foggy day we passed a milestone on which was lettered, "Four miles to Richmond." It was still "on to Richmond" with us what seemed a long way further, and then came a considerable period of hesitancy, in which the command was drawn up for the final dash. The enemy shelled a field near us vigorously, but fortunately, or unfortunately, the fog was so dense that neither party could make accurate observations or do much execution.

For reasons that have passed into history, the attack was not made. We withdrew six miles from the city and went into camp.

I had scarcely begun to enjoy much-needed rest before the Confederates came up in the darkness and shelled us out of such quarters as we had found. We had to leave our boiling coffee behind us - one of the greatest hardships I have ever known. Then followed a long night-ride down the Peninsula, in driving sleet and rain.

The next morning the sun broke out gloriously, warming and drying our chilled, wet forms. Nearly all that day we maintained a line of battle confronting the pursuing enemy. One brigade would take a defensive position, while the other would march about five miles to a commanding point, where it in turn would form a line. The first brigade would then give way, pass through the second, and take position well to the rear. Thus, although retreating, we were always ready to fight. At one point the enemy pressed us closely, and I saw a magnificent cavalry charge down a gentle descent in the road. Every sabre seemed tipped with fire in the brilliant sunshine.

In the afternoon it became evident that there was a body of troops before us. Who or what they were was at first unknown, and for a time the impression prevailed that we should have to cut our way through by a headlong charge. We soon learned, however, that the force was a brigade of colored infantry, sent up to cover our retreat. It was the first time we had seen negro troops, but as the long line of glistening bayonets and light-blue uniforms came into view, prejudices, if any there were, vanished at once, and a cheer from the begrimed troopers rang down our line, waking the echoes. It was a pleasant thing to march past that array of faces, friendly though black, and know we were safe. They represented the F.F.V.'s of Old Virginia, we then wished to see. On the last day of the march my horse gave out, compelling me to walk and lead him.

On the day after our arrival at Yorktown, Kilpatrick gave me despatches for the authorities at Washington. President Lincoln, learning that I had just returned from the raid, sent for me, and I had a memorable interview with him alone in his private room. He expressed profound solicitude for Colonel Dahlgren and his party. They had been detached from the main force, and I could give no information concerning them. We eventually learned of the death of that heroic young officer, Colonel Dahlgren. Although partially helpless from the loss of a leg, he led a daring expedition at the cost of his life.

I expressed regret to the President that the object of the raid had not been accomplished. "Pick the flint, and try it again," said Mr. Lincoln, heartily. I went out from his presence awed by the courage and sublime simplicity of the man. While he gave the impression that he was bearing the nation on his heart, one was made to feel that it was also large enough for sympathy with all striving with him in the humblest way.

My wife joined me in Washington, and few days later accompanied me to the scene of my new labors at

Hampton Hospital, near Fortress Monroe. There were not many patients at that time (March, 1864) in the large barrack wards; but as soon as the Army of the Potomac broke through the Wilderness and approached our vicinity, transports in increasing numbers, laden with desperately wounded men, came to our wharf. During the early summer the wooden barracks were speedily filled, and many tent wards were added. Duty became constant and severe, while the scenes witnessed were often painful in the last degree. More truly than on the field, the real horrors of war are learned from the long agonies in the hospital. While in the cavalry service, I gained in vigor daily; in two months of hospital work I lost thirty pounds. On one day I buried as many as twenty-nine men. Every evening, till the duty became like a nightmare, I followed the dead-cart, filled up with coffins, once, twice, and often thrice, to the cemetery. Eventually an associate chaplain was appointed, who relieved me of this task.

Fortunately, my tastes led me to employ an antidote to my daily work as useful to me as to the patients. Surrounding the hospital was much waste land. This, with the approval of the surgeon in charge, Dr. Ely McMillan, and the aid of the convalescents, I transformed into a garden, and for two successive seasons sent to the general kitchen fresh vegetables by the wagon-load. If reward were needed, the wistful delight with which a patient from the front would regard a raw onion was ample; while for me the care of the homely, growing vegetables and fruit brought a diversion of mind which made life more endurable.

One of the great needs of the patients who had to fight the winning or losing battle of life was good reading, and I speedily sought to obtain a supply. Hearts and purses at the North responded promptly and liberally; publishers threw off fifty per cent from their prices; and I was eventually able to collect, by gift and purchase, about three thousand volumes. In gathering this library, I provided what may be distinctly termed religious reading in abundance; but I also recognized the need of diversion. Long wards were filled with men who had lost a leg or an arm, and who must lie in one position for weeks. To help them get through the time was to help them to live. I therefore made the library rich in popular fiction and genial books of travel and biography. Full sets of Irving, Cooper, Dickens, Thackeray, Scott, Marryat, and other standard works were bought; and many a time I have seen a poor fellow absorbed in their pages while holding his stump lest the jar of a footstep should send a dart of agony to the point of mutilation. My wife gave much assistance in my hospital duties, often reaching and influencing those beyond me. I recall one poor fellow who was actually six months in dying from a very painful wound. Profanity appeared to be his vernacular, and in bitter protest at his fate, he would curse nearly every one and everything. Mrs. Roe's sympathy and attentions changed him very much, and he would listen quietly as long as she would read to him. Some of the hospital attendants, men and women, had good voices, and we organized a choir. Every Sunday afternoon we went from ward to ward singing familiar hymns. It was touching to see rough fellows drawing their blankets over their heads to hide the emotion caused by words and melodies associated, in many instances, with home and mother.

Northern generosity, and, in the main, convalescent labor enabled me to build a large commodious chapel and to make great improvements in the hospital farm. The site of the hospital and garden is now occupied by General Armstrong's Normal and Agricultural Institute for Freedmen, and the chapel was occupied as a place of worship until very recently. Thus a noble and most useful work is being accomplished on the ground consecrated by the life-and-death struggles of so many Union soldiers.

In 1865 the blessed era of peace began, bringing its many changes. In October the hospital became practically empty, and I resigned. The books were sent to Fortress Monroe for the use of the garrison, and I found many of them there long years after, almost worn out from use.

After a little rest and some candidating for a church, I took a small parish at Highland Falls, about a mile from West Point, New York, entering on my labors in January, 1866. In this village my wife and I spent nine very happy years. They were full of trial and many cares, but free from those events which bring the deep shadows into one's life. We soon became engaged in building a new stone church, whose granite walls are so thick, and hard-wood finish so substantial that passing centuries should add only the mellowness of age. The effort to raise funds for this enterprise led me into the lecture-field and here I found my cavalry-raid and army life in general exceedingly useful. I looked around for a patch of garden-ground as instinctively as a duck seeks water. The small plot adjoining the parsonage speedily grew into about three acres, from which eventually came a book entitled "Play and Profit in my Garden."

Up to the year 1871 I had written little for publication

beyond occasional contributions to the New York "Evangelist," nor had I seriously contemplated a literary life. I had always been extremely fond of fiction, and from boyhood had formed a habit of beguiling the solitary hours in weaving crude fancies around people who for any reason interested me. I usually had a mental serial running, to which I returned when it was my mood; but I had never written even a short story. In October, 1871, I was asked to preach for a far uptown congregation in New York, with the possibility of a settlement in view. On Monday following the services of the Sabbath, the officers of the church were kind enough to ask me to spend a week with them and visit among the people. Meantime, the morning papers laid before us the startling fact that the city of Chicago was burning and that its population were becoming homeless. The tidings impressed me powerfully, waking the deepest sympathy. I said to myself, "Here is a phase of life as remarkable as any witnessed during the war." I obeyed the impulse to be on the scene as soon as possible, stated my purpose to my friends, and was soon among the smoking ruins, finding an abiding-place with throngs of others in a partially finished hotel. For days and nights I wandered where a city had been, and among the extemporized places of refuge harboring all classes of people. Late one night I sat for a long time on the steps of Robert Collyer's church and watched the full moon through the roofless walls and shattered steeple. There was not an evidence of life where had been populous streets. It was there and then, as nearly as I can remember, that the vague outlines of my first story, "Barriers Burned Away," began to take form in my mind. I soon returned home, and began to dream and write, giving during the following year such hours as could be withdrawn from many other duties to the construction of the story. I wrote when and where I could - on steamboats, in railway cars, and at all odd hours of leisure, often with long breaks in the work of composition, caused by the pressure of other affairs, again getting up a sort of white heat from incessantly dwelling upon scenes and incidents that had become real to me. In brief, the story took possession of my mind, and grew as naturally as a plant or a weed in my garden.

It will thus be obvious that at nearly middle age, and in obedience to an impulse, I was launched as an author; that I had very slight literary training; and that my appearance as a novelist was quite as great a surprise to myself as to any of my friends. The writing of sermons certainly does not prepare one for the construction of a novel; and to this day certain critics contemptuously dismiss my books as "preaching." During nearly four years of army life, at a period when most young men are forming style and making the acquaintance of literature, I scarcely had a chance to read at all. The subsequent years of the pastorate were too active, except for an occasional dip into a favorite author.

While writing my first story, I rarely thought of the public, the characters and their experiences absorbing me wholly. When my narrative was actually in print, there was wakened a very deep interest as to its reception. I had none of the confidence resulting from the gradual testing of one's power or from association with literary people, and I also was aware that, when published, a book was far away from the still waters of which one's friends are the protecting headlands. That I knew my work to be exceedingly faulty goes without saying; that it was utterly bad, I was scarcely ready to believe. Dr. Field, noted for his pure English diction and taste, would not publish an irredeemable story, and the constituency of the New York "Evangelist" is well known to be one of the most intelligent in the country. Friendly opinions from serial readers were reassuring as far as they went, but of course the great majority of those who followed the story were silent. A writer cannot, like a speaker, look into the eyes of his audience and observe its mental attitude toward his thought. If my memory serves me, Mr. R. R. Bowker was the earliest critic to write some friendly words in the "Evening Mail;" but at first my venture was very generally ignored. Then some unknown friend marked an influential journal published in the interior of the State and mailed it so timely that it reached me on Christmas eve. I doubt if a book was ever more unsparingly condemned than mine in that review, whose final words were, "The story is absolutely nauseating." In this instance and in my salad days I took pains to find out who the writer was, for if his view was correct I certainly should not engage in further efforts to make the public ill. I discovered the reviewer to be a gentleman for whom I have ever had the highest respect as an editor, legislator, and honest thinker. My story made upon him just the impression he expressed, and it would be very stupid on my part to blink the fact. Meantime, the book was rapidly making for itself friends and passing into frequent new editions. Even the editor who condemned the work would not assert that those who bought it were an aggregation of asses. People cannot be found by thousands who will pay a dollar and seventy-five cents for a dime novel or a religious tract. I wished to learn the actual truth more sincerely than any critic to write it, and at last I ventured to take a copy to Mr. George Ripley, of the New York "Tribune." "Here is a man," I thought, "whose fame and position as a critic are recognized by all. If he deigns to notice the book, he will not only say what he thinks, but I shall have much reason to think as he does." Mr. Ripley met the diffident author kindly, asked a few questions, and took the volume. A few weeks later, to my great surprise, he gave over a column to a review of the story. Although not blind to its many faults, he wrote words far more friendly and inspiring than I ever hoped to see; it would seem that the public had sanctioned his verdict. From that day to this these two instances have been types of my experience with many critics, one condemning, another commending. There is ever a third class who prove their superiority by sneering at or ignoring what is closely related to the people. Much thought over my experience led to a conclusion which the passing years confirm: the only thing for a writer is to be himself and take the consequences. Even those who regard me as a literary offender of the blackest dye have never named imitation among my sins.

As successive books appeared, I began to recognize more and more clearly another phase of an author's experience. A writer gradually forms a constituency, certain qualities in his book appealing to certain classes of minds. In my own case, I do not mean classes of people looked at from the social point of view. A writer who takes any hold on popular attention inevitably learns the character of his constituency. He appeals, and minds and temperaments in sympathy respond. Those he cannot touch go on their way indifferently; those he offends may often strike back. This is the natural result of any strong assertion of individuality. Certainly, if I had my choice, I would rather write a book interesting to the young and to the

E. P. Roe

common people, whom Lincoln said "God must love, since He made so many of them." The former are open to influence; the latter can be quickened and prepared for something better. As a matter of fact, I find that there are those in all classes whom my books attract, others who are repelled, as I have said. It is perhaps one of the pleasantest experiences of an author's life to learn from letters and in other ways that he is forming a circle of friends, none the less friendly because personally unknown. Their loyalty is both a safeguard and an inspiration. On one hand, the writer shrinks from abusing such regard by careless work; on the other, he is stimulated and encouraged by the feeling that there is a group in waiting who will appreciate his best endeavor. While I clearly recognize my limitations, and have no wish to emulate the frog in the fable, I can truthfully say that I take increasing pains with each story, aiming to verify every point by experience - my own or that of others. Not long since, a critic asserted that changes in one of my characters, resulting from total loss of memory, were preposterously impossible. If the critic had consulted Ribot's "Diseases of Memory," or some experienced physician, he might have written more justly. I do not feel myself competent to form a valuable opinion as to good art in writing, and I cannot help observing that the art doctors disagree wofully among themselves. Truth to nature and the realities, and not the following of any school or fashion, has ever seemed the safest guide. I sometimes venture to think I know a little about human nature. My active life brought me in close contact with all kinds of people; there was no man in my regiment who hesitated to come to my tent or to talk confidentially by the campfire, while scores of dying men laid bare to me their hearts. I at least know the nature that exists in the human breast. It may be inartistic, or my use of it all wrong. That is a question which time will decide, and I shall accept the verdict. Over twelve years ago, certain oracles, with the voice of fate, predicted my speedy eclipse and disappearance. Are they right in their adverse judgment? I can truthfully say that now, as at the first, I wish to know the facts in the case. The moment an author is conceited about his work, he becomes absurd and is passing into a hopeless condition. If worthy to write at all, he knows that he falls far short of his ideals; if honest, he wishes to be estimated at his true worth, and to cast behind him the mean little Satan of vanity. If he walks under a conscious sense of greatness, he is a ridiculous figure, for beholders remember the literary giants of other days and of his own time, and smile at the airs of the comparatively little man. On the other hand, no self-respecting writer should ape the false deprecating "'umbleness" of Uriah Heep. In short, he wishes to pass, like a coin, for just what he is worth. Mr. Matthew Arnold was ludicrously unjust to the West when he wrote, "The Western States are at this moment being nourished and formed, we hear, on the novels of a native author called Roe." Why could not Mr. Arnold have taken a few moments to look into the bookstores of the great cities of the West, in order to observe for himself how the demand of one of the largest and most intelligent reading publics in the world is supplied? He would have found that the works of Scott and Dickens were more liberally purchased and generally read than in his own land of "distinction." He should have discovered when in this country that American statesmen (?) are so solicitous about the intelligence of their constituents that they give publishers so disposed every opportunity to steal novels describing the nobility and English persons of distinction; that tons of such novels have been sold annually in the West, a thousand to one of the "author called Roe." The simple truth in the case is that in spite of this immense and cheap competition, my novels have made their way and are being read among multitudes of others. No one buys or reads a book under compulsion; and if any one thinks that the poorer the book the better the chance of its being read by the American people, let him try the experiment. When a critic condemns my books, I accept that as his judgment; when another critic and scores of men and women, the peers of the first in cultivation and intelligence, commend the books, I do not charge them with gratuitous lying. My one aim has become to do my work conscientiously and leave the final verdict to time and the public. I wish no other estimate than a correct one; and when the public indicate that they have had enough of Roe, I shall neither whine nor write.

As a rule, I certainly stumble on my stories, as well as stumble through them perhaps. Some incident or unexpected impulse is the beginning of their existence. One October day I was walking on a country road, and a chestnut burr lay in my path. I said to myself, "There is a book in that burr, if I could get it out." With little volition on my part, the story "Opening a Chestnut Burr" took form and was written.

One summer evening, when in New York, I went up to Thomas's Garden, near Central Park, to hear the delicious music he was educating us to appreciate. At a certain point in the programme I noticed that the next piece would be Beethoven's Fifth Symphony, and I glanced around with a sort of congratulatory impulse, as much as to say, "Now we shall have a treat." My attention was immediately arrested and fixed by a young girl who, with the gentleman escorting her, was sitting near by. My first impression of her face was one of marvellous beauty, followed by a sense of dissatisfaction. Such was my distance that I could not annoy her by furtive observation; and I soon discovered that she would regard a stare as a tribute. Why was it that her face was so beautiful, yet so displeasing? Each feature analyzed seemed perfection, yet the general effect was a mocking, ill-kept promise. The truth was soon apparent. The expression was not evil, but frivolous, silly, unredeemed by any genuine womanly grace. She giggled and flirted through the sublime symphony, till in exasperation I went out into the promenade under the open sky. In less than an hour I had my story "A Face Illumined." I imagined an artist seeing what I had seen and feeling a stronger vexation in the wounding of his beauty loving nature; that he learned during the evening that the girl was a relative of a close friend, and that a sojourn at a summer hotel on the Hudson was in prospect. On his return home he conceives the idea of painting the girl's features and giving them a harmonious expression. Then the fancy takes him that the girl is a modern Undine and has not yet received her woman's soul. The story relates his effort to beautify, illumine the face itself by evoking a mind. I never learned who was the actual girl with the features of an angel and the face of a fool.

In the case of "He Fell in Love with His Wife," I merely saw a paragraph in a paper to the effect that a middle-age widower, having found it next to impossible to carry on his farm with hired help, had gone to the county poorhouse and said "If there's a decent woman here, I'll marry her." For years the homely item remained an ungerminating seed in my mind, then started to grow, and the story was written

E. P. Roe

in two months.

My war experience has naturally made the picturesque phase of the Great Conflict attractive material. In the future I hope to avail myself still further of interesting periods in American history.

I find that my love of horticulture and outdoor life has grown with the years. I do not pretend to scientific accuracy or knowledge. On the contrary, I have regarded plants and birds rather as neighbors, and have associated with them. When giving to my parish, I bought a place in the near vicinity of the house which I had spent my childhood. The front windows of our house command a noble view of the Hudson, while on the east and south the Highlands are within rifle-shot. For several years I hesitated to trust solely to literary work for support. As I have said, not a few critics insisted that my books should not be read, and would soon cease to be read. But whether the prediction should prove true or not, I knew in any case that the critics themselves would eat my strawberries; so I made the culture of small fruits the second string to my bow. This business speedily took the form of growing plants for sale, and was developing rapidly, when financial misfortune led to my failure and the devotion of my entire time to writing. Perhaps it was just as well in the end, for my health was being undermined by too great and conflicting demands on my energy. In 1878, at Dr. Holland's request, I wrote a series of papers on small fruits for "Scribner's Magazine" - papers that were expanded into a book entitled "Success with Small Fruits." I now aim merely at an abundant home supply of fruits and vegetables, but in securing this, find pleasure and profit in testing the many varieties catalogued and offered by nurserymen and seedsmen.

About three years ago the editor of "Harper's Magazine" asked me to write one or two papers entitled "One Acre," telling its possessor how to make the most and best of it. When entering on the task, I found there was more in it than I had at first supposed. Changing the title to "The Home Acre," I decided to write a book or manual which might be useful in many rural homes. There are those who have neither time nor inclination to read the volumes and journals devoted to horticulture, who yet have gardens and trees in which they are interested. They wish to learn in the shortest, clearest way just what to do in order to secure success, without going into theories, whys, and wherefores, or concerning themselves with the higher mysteries of garden-lore. This work is now in course of preparation. In brief, my aim is to have the book grow out of actual experience, and not merely my own, either. As far as possible, well-known experts and authorities are consulted on every point. As a natural consequence, the book is growing, like the plants to which it relates. It cannot be written "offhand" or finished "on time" to suit any one except Dame Nature, who, being feminine, is often inscrutable and apparently capricious. The experience of one season is often reversed in the next, and the guide in gardening of whom I am most afraid is the man who is always sure he is right. It was my privilege to have the late Mr. Charles Downing as one of my teachers, and well do I remember how that honest, sagacious, yet docile student of nature would "put on the brakes" when I was passing too rapidly to conclusions. It has always been one of my most cherished purposes to interest people in the cultivation of the soil and rural life. My effort is to "boil down" information to the simplest and most practical form. Last spring, hundreds of varieties of vegetables and small fruits were planted. A carefully

E. P. Roe

written record is being kept from the time of planting until the crop is gathered.

My methods of work are briefly these: I go into my study immediately after breakfast - usually about nine o'clock - and write or study until three or four in the afternoon, stopping only for a light lunch. In the early morning and late afternoon I go around my place, giving directions to the men, and observing the condition of vegetables, flowers, and trees, and the general aspect of nature at the time. After dinner, the evening is devoted to the family, friends, newspapers, and light reading. In former years I wrote at night, but after a severe attack of insomnia this practice was almost wholly abandoned. As a rule, the greater part of a year is absorbed in the production of a novel, and I am often gathering material for several years in advance of writing.

For manuscript purposes I use bound blankbooks of cheap paper. My sheets are thus kept securely together and in place - important considerations in view of the gales often blowing through my study and the habits of a careless man. This method offers peculiar advantages for interpolation, as there is always a blank page opposite the one on which I am writing. After correcting the manuscript, it is put in typewriting and again revised. There are also two revisions of the proof. While I do not shirk the tasks which approach closely to drudgery, especially since my eyesight is not so good as it was, I also obtain expert assistance. I find that when a page has become very familiar and I am rather tired of it, my mind wanders from the close, fixed attention essential to the best use of words. Perhaps few are endowed with both the inventive and the critical faculty. A certain inner sense enables one to know, according to his lights, whether the story itself is true or false; but elegance of style is due chiefly to training, to a cultivation like that of the ear for music. Possibly we are entering on an age in which the people care less for form, for phraseology, than for what seems to them true, real - for what, as they would express it, "takes hold of them." This is no plea or excuse for careless work, but rather a suggestion that the day of prolix, fine, flowery writing is passing. The immense number of well-written books in circulation has made success with careless, slovenly manuscripts impossible. Publishers and editors will not even read, much less publish them. Simplicity, lucidity, strength, a plunge in medias res, are now the qualities and conditions chiefly desired, rather than finely turned sentences in which it is apparent more labor has been expended on the vehicle than on what it contains. The questions of this eager age are, What has he to say? Does it interest us? As an author, I have felt that my only chance of gaining and keeping the attention of men and women was to know, to understand them, to feel with and for them in what constituted their life. Failing to do this, why should a line of my books be read? Who reads a modern novel from sense of duty? There are classics which all must read and pretend to enjoy whether capable of doing so or not. No critic has ever been so daft as to call any of my books a classic. Better books are unread because the writer is not en rapport with the reader. The time has passed when either the theologian, the politician, or the critic can take the American citizen metaphorically by the shoulder and send him along the path in which they think he should go. He has become the most indepen-dent being in the world, good-humoredly tolerant of the beliefs and fancies of others, while reserving, as a matter of course, the right to think for himself.

In appealing to the intelligent American public, choosing for itself among the multitude of books now offered, it is my creed that an author should maintain completely and thoroughly his own individuality, and take the consequences. He cannot conjure strongly by imitating any one, or by representing any school or fashion. He must do his work conscientiously, for his readers know by instinct whether or not they are treated seriously and with respect. Above all, he must understand men and women sufficiently to interest them; for all the "powers that be" cannot compel them to read a book they do not like.

My early experience in respect to my books in the British Dominions has been similar to that of many others. My first stories were taken by one or more publishers without saying "by your leave," and no returns made of any kind. As time passed, Messrs. Ward, Locke & Co., more than any other house, showed a disposition to treat me fairly. Increasing sums were given for successive books. Recently Mr. George Locke visited me, and offered liberal compensation for each new novel. He also agreed to give me five per cent copyright on all my old books published by him, no matter how obtained, in some instances revoking agreements which precluded the making of any such request on my part. In the case of many of these books he has no protection, for they are published by others; but he takes the simple ground that he will not sell any of my books without giving me a share in the profit. Such honorable action should tend to make piracy more odious than ever, on both sides of the sea. Other English firms have offered me the usual royalty, and I now believe that in spite of our House of Mis-Representatives at Washington, the majority of the British publishers are disposed to deal justly and honorably by American writers. In my opinion, the LOWER House in Congress has libelled and slandered the American people by acting as if their constituents, with thievish instincts, chuckled over pennies saved when buying pirated books. This great, rich, prosperous nation has been made a "fence," a receiver of stolen goods, and shamelessly committed to the crime for which poor wretches are sent to jail. Truly, when history is written, and it is learned that the whole power and statesmanship of the government were enlisted in behalf of the pork interest, while the literature of the country and the literary class were contemptuously ignored, it may be that the present period will become known as the Pork Era of the Republic. It is a strange fact that English publishers are recognizing our rights in advance of our own lawmakers.

In relating his experience in the pages of this magazine, Mr. Julian Hawthorne said in effect that one of the best rewards of the literary life was the friends it enabled the writer to make. When giving me his friendship, he proved how true this is. In my experience the literary class make good, genial, honest friends, while their keen, alert minds and knowledge of life in many of its most interesting aspects give an unfailing charm to their society. One can maintain the most cordial and intimate relations with editors of magazines and journals if he will recognize that such relations should have no influence whatever in the acceptance or declination of manuscripts. I am constantly receiving letters from literary aspirants who appear to think that if I will use a little influence their stories or papers would be taken and paid for. I have no such influence, nor do I wish any, in regard to my own work. The conscientious editor's first duty is to his periodical and its constituents, and he would and should be more scrupulous in accepting a manuscript from a friend than from a stranger. To show resentment because a manuscript is returned is absurd, however great may be our disappointment.

Perhaps one of the most perplexing and often painful experiences of an author comes from the appeals of those who hope through him to obtain immediate recognition as writers. One is asked to read manuscripts and commend them to publishers, or at least to give an opinion in regard to them, often to revise or even to rewrite certain portions. I remember that during one month I was asked to do work on the manuscripts of strangers that would require about a year of my time. The maker of such request does not realize that he or she is but one among many, and that the poor author would have to abandon all hope of supporting his family if he tried to comply. The majority who thus appeal to one know next to nothing of the literary life or the conditions of success. They write to the author in perfect good faith, often relating circumstances which touch his sympathies; yet if you tell them the truth about their manuscript, or say you have not time to read it, adding that you have no influence with editors or publishers beyond securing a careful examination of what is written, you feel that you are often set down as a churl, and your inability to comply with their wishes is regarded as the selfishness and arrogance of success. The worried author has also his own compunctions, for while he has tried so often and vainly to secure the recognition requested, till he is in despair of such effort, he still is haunted by the fear that he may overlook some genius whom it would be a delight to guide through what seems a thorny jungle to the inexperienced.

In recalling the past, one remembers when he stood in such sore need of friends that he dislikes even the appearance of passing by on the other side. There are no riches in the world like stanch friends who prove themselves to be such in your need, your adversity, or your weakness. I have some treasured letters received after it had been telegraphed throughout the land that I was a bankrupt and had found myself many thousands of dollars worse off than nothing. The kindly words and looks, the cordial grasp of the hand, and the temporary loan occasionally, of those who stood by me when scarcely sane from overwork, trouble, and, worse than all, from insomnia, can never be forgotten while a trace of memory is left. Soon after my insolvency there came a date when all my interests in my books then published must be sold to the highest bidder. It seemed in a sense like putting my children up at auction; and yet I was powerless, since my interests under contracts were a part of my assets. These rights had been well advertised in the New York and county papers, as the statute required, and the popularity of the books was well known. Any one in the land could have purchased these books from me forever. A friend made the highest bid and secured the property. My rights in my first nine novels became his, legally and absolutely. There was even no verbal agreement between us - nothing but his kind, honest eyes to reassure me. He not only paid the sum he had bidden, but then and there wrote a check for a sum which, with my other assets, immediately liquidated my personal debts, principal and interest. The children of my fancy are again my children, for they speedily earned enough to repay my friend and to enable him to compromise with the holders of indorsed notes in a way satisfactory to them. It so happened that most of these creditors resided in my immediate neighborhood. I determined to fight out the battle in their midst and under their daily observation, and to treat all alike, without regard to their legal claims. Only one creditor tried to make life a burden; but he did his level best. The others permitted me to meet my obligations in my own time and way, and I am grateful for their consideration. When all had received the sum mutually agreed upon, and I had shaken hands with them, I went to the quaint and quiet little city of Santa Barbara, on the Pacific coast, for a change and partial rest. While there, however, I wrote my Charleston story, "The Earth Trembled." In September, 1887, I returned to my home at Cornwall-on-the-Hudson, and resumed my work in a region made dear by the memories of a lifetime. Just now I am completing a Southern story entitled "Miss Lou."

It so happens in my experience that I have discovered one who appears willing to stick closer to me than a brother, and even to pass as my "double," or else he is so helplessly in the hands of his publishers as to be an object of pity. A certain "Edward R. Roe" is also an author, and is suffering cruelly in reputation because his publishers so manage that he is identified with me. By strange coincidence, they hit upon a cover for his book which is almost a facsimile of the cover of my pamphlet novel, "An Original Belle," previously issued. The R in the name of this unfortunate man has been furnished with such a diminutive tail that it passes for a P, and even my friends supposed that the book, offered everywhere for sale, was mine. In many instances I have asked at news stands, "Whose book is that?" The prompt and invariable answer has been, "E. P. Roe's." I have seen book notices in which the volume was ascribed to me in anything but flattering terms. A distinguished judge, in a carefully written opinion, is so uncharitable as to characterize the coincidence in cover as a "fraud," and to say, "No one can look at the covers of the two publications and fail to see evidence of a design to deceive the public and to infringe upon the rights of the publisher and author" - that is, the rights of Messrs. Dodd, Mead would be well, as a rule, for other writers to begin with reputable, honorable publishers and to remain with them. A publisher can do more and better with a line of books than with isolated volumes. When an author's books are scattered, there is not sufficient inducement for any one to push them strongly, nor, as in the case above related, to protect a writer against a "double," should one appear. Authors often know little about business, and should deal with a publisher who will look after their interests as truly as his own. Unbusinesslike habits and methods are certainly not traits to be cultivated, for we often suffer grievously from their existence; yet as far as possible the author should be free from distracting cares. The novelist does his best work when abstracted from the actual world and living in its ideal counterpart which for the time he is imagining. When his creative work is completed, he should live very close to the real world, or else he will be imagining a state of things which neither God nor man had any hand in bringing about.

E. P. Roe

TAKEN ALIVE

CHAPTER I

SOMETHING BEFORE UNKNOWN

Clara Heyward was dressed in deep mourning, and it was evident that the emblems of bereavement were not worn merely in compliance with a social custom. Her face was pallid from grief, and her dark beautiful eyes were dim from much weeping. She sat in the little parlor of a cottage located in a large Californian city, and listened with apathetic expression as a young man pleaded for the greatest and most sacred gift that a woman can bestow. Ralph Brandt was a fine type of young vigorous manhood; and we might easily fancy that his strong, resolute face, now eloquent with deep feeling, was not one upon which a girl could look with indifference. Clara's words, however, revealed the apparent hopelessness of his suit.

"It's of no use, Ralph," she said; "I'm in no mood for such thoughts."

"You don't believe in me; you don't trust me," he resumed sadly. "You think that because I was once wild, and even worse, that I'll not be true to my promises and live an honest life. Have I not been honest when I knew that being so might cost me dear? Have I not told you of my past life and future purposes when I might have concealed almost everything?"

"It's not that, Ralph. I do believe you are sincere; and if the dreadful thing which has broken me down with sorrow had not happened, all might have been as you wish. I should have quite as much confidence in a young man who, like you, has seen evil and turned resolutely away from it, as in one who didn't know much about the world or himself either. What's more, father - "

At the word "father" her listless manner vanished, and she gave way to passionate sobs. "His foul murder is always before me," she wailed. "Oh, we were so happy! he was so kind, and made me his companion! I don't see how I can live without him. I can't think of love and marriage when I remember how he died, and that the villain who killed him is at large and unpunished. What right have I to forget this great wrong and to try to be happy? No, no! the knife that killed him pierced my heart; and it's bleeding all the time. I'm not fit to be any man's wife; and I will not bring my great sorrow into any man's home."

Brandt sprang up and paced the room for a few moments, his brow contracted in deep thought. Then, apparently coming to a decision, he sat down by his companion and took her cold, unresisting hand.

"My poor little girl," he said, kindly, "you don't half understand me yet. I love you all the more because you are heart-broken and pale with grief. That is the reason I have spoken so earnestly to-night. You will grieve yourself to death if left alone; and what good would your death do any one? It would spoil my life. Believe me, I would welcome you to my home with all your sorrow - all the more because of your sorrow; and I'd be so kind and patient that you'd begin to smile again some day. That's what your father would wish if he could speak to you, and not that you should grieve away your life for what can't be helped now. But I have a plan. It's right in my line to capture such scoundrels as the man who murdered your father; and what's more, I know the man, or rather I used to in old times. I've played many a game of euchre with him in which he cheated me out of money that I'd be glad to have now; and I'm satisfied that he does not know of any change in me. I was away on distant detective duty, you know, when your father was killed. I won't ask you to go over the painful circumstances; I can learn them at the prison. I shall try to get permission to search out Bute, desperate and dangerous as he is - "

"Oh, Ralph, Ralph," cried the girl, springing up, her eyes flashing through her tears, "if you will bring my father's murderer to justice, if you will prevent him from destroying other lives, as he surely will, you will find that I can refuse you nothing."

Then she paused, shook her head sadly, and withdrew the hand she had given him. "No," she resumed, "I shouldn't ask this; I don't ask it. As you say, he is desperate and dangerous; and he would take your life the moment he dreamed of your purpose. I should only have another cause for sorrow."

Brandt now smiled as if he were master of the situation. "Why, Clara," he exclaimed, "don't you know that running down and capturing desperadoes is now part of my business?"

"Yes; but you can get plenty of work that isn't so dangerous."

"I should be a nice fellow to ask you to be my wife and yet show I was afraid to arrest your father's murderer. You needn't ask me to do this; you are not going to be responsible for my course in the least. I shall begin operations this very night, and have no doubt that I can get a chance to work on the case. Now don't burden your heart with any thoughts about my danger. I myself owe Bute as big a grudge as I can have against any human being. He cheated me and led me into deviltry years ago, and then I lost sight of him until he was brought to the prison of which your father was one of the keepers. I've been absent for the last three months, you know; but I didn't forget you or your father a day, and you remember I wrote you as soon as I heard of your trouble. I think your father sort of believed in me; he never made me feel I wasn't fit to see you or to be with you, and I'd do more for him living or dead than for any other man."

"He did believe in you, Ralph, and he always spoke well of you. Oh, you can't know how much I lost in him! After mother died he did not leave me to the care of strangers, but gave me most of his time when off duty. He sent me to the best schools, bought me books to read, and took me out evenings instead of going off by himself, as so many men do. He was so kind and so brave; oh, oh! you know he lost his life by trying to do his duty when another man would have given up. Bute and two others broke jail. Father saw one of his assistants stabbed, and he was knocked down himself. He might have remained quiet and escaped with a few bruises; but he caught Bute's foot, and then the wretch turned and stabbed him. He told me all with his poor

E. P. Roe

pale lips before he died. Oh, oh! when shall I forget?"

"You can never forget, dear; I don't ask anything contrary to nature. You were a good daughter, and so I believe you will be a good wife. But if I bring the murderer to justice, you will feel that a great wrong has been righted - that all has been done that can be done. Then you'll begin to think that your father wouldn't wish you to grieve yourself to death, and that as he tried to make you happy while he was living, so he will wish you to be happy now he's gone."

"It isn't a question of happiness. I don't feel as if I could ever be happy again; and so I don't see how I can make you or any one else happy."

"That's my lookout, Clara. I'd be only too glad to take you as you are. Come, now, this is December. If I bring Bute in by Christmas, what will you give me?"

She silently and eloquently gave him her hand; but her lips quivered so she could not speak. He kissed her hand as gallantly as any olden-time knight, then added a little brusquely:

"See here, little girl, I'm not going to bind you by anything that looks like a bargain. I shall attempt all I've said; and then on Christmas, or whenever I get back, I'll speak my heart to you again just as I have spoken now."

"When a man acts as you do, Ralph, any girl would find it hard to keep free. I shall follow you night and day with my thoughts and prayers."

"Well, I'm superstitious enough to believe that I shall

be safer and more successful on account of them. Clara, look me in the eyes before I go."

She looked up to his clear gray eyes as requested.

"I don't ask you to forget one who is dead; but don't you see how much you are to one who is living? Don't you see that in spite of all your sorrow you can still give happiness? Now, be as generous and kind as you can. Don't grieve hopelessly while I'm gone. That's what is killing you; and the thought of it fills me with dread. Try to think that you still have something and some one to live for. Perhaps you can learn to love me a little if you try, and then everything won't look so black. If you find you can't love me, I won't blame you - , and if I lose you as my wife, you won't lose a true, honest friend."

For the first time the girl became vaguely conscious of, the possibility of an affection, a tie superseding all others; she began to see how it was possible to give herself to this man, not from an impulse of gratitude or because she liked him better than any one else, but because of a feeling, new, mysterious, which gave him a sort of divine right in her. Something in the expression of his eyes had been more potent than his words; something subtle, swift as an electric spark had passed from him to her, awakening a faint, strange tumult in the heart she thought so utterly crushed. A few moments before, she could have promised resolutely to be his wife; she could have permitted his embrace with unresponsive apathy. Now she felt a sudden shyness. A faint color stole into her pale face, and she longed to be alone.

"Ralph," she faltered, "you are so generous, I - I don't

know what to say."

"You needn't say anything till I come back. If possible, I will be here by Christmas, for you shouldn't be alone that day with your grief. Good-by."

The hand she gave him trembled, and her face was averted now.

"You will try to love me a little, won't you?"

"Yes," she whispered.

CHAPTER II

A VISITOR AT THE MINE

Ralph Brandt was admirably fitted for the task he had undertaken. With fearlessness he united imperturbable coolness and unwearied patience in pursuit of an object. Few knew him in his character of detective, and no one would have singled him out as an expert in his calling. The more difficult and dangerous the work, the more careless and indifferent his manner, giving the impression to superficial observers of being the very last person to be intrusted with responsible duty. But his chief and others on the force well knew that beneath Brandt's careless demeanor was concealed the relentless pertinacity of a bloodhound on track of its victim. With the trait of dogged pursuit all resemblance to the bloodthirsty animal ceased, and even the worst of criminals found him kind-hearted and good-natured AFTER they were within his power. Failure was an idea not to be entertained. If the man to be caught existed, he could certainly be found, was the principle on which our officer acted.

He readily obtained permission to attempt the capture of the escaped prisoner, Bute; but the murderer had disappeared, leaving no clew. Brandt learned that the slums of large cities and several mining camps had been searched in vain, also that the trains running east had been carefully watched. We need not try to follow his processes of thought, nor seek to learn how he soon came to the conclusion that his man was at some distant mining station working under an assumed name. By a kind of instinct his mind kept reverting to one of these stations with increasing frequency. It was not so remote in respect to mere distance; but it was isolated, off the lines of travel, with a gap of seventy miles between it and what might be termed civilization, and was suspected of being a sort of refuge for hard characters and fugitives from justice. Bute, when last seen, was making for the mountains in the direction of this mine. Invested with ample authority to bring in the outlaw dead or alive, Brandt followed this vague clew.

One afternoon, Mr. Alford, the superintendent of the mine, was informed that a man wished to see him. There was ushered into his private office an elderly gentleman who appeared as if he might be a prospecting capitalist or one of the owners of the mine. The superintendent was kept in doubt as to the character of the visitor for a few moments while Brandt sought by general remarks and leading questions to learn the disposition of the man who must, from the necessities of the case, become to some extent his ally in securing the ends of justice. Apparently the detective was satisfied, for he asked, suddenly:

"By the way, have you a man in your employ by the name of Bute?"

"No, sir," replied Mr. Alford, with a little surprise.

"Have you a man, then, who answers to the following description?" He gave a brief word photograph of the criminal.

"You want this man?" Mr. Alford asked in a low voice.

"Yes."

"Well, really, sir, I would like to know your motive, indeed, I may add, your authority, for - "

"There it is," Brand smilingly remarked, handing the superintendent a paper.

"Oh, certainly, certainly," said Mr. Alford, after a moment. "This is all right; and I am bound to do nothing to obstruct you in the performance of your duty." He now carefully closed the door and added, "What do you want this man for?"

"It's a case of murder."

"Phew! Apparently he is one of the best men on the force."

"Only apparently; I know him well."

Mr. Alford's brow clouded with anxiety, and after a moment he said, "Mr. - how shall I address you?"

"You had better continue to call me by the name under which I was introduced - Brown."

"Well, Mr. Brown, you have a very difficult and hazardous task, and you must be careful how you involve me in your actions. I shall not lay a straw in your way, but I cannot openly help you. It is difficult for me to get labor here at best; and it is understood that I ask no questions and deal with men on the basis simply of their relations to me. As long as I act on this understanding, I can keep public sentiment with me and enforce some degree of discipline. If it were known that I was aiding or abetting you in the enterprise you have in hand, my life would not be worth a rush. There are plenty in camp who would shoot me, just as they would you, should they learn of your design. I fear you do not realize what you are attempting. A man like yourself, elderly and alone, has no better chance of taking such a fellow as you describe Bute to be than of carrying a ton of ore on his back down the mountain. In all sincerity, sir, I must advise you to depart quietly and expeditiously, and give no one besides myself a hint of your errand."

"Will you please step into the outer office and make sure that no one is within earshot?" said Brandt, quietly.

When Mr. Alford returned, the elderly man apparently had disappeared, and a smiling smooth-faced young fellow with short brown hair sat in his place. His host stared, the transformation was so great.

"Mr. Alford," said the detective, "I understand my business and the risks it involves. All I ask of you is that I may not be interfered with so far as you are concerned; and my chief object in calling is to prevent you being surprised by anything you may see or hear. About three miles or thereabouts from here, on the road running east, there is a fellow who keeps a tavern. Do you know him?"

"I know no good of him. He's the worst nuisance I have to contend with, for he keeps some of my men disabled much of the time."

"Well, I knew Bute years ago, and I can make him think I am now what I was then, only worse; and I will induce him to go with me to raid that tavern. If this plan fails, I shall try another, for I am either going to take Bute alive or else get ample proof that he is dead. There may be some queer goings-on before I leave, and all I ask is that you will neither interfere nor investigate. You may be as ignorant and non-committal as you please. I shall report progress to you, however, and may need your testimony, but will see to it that it is given by you as one who had nothing to do with the affair. Now please show me your quarters, so that I can find you at night if need be; also Bute's sleeping-place and the lay of the land to some extent. You'll find that I can take everything in mighty quick. See, I'm the elderly gentleman again," and he resumed his disguise with marvellous celerity.

Mr. Alford led the way through the outer office; and the two clerks writing there saw nothing to awaken the slightest suspicion. The superintendent's cottage stood on the road leading to the mine and somewhat apart from the other buildings. On the opposite side of the highway was a thicket of pines which promised cover until one plunged into the unbroken forest that covered the mountain-side.

Brandt observed this, and remarked, "I've studied the approaches to your place a little at I came along; but I suppose I shall have to give a day or two more to the work before making my attempt."

"Well," rejoined Mr. Alford, who was of rather a social turn and felt the isolation of his life, "why not be my guest for a time? I'll take the risk if you will remain incog, and keep aloof from the men."

"That I should do in any event till ready to act. Thank you for your kindness, for it may simplify my task very much. I will see to it that I do not compromise you. When I'm ready to snare my bird, you can dismiss me a little ostentatiously for New York."

Brandt's horse was now ordered to the stable. The two men entered the cottage, and soon afterward visited the different points of interest, Mr. Alford giving the natural impression that he was showing an interested stranger the appliances for working the mine. At one point he remarked in a low tone, "That's Bute's lodging-place. A half-breed, named Apache Jack, who speaks little English lives with him."

Brandt's seemingly careless and transitory glance rested on a little shanty and noted that it was separated from others of its class by a considerable interval.

"Bute, you say, is on the day-shift."

"Yes, he won't be up till six o'clock."

"I'll manage to see him then without his knowing it."

"Be careful. I take my risk on the ground of your good faith and prudence."

"Don't fear."

CHAPTER III

THWARTED

Brandt maintained his disguise admirably. His presence caused little comment, and he was spoken of as a visiting stockholder of the mine. During his walk with Mr. Alford he appeared interested only in machinery, ores, etc., but his trained eyes made a topographical map of surroundings, and everything centred about Bute's shanty. In the evening, he amply returned his host's hospitality by comic and tragic stories of criminal life. The next day he began to lay his plans carefully, and disappeared soon after breakfast with the ostensible purpose of climbing a height at some distance for the sake of the prospect. He soon doubled round, noting every covert approach to Bute's lodgings. His eye and ear were as quick as an Indian's; but he still maintained, in case he was observed, the manner of an elderly stranger strolling about to view the region.

By noon he felt that he had the immediate locality by heart. His afternoon task was to explore the possibilities of a stream that crossed the mine road something over a mile away, and for this purpose he mounted his horse. He soon reached the shallow ford, and saw that the water was backed up for a considerable distance, and that the shallows certainly

E. P. Roe

extended around a high, jutting rock which hid the stream from that point and beyond from the road. The bed appeared smooth, firm, and sandy, and he waded his horse up the gentle current until he was concealed from the highway. A place, however, was soon reached where the water came tumbling down over impassable rocks; and lie was compelled to ascend the wooded shore. This he did on the side nearest to the mine house, and found that with care he could lead his horse to a point that could not be, he thought, over half a mile from the superintendent's cottage. Here there was a little dell around which the pines grew so darkly and thickly that he determined to make it his covert should he fail in his first attempt. His object now was to see if his estimate of proximity to the mine was correct; and leaving his horse, he pushed up the mountain-side. At last he reached a precipitous ledge. Skirting this a short distance, he found a place of comparatively easy ascent, and soon learned with much satisfaction that he was not over two hundred yards from the thicket opposite Mr. Alford's quarters. These discoveries all favored possible future operations; and he retraced his steps, marking his returning path by bits of white paper, held in place by stones against the high prevailing winds. Near the spot where he had left his horse he found a nook among the rocks in which a fire would be well hidden. Having marked the place carefully with his eye and obtained his bearings, he led his horse back to the stream and reached the unfrequented road again without being observed.

His next task was to discover some kind of a passageway from the mine road to a point on the main highway, leading to the west and out of the mountains. He found no better resource than to strike directly into the forest and travel by points of the compass.

Fortunately, the trees were lofty and comparatively open, and he encountered no worse difficulties than some steep and rugged descents, and at last emerged on the post road at least a mile to the west of the tavern, which stood near its intersection with the mine road; Returning, he again marked out a path with paper as he had before. The sun was now low in the sky; and as he trotted toward the mine, he had but one more precaution to take, and that was to find a place where the trees were sufficiently open to permit him to ride into their shade at night in case he wished to avoid parties upon the road. Having indicated two or three such spots by a single bit of paper that would glimmer in the moonlight, he joined Mr. Alford at supper, feeling that his preparations were nearly complete. When they were alone, he told his host that it would be best not to gratify his curiosity, for then he could honestly say that he knew nothing of any detective's plans or whereabouts.

"I cannot help feeling," said Mr. Alford, "that you are playing with fire over a powder magazine. Now that I know you better, I hate to think of the risk that you are taking. It has troubled me terribly all day. I feel as if we were on the eve of a tragedy. You had better leave quietly in the morning and bring a force later that would make resistance impossible, or else give it up altogether. Why should you throw away your life? I tell you again that if the men get a hint of your character or purpose they will hunt you to death."

"It's a part of my business to incur such risks," replied Brandt, quietly. "Besides, I have a motive in this case which would lead me to take a man out of the jaws of hell."

"That's what you may find you are attempting here. Well, we're in for it now, I suppose, since you are so determined."

"I don't think you will appear involved in the affair at all. In the morning you give me a sack of grain for my horse and some provisions for myself, and then bid farewell to Mr. Brown in the most open and natural manner possible. You may not see me again. It is possible I may have to borrow a horse of you it my scheme to-night don't work. It will be returned or paid for very soon."

"Bute has a pony. He brought it with him, and he and Apache Jack between them manage to keep it. They stable it nights in a little shed back of their shanty."

"I had discovered this, and hope to take the man away on his pony. I understand why Bute keeps the animal. He knew that he might have to travel suddenly and fast."

The next morning Mr. Alford parted with Brandt as had been arranged, the latter starting ostensibly for the nearest railway station. All day long the superintendent was nervous and anxious; but he saw no evidences of suspicion or uneasiness among those in his employ.

Brandt rode at a sharp canter as long as he was in sight, and then approached the stream slowly and warily. When satisfied that he was unobserved, he again passed up its shallow bed around the concealing rock, and sought his hiding-place on the mountain-side. Aware that the coming nights might require ceaseless activity, his first measure was to secure a few hours of sound sleep; and he had so trained himself that he could, as it were, store up rest against long and trying emergencies. The rocks sheltered him against the wind, and a fire gave all the comfort his hardy frame required, as he reposed on his couch of pine-needles. Early in the afternoon he fed his horse, took a hearty meal himself, and concealed the remaining store so that no wild creatures could get at it. At early twilight he returned by way of the stream and hid his horse well back in the woods near the mine. To this he now went boldly, and inquired for Tim Atkins, Bute's assumed name. He was directed to the shanty with which he had already made himself so familiar.

Bute was found alone, and was much surprised at sight of his old gambling acquaintance of better days, for his better days were those of robbery before he had added the deeper stain of murder. Brandt soon allayed active fears and suspicions by giving the impression that in his descensus he had reached the stage of robbery and had got on the scent of some rich booty in the mountains. "But how did you know I was here?" demanded Bute.

"I didn't know it," replied Brandt, adopting his old vernacular; "but I guessed as much, for I knew there was more'n one shady feller in this gang, and I took my chances on findin' you, for, says I to myself, if I can find Bute, I've found the right man to help me crack a ranch when there's some risk and big plunder."

He then disclosed the fact of hearing that the keeper of the tavern had accumulated a good sum of hard money, and was looking out for a chance to send it to a bank. "We can save him the trouble, yer know," he concluded, facetiously.

E. P. Roe

"Well," said Bute, musingly, "I'm gittin' tired of this dog's life, and I reckon I'll go snacks with yer and then put out fer parts unknown. I was paid t'other day, and there ain't much owin' me here. I guess it'll be safer fer me ter keep movin' on, too."

"You may well say that, Bute. I heard below that there was goin' to be some investigations inter this gang, and that there was more'n one feller here whose pictur was on exhibition."

"That so?" said Bute, hastily. "Well, I'll go with yer ter-night, fer it's time I was movin'. I kin tell yer one thing, though - there'll be no investigations here unless a fair-sized regiment makes it. Every man keeps his shooter handy."

"Hanged if we care how the thing turns out. You and me'll be far enough away from the shindy. Now make your arrangements prompt, for we must be on the road by nine o'clock, so we can get through early in the night and have a good start with the swag. My plan is to ambush the whiskey shop, go and demand drinks soon after everybody is gone, and then proceed to business."

"Can't we let my mate, Apache Jack, in with us? I'll stand for him."

"No, no, I don't know anything about Apache Jack; and I can trust you. We can manage better alone, and I'd rather have one-half than one-third."

"Trust me, kin you? you - fool," thought Bute. "So ye thinks I'll sit down and divide the plunder socially with you when I kin give yer a quiet dig in the ribs and take it all. One more man now won't matter. I'm a-goin' ter try fer enough ter-night ter take me well out of these parts."

Bute's face was sinister enough to suggest any phase of evil, and Brandt well knew that he was capable of what he meditated. It was now the policy of both parties, however, to be very friendly, and Bute was still further mellowed by a draught of liquor from Brandt's flask.

They had several games of cards in which it was managed that Bute's winnings should be the larger; and at nine in the evening they started on what was to Bute another expedition of robbery and murder. Mr. Alford, who was on the alert, saw them depart with a deep sigh of relief. The night was cloudy, but the moon gave plenty of light for travelling. Brandt soon secured his horse, and then appeared to give full rein to his careless, reckless spirit.

As they approached the stream, he remarked, "I say, Bute, it's too bad we can't use the pasteboards while on the jog; but I can win a five out of you by an old game of ours. I bet you I can empty my revolver quicker 'n you can."

"We'd better save our amernition and make no noise."

"Oh, pshaw! I always have better luck when I'm free and careless like. It's your sneaking fellers that always get caught. Besides, who'll notice? This little game is common enough all through the mountains, and everybody knows that there's no mischief in such kind of firing. I want to win back some of my money."

"Well, then, take you up; go ahead."

　　　　　　　E. P. Roe

Instantly from Brandt's pistol there were six reports following one another so quickly that they could scarcely be distinguished.

"Now beat that if you can!" cried Brandt, who had a second and concealed revolver ready for an emergency.

"The fool!" thought Bute, "to put himself at the marcy of any man. I can pluck him to-night like a winged pa'tridge;" but he too fired almost as quickly as his companion.

"You only used five ca'tridges in that little game, my friend," said Brandt.

"Nonsense! I fired so quick you couldn't count 'em."

"Now see here, Bute," resumed Brandt, in an aggrieved tone, "you've got to play fair with me. I've cut my eye-teeth since you used to fleece me, and I'll swear you fired only five shots. Let's load and try again."

"What the use of sich - nonsense? You'll swar that you fired the quickest; and of course I'll swar the same, and there's nobody here ter jedge. What's more, Ralph Brandt, I wants you and every man ter know that I always keeps a shot in reserve, and that I never misses. So let's load and jog on, and stop foolin'."

"That scheme has failed," thought Brandt, as he replaced the shells with cartridges.

His purpose was to find a moment when his companion was completely in his power, and it came sooner than he expected. When they drew near the brook, it was evident that Bute's pony was thirsty, for it suddenly darted forward and thrust its nose into the water. Therefore, for an instant, Bute was in advance with his back toward the detective. Covering the fellow with his revolver, Brandt shouted:

"Bute, throw up your hands; surrender, or you are a dead man!"

Instantly the truth flashed through the outlaw's mind. Instead of complying, he threw himself forward over the pony's neck and urged the animal forward. Brandt fired, and Bute fell with a splash into the water. At that moment three miners, returning from the tavern, came shouting to the opposite side of the stream. The frightened pony, relieved of its burden, galloped homeward. Brandt also withdrew rapidly toward the mine for some distance, and then rode into the woods. Having tied his horse well back from the highway, he reconnoitred the party that had so inopportunely interfered with his plans. He discovered that they were carrying Bute, who, from his groans and oaths, was evidently not dead, though he might be mortally wounded. His rescuers were breathing out curses and threats of vengeance against Brandt, now known to be an officer of the law.

"The job has become a little complicated now," muttered Brandt, after they had passed; "and I must throw them off the scent. There will be a dozen out after me soon."

He remounted his horse, stole silently down the road, crossed the stream, and then galloped to the tavern, and calling out the keeper, asked if there was any shorter road out of the mountains than the one leading to the west. Being answered in the negative, he rode hastily away. On reaching the place where he had struck this road the previous day, he entered the woods, followed the rugged trail that he had marked by bits of paper, and slowly approached the mine road again near the point where the stream crossed it. He then reconnoitred and learned that there was evidently a large party exploring the woods between the stream and the mine.

At last they all gathered at the ford for consultation, and Brandt heard one say:

"We're wastin' time beatin' round here. He'd naterly put fer the lowlands as soon as he found he was balked in takin' his man. I move we call on Whiskey Bob, and see if a man's rode that way ter-night."

A call on Whiskey Bob was apparently always acceptable; and the party soon disappeared down the road - some on horses and more on foot. Brandt then quietly crossed the road and gained his retreat on the mountain-side.

"I must camp here now till the fellow dies, and I can prove it, or until I can get another chance," was his conclusion as he rubbed down and fed his horse.

CHAPTER IV

TAKEN ALIVE

After taking some refreshment himself, Brandt decided to go to the thicket opposite the superintendent's house for a little observation. He soon reached this outlook, and saw that something unusual was occurring in the cottage. At last the door opened, and Bute was assisted to his shanty by two men. They had scarcely disappeared before Brandt darted across the road and knocked for admittance.

"Great Scott! you here?" exclaimed Mr. Alford.

"Yes, and here I'm going to stay till I take my man," replied the detective, with a laugh. "Don't be alarmed. I shall not remain in your house, but in the neighborhood."

"You are trifling with your life, and, I may add, with mine."

"Not at all. Come up to your bedroom. First draw the curtains close, and we'll compare notes. I won't stay but a few moments."

Mr. Alford felt that it was best to comply, for some one might come and find them talking in the hall. When

E. P. Roe

Brandt entered the apartment, he threw himself into a chair and laughed in his low careless style as he said, "Well, I almost bagged my game to-night, and would have done so had not three of your men, returning from the tavern, interfered."

"There's a party out looking for you now."

"I know it; but I've put them on the wrong trail. What I want to learn is, will Bute live?"

"Yes; your shot made a long flesh-wound just above his shoulders. A little closer, and it would have cut his vertebrae and finished him. He has lost a good deal of blood, and could not be moved for some days except at some risk."

"You are sure of that?"

"Yes."

"Well, he may have to incur the risk. I only wish to be certain that he will not take it on his own act at once. You'll soon miss him in any event."

"The sooner the better. I wish your aim had been surer."

"That wasn't my good luck. Next time I'll have to shoot closer or else take him alive."

"But you can't stay in this region. They will all be on the alert now."

"Oh, no. The impression will be general to-morrow that I've made for the lowlands as fast as my horse could carry me. Don't you worry. Till I move again, I'm safe enough. All I ask of you now is to keep Bute in his own shanty, and not to let him have more than one man to take care of him if possible. Good-night. You may not see me again, and then again you may."

"Well, now that you are here," said the superintendent, who was naturally brave enough, "spend an hour or two, or else stay till just before daylight. I confess I am becoming intensely interested in your adventure, and would take a hand in it if I could; but you know well enough that if I did, and it became known, I would have to find business elsewhere very suddenly - that is, if given the chance."

"I only wish your passive co-operation. I should be glad, however, if you would let me take a horse, if I must."

"Certainly, as long as you leave my black mare."

Brandt related what had occurred, giving a comical aspect to everything, and then, after reconnoitring the road from a darkened window, regained his cover in safety. He declined to speak of his future plans or to give any clew to his hiding-place, to which he now returned.

During the few remaining hours of darkness and most of the next day, he slept and lounged about his fire. The next night was too bright and clear for anything beyond a reconnoissance, and he saw evidences of an alertness which made him very cautious. He did not seek another interview with Mr. Alford, for now nothing was to be gained by it.

The next day proved cloudy, and with night began a violent storm of wind and rain. Brandt cowered over his fire till nine o'clock, and then taking a slight draught from his flask, chuckled, "This is glorious weather for my work. Here's to Clara's luck this time!"

In little over an hour he started for the mine, near which he concealed his horse. Stealing about in the deep shadows, he soon satisfied himself that no one was on the watch, and then approaching the rear of Bute's shanty, found to his joy that the pony was in the shed. A chink in the board siding enabled him to look into the room which contained his prey; he started as he saw Apache Jack, instantly recognizing in him another criminal for whom a large reward was offered.

"Better luck than I dreamed of," he thought. "I shall take them both; but I now shall have to borrow a horse of Alford;" and he glided away, secured an animal from the stable, and tied it near his own. In a short time he was back at his post of observation. It had now become evident that no one even imagined that there was danger while such a storm was raging. The howling wind would drown all ordinary noises; and Brandt determined that the two men in the shanty should be on their way to jail that night. When he again put his eye to the chink in the wall, Bute was saying:

"Well, no one will start fer the mountings while this storm lasts, but, wound or no wound, I must get out of this as soon as it's over. There's no safety fer me here now."

"Ef they comes fer you, like enough they'll take me," replied Apache Jack, who, now that he was alone with his confederate, could speak his style of English fast enough. His character of half-breed was a disguise which his dark complexion had suggested. "Ter-morrer night, ef it's clar, we'll put out fer the easterd. I know of a shanty in the woods not so very fur from here in which we kin put up till yer's able ter travel furder. Come, now, take a swig of whiskey with me and then we'll sleep; there's no need of our watchin' any longer on a night like this. I'll jest step out an' see ef the pony's safe; sich a storm's 'nuff ter scare him off ter the woods."

"Well, jest lay my shooter on the cha'r here aside me 'fore you go. I feel safer with the little bull-dog in reach."

This the man did, then putting his own revolver on the table, that it might not get wet, began to unbar the door. Swift as a shadow Brandt glided out of the shed and around on the opposite side of the shanty.

An instant later Bute was paralyzed by seeing his enemy enter the open door. Before the outlaw could realize that Brandt was not a feverish vision induced by his wound, the detective had captured both revolvers, and was standing behind the door awaiting Apache Jack's return.

"Hist!" whispered Brandt, "not a sound, or you will both be dead in two minutes."

Bute's nerves were so shattered that he could scarcely have spoken, even if he had been reckless enough to do so. He felt himself doomed; and when brutal natures like his succumb, they usually break utterly. Therefore, he could do no more than shiver with unspeakable

E. P. Roe

dread as if he had an ague.

Soon Apache Jack came rushing in out of the storm, to be instantly confronted by Brandt's revolver. The fellow glanced at the table, and seeing his own weapon was gone, instinctively half drew a long knife.

"Put that knife on the table!" ordered Brandt, sternly. "Do you think I'd allow any such foolishness?"

The man now realized his powerlessness, and obeyed; and Brandt secured this weapon also.

"See here, Apache Jack, or whatever your name is, don't you run your head into a noose. You know I'm empowered to arrest Bute, and you don't know anything about the force I have at hand. All you've got to do is to obey me, an officer of the law, like a good citizen. If you don't, I'll shoot you; and that's all there is about it. Will you obey orders?"

"I no understan'."

"Stop lying! You understand English as well as I do, and I'll suspect YOU if you try that on again. Come, now! I've no time to lose. It's death or obedience!"

"You can't blame a feller fer standin' by his mate," was the sullen yet deprecatory reply.

"I can blame any man, and arrest or shoot him too, who obstructs the law. You must obey me for the next half-hour, to prove that you are not Bute's accomplice."

"He's only my mate, and our rule is ter stand by each other; but, as you say, I can't help myself, and there's no use of my goin' ter jail."

"I should think not," added Brandt, appealing to the fellow's selfish hope of escaping further trouble if Bute was taken. "Now get my prisoner out of bed and dress him as soon as possible,"

"But he ain't able ter be moved. The superintendent said he wasn't."

"That's my business, not yours. Do as I bid you."

"Why don't yer yell fer help?" said Bute, in a hoarse whisper.

"Because he knows I'd shoot him if he did," remarked Brandt, coolly.

"Come, old man," said Jack, "luck's agin yer. Ef there's any hollerin' ter be done, yer's as able ter do that as I be."

"Quick, quick! jerk him out of bed and get him into his clothes. I won't permit one false move."

Jack now believed that his only means of safety was to be as expeditious as possible, and that if Bute was taken safely he would be left unmolested. People of their class rarely keep faith with one another when it is wholly against their interests to do so. Therefore, in spite of the wounded man's groans, he was quickly dressed and his hands tied behind him. As he opened his mouth to give expression to his protests, he found himself suddenly gagged by Brandt, who stood behind him. Then a strap was buckled about his feet, and he lay on the floor helpless and incapable of making a sound.

"Now, Jack," said Brandt, "go before me and bridle and saddle the pony; then bring him to the door."

Jack obeyed.

"Now put Bute upon him. I'll hold his head; but remember I'm covering you with a dead bead all the time."

"No need of that. I'm civil enough now."

"Well, you know we're sort of strangers, and it's no more than prudent for me to be on the safe side till we part company. That's right, strap his feet underneath. Now lead the pony in such directions as I say. Don't try to make off till I'm through with you, or you'll be shot instantly. I shall keep within a yard of you all the time."

They were not long in reaching the horse that Brandt had borrowed, and Jack said, "I s'pose I kin go now."

"First untie Bute's hands so he can guide the pony."

As the fellow attempted to do this, and his two hands were close together, Brandt slipped a pair of light steel handcuffs over his wrists, and the man was in his power. Almost before the new prisoner could recover from his surprise, he was lifted on the borrowed horse, and his legs also tied underneath.

"This ain't fa'r. You promised ter let me go when you got Bute off."

"I haven't got him off yet. Of course I can't let you go right back and bring a dozen men after us. You must be reasonable."

The fellow yelled for help; but the wind swept the sound away.

"If you do that again, I'll gag you too," said Brandt. "I tell you both once more, and I won't repeat the caution, that your lives depend on obedience." Then he mounted, and added, "Bute, I'm going to untie your hands, and you must ride on ahead of me. I'll lead Jack's horse."

In a moment he had his prisoners in the road, and was leaving the mine at a sharp pace. Bute was so cowed and dazed with terror that he obeyed mechanically. The stream was no longer a shallow brook, but a raging torrent which almost swept them away as Brandt urged them relentlessly through it. The tavern was dark and silent as they passed quickly by it. Then Brandt took the gag from Bute's mouth, and he groaned, cursed, and pleaded by turns. Hour after hour he urged them forward, until at last Bute gave out and fell forward on the pony's neck. Brandt dismounted and gave the exhausted man a draught from his flask.

"Oh, shoot me and have done with it!" groaned Bute; "I'd rather be shot than hanged anyhow."

"Couldn't think of it," replied the detective, cheerily. "My rule is to take prisoners alive, so that they can have a fair trial and be sure that they get justice. I'd take you the rest of the way in a bed if I could, but if you can't sit up, I'll have to tie you on. We'll reach a friend of mine by daylight, and then you can ride in a wagon, so brace up."

This the outlaw did for a time, and then he gave out utterly and was tied more securely to the pony. Out of compassion, Brandt thereafter travelled more slowly; and when the sun was an hour high, he led his forlorn captives to the house of a man whom he knew could be depended upon for assistance. After a rest sufficient to give Bute time to recover somewhat, the remainder of the journey was made without any incident worth mentioning, and the prisoners were securely lodged in jail on the evening of the 24th of December.

CHAPTER V

WHAT BRANDT SAW CHRISTMAS EVE

Brandt's words and effort had had their natural effect on the mind of Clara Heyward. They proved an increasing diversion of her thoughts, and slowly dispelled the morbid, leaden grief under which she had been sinking. Her new anxiety in regard to her lover's fortune and possible fate was a healthful counter-irritant. Half consciously she yielded to the influence of his strong, hopeful spirit, and almost before she was aware of it, she too began to hope. Chief of all, his manly tenderness and unbargaining love stole into her heart like a subtle balm; and responsive love, the most potent of remedies, was renewing her life. She found herself counting the days and then the hours that must intervene before the 25th. On Christmas eve her woman's nature triumphed, and she instinctively added such little graces to her toilet as her sombre costume permitted. She also arranged her beautiful hair in the style which she knew he admired. He might come; and she determined that his first glance should reveal that he was not serving one who was coldly apathetic to his brave endeavor and loyalty.

Indeed, even she herself wondered at the changes that had taken place during the brief time which had elapsed since their parting. There was a new light in

E. P. Roe

her eyes, and a delicate bloom tinged her cheeks.

"Oh," she murmured, "it's all so different now that I feel that I can live for him and make him happy."

She was sure that she could welcome him in a way that would assure him of the fulfilment of all his hopes; but when he did come with his eager, questioning eyes, she suddenly found herself under a strange restraint, tongue-tied and embarrassed. She longed to put her arms about his neck and tell him all - the new life, the new hope which his look of deep affection had kindled; and in effort for self-control, she seemed to him almost cold. He therefore became perplexed and uncertain of his ground, and took refuge in the details of his expedition, meanwhile mentally assuring himself that he must keep his word and put no constraint on the girl contrary to the dictates of her heart.

As his mind grew clearer, his keen observation began to reveal hopeful indications. She was listening intently with approval, and something more in her expression, he dared to fancy. Suddenly he exclaimed, "How changed you are for the better, Clara! You are lovelier to-night than ever you were. What is it in your face that is so sweet and bewildering? You were a pretty girl before; now you are a beautiful woman."

The color came swiftly at his words, and she faltered as she averted her eyes, "Please go on with your story, Ralph. You have scarcely begun yet. I fear you were in danger."

He came and stood beside her. "Clara," he pleaded, "look at me."

Hesitatingly she raised her eyes to his.

"Shall I tell you what I hope I see?"

The faintest suggestion of a smile hovered about her trembling lips.

"I hope I see what you surely see in mine. Come, Clara, you shall choose before you hear my story. Am I to be your husband or friend? for I've vowed that you shall not be without a loyal protector."

"Ralph, Ralph," she cried, springing up and hiding her face on his shoulder, "I have no choice at all. You know how I loved papa; but I've learned that there's another and different kind of love. I didn't half understand you when you first spoke; now I do. You will always see in my eyes what you've seen to-night."

E. P. Roe

FOUND YET LOST

CHAPTER I

LOVE IN THE WILDERNESS

Hopeless indeed must that region be which May cannot clothe with some degree of beauty and embroider with flowers. On the 5th day of the month the early dawn revealed much that would charm the eyes of all true lovers of nature even in that section of Virginia whose characteristics so grimly correspond with its name - The Wilderness. The low pines and cedars, which abound everywhere, had taken a fresh green; the deciduous trees, the tangled thickets, impenetrable in many places by horse or man, were putting forth a new, tender foliage, tinted with a delicate semblance of autumn hues. Flowers bloomed everywhere, humbly in the grass close to the soil as well as on the flaunting sprays of shrubbery and vines, filling the air with fragrance as the light touched and expanded the petals. Wood-thrushes and other birds sang as melodiously and contentedly as if they had selected some breezy upland forest for their nesting-place instead of a region which has become a synonym for gloom, horror, and death.

Lonely and uninhabited in its normal condition, this

forbidding wilderness had become peopled with thousands of men. The Army of the Potomac was penetrating and seeking to pass through it. Vigilant General Lee had observed the movement, and with characteristic boldness and skill ordered his troops from their strong intrenchments on Mine Run toward the Union flank. On this memorable morning the van of his columns wakened from their brief repose but a short distance from the Federal bivouac. Both parties were unconscious of their nearness, for with the exception of a few clearings the dense growth restricted vision to a narrow range. The Union forces were directed in their movements by the compass, as if they were sailors on a fog-enshrouded sea; but they well knew that they were seeking their old antagonist, the Army of Northern Virginia, and that the stubborn tug-of-war might begin at any moment.

When Captain Nichol shook off the lethargy of a brief troubled sleep, he found that the light did not banish his gloomy impressions. Those immediately around him were still slumbering, wrapped in their blankets. Few sounds other than the voices of the awakening birds broke the silence. After a little thought he drew his notebook from his pocket and wrote as follows:

"MY DARLING HELEN - I obey an impulse to write to you this morning. It is scarcely light enough to see as yet; but very soon we shall be on the move again to meet - we known not what, certainly heavy, desperate fighting. I do not know why I am so sad. I have faced the prospect of battles many times before, and have passed through them unharmed, but now I am depressed by an unusual foreboding. Naturally my thoughts turn to you. There was no formal engagement between us when I said those words (so hard to speak) of farewell, nor have I sought to bind you since. Every month has made more clear the uncertainty of life in my calling; and I felt that I had no right to lay upon you any restraint other than that of your own feelings. If the worst happened you would be free as far as I was concerned, and few would know that we had told each other of our love. I wish to tell you of mine once more - not for the last time, I hope, but I don't know. I do love you with my whole heart and soul; and if I am to die in this horrible wilderness, where so many of my comrades died a year ago, my last thoughts will be of you and of the love of God, which your love has made more real to me. I love you too well to wish my death, should it occur, to spoil your young life. I do not ask you to forget me - that would be worse than death, but I ask you to try to be happy and to make others happy as the years pass on. This bloody war will come to an end, will become a memory, and those who perish hope to be remembered; but I do not wish my memory to hang like a cloud over the happy days of peace. I close, my darling, in hope, not fear - hope for you, hope for me, whatever may happen to-day or on coming days of strife. It only remains for me to do my duty. I trust that you will also do yours, which may be even harder. Do not give way to despairing grief if I cannot come back to you in this world. Let your faith in God and hope of a future life inspire and strengthen you in your battles, which may require more courage and unselfishness than mine.

"Yours, either in life or death, ALBERT NICHOL."

He made another copy of this letter, put both in envelopes, and addressed them, then sought two men of his company who came from his native village. They were awake now and boiling their coffee. The officer and the privates had grown up as boys together with little difference of social standing in the democratic town. When off duty, there still existed much of the old familiarity and friendly converse, but when Captain Nichol gave an order, his townsmen immediately became conscious that they were separated from him by the iron wall of military discipline. This characteristic did not alienate his old associates. One of the men hit the truth fairly in saying: "When Cap speaks as Cap, he's as hard and sharp as a bayonet-point; but when a feller is sick and worn out 'tween times you'd think your granny was coddlin' yer."

It was as friend and old neighbor that Nichol approached Sam and Jim Wetherby, two stalwart brothers who had enlisted in his company. "Boys," he said, "I have a favor to ask of you. The Lord only knows how the day will end for any of us. We will take our chances and do our duty, as usual. I hope we may all boil coffee again to-night; but who knows? Here are two letters. If I should fall, and either or both of you come out all right, as I trust you will, please forward them. If I am with you again to-night, return them to me."

"Come, Captain," said Jim, heartily, "the bullet isn't molded that can harm you. You'll lead us into Richmond yet."

"It will not be from lack of goodwill if I don't. I like your spirit; and I believe the army will get there this time whether I'm with it or not. Do as I ask. There is no harm in providing against what may happen. Make your breakfast quickly, for orders may come at any moment;" and he strode away to look after the general readiness of his men.

The two brothers compared the address on the letters and laughed a little grimly. "Cap is a-providing, sure enough," Sam Wetherby remarked. "They are both written to the pretty Helen Kemble that he used to make eyes at in the singing-school. I guess he thinks that you might stop a bullet as well as himself, Jim."

"It's clear he thinks your chances for taking in lead are just as good," replied Jim. "But come, I'm one of them fellows that's never hit till I am hit. One thing at a time, and now it's breakast."

"Well, hanged if I want to charge under the lead of any other captain!" remarked Sam, meditatively sipping his coffee. "If that girl up yonder knows Cap's worth, she'll cry her eyes out if anything happens to him."

A few moments later the birds fled to the closest cover, startled by the innumerable bugles sounding the note of preparation. Soon the different corps, divisions, and brigades were upon their prescribed lines of march. No movement could be made without revealing the close proximity of the enemy. Rifle-reports from skirmish lines and reconnoitring parties speedily followed. A Confederate force was developed on the turnpike leading southwest from the old Wilderness Tavern; and the fighting began. At about eight o'clock Grant and Meade came up and made their headquarters beneath some pine-trees near the tavern. General Grant could scarcely believe at first that Lee had left his strong intrenchments to give battle in a region little better than a jungle; but he soon had ample and awful proof of the fact. Practically unseen by each other, the two armies grappled like giants in the dark. So thick were the trees and undergrowth that a soldier on a battle line could rarely see a thousand men on either side of him, yet nearly two hundred thousand men matched their deadly strength that day. Hundreds fell, died, and were hidden forever from human eyes.

Thinking to sweep away the rear-guard of Lee's retreating army, Grant ordered a strong advance on the pike in the afternoon. At first it was eminently successful, and if it had been followed up vigorously and steadily, as it undoubtedly would have been if the commander had known what was afterward revealed, it might have resulted in severe disaster to the Confederates. The enemy was pressed back rapidly; and the advancing Union forces were filled with enthusiasm. Before this early success culminated, genuine sorrow saddened every one in Captain Nichol's company. With his face toward the enemy, impetuously leading his men, he suddenly dropped his sword and fell senseless. Sam and Jim Wetherby heard a shell shrieking toward them, and saw it explode directly over their beloved leader. They rushed to his side; blood was pouring over his face, and it also seemed to them that a fragment of the shell had fatally wounded him in the forehead.

"Poor Cap, poor, brave Cap!" ejaculated Sam. "He didn't give us those letters for nothing."

"A bad job, an awfully bad job for us all! curse the eyes that aimed that shell!" growled practical Jim. "Here, take hold. We'll put him in that little dry ditch we just passed, and bury him after the fight, if still on our pins. We can't leave him here to be tramped on."

This they did, then hastily rejoined their company,

E. P. Roe

which had swept on with the battle line. Alas! that battle line and others also were driven back with terrible slaughter before the day closed. Captain Nichol was left in the ditch where he had been placed, and poor Sam Wetherby lay on his back, staring with eyes that saw not at a shattered bird's nest in the bushes above his head. The letter in his pocket mouldered with him.

Jim's begrimed and impassive face disguised an aching heart as he boiled his coffee alone that night. Then, although wearied almost to exhaustion, he gave himself no rest until he had found what promised to be the safest means of forwarding the letter in his pocket.

CHAPTER II

LOVE AT HOME

Long years before the war, happy children were growing in the village of Alton. They studied the history of wars much as they conned their lessons in geography. Scenes of strife belonged to the past, or were enacted among people wholly unlike any who dwelt in their peaceful community. That Americans should ever fight each other was as undreamed of as that the minister should have a pitched battle in the street with his Sunday-school superintendent. They rejoiced mildly when in their progress through the United States history they came to pages descriptive of Indian wars and the Revolutionary struggle, since they found their lessons then more easily remembered than the wordy disputes and little understood decisions of statesmen. The first skating on the pond was an event which far transcended in importance anything related between the green covers of the old history book, while to Albert Nichol the privilege of strapping skates on the feet of little Helen Kemble, and gliding away with her over the smooth ice, was a triumph unknown by any general. He was the son of a plain farmer, and she the daughter of the village banker. Thus, even in childhood, there was thrown around her the glamour of position and reputed wealth - advantages which have their value among the most democratic folk, although

E. P. Roe

slight outward deference may be paid to their possessors. It was the charming little face itself, with its piquant smiles and still more piquant pouts, which won Albert's boyish admiration. The fact that she was the banker's daughter only fired his ambition to be and to do something to make her proud of him.

Hobart Martine, another boy of the village, shared all his schoolmate's admiration for pretty Nellie, as she was usually called. He had been lame from birth, and could not skate. He could only shiver on the bank or stamp around to keep himself warm, while the athletic Al and the graceful little girl passed and repassed, quite forgetting him. There was one thing he could do; and this pleasure he waited for till often numb with cold. He could draw the child on his sled to her home, which adjoined his own.

When it came his turn to do this, and he limped patiently through the snow, tugging at the rope, his heart grew warm as well as his chilled body. She was a rather imperious little belle with the other boys, but was usually gentle with him because he was lame and quiet. When she thanked him kindly and pleasantly at her gate, he was so happy that he could scarcely eat his supper. Then his mother would laugh and say, "You've been with your little sweetheart." He would flush and make no reply.

How little did those children dream of war, even when studying their history lessons! Yet Albert Nichol now lay in the Wilderness jungle. He had done much to make his little playmate proud of him. The sturdy boy developed into a manly man. When he responded to his country's call and raised a company among his old friends and neighbors, Helen Kemble exulted over him tearfully. She gave him the highest tribute within her power and dearest possession -her heart. She made every campaign with him, following him with love's untiring solicitude through the scenes he described, until at last the morning paper turned the morning sunshine into mockery and the songs of the birds into dirges. Captain Nichol's name was on the list of the killed.

With something of the same jealousy, developed and intensified, which he had experienced while watching Albert glide away on the ice with the child adored in a dumb, boyish way, Hobart had seen his old schoolmate depart for the front. Then his rival took the girl from him; now he took her heart. Martine's lameness kept him from being a soldier. He again virtually stood chilled on the bank, with a cold, dreary, hopeless feeling which he believed would benumb his life. He did not know, he was not sure that he had lost Helen beyond hope, until those lurid days when men on both sides were arming and drilling for mutual slaughter. She was always so kind to him, and her tones so gentle when she spoke, that in love's fond blindness he had dared to hope. He eventually learned that she was only sorry for him. He did not, could not, blame her, for he needed but to glance at Nichol's stalwart form, and recall the young soldier's record, in order to know that it would be strange indeed if the girl had chosen otherwise. He would have been more than human if there had not been some bitterness in his heart; but he fought it down honestly, and while pursuing his peaceful avocations engaged in what he believed would be a lifelong battle. He smiled at the girl across the garden fence and called out his cheery "Good-morning." He was her frequent companion by the fireside or on the piazza, according to the season; and

E. P. Roe

he alone of the young men was welcome, for she had little sympathy for those who remained at home without his excuse. He was so bravely her friend, keeping his great love so sternly repressed that she only felt it like a genial warmth in his tones and manner, and believed that he was becoming in truth what he seemed, merely a friend.

On that terrible May morning he was out in the garden and heard her wild, despairing cry as she read the fatal words. He knew that a heavy battle had been begun, and was going down to the gate for his paper, which the newsboy had just left. There was no need of opening it, for the bitter cry he had heard made known to him the one item of intelligence compared with which all else for the time became insignificant. Was it the Devil that inspired a great throb of hope in his heart? At any rate he thought it was, and ground his heel into the gravel as if the serpent's head was beneath it, then limped to Mr. Kemble's door.

The old banker came out to meet him, shaking his gray head and holding the paper in his trembling hand. "Ah!" he groaned, "I've feared it, I've feared it all along, but hoped that it would not be. You've seen Nichol's name - " but he could not finish the sentence.

"No, I have seen nothing; I only heard Helen's cry. That told the whole story."

"Yes. Well, her mother's with her. Poor girl! poor girl! God grant it isn't her death-blow too. She has suffered too much under this long strain of anxiety."

A generous resolve was forming in Martine's mind, and he said earnestly, "We must tide her through this terrible shock. There may be some mistake; he may be only wounded. Do not let her give up hope absolutely. I'll drop everything and go to the battlefield at once. If the worst has in truth happened, I can bring home his remains, and that would be a comfort to her. A newspaper report, made up hastily in the field, is not final. Let this hope break the cruel force of the blow, for it is hard to live without hope."

"Well, Hobart, you ARE a true friend. God bless and reward you! If nothing comes of it for poor Nichol, as I fear nothing will, your journey and effort will give a faint hope to Nellie, and, as you say, break the force of the blow. I'll go and tell her."

Martine went into the parlor, which Helen had decorated with mementoes of her soldier lover. He was alone but a few moments before he heard hasty steps. Helen entered with hot, tearless eyes and an agonized, imploring expression.

"What!" she cried, "is it true that you'll go?"

"Yes, Helen, immediately. I do not think there's reason for despair."

"Oh, God bless you! friend, friend! I never knew what the word meant before. Oh, Hobart, no sister ever lavished love on a brother as I will love you if you bring back my Albert;" and in the impulse of her overwhelming gratitude she buried her face on his shoulder and sobbed aloud. Hope already brought the relief of tears.

He stroked the bowed head gently, saying, "God is my witness, Helen, that I will spare no pains and shrink from no danger in trying to find Captain Nichol. I have known of many instances where the first reports of battles proved incorrect;" and he led her to a chair.

"It is asking so much of you," she faltered.

"You have asked nothing, Helen. I have offered to go, and I AM going. It is a little thing for me to do. You know that my lameness only kept me from joining Captain Nichol's company. Now try to control your natural feelings like a brave girl, while I explain my plans as far as I have formed them."

"Yes, yes! Wait a few moments. Oh, this pain at my heart! I think it would have broken if you hadn't come. I couldn't breathe; I just felt as if sinking under a weight."

"Take courage, Helen. Remember Albert is a soldier."

"IS, IS! Oh, thanks for that little word! You do not believe that he is gone and lost to me?"

"I cannot believe it yet. We will not believe it. Now listen patiently, for you will have your part to do."

"Yes, yes; if I could only do something! That would help me so much. Oh, if I could only go with you!"

"That would not be best or wise, and might defeat my efforts. I must be free to go where you could not - to visit places unsafe for you. My first step must be to get letters to our State Senator. Your father can write one, and I'll get one or two others. The Senator will give me a letter to the Governor, who in turn will accredit me to the authorities at Washington and the officer in command on the battlefield. You know I shall need passes. Those who go to the extreme front must be able to account for themselves. I will keep in telegraphic communication with you, and you may receive additional tidings which will aid me in my search. Mr. Kemble!" he concluded, calling her father from his perturbed pacing up and down the hall.

"Ah!" said the banker, entering, "this is a hundred-fold better than despairing, useless grief. I've heard the gist of what Hobart has said, and approve it. Now I'll call mother, so that we may all take courage and get a good grip on hope."

They consulted together briefly, and in the prospect of action, Helen was carried through the first dangerous crisis in her experience.

CHAPTER III

"DISABLED"

Mrs. Martine grieved over her son's unexpected resolve. In her estimation he was engaging in a very dangerous and doubtful expedition. Probably mothers will never outgrow a certain jealousy when they find that another woman has become first in the hearts of their sons. The sense of robbery was especially strong in this case, for Mrs. Martine was a widow, and Hobart an only and idolized child.

The mother speedily saw that it would be useless to remonstrate, and tearfully aided him in his preparations. Before he departed, he won her over as an ally. "These times, mother, are bringing heavy burdens to very many, and we should help each other bear them. You know what Helen is to me, and must be always. That is something which cannot be changed. My love has grown with my growth and become inseparable from my life. I have my times of weakness, but think I can truly say that I love her so well that I would rather make her happy at any cost to myself. If it is within my power, I shall certainly bring Nichol back, alive or dead. Prove your love to me, mother, by cheering, comforting, and sustaining that poor girl. I haven't as much hope of success as I tried to give her, but she needs hope now; she must have it, or there is no assurance against disastrous effects on her health and mind. I couldn't bear that."

"Well, Hobart, if he is dead, she certainly ought to reward you some day."

"We must not think of that. The future is not in our hands. We can only do what is duty now."

Noble, generous purposes give their impress to that index of character, the human face. When Martine came to say good-by to Helen, she saw the quiet, patient cripple in a new light. He no longer secured her strong affection chiefly on the basis of gentle, womanly commiseration. He was proving the possession of those qualities which appeal strongly to the feminine nature; he was showing himself capable of prompt, courageous action, and his plain face, revealing the spirit which animated him, became that of a hero in her eyes. She divined the truth - the love so strong and unselfish that it would sacrifice itself utterly for her. He was seeking to bring back her lover when success in his mission would blot out all hope for him. The effect of his action was most salutary, rousing her from the inertia of grief and despair. "If a mere friend," she murmured, "can be so brave and self-forgetful, I have no excuse for giving away utterly."

She revealed in some degree her new impressions in parting. "Hobart," she said, holding his hand in both of hers, "you have done much to help me. You have not only brought hope, but you have also shown a spirit which would shame me out of a selfish grief. I cannot now forget the claims of others, of my dear father and mother here, and I promise you that I will try to be brave like you, like Albert. I shall not become a weak, helpless burden, I shall not sit still and wring idle hands when others are heroically doing and suffering. Good-by, my friend, my brother. God help us all!"

He felt that she understood him now as never before; and the knowledge inspired a more resolute purpose, if this were possible. That afternoon he was on his way. There came two or three days of terrible suspense for Helen, relieved only by telegrams from Martine as he passed from point to point. The poor girl struggled as a swimmer breasts pitiless waves intervening between him and the shore. She scarcely allowed herself an idle moment; but her effort was feverish and in a measure the result of excitement. The papers were searched for any scrap of intelligence, and the daily mail waited for until the hours and minutes were counted before its arrival.

One morning her father placed Nichol's letter in her hands. They so trembled in the immense hope, the overwhelming emotion which swept over her at sight of the familiar handwriting, that at first she could not open it. When at last she read the prophetic message, she almost blotted out the writing with her tears, moaning, "He's dead, he's dead!" In her morbid, overwrought condition, the foreboding that had been in the mind of the writer was conveyed to hers; and she practically gave up hope for anything better than the discovery and return of his remains. Her father, mother, and intimate friends tried in vain to rally her; but the conviction remained that she had read her lover's farewell words. In spite of the most pathetic and strenuous effort, she could not keep up any longer, and sobbed till she slept in utter exhaustion.

On the following day, old Mr. Wetherby came into the

bank. The lines about his mouth were rigid with suppressed feeling. He handed Mr. Kemble a letter, saying in a husky voice, "Jim sent this. He says at the end I was to show it to you." The scrawl gave in brief the details about Captain Nichol already known to the reader, and stated also that Sam Wetherby was missing. "All I know is," wrote the soldier, "that we were driven back, and bullets flew like hail. The brush was so thick I couldn't see five yards either way when I lost sight of Sam."

The colonel of the regiment also wrote to Captain Nichol's father, confirming Private Wetherby's letter. The village had been thrown into a ferment by the tidings of the battle and its disastrous consequences. There was bitter lamentation in many homes. Perhaps the names of Captain Nichol and Helen were oftenest repeated in the little community, for the fact of their mutual hopes was no longer a secret. Even thus early some sagacious people nodded their heads and remarked, "Hobart Martine may have his chance yet." Helen Kemble believed without the shadow of a doubt that all the heart she had for love had perished in the wilderness.

The facts contained in Jim Wetherby's letter were telegraphed to Martine, and he was not long in discovering confirmation of them in the temporary hospitals near the battlefield. He found a man of Captain Nichol's company to whom Jim had related the circumstances. For days the loyal friend searched laboriously the horrible region of strife, often sickened nearly unto death by the scenes he witnessed, for his nature had not been rendered callous by familiarity with the results of war. Then instead of returning home, he employed the influence given by his letters and passes, backed by his own earnest pleading, to obtain permission for a visit to Nichol's regiment. He found it under fire; and long afterward Jim Wetherby was fond of relating how quietly the lame civilian listened to the shells shrieking over and exploding around him. Thus Martine learned all that could be gathered of Nichol's fate, and then, ill and exhausted, he turned his face northward. He felt that it would be a hopeless task to renew his search on the battlefield, much of which had been burned over. He also had the conviction it would be fatal to him to look upon its unspeakable horrors, and breathe again its pestilential air.

He was a sick man when he arrived at home, but was able to relate modestly in outline the history of his efforts, softening and concealing much that he had witnessed. In the delirium of fever which followed, they learned more fully of what he had endured, of how he had forced himself to look upon things which, reproduced in his ravings, almost froze the blood of his watchers.

Helen Kemble felt that her cup of bitterness had been filled anew, yet the distraction of a new grief, in which there was a certain remorseful self-reproach, had the effect of blunting the sharp edge of her first sorrow. In this new cause for dread she was compelled in some degree to forget herself. She saw the intense solicitude of her father and mother, who had been so readily accessory to Martine's expedition; she also saw that his mother's heart was almost breaking under the strain of anxiety. His incoherent words were not needed to reveal that his effort had been prompted by his love. She was one of his watchers, patiently enduring the expressions of regret which the mother in her sharp agony could not repress. Nichol's last letter was now known by heart, its every word felt to be prophetic. She had indeed been called upon to exercise courage and fortitude greater than he could manifest even in the Wilderness battle. Although she often faltered, she did not fail in carrying out his instructions. When at last Martine, a pallid convalescent, could sit in the shade on the piazza, she looked older by years, having, besides, the expression seen in the eyes of some women who have suffered much, and can still suffer much more. In the matter relating to their deepest consciousness, no words had passed between them. She felt as if she were a widow, and hoped he would understand. His full recognition of her position, and acceptance of the fact that she did and must mourn for her lover, his complete self-abnegation, brought her a sense of peace.

The old clock on the landing of the stairway measured off the hours and days with monotonous regularity. Some of the hours and days had been immeasurably longer than the ancient timekeeper had indicated; but in accordance with usual human experiences, they began to grow shorter. Poignant sorrow cannot maintain its severity, or people could not live. Vines, grasses, and flowers covered the graves in Virginia; the little cares, duties, and amenities of life began to screen at times the sorrows that were nevertheless ever present.

"Hobart," Helen said one day in the latter part of June, "do you think you will be strong enough to attend the commemorative services next week? You know they have been waiting for you."

"Yes," he replied quietly; "'and they should not have

E. P. Roe

delayed them so long. It is very sad that so many others have been added since - since - "

"Well, you have not been told, for we have tried to keep every depressing and disquieting influence from you. Dr. Barnes said it was very necessary, because you had seen so much that you should try to forget. Ah, my friend, I can never forget what you suffered for me! Captain Nichol's funeral sermon was preached while you were so ill. I was not present - I could not be. I've been to see his mother often, and she understands me. I could not have controlled my grief, and I have a horror of displaying my most sacred feelings in public. Father and the people also wish you to be present at the general commemorative services, when our Senator will deliver a eulogy on those of our town who have fallen; but I don't think you should go if you feel that it will have a bad effect on you."

"I shall be present, Helen. I suppose my mind has been weak like my body; but the time has come when I must take up life again and accept its conditions as others are doing. You certainly are setting me a good example. I admit that my illness has left a peculiar repugnance to hearing and thinking about the war; it all seemed so very horrible. But if our brave men can face the thing itself, I should be weak indeed if I could not listen to a eulogy of their deeds."

"I am coming to think," resumed Helen, thoughtfully, "that the battle line extends from Maine to the Gulf, and that quiet people like you and me are upon it as truly as the soldiers in the field. I have thought that perhaps the most merciful wounds are often those which kill outright."

"I can easily believe that," he said.

His quiet tone and manner did not deceive her, and she looked at him wistfully as she resumed, "But if they do not kill, the pain must be borne patiently, even though we are in a measure disabled."

"Yes, Helen; and you are disabled in your power to give me what I can never help giving you. I know that. I will not misjudge or presume upon your kindness. We are too good friends to affect any concealments from each other."

"You have expressed my very thought. When you spoke of accepting the conditions of life, I hoped you had in mind what you have said - the conditions of life as they ARE, as we cannot help or change them. We both have got to take up life under new conditions."

"You have; not I, Helen."

Tears rushed to her eyes as she faltered, "I would be transparently false should I affect not to know. What I wish you to feel through the coming months and years is that I cannot - that I am disabled by my wound."

"I understand, Helen. We can go on as we have begun. You have lost, as I have not, for I have never possessed. You will be the greater sufferer; and it will be my dear privilege to cheer and sustain you in such ways as are possible to a simple friend."

She regarded him gratefully, and for the first time since that terrible May morning the semblance of a smile briefly illumined her face.

CHAPTER IV

MARTINE SEEKS AN ANTIDOTE

It can readily be understood that Martine in his expedition to the South had not limited his efforts solely to his search for Captain Nichol. Wherever it had been within his power he had learned all that he could of other officers and men who had come from his native region; and his letters to their relatives had been in some instances sources of unspeakable comfort. In his visit to the front he had also seen and conversed with his fellow-townsmen, some of whom had since perished or had been wounded. As he grew stronger, Helen wrote out at his dictation all that he could remember concerning these interviews; and these accounts became precious heirlooms in many families.

On the Fourth of July the commemorative oration was delivered by the Senator, who proved himself to be more than senator by his deep, honest feeling and good taste. The "spread eagle" element was conspicuously absent in his solemn, dignified, yet hopeful words. He gave to each their meed of praise. He grew eloquent over the enlisted men who had so bravely done their duty without the incentive of ambition. When he spoke of the honor reflected on the village by the heroism of Captain Nichol, the hearts of the people glowed with gratitude and pride; but thoughts of pity came to all as they remembered the girl, robed in black, who sat with bowed head among them.

"I can best bring my words to a close," said the Senator, "by reading part of a letter written by one of your townsmen, a private in the ranks, yet expressive of feelings inseparable from our common human nature:

"DEAR FATHER - You know I ain't much given to fine feelings or fine words. Poor Sam beat me all holler in such things; but I want you and all the folks in Alton to know that you've got a regular soldier at home. Of course we were all glad to see Bart Martine; and we expected to have a good-natured laugh at his expense when the shells began to fly. Soldiers laugh, as they eat, every chance they get, 'cause they remember it may be the last one. Well, we knew Bart didn't know any more about war than a chicken, and we expected to see him get very nervous and limp off to the rear on the double quick. He didn't scare worth a cent. When a shell screeched over our heads, he just waited till the dinged noise was out of our ears and then went on with his questions about poor Cap and Sam and the others from our town. We were supporting a battery, and most of us lying down. He sat there with us a good hour, telling about the folks at home, and how you were all following us with your thoughts and prayers, and how you all mourned with those who lost friends, and were looking after the children of the killed and wounded. Fact is, before we knew it we were all on our feet cheering for Alton and the folks at home and the little lame man, who was just as good a soldier as any of us. I tell you he heartened up the boys, what's left of us. I'm sorry to hear he's so sick. If he should die, bury

E. P. Roe

him with a soldier's honors. JAMES WETHERBY."

"These plain, simple, unadorned words," concluded the Senator, "need no comment. Their force and significance cannot be enhanced by anything I can say. I do not know that I could listen quietly to shrieking and exploding shells while I spoke words of courage and good cheer; but I do know that I wish to be among the foremost to honor your modest, unassuming townsman, who could do all this and more."

Martine was visibly distressed by this unexpected feature in the oration and the plaudits which followed. He was too sad, too weak in body and mind, and too fresh from the ghastly battlefield, not to shrink in sensitive pain from personal and public commendation. He evaded his neighbors as far as possible and limped hastily away.

He did not see Helen again till the following morning, for her wound had been opened afresh, and she spent the remainder of the day and evening in the solitude of her room. Martine was troubled at this, and thought she felt as he did.

In the morning she joined him on the piazza. She was pale from her long sad vigil, but renewed strength and a gentle patience were expressed in her thin face.

"It's too bad, Helen," he broke out in unwonted irritation. "I wouldn't have gone if I had known. It was a miserable letting down of all that had gone before - that reference to me."

Now she smiled brightly as she said, "You are the only

one present who thought so. Has this been worrying you?"

"Yes, it has. If the speaker had seen what I saw, he would have known better. His words only wounded me."

"He judged you by other men, Hobart. His words would not have wounded very many. I'm glad I heard that letter - that I have learned what I never could from you. I'm very proud of my friend. What silly creatures women are, anyway! They want their friends to be brave, yet dread the consequences of their being so beyond words."

"Well," said Martine, a little grimly, "I'm going to my office to-morrow. I feel the need of a long course of reading in Blackstone."

"You must help keep me busy also," was her reply.

"I've thought about that; yes, a great deal. You need some wholesome, natural interest that is capable of becoming somewhat absorbing. Is it strange that I should recommend one phase of my hobby, flowers? You know that every tree, shrub, and plant on our little place is a sort of a pet with me. You are fond of flowers, but have never given much thought to their care, leaving that to your gardener. Flowers are only half enjoyed by those who do not cultivate them, nurse, or pet them. Then there is such an infinite variety that before you know it your thoughts are pleasantly occupied in experimenting with even one family of plants. It is an interest which will keep you much in the open air and bring you close to Mother Nature."

The result of this talk was that the sad-hearted girl first by resolute effort and then by a growing fondness for the tasks, began to take a personal interest in the daily welfare of her plants. Martine and her father were always on the look-out for something new and rare; and as winter approached, the former had a small conservatory built on the sunny side of the house. They also gave her several caged song-birds, which soon learned to recognize and welcome her. From one of his clients Martine obtained a droll-looking dog that seemed to possess almost human intelligence. In the daily care of living things and dependent creatures that could bloom or be joyous without jarring upon her feelings, as would human mirth or gayety, her mind became wholesomely occupied part of each day; she could smile at objects which did not know, which could not understand.

Still, there was no effort on her part to escape sad memories or the acts and duties which revived them. A noble monument had been erected to Captain Nichol, and one of her chief pleasures was to decorate it with the flowers grown under her own care. Few days passed on which she did not visit one of the families who were or had been represented at the front, while Mrs. Nichol felt that if she had lost a son she had in a measure gained a daughter. As the months passed and winter was wellnigh spent, the wise gossips of the village again began to shake their heads and remark, "Helen Kemble and Bart Martine are very good friends; but I guess that's all it will amount to - all, at any rate, for a long time."

All, for all time, Helen had honestly thought. It might easily have been for all time had another lover sought her, or if Martine himself had become a wooer and so put her on her guard. It was his patient acceptance of what she had said could not be helped, his self-forgetfulness, which caused her to remember his need - a need greatly increased by a sad event. In the breaking up of winter his mother took a heavy cold which ended in pneumonia and death.

The gossips made many plans for him and indulged in many surmises as to what lie would do; but he merely engaged the services of an old woman as domestic, and lived on quietly as before. Perhaps he grew a little morbid after this bereavement and clung more closely to his lonely hearth.

This would not be strange. Those who dwell among shadows become ill at ease away from them. Helen was the first to discover this tendency, and to note that he was not rallying as she had hoped he would. He rarely sought their house except by invitation, and then often lapsed into silences which he broke with an evident effort. He never uttered a word of complaint or consciously appealed for sympathy, but was slowly yielding to the steady pressure of sadness which had almost been his heritage. She would have been less than woman if, recalling the past and knowing so well the unsatisfied love in his heart, she had not felt for him daily a larger and deeper commiseration. When the early March winds rattled the casements, or drove the sleety rain against the windows, she saw him in fancy sitting alone brooding, always brooding.

One day she asked abruptly, "Hobart, what are you thinking about so deeply when you are looking at the fire?"

A slow, deep flush came into his face, and he hesitated

in his answer. At last he said, "I fear I'm getting into a bad mood, and think I must do something decided. Well, for one thing, the continuance of this war weighs upon my spirit. Men are getting so scarce that I believe they will take me in some capacity. Now that mother is not here, I think I ought to go."

"Oh, Hobart, we would miss you so!" she faltered.

He looked up with a smile. "Yes, Helen, I think you would - not many others, though. You have become so brave and strong that you do not need me any more."

"I am not so brave and strong as I seem. If I were, how did I become so? With the tact and delicacy of a woman, yet with the strength of a man, you broke the crushing force of the first blow, and have helped me ever since."

"You see everything through a very friendly medium. At any rate I could not have been content a moment if I had not done all in my power. You do not need me any longer; you have become a source of strength to others. I cannot help seeing crowded hospital wards; and the thought pursues me that in one of them I might do something to restore a soldier to his place in the field or save him for those at home. I could at least be a hospital nurse, and I believe it would be better for me to be doing some such work."

"I believe it would be better for me also," she answered, her eyes full of tears.

"No, Helen - no, indeed. You have the higher mission of healing the heart-wounds which the war is making in your own vicinity. You should not think of leaving your father and mother in their old age, or of filling their days with anxiety which might shorten their lives."

"It will be very hard for us to let you go. Oh, I did not think I would have to face this also!"

He glanced at her hastily, for there was a sharp distress in her tone, of which she was scarcely conscious herself. Then, as if recollecting himself, he reasoned gently and earnestly: "You were not long in adopting the best antidote for trouble. In comforting others, you have been comforted. The campaign is opening in Virginia; and I think it would be a good and wholesome thing for me to be at work among the wounded. If I can save one life, it will be such a comfort after the war is over."

"Yes," she replied, softly; "the war will be over some day. Albert, in his last letter, said the war would cease, and that happy days of peace were coming. How they can ever be happy days to some I scarcely know; but he seemed to foresee the future when he wrote."

"Helen, I'm going. Perhaps the days of peace will be a little happier if I go."

CHAPTER V

SECOND BLOOM

Martine carried out his purpose almost immediately, seeking the temporary and most exposed hospitals on the extreme left of Grant's army before Petersburg. Indeed, while battles were still in progress he would make his way to the front and become the surgeon's tireless assistant. While thus engaged, even under the enemy's fire, he was able to render services to Jim Wetherby which probably saved the soldier's life. Jim lost his right arm, but found a nurse who did not let him want for anything till the danger point following amputation had passed. Before many weeks he was safe at home, and from him Helen learned more of Martine's quiet heroism than she could ever gather from his letters. In Jim Wetherby's estimation, Cap and Bart Martine were the two heroes of the war.

The latter had found the right antidote. Not a moment was left for morbid brooding. On every side were sharp physical distress, deadly peril to life and limb, pathetic efforts to hold ground against diseases or sloughing wounds. In aiding such endeavor, in giving moral support and physical care, Martine forgot himself. Helen's letters also were an increasing inspiration. He could scarcely take up one of them and say, "Here her words begin to have a warmer tinge of feeling;" but as spring advanced, imperceptibly yet surely, in spite of pauses and apparent retrogressions, just so surely she revealed a certain warmth of sympathy. He was engaged in a work which made it easy for her to idealize him. His unselfish effort to help men live, to keep bitter tears from the eyes of their relatives, appealed most powerfully to all that was unselfish in her nature, and she was beginning to ask, "If I can make this man happier, why should I not do so?" Nichol's letter gained a new meaning in the light of events: "I do not ask you to forget me - that would be worse than death - but I ask you to try to be happy and to make others happy."

"A noble, generous nature prompted those words," she now often mused. "How can I obey their spirit better than in rewarding the man who not only has done so much for me, but also at every cost sought to rescue him?"

In this growing disposition she had no innate repugnance to overcome, nor the shrinking which can neither be defined nor reasoned against. Accustomed to see him almost daily from childhood, conscious for years that he was giving her a love that was virtually homage, she found her heart growing very compassionate and ready to yield the strong, quiet affection which she believed might satisfy him. This had come about through no effort on her part, from no seeking on his, but was the result of circumstances, the outgrowth of her best and most unselfish feelings.

But the effect began to separate itself in character from its causes. All that had gone before might explain why she was learning to love him, and be sufficient reason for this affection, but a woman's love, even that quiet

E. P. Roe

phase developing in Helen's heart, is not like a man's conviction, for which he can give his clear-cut reasons. It is a tenderness for its object - a wish to serve and give all in return for what it receives.

Martine vaguely felt this change in Helen long before he understood it. He saw only a warmer glow of sisterly affection, too high a valuation of his self-denying work, and a more generous attempt to give him all the solace and support within her power.

One day in July, when the war was well over and the field hospitals long since broken up, he wrote from Washington, where he was still pursuing his labors:

"My work is drawing to a close. Although I have not accomplished a tithe of what I wished to do, and have soon so much left undone, I am glad to remember that I have alleviated much pain and, I think, saved some lives. Such success as I have had, dear Helen, has largely been due to you. Your letters have been like manna. You do not know - it would be impossible for you to know - the strength they have given, the inspiration they have afforded. I am naturally very weary and worn physically, and the doctors say I must soon have rest; but your kind words have been life-giving to my soul. I turn to them from day to day as one would seek a cool, unfailing spring. I can now accept life gratefully with the conditions which cannot be changed. How fine is the influence of a woman like you! What deep springs of action it touches! When waiting on the sick and wounded, I try to blend your womanly nature with my coarser fibre. Truly, neither of us has suffered in vain if we learn better to minister to others. I cannot tell you how I long to see the home gardens again; and it now seems that just to watch you in yours will be unalloyed happiness."

Helen smiled over this letter with sweet, deep meanings in her eyes.

One August evening, as the Kemble family sat at tea, he gave them a joyous surprise by appearing at the door and asking in a matter-of-fact voice, "Can you put an extra plate on the table?"

There was no mistaking the gladness of her welcome, for it was as genuine as the bluff heartiness of her father and the gentle solicitude of her mother, who exclaimed, "Oh, Hobart, how thin and pale you are!"

"A few weeks' rest at home will remedy all that," he said. "The heat in Washington was more trying than my work."

"Well, thank the Lord! you ARE at home once more," cried the banker. "I was thinking of drawing on the authorities at Washington for a neighbor who had been loaned much too long."

"Helen," said Martine, with pleased eyes, "how well you look! It is a perfect delight to see color in your cheeks once more. They are gaining, too, their old lovely roundness. I'm going to say what I think right out, for I've been with soldiers so long that I've acquired their bluntness."

"It's that garden work you lured me into," she explained. "I hope you won't think your plants and trees have been neglected."

"Have you been keeping my pets from missing me?"

"I guess they have missed you least of all. Helen has seen to it that they were cared for first," said Mrs. Kemble, emphatically.

"You didn't write about that;" and he looked at the girl gratefully.

"Do you think I could see weeds and neglect just over the fence?" she asked, with a piquant toss of her head.

"Do you think I could believe that you cared for my garden only that your eyes might not be offended?"

"There, I only wished to give you a little surprise. You have treated us to one by walking in with such delightful unexpectedness, and so should understand. I'll show you when you are through supper."

"I'm through now;" and he rose with a promptness most pleasing to her. His gladness in recognizing old and carefully nurtured friends, his keen, appreciative interest in the new candidates for favor that she had planted, rewarded her abundantly.

"Oh," he exclaimed, "what a heavenly exchange from the close, fetid air of hospital wards! Could the first man have been more content in his divinely planted garden?"

She looked at him shyly and thought, "Perhaps when you taste of the fruit of knowledge the old story will have a new and better meaning."

She now regarded him with a new and wistful interest, no longer seeing him through the medium of friendship only. His face, thin and spiritualized, revealed his soul without disguise. It was the countenance of one who had won peace through the divine path of ministry - healing others, himself had been healed. She saw also his unchanged, steadfast love shining like a gem over which flows a crystal current. Its ray was as serene as it was undimmed. It had taken its place as an imperishable quality in his character - a place which it would retain without vicissitude unless some sign from her called it into immediate and strong manifestation. She was in no haste to give this. Time was touching her kindly; the sharp, cruel outlines of the past were softening in the distance, and she was content to remember that the treasure was hers when she was ready for it - a treasure more valued daily.

With exultation she saw him honored by the entire community. Few days passed without new proofs of the hold he had gained on the deepest and best feelings of the people. She who once had pitied now looked up to him as the possessor of that manhood which the most faultless outward semblance can only suggest.

Love is a magician at whose touch the plainest features take on new aspects. Helen's face had never been plain. Even in its anguish it had produced in beholders the profound commiseration which is more readily given when beauty is sorrowful. Now that a new life at heart was expressing itself, Martine, as well as others, could not fail to note the subtile changes. While the dewy freshness of her girlish bloom was absent, the higher and more womanly qualities were now revealing themselves. Her nature had been deepened by her experiences, and the harmony of her life was all the sweeter for its minor chords.

To Martine she became a wonderful mystery, and he

almost worshipped the woman whose love he believed buried in an unknown grave, but whose eyes were often so strangely kind. He resumed his old life, but no longer brooded at home, when the autumn winds began to blow. He recognized the old danger and shunned it resolutely. If he could not beguile his thoughts from Helen, it was but a step to her home, and her eyes always shone with a luminous welcome. Unless detained by study of the legal points of some case in hand, he usually found his way over to the Kemble fireside before the evening passed, and his friends encouraged him to come when he felt like it. The old banker found the young man exceedingly companionable, especially in his power to discuss intelligently the new financial conditions into which the country was passing. Helen would smile to herself as she watched the two men absorbed in questions she little understood, and observed her mother nodding drowsily over her knitting. The scene was so peaceful, so cheery, so hopeful against the dark background of the past, that she could not refrain from gratitude. Her heart no longer ached with despairing sorrow, and the anxious, troubled expression had faded out of her parents' faces.

"Yes," she would murmur softly to herself, "Albert was right; the bloody war has ceased, and the happy days of peace are coming. Heaven has blessed him and made his memory doubly blessed, in that he had the heart to wish them to be happy, although he could not live to see them. Unconsciously he took the thorns out of the path which led to his friend and mine. How richly father enjoys Hobart's companionship! He will be scarcely less happy - when he knows - than yonder friend, who is such a very scrupulous friend. Indeed, how either is ever going to know I scarcely see, unless

I make a formal statement."

Suddenly Martine turned, and caught sight of her expression.

"All I have for your thoughts! What wouldn't I give to know them!"

Her face became rosier than the firelight warranted as she laughed outright and shook her head.

"No matter," he said; "I am content to hear you laugh like that."

"Yes, yes," added the banker; "Helen's laugh is sweeter to me than any music I ever heard. Thank God! we all can laugh again. I am getting old, and in the course of nature must soon jog on to the better country. When that time comes, the only music I want to hear from earth is good, honest laughter."

"Now, papa, hush that talk right away," cried Helen, with glistening eyes.

"What's the matter?" Mrs. Kemble asked, waking up.

"Nothing, my dear, only it's time for us old people to go to bed."

"Well, I own that it would be more becoming to sleep there than to reflect so unfavorably on your conversation. Of late years talk about money matters always puts me to sleep."

"That wasn't the case, was it, my dear, when we tried to stretch a thousand so it would reach from one

January to another?"

"I remember," she replied, smiling and rolling up her knitting, "that we sometimes had to suspend specie payments. Ah, well, we were happy."

When left alone, it was Helen's turn to say, "Now your thoughts are wool-gathering. You don't see the fire when you look at it that way."

"No, I suppose not," replied Martine. "I'll be more frank than you. Your mother's words, 'We were happy,' left an echo in my mind. How experience varies! It is pleasant to think that there are many perfectly normal, happy lives like those of your father and mother."

"That's one thing I like in you, Hobart. You are so perfectly willing that others should be happy."

"Helen, I agree with your father. Your laugh WAS music, the sweetest I ever heard. I'm more than willing that you should be happy. Why should you not be? I have always felt that what he said was true - what he said about the right to laugh after sorrow - but it never seemed so true before. Who could wish to leave blighting sorrow after him? Who could sing in heaven if he knew that he had left tears which could not be dried on earth?"

"You couldn't," she replied with bowed head.

"Nor you, either; nor the brave man who died, to whom I only do justice in believing that he would only be happier could he hear your laugh. Your father's wholesome, hearty nature should teach us to banish every morbid tendency. Let your heart grow as light as it will, my friend. Your natural impulses will not lead you astray. Good-night."

"You feel sure of that?" she asked, giving him a hand that fluttered in his, and looking at him with a soft fire in her eyes.

"Oh, Helen, how distractingly beautiful you are! You are blooming again like your Jack-roses when the second growth pushes them into flower. There; I must go. If I had a stone in my breast instead of a heart - Good-night. I won't be weak again."

E. P. Roe

CHAPTER VI

MORE THAN REWARD

Helen Kemble's character was simple and direct She was one who lived vividly in the passing hour, and had a greater capacity for deep emotions than for retaining them. The reputation for constancy is sometimes won by those incapable of strong convictions. A scratch upon a rock remains in all its sharpness, while the furrow that has gone deep into the heart of a field is eventually almost hidden by a new flowering growth. The truth was fully exemplified in Helen's case; and a willingness to marry her lifelong lover, prompted at first by a spirit of self-sacrifice, had become, under the influence of daily companionship, more than mere assent. While gratitude and the wish to see the light of a great, unexpected joy come into his eyes remained her chief motives, she had learned that she could attain a happiness herself, not hoped for once, in making him happy.

He was true to his word, after the interview described in the preceding chapter. He did not consciously reveal the unappeased hunger of his heart, but her intuition was never at fault a moment.

One Indian-summer-like morning, about the middle of October, he went over to her home and said, "Helen, what do you say to a long day's outing? The foliage is at its brightest, the air soft as that of June. Why not store up a lot of this sunshine for winter use?"

"Yes, Helen, go," urged her mother. "I can attend to everything."

"A long day, did you stipulate?" said the girl in ready assent; "that means we should take a lunch. I don't believe you ever thought of that."

"We could crack nuts, rob apple-orchards, or if driven to extremity, raid a farmhouse."

"You have heard too much from the soldiers about living off the country. I'd rather raid mamma's cupboard before we start. I'll be ready as soon as you are."

He soon appeared in his low, easy phaeton; and she joined him with the presentiment that there might be even greater gladness in his face by evening than it now expressed. While on the way to the brow of a distant hill which would be their lunching place, they either talked with the freedom of old friends or lapsed into long silences.

At last he asked, "Isn't it a little odd that when with you the sense of companionship is just as strong when you are not talking?"

"It's a comfort you are so easily entertained. Don't you think I'm a rather moderate talker for a woman?"

"Those that talk the most are often least entertaining. I've thought a good deal about it - the unconscious influence of people on one another. I don't mean influence in any moral sense, but in the power to make one comfortable or uncomfortable, and to produce a sense of restfulness and content or to make one ill at ease and nervously desirous of escape."

"And you have actually no nervous desire to escape, no castings around in your mind for an excuse to turn around and drive home?"

"No one could give a surer answer to your question than yourself. I've been thinking of something pleasanter than my enjoyment."

"Well?"

"That your expression has been a very contented one during the last hour. I am coming to believe that you can accept my friendship without effort. You women are all such mysteries! One gets hold of a clew now and then. I have fancied that if you had started out in the spirit of self-sacrifice that I might have a pleasant time, you would be more conscious of your purpose. Even your tact might not have kept me from seeing that you were exerting yourself; but the very genius of the day seems to possess you. Nature is not exerting herself in the least. No breath of air is stirring; all storms are in the past or the future. With a smile on her face, she is just resting in serene content, as you were, I hope. She is softening and obscuring everything distant by an orange haze, so that the sunny present may be all the more real. Days like these will do you good, especially if your face and manner reveal that you can be as truly at rest as Nature."

"Yet what changes may soon pass over the placid scene!"

"Yes, but don't think of them."

"Well, I won't - not now. Yes, you are becoming very penetrating. I am not exerting myself in the least to give you a pleasant time. I am just selfishly and lazily content."

"That fact gives me so much more than content that it makes me happy."

"Hobart, you are the most unselfish man I ever knew."

"Nonsense!"

They had reached their picnic-ground - the edge of a grove whose bright-hued foliage still afforded a grateful shade. The horse was unharnessed and picketed so that he might have a long range for grazing. Then Martine brought the provision basket to the foot of a great oak, and sat down to wait for Helen, who had wandered away in search of wild flowers. At last she came with a handful of late-blooming closed gentians.

"I thought these would make an agreeable feature in your lunch."

"Oh, you are beginning to exert yourself."

"Yes, I have concluded to, a little. So must you, to the extent of making a fire. The rest will be woman's work. I propose to drink your health in a cup of coffee."

"Ah, this is unalloyed," he cried, sipping it later on.

"The coffee?"

"Yes, and everything. We don't foresee the bright days any more than the dark ones. I did not dream of this in Virginia."

"You are easily satisfied. The coffee is smoky, the lunch is cold, winter is coming, and - "

"And I am very happy," he said.

"It would be a pity to disturb your serenity."

"Nothing shall disturb it to-day. Peace is one of the rarest experiences in this world. I mean only to remember that our armies are disbanded and that you are at rest, like Nature."

She had brought a little book of autumn poems, and after lunch read to him for an hour, he listening with the same expression of quiet satisfaction. As the day declined, she shivered slightly in the shade. He immediately arose and put a shawl around her.

"You are always shielding me," she said gently.

"One can do so little of that kind of thing," he replied, "not much more than show intent."

"Now you do yourself injustice." After a moment's hesitancy she added, "I am not quite in your mood to-day, and even Nature, as your ally, cannot make me forget or even wish to forget."

"I do not wish you to forget, but merely cease to remember for a little while. You say Nature is my ally. Listen: already the wind is beginning to sigh in the branches overhead. The sound is low and mournful, as if full of regret for the past and forebodings for the future. There is a change coming. All that I wished or could expect in you was that this serene, quiet day would give you a respite - that complete repose in which the wounded spirit is more rapidly healed and strengthened for the future."

"Have you been strengthened? Have you no fears for the future?"

"No fears, Helen. My life is strong in its negation. The man who is agitated by hopes and fears, who is doomed to disappointments, is the one who has not recognized his limitations, who has not accepted well-defined conditions."

"Hobart, I'm going to put you on your honor now. Remember, and do not answer hastily," and her gaze into his face was searching. Although quiet and perfectly self-controlled, the rich color mounted to her very brow.

"Well, Helen," he asked wonderingly.

"Imagine it possible," she continued with the same earnest gaze, "that you were a woman who has loved as I have loved, and lost as I have. The circumstances are all known, and you have only to recall them. If a man had loved you as you have loved me - "

"But, Helen, can you not believe in a love so strong that it does not ask - "

By a gesture she checked him and repeated, "But if a man had loved you as you have loved me - remember now, on your honor - would you permit him to love with no better reward than the consciousness of being a solace, a help, a sort of buffer between you and the ills of life?"

"But, Helen, I am more than that: I am your friend."

"Indeed you are, the best a woman ever had, or I could not speak as I am doing. Yet what I say is true. From the first it has been your sleepless aim to stand between me and trouble. What have I ever done for you?"

"In giving me your friendship - "

Again she interrupted him, saying, "That virtually means giving you the chance for continued self-sacrifice. Any man or woman in the land would give you friendship on such terms, YOUR terms with me. But you do not answer my question; yet you have answered it over and over again. Were you in my place with your unselfish nature, you could not take so very much without an inevitable longing to return all in your power."

He was deeply agitated. Burying his face in his hands, he said hoarsely, "I must not look at you, or my duty may be too hard. Ah, you are banishing peace and serenity now with a vengeance! I recognize your motive - whither your thoughts are tending. Your conscience, your pity, your exaggerated gratitude are driving you to contemplate a self-sacrifice compared with which mine is as nothing. Yet the possibility of what you suggest is so sweet, so - oh, it is like the reward of heaven for a brief life!" Then he bowed his head lower and added slowly, as if the words were forced from him, "No, Helen, you shall not reward me.

I cannot take as pay, or 'return,' as you express it, the reward that you are meditating. I must not remember in after years that my efforts in your behalf piled up such a burdensome sense of obligation that there was but one escape from it."

She came to his side, and removing his hands from his face, retained one of them as she said, gently, "Hobart, I am no longer a shy girl. I have suffered too deeply, I have learned too thoroughly how life may be robbed of happiness, and for a time, almost of hope, not to see the folly of letting the years slip away, unproductive of half what they might yield to you and me. I understand you; you do not understand me, probably because your ideal is too high. You employed an illustration in the narrowest meaning. Is heaven given only as a reward? Is not every true gift an expression of something back of the gift, more than the gift?"

"Helen!"

"Yes, Hobart, in my wish to make you happier I am not bent on unredeemed self-sacrifice. You have been the most skilful of wooers."

"And you are the divinest of mysteries. How have I wooed you?"

"By not wooing at all, by taking a course which compelled my heart to plead your cause, by giving unselfish devotion so unstintedly that like the rain and dew of heaven, it has fostered a new life in my heart, different from the old, yet sweet, real, and precious. I have learned that I can be happier in making you happy. Oh, I shall be no martyr. Am I inconstant because time and your ministry have healed the old wound - because the steady warmth and glow of your love has kindled mine?"

He regarded her with a gaze so rapt, so reverent, so expressive of immeasurable gratitude that her eyes filled with tears. "I think you do understand me," she whispered.

He kissed her hand in homage as he replied, "A joy like this is almost as hard to comprehend at first as an equally great sorrow. My garden teaches me to understand you. A perfect flower-stalk is suddenly and rudely broken. Instead of dying, it eventually sends out a little side-shoot which gives what bloom it can."

"And you will be content with what it can give?"

"I shall be glad with a happiness which almost terrifies me. Only God knows how I have longed for this."

That evening the old banker scarcely ceased rubbing his hands in general felicitation, while practical, house-wifely Mrs. Kemble already began to plan what she intended to do toward establishing Helen in the adjoining cottage.

Now that Martine believed his great happiness possible, he was eager for its consummation. At his request the 1st of December was named as the wedding day. "The best that a fireside and evening lamp ever suggested will then come true to me," ha urged. "Since this can be, life is too short that it should not be soon."

Helen readily yielded. Indeed, they were all so absorbed in planning for his happiness as to be oblivious of the rising storm. When at last the girl went to her room, the wind sighed and wailed so mournfully around the house as to produce a feeling of depression and foreboding.

CHAPTER VII

YANKEE BLANK

The wild night storm which followed the most memorable day of his life had no power to depress Martine. In the wavy flames and glowing coals of his open fire he saw heavenly pictures of the future. He drew his mother's low chair to the hearth, and his kindled fancy placed Helen in it. Memory could so reproduce her lovely and familiar features that her presence became almost a reality. In a sense he watched her changing expression and heard her low, mellow tones. The truth that both would express an affection akin to his own grew upon his consciousness like the incoming of a sun-lighted tide. The darkness and storm without became only the background of his pictures, enhancing every prophetic representation. The night passed in ecstatic waking dreams of all that the word "home" suggests when a woman, loved as he loved Helen, was its architect.

The days and weeks which followed were filled with divine enchantment; the prosaic world was trans-figured; the intricacies of the law were luminous with the sheen of gold, becoming the quartz veins from which he would mine wealth for Helen; the plants in his little rose-house were cared for with caressing tenderness because they gave buds which would be worn over the heart now throbbing for him. Never did mortal know such unalloyed happiness as blessed Martine, as he became daily more convinced that Helen was not giving herself to him merely from the promptings of compassion.

At times, when she did not know he was listening, he heard her low, sweet laugh; and it had a joyous ring and melody which repeated itself like a haunting refrain of music. He would say smilingly, "It is circumstantial evidence, equivalent to direct proof."

Helen and her mother almost took possession of his house while he was absent at his office, refurnishing and transforming it, yet retaining with reverent memory what was essentially associated with Mrs. Martine. The changing aspects of the house did not banish the old sense of familiarity, but were rather like the apple-tree in the corner of the garden when budding into new foliage and flower. The banker's purse was ever open for all this renovation, but Martine jealously persisted in his resolve to meet every expense himself. Witnessing his gladness and satisfaction, they let him have his way, he meanwhile exulting over Helen's absorbed interest in the adornment of her future home.

The entire village had a friendly concern in the approaching wedding; and the aged gossips never tired of saying, "I told you so," believing that they understood precisely how it had all come about. Even Mrs. Nichol aquiesced with a few deep sighs, assuring herself, "I suppose it's natural. I'd rather it was Bart Martine than anybody else."

A few days before the 1st of December, Martine

received a telegram from an aged uncle residing in a distant State. It conveyed a request hard to comply with, yet he did not see how it could be evaded. The despatch was delivered in the evening while he was at the Kembles', and its effect upon the little group was like a bolt out of a clear sky. It ran:

"Your cousin dangerously ill at - Hospital, Washington. Go to him at once, if possible, and telegraph me to come, if necessary."

Hobart explained that this cousin had remained in the army from choice, and that his father, old and feeble, naturally shrank from a journey to which he was scarcely equal. "My hospital experience," he concluded, "leads him to think that I am just the one to go, especially as I can get there much sooner than he. I suppose he is right. Indeed, I do not know of any one else whom he could call upon. It certainly is a very painful duty at this time."

"I can't endure to think of it," Helen exclaimed.

"It's a clear question of conscience, Helen," he replied gently. "Many years have passed since I saw this cousin, yet he, and still more strongly his father, have the claims of kinship. If anything should happen which my presence could avert, you know we should both feel bad. It would be a cloud upon our happiness. If this request had come before you had changed everything for me, you know I would have gone without a moment's hesitation. Very gratitude should make me more ready for duty;" yet he signed deeply.

"But it may delay the wedding, for which the invitations have gone out," protested Mrs. Kemble.

"Possibly it may, if my cousin's life is in danger."
Then, brightening up, he added: "Perhaps I shall find
that I can leave him in good care for a short time, and
then we can go to Washington on our wedding trip. I
would like to gain associations with that city different
from those I now have."

"Come now," said the banker, hopefully, "if we must
face this thing, we must. The probabilities are that it
will turn out as Hobart says. At worst it can only be a
sad interruption and episode. Hobart will be better
satisfied in the end if he does what he now thinks
his duty."

"Yours is the right view," assented the young man,
firmly. "I shall take the midnight train, and telegraph
as soon as I have seen my cousin and the hospital
surgeon."

He went home and hastily made his preparations; then,
with valise in hand, returned to the Kembles'. The old
people bade him Godspeed on his journey, and
considerately left him with his affianced.

"Hobart," Helen entreated, as they were parting, "be
more than ordinarily prudent. Do not take any risks,
even the most trivial, unless you feel you must.
Perhaps I'm weak and foolish, but I'm possessed with a
strange, nervous dread. This sudden call of duty - for
so I suppose I must look upon it - seems so
inopportune;" and she hid her tears on his shoulder.

"You are taking it much too seriously, darling," he
said, gently drawing her closer to him.

"Yes, my reason tells me that I am. You are only going

on a brief journey, facing nothing that can be called danger. Yet I speak as I feel - I cannot help feeling. Give me glad reassurance by returning quickly and safely. Then hereafter I will laugh at forebodings."

"There, you need not wait till I reach Washington. You shall hear from me in the morning, and I will also telegraph when I have opportunity on my journey."

"Please do so, and remember that I could not endure to have my life impoverished again."

Late the following evening, Martine inquired his way to the bedside of his cousin, and was glad indeed to find him convalescent. His own experienced eyes, together with the statement of the sick man and wardmaster, convinced him that the danger point was well passed. In immense relief of mind he said cheerily, "I will watch to-night"; and so it was arranged.

His cousin, soothed and hushed in his desire to talk, soon dropped into quiet slumber, while Martine's thronging thoughts banished the sense of drowsiness. A shaded lamp burned near, making a circle of light and leaving the rest of the ward dim and shadowy. The scene was very familiar, and it was an easy effort for his imagination to place in the adjoining cots the patients with whom, months before, he had fought the winning or losing battle of life. While memory sometimes went back compassionately to those sufferers, his thoughts dwelt chiefly upon the near future, with its certainty of happiness - a happiness doubly appreciated because his renewed experience in the old conditions of his life made the home which awaited him all the sweeter from contrast. He could scarcely believe that he was the same man who in places like this had sought to forget the pain of bereavement and of denial of his dearest wish - he who in the morning would telegraph Helen that the wedding need not even be postponed, or any change made in their plans.

The hours were passing almost unnoted, when a patient beyond the circle of light feebly called for water. Almost mechanically Hobart rose to get it, when a man wearing carpet slippers and an old dressing-gown shuffled noiselessly into view.

"Captain Nichol!" gasped Martine, sinking back, faint and trembling, in his chair.

The man paid no attention, but passed through the circle of light to the patient, gave him a drink, and turned. Martine stared with the paralysis of one looking upon an apparition.

When the figure was opposite to him, he again ejaculated hoarsely, "Captain Nichol!"

The form in slippers and gray ghostly dressing-gown turned sleepy eyes upon him without the slightest sign of recognition, passed on, and disappeared among the shadows near the wardmaster's room.

A blending of relief and fearful doubt agitated Martine. He knew he had been wide awake and in the possession of every faculty - that his imagination had been playing him no tricks. He was not even thinking of Nichol at the time; yet the impression that he had looked upon and spoken to his old schoolmate, to Helen's dead lover, had been as strong as it was instantaneous. When the man had turned, there had been an unnatural expression, which in a measure dispelled the illusion. After a moment of thought which scorched his brain, he rose and followed the man's steps, and was in time to see him rolling himself in his blanket on the cot nearest the door. From violent agitation, Martine unconsciously shook the figure outlined in the blanket roughly, as he asked, "What's your name?"

"Yankee Blank, doggone yer! Kyant you wake a feller 'thout yankin' 'im out o' baid? What yer want?"

"Great God!" muttered Hobart, tottering back to his seat beside his sleeping cousin, "was there ever such a horrible, mocking suggestion of one man in another? Yankee Blank - what a name! Southern accent and vernacular, yet Nichol's voice! Such similarity combined with such dissimilarity is like a nightmare. Of course it's not Nichol. He was killed nearly two years ago. I'd be more than human if I could wish him back now; but never in my life have I been so shocked and startled. This apparition must account for itself in the morning."

But he could not wait till morning; he could not control himself five minutes. He felt that he must banish that horrible semblance of Nichol from his mind by convincing himself of its absurdity.

He waited a few moments in order to compose his nerves, and then returned. The man had evidently gone to sleep.

"What a fool I am!" Martine again muttered. "Let the poor fellow sleep. The fact that he doesn't know me is proof enough. The idea of wanting any proof! I can investigate his case in the morning, and, no doubt, in broad light that astonishing suggestion of Nichol will disappear."

He was about to turn away when the patient who had called for water groaned slightly. As if his ears were as sensitive to such sounds as those of a mother who hears her child even when it stirs, the man arose. Seeing Martine standing by him, he asked in slight irritation, "What yer want? Why kyant yer say what yer want en have done 'th it? Lemme 'tend ter that feller yander firs'. We uns don't want no mo' stiffs;" and he shuffled with a peculiar, noiseless tread to the patient whose case seemed on his mind. Martine followed, his very hair rising at the well-remembered tones, and the mysterious principle of identity again revealed within the circle of light.

"This is simply horrible!" he groaned inwardly, "and I must have that man account for himself instantly."

"Now I'll 'tend ter yer, but yer mout let a feller sleep when he kin,"

"Don't you know me?" faltered Martine, overpowered.

"Naw."

"Please tell me your real name, not your nickname."

"Ain' got no name 'cept Yankee Blank. What's the matter with yer, anyhow?"

"Didn't you ever hear of Captain Nichol?"

"Reckon not. Mout have. I've nussed mo' cap'ins than I kin reckerlect."

"Are you a hospital nurse?"

"Sorter 'spect I am. That's what I does, anyhow. Have you anything agin it? Don't yer come 'ferin' round with me less yer a doctor, astin' no end o' questions. Air you a new doctor?"

"My name is Hobart Martine," the speaker forced himself to say, expecting fearfully a sign of recognition, for the impression that it was Nichol grew upon him every moment, in spite of apparent proof to the contrary.

"Hump! Hob't Ma'tine. Never yeared on yer. Ef yer want ter chin mo' in the mawnin', I'll be yere."

"Wait a moment, Yan - "

"Yankee Blank, I tole yer."

"Well, here's a dollar for the trouble I'm making you," and Martine's face flushed with shame at the act, so divided was his impression about the man.

Yankee Blank took the money readily, grinned, and said, "Now I'll chin till mawnin' ef yer wants hit."

"I won't keep you long. You remind me of - of - well, of Captain Nichol."

"He must 'a' been a cur'ous chap. Folks all say I'm a cur'ous chap."

"Won't you please tell me all that you can remember about yourself?"

"'Tain't much. Short hoss soon curried. Allus ben in hospitals. Had high ole jinks with a wound on my haid. Piece o' shell, they sez, cut me yere," and he pointed to a scar across his forehead. "That's what they tole me. Lor'! I couldn't mek much out o' the gibberish I firs' year, en they sez I talked gibberish too. But I soon got the hang o' the talk in the hospital. Well, ez I wuz sayin', I've allus been in hospitals firs' one, then anuther. I got well, en the sojers call me Yankee Blank en set me waitin' on sick uns en the wounded. That's what I'm a-doin' now."

"You were in Southern hospitals?"

"I reckon. They called the place Richman."

"Why did you come here?"

"Kaze I wuz bro't yere. They said I was 'changed.'"

"Exchanged, wasn't it?"

"Reckon it was. Anyhow I wuz bro't yere with a lot o' sick fellers. I wuzn't sick. For a long time the doctors kep' a-pesterin' me with questions, but they lemme 'lone now. I 'spected you wuz a new doctor, en at it agin."

"Don't you remember the village of Alton?"

The man shook his head.

"Don't you - " and Martine's voice grew husky - "don't

you remember Helen Kemble?"

"A woman?"

"Yes."

"Never yeared on her. I only reckerlect people I've seen in hospitals. Women come foolin' roun' some days, but Lor'! I kin beat any on 'em teekin' keer o' the patients; en wen they dies, I kin lay 'em out. You ast the wardmaster ef I kant lay out a stiff with the best o' 'em."

"That will do. You can go to sleep now."

"All right, Doc. I call everybody doc who asts sech a lot o' questions." He shuffled to his cot and was soon asleep.

CHAPTER VIII

"HOW CAN I?"

Martine sank into his chair again. Although the conversation had been carried on in low tones, it was the voice of Nichol that he had heard. Closer inspection of the slightly disfigured face proved that, apart from the scar on the forehead, it was the countenance of Nichol. A possible solution of the mystery was beginning to force itself in Hobart's reluctant mind. When Nichol had fallen in the Wilderness, the shock of his injury had rendered him senseless and caused him to appear dead to the hasty scrutiny of Sam and Jim Wetherby. They were terribly excited and had no time for close examination. Nichol might have revived, have been gathered up with the Confederate wounded, and sent to Richmond. There was dire and tremendous confusion at that period, when within the space of two or three days tens of thousands were either killed or disabled. In a Southern hospital Nichol might have recovered physical health while, from injury to the brain, suffering complete eclipse of memory. In this case he would have to begin life anew, like a child, and so would pick up the vernacular and bearing of the enlisted men with whom he would chiefly associate.

Because he remembered nothing and know nothing, he

E. P. Roe

may at first have been tolerated as a "cur'ous chap," then employed as he had explained. He could take the place of a better man where men were greatly needed.

This theory could solve the problem; and Martine's hospital experience prepared his mind to understand what would be a hopeless mystery to many. He was so fearfully excited that be could not remain in the ward. The very proximity to this strange being, who had virtually risen from the dead and appeared to him of all others, was a sort of torture in itself.

What effect would this discovery have on his relations to Helen? He dared not think yet he must think. Already the temptation of his life was forming in his mind. His cousin was sleeping; and with a wild impatience to escape, to get away from all his kind, he stole noiselessly out into the midnight and deserted streets. On, on he went, limping he knew not, cared not where, for his passion and mental agony drove him hither and thither like a leaf before a fitful gale.

"No one knows of this," he groaned. "I can still return and marry Helen. But oh, what a secret to carry!"

Then his heart pleaded. "This is not the lover she lost - only a horrible, mocking semblance. He has lost his own identity; he does not even know himself - would not know her. Ah! I'm not sure of that. I would be dead indeed if her dear features did not kindle my eyes in recognition. It may be that the sight of her face is the one thing essential to restore him. I feel this would be true were it my case. But how can I give her up now? How can? - how can I? Oh, this terrible journey! No wonder Helen had forebodings. She loves me; she is mine. No one else has so good a right. We were to be married only a few hours hence. Then she whom I've loved from childhood would make my home a heaves on earth. And yet - and yet - " Even in the darkness he buried his face in his hands, shuddered, moaned, writhed, and grated his teeth in the torment of the conflict.

Hour after hour he wavered, now on the point of yielding, then stung by conscience into desperate uncertainty. The night was cold, the howling wind would have chilled him at another time, but during his struggle great drops of sweat often poured from his face. Only the eye of God saw that battle, the hardest that was fought and won during the war.

At last, when well out of the city, he lifted his agonized eyes and saw the beautiful hues of morning tingeing the east. Unconsciously, he repeated the sublime, creative words, "Let there be light." It came to him. With the vanishing darkness, he revolted finally against the thought of any shadows existing between him and Helen. She should have all the light that he had, and decide her own course. He had little hope that she would wed him, even if she did not marry Nichol in his present condition - a condition probably only temporary and amenable to skilful treatment.

Wearily he dragged his lame foot back to a hotel in the populous party of the city, and obtained food and wine, for he was terribly exhausted. Next he telegraphed Mr. Kemble:

"Arrived last evening. The wedding will have to be postponed. Will explain later."

"It's the best I can do now," he muttered. "Helen will

think it is all due to my cousin's illness." Then he returned to the hospital and found his relative in a state of wonderment at his absence, but refreshed from a good night's rest. Yankee Blank was nowhere to be seen.

"Hobart," exclaimed his cousin, "you look ill - ten years older than you did last night."

"You see me now by daylight," was the quiet reply. "I am not very well."

"It's a perfect shame that I've been the cause of so much trouble, especially when it wasn't necessary."

"Oh, my God!" thought Martine, "there was even no need of this fatal journey." But his face had become grave and inscrutable, and the plea of ill-health reconciled his cousin to the necessity of immediate return. There was no good reason for his remaining, for by a few additional arrangements his relative would do very well and soon be able to take care of himself. Martine felt that lie could not jeopardize his hard-won victory by delay, which was as torturing as the time intervening between a desperate surgical operation and the knowledge that it is inevitable.

After seeing that his cousin made a good breakfast, he sought a private interview with the wardmaster. He was able to extract but little information about Yankee Blank more than the man had given himself. "Doctors say he may regain his memory at any time, or it may be a long while, and possibly never," was the conclusion.

"I think I know him," said Martine. "I will bring

physician from the city to consult this morning with the surgeon in charge."

"I'm glad to hear it," was the reply. "Something would have to be done soon. He is just staying on here and making himself useful to some extent."

When Martine re-entered the ward, Yankee Blank appeared, grinned, and said affably, "Howdy." Alas! a forlorn, miserable hope that he might have been mistaken was banished from Hobart's mind now that he saw Nichol in the clear light of day. The scar across his forehead and a change of expression, denoting the eclipse of fine, cultivated manhood, could not disguise the unmistakable features. There was nothing to be done but carry out as quickly as possible the purpose which had cost him so dear.

He first telegraphed his uncle to dismiss further anxiety, and that his son would soon be able to visit him. Then the heavy-hearted man sought a physician whom he knew well by reputation.

The consultation was held, and Nichol (as he may be more properly named hereafter) was closely questioned and carefully examined. The result merely confirmed previous impressions. It was explained, as far as explanation can be given of the mysterious functions of the brain, that either the concussion of the exploding shell or the wound from a flying fragment had paralyzed the organ of memory. When such paralysis would cease, if ever, no one could tell. The power to recall everything might return at any moment or it might be delayed indefinitely. A shock, a familiar face, might supply the potency required, or restoration come through the slow, unseen processes of nature.

Martine believed that Helen's face and voice would accomplish everything.

He was well known to the medical authorities and had no difficulty in securing belief that he had identified Nichol. He also promised that abundant additional proof should be sent on from Alton, such certainty being necessary to secure the officer's back pay and proper discharge from the service. The surgeon then addressed the man so strangely disabled, "You know I'm in charge of this hospital?"

"I reckon," replied Nichol, anxiously, for the brief experience which he could recall had taught him that the authority of the surgeon-in-chief was autocratic.

"Well, first, you must give up the name of Yankee Blank. Your name hereafter is Captain Nichol."

"All right, Doctor. I'll be a gin'ral ef you sez so."

"Very well; remember your name is Captain Nichol. Next, you must obey this man and go with him. You must do just what he says in all respects. His name is Mr. Hobart Martine."

"Yes, he tole me las' night, Hob't Ma'tine. He took on mighty cur'ous after seein' me."

"Do you understand that you are to mind, to obey him in all respects just as you have obeyed me?"

"I reckon. Will he tek me to anuther hospital?"

"He will take you where you will be well cared for and treated kindly." Having written Nichol's discharge from the hospital, the surgeon turned to other duties.

Martine informed his cousin, as far as it was essential, of the discovery he had made and of the duties which it imposed, then took his leave. Nichol readily accompanied him, and with the exception of a tendency to irritation at little things, exhibited much of the good-natured docility of a child. Martine took him to a hotel, saw that he had a bath, put him in the hands of a barber, and then sent for a clothier. When dressed in clean linen and a dark civilian suit, the appearance of the man was greatly improved. Hobart had set his teeth, and would entertain no thought of compromise with his conscience. He would do by Nichol as he would wish to be done by if their relations were reversed. Helen should receive no greater shock than was inevitable, nor should Nichol lose the advantage of appearing before her in the outward aspect of a gentleman.

Martine then planned his departure so that he would arrive at Alton in the evening - the evening of the day on which he was to have been married. He felt that Mr. Kemble should see Nichol first and hear the strange story; also that the father must break the news to the daughter, for he could not. It was a terrible journey to the poor fellow, for during the long hours of inaction he was compelled to face the probable results of his discovery. The sight of Nichol and his manner was intolerable; and in addition, he was almost as much care as a child. Everything struck him as new and strange, and he was disposed to ask numberless questions. His vernacular, his alternations of amusement and irritation, and the oddity of his ignorance concerning things which should be simple or familiar to a grown man, attracted the attention of his

E. P. Roe

fellow-passengers. It was with difficulty that Martine, by his stern, sad face and a cold, repelling manner, kept curiosity from intruding at every point.

At last, with heart beating thickly, he saw the lights of Alton gleaming in the distance. It was a train not often used by the villagers, and fortunately no one had entered the car who knew him; even the conductor was a stranger. Alighting at the depot, he hastily took a carriage, and with his charge was driven to the private entrance of the hotel. Having given the hackman an extra dollar not to mention his arrival till morning, he took Nichol into the dimly-lighted and deserted parlor and sent for the well-known landlord. Mr. Jackson, a bustling little man, who, between the gossip of the place and his few guests, never seemed to have a moment's quiet, soon entered. "Why, Mr. Martine," he exclaimed, "we wasn't a-lookin' for you yet. News got around somehow that your cousin was dyin' in Washington and that your weddin' was put off too - Why! you look like a ghost, even in this light," and he turned up the lamp.

Martine had told Nichol to stand by a window with his back to the door. He now turned the key, pulled down the curtain, then drew his charge forward where the light fell clear upon his face, and asked, "Jackson, who is that?"

The landlord stared, his jaw fell from sheer astonishment, as he faltered, "Captain Nichol!"

"Yes," said Nichol, with a pleased grin, "that's my new name! Jes' got it, like this new suit o' clo's, bes' I ever had, doggoned ef they ain't. My old name was Yankee Blank."

"Great Scott!" ejaculated Jackson; "is he crazy?"

"Look yere," cried Nichol; "don' yer call me crazy or I'll light on yer so yer won't fergit it."

"There, there!" said Martine, soothingly, "Mr. Jackson doesn't mean any harm. He's only surprised to see you home again."

"Is this home? What's home?"

"It's the town where you were brought up. We'll make you understand about it all before long. Now you shall have some supper. Mr. Jackson is a warm friend of yours, and will see that you have a good one."

"I reckon we'll get on ef he gives me plenty o' fodder. Bring it toreckly, fer I'm hungry. Quit yer starin', kyant yer?" "Don't you know me, Captain Nichol? Why, I - "

"Naw. Never seed ner yeared on yer. Did I ever nuss yer in a hospital? I kyant reckerlect all on 'em. Get we uns some supper."

"That's the thing to do first, Jackson," added Martine, "Show us upstairs to a private room and wait on us yourself. Please say nothing of this till I give you permission."

They were soon established in a suitable apartment, in which a fire was kindled. Nichol took a rocking-chair and acquiesced in Martine's going out on the pretext of hastening supper.

The landlord received explanations which enabled him to co-operate with Martine. "I could not," said the latter, "take him to his own home without first preparing his family. Neither could I take him to mine for several reasons."

"I can understand some of 'em, Mr. Martine. Why, great Scott! How about your marriage, now that - "

"We won't discuss that subject. The one thing for you to keep in mind is that Nichol lost his memory at the time of his wound. He don't like to be stared at or thought strange. You must humor him much as you would a child. Perhaps the sight of familiar faces and scenes will restore him. Now copy this note in your handwriting and send it to Mr. Kemble. Tell your messenger to be sure to put it into the banker's hands and no other's," and he tore from his note-book a leaf on which was pencilled the following words:

"MR. KEMBLE:

"DEAR SIR - A sick man at the hotel wishes to see you on important business. Don't think it's bad news about Mr. Martine, because it isn't. Please come at once and oblige, HENRY JACKSON."

CHAPTER IX

SHADOWS OF COMING EVENTS

This first day of winter, her fatal wedding-day, was a sad and strange one to Helen Kemble. The sun was hidden by dark clouds, yet no snow fell on the frozen ground. She had wakened in the morning with a start, oppressed by a disagreeable yet forgotten dream. Hastily dressing, she consoled herself with the hope of a long letter from Martine, explaining everything and assuring her of his welfare; but the early mail brought nothing. As the morning advanced, a telegram from Washington, purposely delayed, merely informed her that her affianced was well and that full information was on its way.

"He has evidently found his cousin very low, and needing constant care," she had sighingly remarked at dinner.

"Yes, Nellie," said the banker, cheerily, "but it is a comfort he is well. No doubt you are right about his cousin, and it has turned out as Hobart feared. In this case it is well he went, for he would always have reproached himself if he had not. The evening mail will probably make all clear."

"It has been so unfortunate!" complained Mrs. Kemble.

E. P. Roe

"If it had only happened a little earlier, or a little later! To have all one's preparations upset and one's plans frustrated is exasperating. Were it not for that journey, Helen would have been married by this time. People come ostensibly to express sympathy, but in reality to ask questions."

"I don't care about people," said Helen, "but the day has been so different from what we expected that it's hard not to yield to a presentiment of trouble. It is so dark and gloomy that we almost need a lamp at midday."

"Well, well," cried hearty Mr. Kemble, "I'm not going to cross any bridges till I come to them. That telegram from Hobart is all we need, to date. I look at things as I do at a bank-bill. If its face is all right, and the bill itself all right, that's enough. You women-folks have such a lot of moods and tenses! Look at this matter sensibly. Hobart was right in going. He's doing his duty, and soon will be back with mind and conscience at rest. It isn't as if he were ill himself."

"Yes, papa, that's just the difference; we women feel, and you men reason. What you say, though, is a good wholesome antidote. I fear I'm a little morbid to-day."

After dinner she and her mother slipped over to the adjoining cottage, which had been made so pretty for her reception. While Mrs. Kemble busied herself here and there, Helen kindled a fire on the hearth of the sitting-room and sat down in the low chair which she knew was designed for her. The belief that she would occupy it daily and be at home, happy herself and, better far, making another, to whom she owed so much, happy beyond even his fondest hope, brought smiles to her face as she watched the flickering blaze.

"Yes," she murmured, "I can make him happier even than he dreams. I know him so well, his tastes, his habits, what he most enjoys, that it will be an easy task to anticipate his wishes and enrich his life. Then he has been such a faithful, devoted friend! He shall learn that his example had not been lost on me,"

At this moment the wind rose in such a long mournful, human-like sigh about the house that she started up and almost shuddered. When the evening mail came and brought no letter, she found it hard indeed not to yield to deep depression. In vain her father reasoned with her. "I know all you say sounds true to the ear," she said, "but not to my heart. I can't help it; but I am oppressed with a nervous dread of some impending trouble."

They passed the early hours of the evening as best they could, seeking to divert each other's thoughts. It had been long since the kind old banker was so garrulous, and Helen resolved to reward him by keeping up. Indeed, she shrank from retiring, feeling that through the sleepless night she would be the prey of all sorts of wretched fancies. Never once did her wildest thoughts suggest what had happened, or warn her of the tempest soon to rage in her breast.

Then came the late messenger with the landlord's copied note. She snatched it from the bearer's hand before he could ring the bell, for her straining ears had heard his step even on the gravel walk. Tremblingly she tore open, the envelope in the hall without looking at the address.

"Mr. Jackson said how I was to give it to your father," protested the messenger.

"Well, well," responded Mr. Kemble, perturbed and anxious, "I'm here. You can go unless there's an answer required.'

"Wasn't told nothin' 'bout one," growled the departing errand-boy.

"Give the note to me, Helen," said her father. "Why do you stare at it so?"

She handed it to him without a word, but looked searchingly in his face, and so did his wife, who had joined him.

"Why, this is rather strange," he said.

"I think it is," added Helen, emphatically.

Mrs. Kemble took the note and after a moment ejaculated: "Well, thank the Lord! it isn't about Hobart."

"No, no," said the banker, almost irritably. "We've all worried about Hobart till in danger of making fools of ourselves. As if people never get sick and send for relatives, or as if letters were never delayed! Why, bless me! haven't we heard to-day that he was well? and hasn't Jackson, who knows more about other people's business than his own, been considerate enough to say that his request has nothing to do with Hobart? It is just as he says, some one is sick and wants to arrange about money matters before banking hours to-morrow. There, it isn't far. I'll soon be back."

"Let me go with you, father," pleaded Helen. "I can stay with Mrs. Jackson or sit in the parlor till you are through."

"Oh, no, indeed."

"Papa, I AM going with you," said Helen, half-desperately. "I don't believe I am so troubled for nothing. Perhaps it's a merciful warning, and I may be of use to you."

"Oh, let her go, father," said his wife. "She had better be with you than nervously worrying at home. I'll be better satisfied if she is with you."

"Bundle up well, then, and come along, you silly little girl."

Nichol was too agreeably occupied with his supper to miss Hobart, who watched in the darkened parlor for the coming of Mr. Kemble. At last he saw the banker passing through the light streaming from a shop-window, and also recognized Helen at his side. His ruse in sending a note purporting to come from the landlord had evidently failed; and here was a new complication. He was so exhausted in body and mind that he felt he could not meet the girl now without giving way utterly. Hastily returning to the room in which were Nichol and Jackson, he summoned the latter and said, "Unfortunately, Miss Kemble is coming with her father. Keep your counsel; give me a light in another private room; detain the young lady in the parlor, and then, bring Mr. Kemble to me."

"Ah, glad to see you, Mr. Kemble," said the landlord, a moment or two later, with reassuring cheerfulness;

"you too, Miss Helen. That's right, take good care of the old gentleman. Yes, we have a sick man here who wants to see you, sir. Miss Helen, take a seat in the parlor by the fire while I turn up the lamp. Guess you won't have to wait long."

"Now, Helen," said her father, smiling at her significantly, "can you trust me out of your sight to go upstairs with Mr. Jackson?"

Much relieved, she smiled in return and sat down to wait.

"Who is this man, Jackson?" Mr. Kemble asked on the stairs.

"Well, sir, he said he would explain everything."

A moment later the banker needed not Martine's warning gesture enjoining silence, for he was speechless with astonishment.

"Mr. Jackson," whispered Martine, "will you please remain in the other room and look after your patient?"

"Hobart," faltered Mr. Kemble, "in the name of all that's strange, what does this mean?"

"It is indeed very strange, sir. You must summon all your nerve and fortitude to help us through. Never before were your strength and good strong common-sense more needed. I've nearly reached the end of my endurance. Please, sir, for Helen's sake, preserve your self-control and the best use of all your faculties, for you must now advise. Mr. Kemble, Captain Nichol is alive."

The banker sank into a chair and groaned. "This would have been glad news to me once; I suppose it should be so now. But how, how can this be?"

"Well, sir, as you say, it should be glad news; it will be to all eventually. I am placed in a very hard position; but I have tried to do my duty, and will."

"Why, Hobart, my boy, you look more worn than you did after your illness. Merciful Heaven! what a complication!"

"A far worse one than you can even imagine. Captain Nichol wouldn't know you. His memory was destroyed at the time of the injury. All before that is gone utterly;" and Martine rapidly narrated what is already known to the reader, concluding, "I'm sorry Helen came with you, and I think you had better get her home as soon as possible. I could not take him to my home for several reasons, or at least I thought it best not to. It is my belief that the sight of Helen, the tones of her voice, will restore him; and I do not think it best for him to regain his consciousness of the past in a dwelling prepared for Helen's reception as my wife. Perhaps later on, too, you will understand why I cannot see him there. I shall need a home, a refuge with no such associations. Here, on this neutral ground, I thought we could consult, and if necessary send for his parents to-night. I would have telegraphed you, but the case is so complicated, so difficult. Helen must be gradually prepared for the part she must take. Cost me what it may, Nichol must have his chance. His memory may come back instantly and he recall everything to the moment of his injury. What could be more potent to effect this than the sight and voice of Helen? No one here except Jackson is now aware of his condition. If

E. P. Roe

she can restore him, no one else, not even his parents, need know anything about it, except in a general way. It will save a world of disagreeable talk and distress. At any rate, this course seemed the best I could hit upon in my distracted condition."

"Well, Hobart, my poor young friend, you have been tried as by fire," said Mr. Kemble, in a voice broken by sympathy; "God help you and guide us all in this strange snarl! I feel that the first thing to be done is to get Helen home. Such tidings as yours should be broken to her in that refuge only."

"I agree with you most emphatically, Mr. Kemble. In the seclusion of her own home, with none present except yourself and her mother, she should face this thing and nerve herself to act her part, the most important of all. If she cannot awaken Captain Nichol's memory, it is hard to say what will, or when he will be restored."

"Possibly seeing me, so closely associated with her, may have the same effect," faltered the banker.

"I doubt it; but we can try it. Don't expect me to speak while in the hallway. Helen, no doubt, is on the alert, and I cannot meet her to-night. I am just keeping up from sheer force of will. You must try to realize it. This discovery will change everything for me. Helen's old love will revive in all-absorbing power. I've faced this in thought, but cannot in reality NOW - I simply CANNOT. It would do no good. My presence would be an embarrassment to her, and I taxed beyond mortal endurance. You may think me weak, but I cannot help it. As soon as possible I must put you, and if you think best, Captain Nichol's father, in charge of the situation.

Jackson can send for his father at once if you wish."

"I do wish it immediately. I can't see my way through. this. I would like Dr. Barnes' advice and presence also."

"I think it would be wise, sir. The point I wish to make is that I have done about all that I now can in this affair. My further presence is only another complication. At any rate, I must have a respite - the privilege of going quietly to my own home as soon as possible."

"Oh, Hobart, my heart aches for you; it just ACHES for you. You have indeed been called upon to endure a hundredfold too much in this strange affair. How it will all end God only knows. I understand you sufficiently. Leave the matter to me now. We will have Dr. Barnes and Mr. and Mrs. Nichol here as soon as can be. I suppose I had better see the captain a few moments and then take Helen home."

Martine led the way into the other apartment, where Nichol, rendered good-natured by his supper and a cigar, was conversing sociably with the landlord. Mr. Kemble fairly trembled as he came forward, involuntarily expecting that the man so well known to him must give some sign of recognition.

Nichol paid no heed to him. He had been too long accustomed to see strangers coming and going to give them either thought or attention.

"I say, Hob't Ma'tine," he began, "don' yer cuss me fer eatin' all the supper. I 'lowed ter this Jackson, as yer call 'im, that yer'd get a bite somewhar else, en he 'lowed yer would."

"All right, Nichol; I'm glad you had a good supper."

"I say, Jackson, this Ma'tine's a cur'ous chap - mo
cur'ous than I be, I reckon. He's been actin' cur'ous
ever since he seed me in the horspital. It's all cur'ous.
'Fore he come, doctors en folks was trying ter fin' out
'bout me, en this Ma'tine 'lows he knows all 'bout me.
Ef he wuzn't so orful glum, he'd be a good chap anuff,
ef he is cur'ous. Hit's all a-changin' somehow, en yet'
tisn't. Awhile ago nobody knowd 'bout me, en they
wuz allus a-pesterin' of me with questions. En now
Ma'tine en you 'low you know 'bout me, yet you ast
questions jes' the same. Like anuff this man yere,"
pointing with his cigar to Mr. Kemble, who was
listening with a deeply-troubled face, "knows 'bout me
too, yet wants to ast questions. I don' keer ef I do say
it, I had better times with the Johnnies that call me
Yankee Blank than I ever had sence. Well, ole duffer
[to Mr. Kemble], ast away and git yer load off'n yer
mind. I don't like glum faces roun' en folks jes'
nachelly bilin' over with questions."

"No, Captain Nichol," said the banker, gravely and
sadly, "I've no questions to ask. Good-by for the
present."

Nichol nodded a careless dismissal and resumed his
reminiscences with Jackson, whose eager curiosity and
readiness to laugh were much more to his mind.

Following the noise made by closing the door, Helen's
voice rang up from the hall below, "Papa!"

"Yes, I'm coming, dear," he tried to answer cheerily.

Then he wrung Martine's hand and whispered, "Send for Dr. Barnes. God knows you should have relief. Tell Jackson also to have a carriage go for Mr. Nichol at once. After the doctor comes you may leave all in our hands. Good-by."

Martine heard the rustle of a lady's dress and retired precipitately.

CHAPTER X

"YOU CANNOT UNDERSTAND"

With an affectation of briskness he was far from feeling, Mr. Kemble came down the stairs and joined his daughter in the hall. He had taken pains to draw his hat well over his eyes, anticipating and dreading her keen scrutiny, but, strange to say, his troubled demeanor passed unnoticed. In the interval of waiting Helen's thoughts had taken a new turn. "Well, papa," she began, as they passed into the street, "I am curious to know about the sick man. You stayed an age, but all the same I'm glad I came with you. Forebodings, presentiments, and all that kind of thing seemed absurd the moment I saw Jackson's keen, mousing little visage. His very voice is like a ray of garish light entering a dusky, haunted room. Things suggesting ghosts and hobgoblins become ridiculously prosaic, and you are ashamed of yourself and your fears."

"Yes, yes," replied Mr. Kemble, yielding to irritation in his deep perplexity, "the more matter-of-fact we are the better we're off. I suppose the best thing to do is just to face what happens and try to be brave."

"Well, papa, what's happened to annoy you to-night? Is this sick man going to make you trouble?"

"Like enough. I hope not. At any rate, he has claims which I must meet."

"Don't you think you can meet them?" was her next anxious query, her mind reverting to some financial obligation.

"We'll see. You and mother'll have to help me out, I guess. I'll tell you both when we get home;" and his sigh was so deep as to be almost a groan.

"Papa," said Helen, earnestly pressing his arm, "don't worry. Mamma and I will stand by you; so will Hobart. He is the last one in the world to desert one in any kind of trouble."

"I know that, no one better; but I fear he'll be in deeper trouble than any of us. The exasperating thing is that there should be any trouble at all. If it had only happened before - well, well, I can't talk here in the street. As you say, you must stand by me, and I'll do the best I can by you and all concerned."

"Oh, papa, there was good cause for my foreboding."

"Well, yes, and no. I don't know. I'm at my wits' end. If you'll be brave and sensible, you can probably do more than any of us."

"Papa, papa, something IS the matter with Hobart," and she drew him hastily into the house, which they had now reached.

Mrs. Kemble met them at the door. Alarmed at her husband's troubled face, she exclaimed anxiously, "Who is this man? What did he want?"

"Come now, mother, give me a chance to get my breath. We'll close the doors, sit down, and talk it all over."

Mrs. Kemble and her daughter exchanged an apprehensive glance and followed with the air of being prepared for the worst.

The banker sat down and wiped the perspiration from his brow, then looked dubiously at the deeply anxious faces turned toward him. "Well," he said, "I'm going to tell you everything as far as I understand it. Now I want to see if you two can't listen calmly and quietly and not give way to useless feeling. There's much to be done, and you especially, Helen, must be in the right condition to do it."

"Oh, papa, why torture me so? Something HAS happened to Hobart. I can't endure this suspense."

"Something has happened to us all," replied her father, gravely. "Hobart has acted like a hero, like a saint; so must you. He is as well and able to go about as you are. I've seen him and talked with him."

"He saw you and not me?" cried the girl, starting up.

"Helen, I entreat, I command you to be composed and listen patiently. Don't you know him well enough to be sure he had good reasons - "

"I can't imagine a reason," was the passionate reply, as she paced the floor. "What reason could keep me from him? Merciful Heaven! father, have you forgotten that I was to marry him to-day? Well," she added hoarsely, standing before him with hands clinched in her effort at self-restraint, "the reason?"

"Poor fellow! poor fellow! he has not forgotten it," groaned Mr. Kemble. "Well, I might as well out with it. Suppose Captain Nichol was not killed after all?"

Helen sank into a chair as if struck down as Nichol had been himself. "What!" she whispered; and her face was white indeed.

Mrs. Kemble rushed to her husband, demanding, "Do you mean to tell us that Captain Nichol is alive?"

"Yes; that's just the question we've got to face."

"It brings up another question," replied his wife, sternly. "If he's been alive all this time, why did he not let us know? As far as I can make out, Hobart has found him in Washington - "

"Helen," cried her father to the trembling girl, "for Heaven's sake, be calm!"

"He's alive, ALIVE!" she answered, as if no other thought could exist in her mind. Her eyes were kindling, the color coming into her face, and her bosom throbbed quickly as if her heart would burst its bonds. Suddenly she rushed to her father, exclaiming, "He was the sick man. Oh, why did you not let me see him?"

"Well, well!" ejaculated Mr. Kemble, "Hobart was right, poor fellow! Yes, Helen, Captain Nichol is the sick man, not dangerously ill, however. You are giving ample reason why you should not see him yet; and I tell you plainly you can't see him till you are just as composed as I am."

She burst into a joyous, half-hysterical laugh as she exclaimed, "That's not asking much. I never saw you so moved, papa. Little wonder! The dead is alive again! Oh, papa, papa, you don't understand me at all! Could I hear such tidings composedly - I who have wept so many long nights and days over his death? I must give expression to overwhelming feeling here where it can do no harm, but if I had seen him - when I do see him - ah! he'll receive no harm from me."

"But, Helen, think of Hobart," cried Mrs. Kemble, in sharp distress.

"Mother, mother, I cannot help it. Albert is alive, ALIVE! The old feeling comes back like the breaking up of the fountains of the great deep. You cannot know, cannot understand; Hobart will. I'm sorry, SORRY for him; but he will understand. I thought Albert was dead; I wanted to make Hobart happy. He was so good and kind and deserving that I did love him in a sincere, quiet way, but not with my first love, not as I loved Albert. I thought my love was buried with him; but it has burst the grave as he has. Papa, papa, let me go to him, now, NOW! You say he is sick; it is my place to nurse him back to life. Who has a better right? Why do you not bring him here?"

"Perhaps it will be best, since Helen feels so," said Mr. Kemble, looking at his wife.

"Well, I don't know," she replied with a deep sigh. "We certainly don't wish the public to be looking on any more than we can help. He should be either here or at his own home."

"There's more reason for what you say than you think," Mr. Kemble began.

"There, papa," interrupted Helen, "I'd be more or less than human if I could take! this undreamed-of news quietly, I can see how perplexed and troubled you've been, and how you've kindly tried to prepare me for the tidings. You will find that I have strength of mind to meet all that is required of me. It is all simpler to me than to you, for in a matter of this kind the heart is the guide, indeed, the only guide. Think! If Albert had come back months ago; if Hobart had brought him back wounded and disabled - how would we have acted? Only our belief in his death led to what has happened since, and the fact of life changes everything back to - "

"Now, Helen, stop and listen to me," said her father, firmly. "In one sense the crisis is over, and you've heard the news which I scarcely knew how to break to you. You say you will have strength of mind to meet what is required of you. I trust you may. But it's time you understood the situation as far as I do. Mother's words show she's off the track in her suspicion. Nichol is not to blame in any sense. He is deserving of all sympathy, and yet - oh, dear, it is such a complication!" and the old man groaned as he thought of the personality who best knew himself as Yankee Blank. "The fact is," he resumed to his breathless listeners, "Nichol is not ill at all physically. His mind is affected - "

Mrs. Kemble sank back in her chair, and Helen uttered a cry of dismay.

"Yes, his mind is affected peculiarly. He remembers

E. P. Roe

nothing that happened before he was wounded. You must realize this, Helen; you must prepare yourself for it. His loss of memory is much more sad than if he had lost an arm or a leg. He remembers only what he has picked up since his injury."

"Then, then, he's not insane?" gasped Helen.

"No, no, I should say not," replied her father, dubiously; "yet his words and manner produce much the same effect as if he were - even a stronger effect."

"Oh, this is dreadful!" cried his wife.

"Dreadful indeed, but not hopeless, you know. Keep in mind doctors say that his memory may come back at any time; and Hobart has the belief that the sight and voice of Helen will bring it back."

"God bless Hobart," said Helen, with a deep breath, "and God help him! His own love inspired that belief. He's right; I know he's right."

"Well, perhaps he is. I don't know. I thought Nichol would recognize me; but there wasn't a sign."

"Oh, papa," cried Helen, smiling through her tears, "there are some things which even your experience and wisdom fail in. Albert will know me. We have talked long enough; now let us act."

"You don't realize it all yet, Helen; you can't. You must remember that Nichol regained consciousness in a Southern hospital. He has learned to talk and act very much like such soldiers as would associate with him."

"The fact that he's alive and that I now may restore him is enough, papa."

"Well, I want Dr. Barnes present when you meet him."

"Certainly; at least within call."

"I must stipulate too," said Mrs. Kemble. "I don't wish the coming scenes to take place in a hotel, and under the eyes of that gossip, Jackson. I don't see why Hobart took him there."

"I do," said Mr. Kemble, standing up for his favorite. "Hobart has already endured more than mortal man ought, yet he has been most delicately considerate. No one but Jackson and Dr. Barnes know about Nichol and his condition. I have also had Nichol's father and mother sent for on my own responsibility, for they should take their share of the matter. Hobart believes that Helen can restore Nichol's memory. This would simplify everything and save many painful impressions. You see, it's such an obscure trouble, and there should be no ill-advised blundering in the matter. The doctors in Washington told Hobart that a slight shock, or the sight of an object that once had the strongest hold upon his thoughts - well, you understand."

"Yes," said Helen, "I DO understand. Hobart is trying to give Albert the very best chance. Albert wrote that his last earthly thoughts would be of me. It is but natural that my presence should kindle those thoughts again. It was like Hobart, who is almost divine in his thoughtfulness of others, to wish to shield Albert from the eyes of even his own father and mother until he could know them, and know us all. He was only taken to the hotel that we all might understand and be

E. P. Roe

prepared to do our part. Papa, bring Albert here and let his father and mother come here also. He should be sacredly shielded in his infirmity, and give a every chance to recover before being seen by others; and please, papa, exact from Jackson a solemn promise not to tattle about Albert."

"Yes, yes; but we have first a duty to perform. Mother, please prepare a little lunch, and put a glass of your old currant wine on the tray. Hobart must not come to a cold, cheerless home. I'll go and have his old servant up and ready to receive him."

"No, mamma, that is still my privilege," said Helen, with a rush, of tears. "Oh, I'm so sorry, SORRY for him! but neither he nor I can help or change what is, what's true."

When the tray was ready, she wrote and sealed these words:

"God bless you, Hobart; God reward you! You have made me feel to-night that earth is too poor, and only heaven rich enough to reward you.

"HELEN."

CHAPTER XI

MR. KEMBLE'S APPEAL

It often happens that the wife's disposition is an antidote to her husband: and this was fortunately true of Mrs. Jackson. She was neither curious nor gossiping, and with a quick instinct that privacy was desired by Martine, gave at an early hour her orders to close the house for the night. The few loungers, knowing that she was autocratic, slouched off to other resorts. The man and maids of all work were kept out of the way, while she and her husband waited on their unexpected guests. After Mr. Kemble's departure, the errand-boy was roused from his doze behind the stove and seat for Dr. Barnes; then Jackson wrote another note at Martine's dictation:

"MR. WILLIAM NICHOL:

"DEAR SIR - A relative of yours is sick at my house. He came on the evening train. You and your wife had better come at once in the carriage."

Martine retired to the room in which he had seen Mr. Kemble, that he might compose himself before meeting the physician. The sound of Helen's voice, the mere proximity of the girl who at this hour was to have been his wife had not "old chaos" come again for him, were by no means "straws" in their final and crushing weight. Motionless, yet with mind verging on distraction, he sat in the cold, dimly lighted room until aroused by the voice of Dr. Barnes.

"Why, Hobart!" cried his old friend, starting at the bloodshot eyes and pallid face of the young man, "what is the matter? You need me, sure enough, but why on earth are you shivering in this cold room at the hotel?"

Martine again said to Jackson: "Don't leave him," and closed the door. Then, to the physician: "Dr. Barnes, I am ill and worn-out. I know it only too well. You must listen carefully while I in brief tell you why you were sent for; then you and others must take charge and act as you think best. I'm going home. I must have rest and a respite. I must be by myself;" and he rapidly began to sketch his experiences in Washington.

"Hold!" said the sensible old doctor, who indulged in only a few strong exclamations of surprise, which did not interrupt the speaker, "hold! You say you left the ward to think it over, after being convinced that you had discovered Nichol. Did you think it over quietly?"

"Quietly!" repeated Martine, with intense bitterness. "Would a man, not a mummy, think over such a thing quietly? Judge me as you please, but I was tempted as I believe never man was before. I fought the Devil till morning."

"I thought as much," said the doctor, grasping Martine's hand, then slipping a finger on his pulse. "You fought on foot too, didn't you?"

"Yes, I walked the streets as if demented."

"Of course. That in part accounts for your exhaustion. Have you slept much since?"

"Oh, Doctor, let me get through and go home!"

"No, Hobart, you can't get through with me till I am with you. My dear fellow, do you think that I don't understand and sympathize with you? There's no reason why you should virtually risk your life for Captain Nichol again. Take this dose of quinine at once, and then proceed. I can catch on rapidly. First answer, how much have you slept since?"

"The idea of sleep! You can remedy this, Doctor, after my part in this affair is over. I must finish now. Helen may return, and I cannot meet her, nor am I equal to seeing Mr. and Mrs. Nichol. My head feels queer, but I'll get through somehow, if the strain is not kept up too long;" and he finished in outline his story. In conclusion he said, "You will understand that you are now to have charge of Nichol. He is prepared by his experience to obey you, for he has always been in hospitals, where the surgeon's will is law. Except with physicians, he has a sort of rough waywardness, learned from the soldiers."

"Yes, I understand sufficiently now to manage. You put him in my charge, then go home, and I'll visit you as soon as I can."

"One word more, Doctor. As far as you think best, enjoin reticence on Jackson. If the sight of Helen restores Nichol, as I believe it will, little need ever be said about his present condition. Jackson would not dare to disobey a physician's injunction."

"Don't you dare disobey them, either. I'll manage him too. Come."

Nichol had slept a good deal during the latter part of his journey, and now was inclined to wakefulness - a tendency much increased by his habit of waiting on hospital patients at night. In the eager and curious Jackson he had a companion to his mind, who stimulated in him a certain child-like vanity.

"Hello, Ma'tine," he said, "ye're gittin' tired o' me, I reckon, ye're off so much. I don't keer. This yere Jackson's a lively cuss, en I 'low we'll chin till mawnin'."

"Yes, Nichol, Mr. Jackson is a good friend of yours; and here is another man who is more than a friend. You remember what the surgeon at the hospital said to you?"

"I reckon," replied Nichol, anxiously. "Hain't I minded yer tetotally?"

"Yes, you have done very well indeed - remarkably well, since you knew I was not a doctor. Now this man is a doctor - the doctor I was to bring you to. You won't have to mind me any more, but you must mind this man, Dr. Barnes, in all respects, just as you did the doctors in the hospitals. As long as you obey him carefully he will be very good to you."

"Oh, I'll mind, Doctor," said Nichol, rising and assuming the respectful attitude of a hospital nurse. "We uns wuz soon larned that't wuzn't healthy to go agin the doctor. When I wuz Yankee Blank, 'fo' I got ter be cap'n, I forgot ter give a Johnny a doze o' med'cine, en I'm doggoned ef the doctor didn't mek me tek it myse'f. Gee wiz! sech a time ez I had! Hain't give the doctors no trouble sence."

"All right, Captain Nichol," said Dr. Barnes, quietly, "I understand my duties, and I see that you understand yours. As you say, doctors must be obeyed, and I already see that you won't make me or yourself any trouble. Good-night, Hobart, I'm in charge now."

"Good-night, Doctor. Mr. Jackson, I'm sure you will carry out Dr. Barnes' wishes implicitly."

"Yer'd better, Jackson," said Nichol, giving him a wink. "A doctor kin give yer high ole jinks ef ye're not keerful."

Martine now obeyed the instinct often so powerful in the human breast as well as in dumb animals, and sought the covert, the refuge of his home, caring little whether he was to live or die. When he saw the lighted windows of Mr. Kemble's residence, he moaned as if in physical pain. A sudden and immeasurable longing to see, to speak with Helen once before she was again irrevocably committed to Nichol, possessed him. He even went to her gate to carry out his impulse, then curbed himself and returned resolutely to his dwelling. As soon as his step was on the porch, the door opened and Mr. Kemble gave him the warm grasp of friendship. Without a word, the two men entered the sitting-room, sat down by the ruddy fire, and looked at each other, Martine with intense, questioning anxiety in his haggard face. The banker nodded gravely as he said, "Yes, she knows."

"It's as I said it would be?" Martine added huskily, after a moment or two.

"Well, my friend, she said you would understand her better than any one else. She wrote you this note."

Martine's hands so trembled that he could scarcely break the seal. He sat looking at the tear-blurred words some little time, and grew evidently calmer, then faltered, "Yes, it's well to remember God at such a time. He has laid heavy burdens upon me. He is responsible for them, not I. If I break, He also will be responsible."

"Hobart," said Mr. Kemble, earnestly, "you must not break under this, for our sake as well as your own. I have the presentiment that we shall all need you yet, my poor girl perhaps most of all. She doesn't, she can't realize it. Now, the dead is alive again. Old girlish impulses and feelings are asserting themselves. As is natural, she is deeply excited; but this tidal wave of feeling will pass, and then she will have to face both the past and future. I know her well enough to be sure she could never be happy if this thing wrecked you. And then, Hobart," and the old man sank his voice to a whisper, "suppose - suppose Nichol continues the same."

"He cannot," cried Martine, almost desperately. "Oh, Mr. Kemble, don't suggest any hope for me. My heart tells me there is none, that there should not be any. No, she loved him as I have loved her from childhood. She is right. I do understand her so well that I know what the future will be."

"Well," said Mr. Kemble, firmly, as he rose, "she shall

never marry him as he is, with my consent. I don't feel your confidence about Helen's power to restore him. I tell you, Hobart, I'm in sore straits. Helen is the apple of my eye. She is the treasure of our old age. God knows I remember what you have done for her and for us in the past; and I feel that we shall need you in the future. You've become like a son to mother and me, and you must stand by us still. Our need will keep you up and rally you better than all Dr. Barnes' medicine. I know you well enough to know that. But take the medicine all the same; and above all things, don't give way to anything like recklessness and despair. As you say, God has imposed the burden. Let him give you the strength to bear it, and other people's burdens too, as you have in the past. I must go now. Don't fail me."

Wise old Mr. Kemble had indeed proved the better physician. His misgivings, fears, and needs, combined with his honest affection, had checked the cold, bitter flood of despair which had been overwhelming Martine. The morbid impression that he would be only another complication, and of necessity an embarrassment to Helen and her family, was in a measure removed. Mere words of general condolence would not have helped him; an appeal like that to the exhausted soldier, and the thought that the battle for him was not yet over, stirred the deep springs of his nature and slowly kindled the purpose to rally and be ready. He rose, ate a little of the food, drank the wine, then looked around the beautiful apartment prepared for her who was to have been his wife, "I have grown weak and reckless," he said. "I ought to have known her well enough - I do know her so well - as to be sure that I would cloud her happiness if this thing destroyed me."

CHAPTER XII

"YOU MUST REMEMBER"

Mr. And Mrs. Nichol wonderingly yet promptly complied with the request for their presence, meantime casting about in their minds as to the identity of the relative who had summoned them so unexpected. Mr. Kemble arrived at the hotel at about the same moment as they did, and Jackson was instructed to keep the carriage in waiting. "It was I who sent for you and your wife," said the banker. "Mr. Martine, if possible, would have given you cause for a great joy only; but I fear it must be tempered with an anxiety which I trust will not be long continued;" and he led the way into the parlor.

"Is it - can it be about Albert?" asked Mrs. Nichols trembling, and sinking into a chair.

"Yes, Mrs. Nichol. Try to keep your fortitude, for perhaps his welfare depends upon it."

"Oh, God be praised! The hope of this never wholly left me, because they didn't find his body."

Dr. Barnes came down at once, and with Mr. Kemble tried to soothe the strong emotions of the parents, while at the same time enlightening them as to their son's discovery and condition.

"Well," said Mr. Nichol, in strong emphasis; "Hobart Martine is one of a million."

"I think he ought to have brought Albert right to me first," Mrs. Nichol added, shaking her head and wiping her eyes. "After all, a mother's claim - "

"My dear Mrs. Nichol," interrupted Dr. Barnes, "there was no thought of undervaluing your claim on the part of our friend Hobart. He has taken what he believed, and what physicians led him to believe, was the best course to restore your son. Besides, Mr. Martine is a very sick man. Even now he needs my attention more than Captain Nichol. You must realize that he was to have married Miss Kemble to-day; yet he brings back your son, sends for Mr. Kemble in order that his daughter, as soon as she can realize the strange truth, may exert her power. He himself has not seen the girl who was to have been his bride."

"Wife, wife," said Mr. Nichol, brokingly, "no mortal man could do more for us than Hobart Martine, God bless him!"

"Mrs. Nichol," began Mr. Kemble, "my wife and Helen both unite in the request that you and your husband bring your son at once to our house; perhaps you would rather meet him in the privacy - "

"Oh, no, no!" she cried, "I cannot wait. Please do not think I am insensible to all this well-meant kindness; but a mother's heart cannot wait. He'll know ME - me who bore him and carried him on my breast."

"Mrs. Nichol, you shall see him at once," said the doctor. "I hope it will be as you say; but I'm compelled to tell you that you may be disappointed. There's no certainty that this trouble will pass away at once under any one's influence. You and your husband come with me. Mr. Kemble, I will send Jackson down, and so secure the privacy which you would kindly provide. I will be present, for I may be needed."

He led the way, the mother following with the impetuosity and abandon of maternal love, and the father with stronger and stranger emotions than he had ever known, but restrained in a manner natural to a quiet, reticent man. They were about to greet one on whom they had once centred their chief hopes and affection, yet long mourned as dead. It is hard to imagine the wild tumult of their feelings. Not merely by words, but chiefly by impulse, immediate action, could they reveal how profoundly they were moved.

With kindly intention, as he opened the door of the apartment, the doctor began, "Mr. Jackson, please leave us a few - "

Mrs. Nichol saw her son and rushed upon him, crying, "Albert, Albert!" It was enough at that moment that she recognized him; and the thought that he would not recognize her was banished. With an intuition of heart beyond all reasoning, she felt that he who had drawn his life from her must know her and respond to nature's first strong tie.

In surprise, Nichol had risen, then was embarrassed to find an elderly woman sobbing on his breast and addressing him in broken, endearing words by a name utterly unfamiliar. He looked wonderingly at his father, who stood near, trembling and regarding him through tear-dimmed eyes with an affectionate interest, impressive even to his limited perceptions.

"Doctor," he began over his mother's head, "what in thunder does all this here mean? Me 'n' Jackson was chinnin' comf't'bly, when sud'n you uns let loose on me two crazy old parties I never seed ner yeared on. Never had folks go on so 'bout me befo'. Beats even that Hob't Ma'tine," and he showed signs of rising irritation.

"Albert, Albert!" almost shrieked Mrs. Nichol, "don't you know me - ME, your own mother?"

"Naw."

At the half-indignant, incredulous tone, yet more than all at the strange accent and form of this negative, the poor woman was almost beside herself. "Merciful God!" she cried, "this cannot be;" and she sank into a chair, sobbing almost hysterically.

For reasons of his own, Dr. Barnes did not interfere. Nature in powerful manifestations was actuating the parents; and he decided, now that things had gone so far, to let the entire energy of uncurbed emotion, combined with all the mysterious affinity of the closest kinship, exert its influence on the clogged brain of his patient.

For a few moments Mrs. Nichol was too greatly over-come to comprehend anything clearly; her husband, on the other hand, was simply wrought up to his highest capacity for action. His old instinct of authority returned, and he seized his son's hand and began, "Now, see here, Albert, you were wounded in your head - "

"Yes, right yere," interrupted Nichol, pointing to his scar. "I knows all 'bout that, but I don't like these goin's on, ez ef I wuz a nachel-bawn fool, en had ter bleve all folks sez. I've been taken in too often. When I wuz with the Johnnies they'd say ter me, 'Yankee Blank, see that ar critter? That's a elephant.' When I'd call it a elephant, they'd larf an' larf till I flattened out one feller's nose. I dunno nothin' 'bout elephants; but the critter they pinted at wuz a cow. Then one day they set me ter scrubbin' a nigger to mek 'im white, en all sech doin's, till the head-doctor stopped the hull blamed nonsense. S'pose I be a cur'ous chap. I ain't a nachel-bawn ijit. When folks begin ter go on, en do en say things I kyant see through, then I stands off en sez, 'Lemme 'lone.' The hospital doctors wouldn't 'low any foolin' with me 't all."

"I'm not allowing any fooling with you," said Dr. Barnes, firmly. "I wish you to listen to that man and woman, and believe all they say. The hospital doctors would give you the same orders."

"All right, then," assented Nichol, with a sort of grimace of resignation. "Fire away, old man, an' git through with yer yarn so Jackson kin come back. I wish this woman wouldn't take on so. Hit makes me orful oncomf't'ble, doggoned ef hit don't."

The rapid and peculiar utterance, the seemingly unfeeling words of his son, stung the father into an ecstasy of grief akin to anger. A man stood before him, as clearly recognized as his own image in a mirror. The captain was not out of his mind in any familiar sense of the word; he remembered distinctly what had happened for months past. He must recall, he must be MADE to recollect the vital truths of his life on which not only his happiness but that of others depended. Although totally ignorant of what the wisest can explain but vaguely, Mr. Nichol was bent on restoring his son by the sheer force of will, making him remember by telling him what he should and must recall. This he tried to do with strong, eager insistence. "Why, Albert," he urged, "I'm your father; and that's your mother."

Nichol shook his head and looked at the doctor, who added gravely, "That's all true."

"Yes," resumed Mr. Nichol, with an energy and earnestness of utterance which compelled attention. "Now listen to reason. As I was saying, you were wounded in the head, and you have forgotten what happened before you were hurt. But you must remember, you must, indeed, or you will break your mother's heart and mine, too."

"But I tell yer, I kyant reckerlect a thing befo' I kinder waked up in the hospital, en the Johnnies call me Yankee Blank. I jes' wish folks would lemme alone on that pint. Hit allus bothers me en makes me mad. How kin I reckerlect when I kyant?" and he began to show signs of strong vexation.

Dr. Barnes was about to interfere when Mrs. Nichol, who had grown calmer, rose, took her son's hand, and said brokenly: "Albert, look me in the face, your mother's face, and try, TRY with all your heart and soul and mind. Don't you remember ME?"

It was evident that her son did try. His brow wrinkled in the perplexed effort, and he looked at her fixedly for a moment or more; but no magnetic current from his mother's hand, no suggestion of the dear features which had bent over him in childhood and turned toward him in love and pride through subsequent years found anything in his arrested consciousness answering to her appeal.

The effort and its failure only irritated him, and he broke out: "Now look yere, I be as I be. What's the use of all these goin's on? Doctor, if you sez these folks are my father and mother, so be it. I'm learning somethin' new all the time. This ain't no mo' quar, I s'pose, than some other things. I've got to mind a doctor, for I've learned that much ef I hain t nuthin' else, but I want you uns to know that I won't stan' no mo' foolin'. Doctors don't fool me, en they've got the po'r ter mek a feller do ez they sez, but other folks is got ter be keerful how they uses me."

Mrs. Nichol again sank into her chair and wept bitterly; her husband at last remained silent in a sort of inward, impotent rage of grief. There was their son, alive and in physical health, yet between him and them was a viewless barrier which they could not break through.

The strange complications, the sad thwartings of hope which must result unless he was restored, began to loom already in the future.

Dr. Barnes now came forward and said: "Captain Nichol, you are as you are at this moment, but you must know that you are not what you were once. We are trying to restore you to your old self. You'd be a great deal better off if we succeed. You must help us all you can. You must be patient, and try all the time to recollect. You know I am not deceiving you, but seeking to help you. You don't like this. That doesn't matter. Didn't you see doctors do many things in hospitals which the patients didn't like?"

"I reckon," replied Nichol, growing reasonable at once when brought on familiar ground.

"Well, you are my patient. I may have to do some disagreeable things, but they won't hurt you. It won't be like taking off an arm or a leg. You have seen that done, I suppose?"

"You bet!" was the eager, proud reply. "I used to hold the fellows when they squirmed."

"Now hold yourself. Be patient and good-natured. While we are about it, I want to make every appeal possible to your lost memory, and I order you to keep on trying to remember till I say: 'Through for the present.' If we succeed, you'll thank me all the days of your life. Anyhow, you must do as I say."

"Oh, I know that."

"Well, then, your name is Captain Nichol. This is Mr. Nichol, your father; this lady is your mother. Call them father and mother when you speak to them. Always speak kindly and pleasantly. They'll take you to a pleasant home when I'm through with you, and you must mind them. They'll be good to you everyway."

Nichol grinned acquiescence and said: "All right, Doctor."

"Now you show your good sense. We'll have you sound and happy yet." The doctor thought a moment and then asked: "Mr. Nichol, I suppose that after our visit to Mr. Kemble, you and your wife would prefer to take your son home with you?"

"Certainly," was the prompt response.

"I would advise you to do so. After our next effort, however it results, we all will need rest and time for thought. Captain, remain here a few moments with your father and mother. Listen good-naturedly and answer pleasantly to whatever they may say to you. I will be back soon."

CHAPTER XIII

"I'M HELEN"

Dr. Barnes descended the stairs to the parlor where Mr. Kemble impatiently awaited him. "Well?" said the banker, anxiously.

"I will explain while on the way to your house. The carriage is still ready, I suppose?" to Jackson.

"Yes," was the eager reply; "how did he take the meeting of his parents?"

"In the main as I feared. He does not know them yet. Mr. Jackson, you and I are somewhat alike in one of our duties. I never talk about my patients. If I did, I ought to be drummed out of the town instead of ever being called upon again. Of course you feel that you should not talk about your guests. You can understand why the parties concerned in this matter would not wish to have it discussed in the village."

"Certainly, Doctor, certainly," replied Jackson, reddening, for he knew something of his reputation for gossip. "This is no ordinary case."

"No, it is not. Captain Nichol and his friends would never forgive any one who did not do right by them

E. P. Roe

now. In about fifteen minutes or so I will return. Have the carriage wait for me at Mr. Kemble's till again wanted. You may go back to the captain and do your best to keep him wide-awake."

Jackson accompanied them to the conveyance and said to the man on the box: "Obey all Dr. Barnes's orders."

As soon as the two men were seated, the physician began: "Our first test has failed utterly;" and he briefly narrated what had occurred, concluding, "I fear your daughter will have no better success. Still, it is perhaps wise to do all we can, on the theory that these sudden shocks may start up the machinery of memory. Nichol is excited; such powers as he possesses are stimulated to their highest activity, and he is evidently making a strong effort to recall the past, I therefore now deem it best to increase the pressure on his brain to the utmost. If the obstruction does not give way, I see no other course than to employ the skill of experts and trust to the healing processes of time."

"I am awfully perplexed, Doctor," was the reply. "You must be firm with me on one point, and you know your opinion will have great weight. Under no sentimental sense of duty, or even of affection, must Helen marry Nichol unless he is fully restored and given time to prove there is no likelihood of any return of this infirmity."

"I agree with you emphatically. There is no reason for such self-sacrifice on your daughter's part. Nichol would not appreciate it. He is not an invalid; on the contrary, a strong, muscular man, abundantly able to take care of himself under the management of his family."

"He has my profound sympathy," continued Mr. Kemble, "but giving that unstintedly is a very different thing from giving him my only child."

"Certainly. Perhaps we need not say very much to Miss Helen on this point at present. Unless he becomes his old self she will feel that she has lost him more truly than if he were actually dead. The only deeply perplexing feature in the case is its uncertainty. He may be all right before morning, and he may never recall a thing that happened before the explosion of that shell."

The carriage stopped, and Mr. Kemble hastily led the way to his dwelling. Helen met them at the door. "Oh, how long you have been!" she protested; "I've just been tortured by suspense."

Dr. Barnes took her by the hand and led her to the parlor. "Miss Helen," he said gravely, "if you are not careful you will be another patient on my hands. Sad as is Captain Nichol's case, he at least obeys me implicitly; so must you. Your face is flushed, your pulse feverish, and - "

"Doctor," cried the girl, "you can't touch the disease till you remove the cause. Why is he kept so long from me?"

"Helen, child, you MUST believe that the doctor - that we all - are doing our best for you and Nichol," said Mr. Kemble, anxiously. "His father and mother came to the hotel. It was but natural that they should wish to see him at once. How would we feel?"

"Come, Helen, dear, you must try to be more calm,"

E. P. Roe

urged the mother, gently, with her arm around her daughter's neck. "Doctor, can't you give her something to quiet her nerves?"

"Miss Helen, like the captain, is going to do just as I say, aren't you? You can do more for yourself than I can do for you. Remember, you must act intelligently and cooperate with me. His father, and especially his mother, exhibited the utmost degree of emotion and made the strongest appeals without effect. Now we must try different tactics. All must be quiet and nothing occur to confuse or irritate him."

"Ah, how little you all understand me! The moment you give me a chance to act I can be as calm as you are. It's this waiting, this torturing suspense that I cannot endure. Hobart would not have permitted it. He knows, he understands. Every effort will fail till Albert sees me. It will be a cause for lasting gratitude to us both that I should be the one to restore him. Now let me manage. My heart will guide me better than your science."

"What will you do?" inquired her father, in deep solicitude.

"See, here's his picture," she replied, taking it from a table near - "the one he gave me just before he marched away. Let him look at that and recall himself. Then I will enter. Oh, I've planned it all! My self-control will be perfect. Would I deserve the name of woman if I were weak or hysterical? No, I would do my best to rescue any man from such a misfortune, much more Albert, who has such sacred claims."

"That's a good idea of yours about the photograph.

Well, I guess I must let Nature have her own way again, only in this instance I advise quiet methods."

"Trust me, Doctor, and you won't regret it."

"Nerve yourself then to do your best, but prepare to be disappointed for the present. I do not and cannot share in your confidence."

"Of course you cannot," she said, with a smile which illuminated her face into rare beauty. "Only love and faith could create my confidence."

"Miss Helen," was the grave response, "would love and faith restore Captain Nichol's right arm if he had lost it?"

"Oh, but that's different," she faltered.

"I don't know whether it is or not. We are experimenting. There may be a physical cause obstructing memory which neither you nor any one can now remove. Kindness only leads me to temper your hope."

"Doctor," she said half-desperately, "it is not hope; it is belief. I could not feel as I do if I were to be disappointed."

"Ah, Miss Helen, disappointment is a very common experience. I must stop a moment and see one who has learned this truth pretty thoroughly. Then I will bring Nichol and his parents at once."

Tears filled her eyes. "Yes, I know," she sighed; "my heart just bleeds for him, but I cannot help it. Were I not sure that Hobart understands me better than any one else, I should be almost distracted. This very thought of him nerves me. Think what he did for Albert from a hard sense of duty. Can I fail? Good-by, and please, PLEASE hasten."

Martine rose to greet the physician with a clear eye and a resolute face. "Why, why!" cried Dr. Barnes, cheerily, "you look a hundred per cent better. That quinine - "

"There, Doctor, I don't undervalue your drugs; but Mr. Kemble has been to see me and appealed to me for help - to still be on hand if needed. Come, I've had my hour for weakness. I am on the up-grade now. Tell me how far the affair has progressed."

"Haven't time, Hobart. Since Mr. Kemble's treatment is so efficacious, I'll continue it. You will be needed, you will indeed, no matter how it all turns out. I won't abandon my drugs, either. Here, take this."

Martine took the medicine as administered. "Now when you feel drowsy, go to sleep," added the doctor.

"Tell me one thing - has she seen him yet?"

"No; his father and mother have, and he does not know them. It's going to be a question of time, I fear."

"Helen will restore him."

"So she believes, or tries to. I mercifully shook her faith a little. Well, she feels for you, old fellow. The belief that you understand her better than any one has great sustaining power."

"Say I won't fail her; but I entreat that you soon let me know the result of the meeting."

"I'll come in," assented the doctor, as he hastily departed. Then he added sotto voce, "If you hear anything more under twelve or fifteen hours, I'm off my reckoning."

Re-entering the carriage, he was driven rapidly to the hotel. Jackson had played his part, and had easily induced Nichol to recount his hospital experience in the presence of his parents, who listened in mingled wonder, grief, and impotent protest.

"Captain, put on your overcoat and hat and come with me," said the doctor, briskly. "Your father and mother will go with us."

"Good-by, Jackson," said Nichol, cordially. "Ye're a lively cuss, en I hopes we'll have a chaince to chin agin."

With a blending of hope and of fear, his parents followed him. The terrible truth of his sensibility to all that he should recognize and remember became only the more appalling as they comprehended it. While it lost none of its strangeness, they were compelled to face and to accept it as they could not do at first.

"Now, Captain," said the doctor, after they were seated in the carriage, "listen carefully to me. It is necessary that you recall what happened before you were wounded. I tell you that you must do it if you can, and you know doctors must be obeyed."

"Look yere, Doctor, ain't I a-tryin'? but I tell yer hit's

like tryin' ter lift myself out o' my own boots."

"Mind, now, I don't say you must remember, only try your best. You can do that?"

"I reckon."

"Well, you are going to the house of an old friend who knew you well before you were hurt. You must pay close heed to all she says just as you would to me. You must not say any rude, bad words, such as soldiers often use, but listen to every word she says. Perhaps you'll know her as soon as you see her. Now I've prepared you. I won't be far off."

"Don't leave me, Doctor. I jes' feels nachelly muxed up en mad when folks pester me 'bout what I kyant do."

"You must not get angry now, I can tell you. That would never do at all. I FORBID it."

"There, there now, Doctor, I won't, doggone me ef I will," Nichol protested anxiously.

Mr. Kemble met them at the door, and the captain recognized him instantly.

"Why, yere's that sensible ole feller what didn't want to ast no questions," he exclaimed.

"You are right, Captain Nichol, I have no questions to ask."

"Well, ef folks wuz all like you I'd have a comf't'ble time"

"Come with me, Captain," said the physician, leading the way into the parlor. Mr. Kemble silently ushered Mr. and Mrs. Nichol into the sitting-room on the opposite side of the hall and placed them in the care of his wife. He then went into the back parlor in which was Helen, now quiet as women so often are in emergencies. Through a slight opening between the sliding-door she looked, with tightly clasped hands and parted lips, at her lover. At first she was conscious of little else except the overwhelming truth that before her was one she had believed dead. Then again surged up with blinding force the old feeling which had possessed her when she saw him last - when he had impressed his farewell kiss upon her lips. Remembering the time for her to act was almost at hand, she became calm - more from the womanly instinct to help him than from the effort of her will.

Dr. Barnes said to Nichol, "Look around. Don't you think you have seen this room before? Take your time and try to remember."

The captain did as he was bidden, but soon shook his head. "Hit's right purty, but I don't reckerlect."

"Well, sit down here, then, and look at that picture. Who is it?"

"Why, hit's me - me dressed up as cap'n," ejaculated Nichol, delightedly.

"Yes, that was the way you looked and dressed before you were wounded."

"How yer talk! This beats anythin' I ever yeared from the Johnnies."

"Now, Captain Nichol, you see we are not deceiving you. We called you captain. There's your likeness, taken before you were hurt and lost your memory, and you can see for yourself that you were a captain. You must think how much there is for you to try to remember. Before you went to the war, long before you got hurt, you gave this likeness of yourself to a young lady that you thought a great deal of. Can't you recall something about it?"

Nichol wrinkled his scarred forehead, scratched his head, and hitched uneasily in his chair, evidently making a vain effort to penetrate the gloom back of that vague awakening in the Southern hospital. At last he broke out in his usual irritation, "Naw, I kyant, doggon - "

"Hush! you must not use that word here. Don't be discouraged. You are trying; that's all I ask," and the doctor laid a soothing hand on his shoulder. "Now, Captain, I'll just step in the next room. You think quietly as you can about the young lady to whom you gave that picture of yourself."

Nichol was immensely pleased with his photograph, and looked at it in all its lights. While thus gratifying a sort of childish vanity, Helen entered noiselessly, her blue eyes, doubly luminous from the pallor of her face, shining like sapphires. So intent was her gaze that one might think it would "kindle a soul under the ribs of death."

At last Nichol became conscious of her presence and started, exclaiming, "Why, there she is herself."

"OH, Albert, you DO know me," cried the girl, rushing

toward him with outstretched hand.

He took it unhesitatingly, saying with a pleased wonder, "Well, I reckon I'm comin' round. Yer the young lady I give this picture to?"

"I'm Helen," she breathed, with an indescribable accent of tenderness and gladness.

"Why, cert'ny. The doctor tole me 'bout you."

"But you remember me yourself?" she pleaded. "You remember what you said to me when you gave me this picture?" and she looked into his eyes with an expression which kindled even his dull senses.

"Oh, shucks!" he said slowly, "I wish I could. I'd like ter 'blige yer, fer ye're right purty, en I am a-tryin' ter mind the doctor."

Such a sigh escaped her that one might think her heart and hope were going with it. The supreme moment of meeting had come and gone, and he did not know her; she saw and felt in her inmost soul that he did not. The brief and illusive gleam into the past was projected only from the present, resulting from what he had been told, not from what he recalled.

She withdrew her hand, turned away, and for a moment or two her form shook with sobs she could not wholly stifle. He looked on perplexed and troubled, then broke out, "I jes' feels ez ef I'd split my blamed ole haid open - "

She checked him by a gesture. "Wait," she cried, "sit down." She took a chair near him and hastily wiped

E. P. Roe

her eyes. "Perhaps I can help you remember me. You will listen closely, will you not?"

"I be dog - oh, I forgot," and he looked toward the back parlor apprehensively. "Yes, mees, I'll do anythin' yer sez."

"Well, once you were a little boy only so high, and I was a little girl only so high. We both lived in this village and we went to school together. We studied out of the same books together. At three o'clock in the afternoon school was out, and then we put our books in our desks and the teacher let us go and play. There was a pond of water, and it often froze over with smooth black ice. You and I used to go together to that pond; and you would fasten my skates on my feet - "

"Hanged ef I wouldn't do it agin," he cried, greatly pleased. "Yer beats 'em all. Stid o' astin' questions, yer tells me all 'bout what happened. Why, I kin reckerlect it all ef I'm tole often anuff."

With a sinking heart she faltered on, "Then you grew older and went away to school, and I went away to school. We had vacations; we rode on horseback together. Well, you grew to be as tall as you are now; and then came a war and you wore a captain's uniform, like - like that you see in your likeness, and - and - " she stopped. Her rising color became a vivid flush; she slowly rose as the thought burned its way into her consciousness that she was virtually speaking to a stranger. Her words were bringing no gleams of intelligence into his face; they were throwing no better, no stronger light upon the past than if she were telling the story to a great boy. Yet he was not a boy. A man's face was merely disfigured (to her eyes) by a grin of pleasure instead of a pleased smile; and a man's eyes were regarding her with an unwinking stare of admiration. She was not facing her old playmate, her old friend and lover, but a being whose only consciousness reached back but months, through scenes, associations coarse and vulgar like himself. She felt this with an intuition that was overwhelming. She could not utter another syllable, much less speak of the sacred love of the past. "O God!" she moaned in her heart, "the man has become a living grave in which his old self is buried. Oh, this is terrible, terrible!"

As the truth grew upon her she sprang away, wringing her hands and looking upon him with an indescribable expression of pity and dread. "Oh," she now moaned aloud, "if he had only come back to me mutilated in body, helpless! but this change - "

She fled from the room, and Nichol stared after her in perplexed consternation.

E. P. Roe

CHAPTER XIV

"FORWARD! COMPANY A"

When Mrs. Kemble was left alone with Captain Nichol's parents in the sitting-room, she told them of Helen's plan of employing the photograph in trying to recall their son to himself. It struck them as an unusually effective method. Mrs. Kemble saw that their anxiety was so intense that it was torture for them to remain in suspense away from the scene of action. It may be added that her own feelings also led her to go with them into the back parlor, where all that was said by Nichol and her daughter could be heard. Her solicitude for Helen was not less than theirs for their son; and she felt the girl might need both motherly care and counsel. She was opposed even more strenuously than her husband to any committal on the daughter's part to her old lover unless he should become beyond all doubt his former self. At best, it would be a heavy cross to give up Martine, who had won her entire affection. Helen's heart presented a problem too deep for solution. What would - what could - Captain Nichol be to her child in his present condition, should it continue?

It was but natural, therefore, that she and her husband should listen to Helen's effort to awaken memories of the past with profound anxiety. How far would she go?

If Nichol were able to respond with no more appreciative intelligence than he had thus far manifested, would a sentiment of pity and obligation carry her to the point of accepting him as he was, of devoting herself to one who, in spite of all their commiseration and endeavors to tolerate, might become a sort of horror in their household! It was with immense relief that they heard her falter in her story, for they quickly divined that there was nothing in him which responded to her effort. When they heard her rise and moan, "If he had only come back to me mutilated in body, helpless! but this change - " they believed that she was meeting the disappointment as they could wish.

Mr. and Mrs. Nichol heard the words also, and while in a measure compelled to recognize their force, they conveyed a meaning hard to accept. The appeal upon which so much hope had been built had failed. In bitterness of soul, the conviction grew stronger that their once brave, keen-minded son would never be much better than an idiot.

Then Helen appeared among them as pale, trembling, and overwhelmed as if she had seen a spectre. In strong reaction from her effort and blighted hope she was almost in a fainting condition. Her mother's arms received her and supported her to a lounge; Mrs. Nichol gave way to bitter weeping; Mr. Kemble wrung the father's hand in sympathy, and then at his wife's request went for restoratives. Dr. Barnes closed the sliding-doors and prudently reassured Nichol: "You have done your best, Captain, and that is all I asked of you. Remain here quietly and look at your picture for a little while, and then you shall have a good long rest."

"I did try, Doctor," protested Nichol, anxiously. "Gee wiz! I reckon a feller orter try ter please sech a purty gyurl. She tole me lots. Look yere, Doctor, why kyan't I be tole over en over till I reckerlect it all?"

"Well, we'll see, Captain. It's late now, and we must all have a rest. Stay here till I come for you."

Nichol was so pleased with his photograph that he was well content in its contemplation. The physician now gave his attention to Helen, who was soon so far restored as to comprehend her utter failure. Her distress was great indeed, and for a few moments diverted the thoughts of even Mr. and Mrs. Nichol from their own sad share in the disappointment.

"Oh, oh!" sobbed Helen, "this is the bitterest sorrow the war has brought us yet."

"Well, now, friends," said Dr. Barnes, "it's time I had my say and gave my orders. You must remember that I have not shared very fully in your confidence that the captain could be restored by the appeals you have made; neither do I share in this abandonment to grief now. As the captain says, he is yet simply unable to respond. We must patiently wait and see what time and medical skill can do for him. There is no reason whatever for giving up hope. Mrs. Kemble, I would advise you to take Miss Helen to her room, and you, Mr. Nichol, to take your wife and son home. I will call in the morning, and then we can advise further."

His counsel was followed, the captain readily obeying when told to go with his parents. Then the physician stepped over to Martine's cottage and found, as he supposed, that the opiate and exhausted nature had brought merciful oblivion.

It was long before Helen slept, nor would she take anything to induce sleep. She soon became quiet, kissed her mother, and said she wished to be alone. Then she tried to look at the problem in all its aspects, and earnestly asked for divine guidance. The decision reached in the gray dawn brought repose of mind and body.

It was late in the afternoon when Martine awoke with a dull pain in his head and heart. As the consciousness of all that had happened returned, he remembered that there was good reason for both. His faithful old domestic soon prepared a dainty meal, which aided in giving tone to his exhausted system. Then he sat down by his fire to brace himself for the tidings he expected to hear. Helen's chair was empty. It would always be hers, but hope was gone that she would smile from it upon him during the long winter evenings. Already the room was darkening toward the early December twilight, and he felt that his life was darkening in like manner. He was no longer eager to hear what had occurred. The mental and physical sluggishness which possessed him was better than sharp pain; he would learn all soon enough - the recognition, the beginning of a new life which inevitably would drift further and further from him. His best hope was to get through the time, to endure patiently and shape his life so as to permit as little of its shadow as possible to fall upon hers. But as he looked around the apartment and saw on every side the preparations for one who had been his, yet could be no longer, his fortitude gave way, and he buried his face in his hands.

So deep was his painful revery that he did not hear the

E. P. Roe

entrance of Dr. Barnes and Mr. Kemble. The latter laid a hand upon his shoulder and said kindly, "Hobart, my friend, it is just as I told you it would be. Helen needs you and wishes to see you."

Martine started up, exclaiming, "He must have remembered her."

Mr. Kemble shook his head. "No, Hobart," said the doctor, "she was as much of a stranger to him as you were. There were, of course, grounds for your expectation and hers also, but we prosaic physiologists have some reason for our doubtings as well as you for your beliefs. It's going to be a question of time with Nichol. How are you yourself? Ah, I see," he added, with his finger on his patient's pulse. "With you it's going to be a question of tonics."

"Yes, I admit that," Martine replied, "but perhaps of tonics other than those you have in mind. You said, sir [to Mr. Kemble], that Helen wished to see me?"

"Yes, when you feel well enough."

"I trust you will make yourselves at home," said Martine, hastily preparing to go out.

"But don't you wish to hear more about Nichol?" asked the doctor, laughing.

"Not at present. Good-by."

Yet he was perplexed how to meet the girl who should now have been his wife; and he trembled with strange embarrassment as he entered the familiar room in which he had parted from her almost on the eve of their wedding. She was neither perplexed nor embarrassed, for she had the calmness of a fixed purpose. She went swiftly to him, took his hand, led him to a chair, then sat down beside him. He looked at her wonderingly and listened sadly as she asked, "Hobart, will you be patient with me again?"

"Yes," he replied after a moment, yet he sighed deeply in foreboding.

Tears came into her eyes, yet her voice did not falter as she continued: "I said last night that you would understand me better than any one else; so I believe you will now. You will sustain and strengthen me in what I believe to be duty."

"Yes, Helen, up to the point of such endurance as I have. One can't go beyond that."

"No, Hobart, but you will not fail me, nor let me fail. I cannot marry Captain Nichol as he now is" - there was an irrepressible flash of joy in his dark eyes - "nor can I," she added slowly and sadly, "marry you." He was about to speak, but she checked him and resumed. "Listen patiently to me first. I have thought and thought long hours, and I think I am right. You, better than I, know Captain Nichol's condition - its sad contrast to his former noble self. The man we once knew is veiled, hidden, lost - how can we express it? But he exists, and at any time may find and reveal himself. No one, not even I, can revolt at what he is now as he will revolt at it all when his true consciousness returns. He has met with an immeasurable misfortune. He is infinitely worse off than if helpless - worse off than if he were dead, if this condition is to last; but it may not last. What would he think of me if I should desert him now and leave him nothing to remember but a condition of which he could only think with loathing? I will hide nothing from you, Hobart, my brave, true friend - you who have taught me what patience means. If you had brought him back utterly helpless, yet his old self in mind, I could have loved him and married him, and you would have sustained me in that course. Now I don't know. My future, in this respect, is hidden like his. The shock I received last night, the revulsion of feeling which followed, leaves only one thing clear. I must try to do what is right by him; it will not be easy. I hope you will understand. While I have the deepest pity that a woman can feel, I shrink from him NOW, for the contrast between his former self and his present is so terrible. Oh, it is such a horrible mystery! All Dr. Barnes's explanations do not make it one bit less mysterious and dreadful. Albert took the risk of this; he has suffered this for his country. I must suffer for him; I must not desert him in his sad extremity. I must not permit him to awake some day and learn from others what he now is, and that I, the woman he loved, of all others, left him to his degradation. The consequences might be more fatal than the injury which so changed him. Such action on my part might destroy him morally. Now his old self is buried as truly as if he had died. I could never look him in the face again if I left him to take his chances in life with no help from me, still less if I did that which he could scarcely forgive. He could not understand all that has happened since we thought him dead. He would only remember that I deserted him in his present pitiable plight. Do you understand me, Hobart?"

"I must, Helen."

"I know how hard it is for you. Can you think I forget this for a moment? Yet I send for you to help, to sustain me in a purpose which changes our future so greatly. Do you not remember what you said once about accepting the conditions of life as they are? We must do this again, and make the best of them."

"But if - suppose his memory does not come back. Is there to be no hope?"

"Hobart, you must put that thought from you as far as you can. Do you not see whither it might lead? You would not wish Captain Nichol to remain as he is?"

"Oh," he cried desperately, "I'm put in a position that would tax any saint in the calendar."

"Yes, you are. The future is not in our hands. I can only appeal to you to help me do what I think is right NOW."

He thought a few moments, took his resolve, then gave her his hand silently. She understood him without a word.

The news of the officer's return and of his strange condition was soon generally known in the village; but his parents, aided by the physician, quickly repressed those inclined to call from mere curiosity. At first Jim Wetherby scouted the idea that his old captain would not know him, but later had to admit the fact with a wonder which no explanations satisfied. Nichol immediately took a fancy to the one-armed veteran, who was glad to talk by the hour about soldiers and hospitals.

Before any matured plan for treatment could be adopted Nichol became ill, and soon passed into the delirium of fever. "The trouble is now clear enough," Dr. Barnes explained. "The captain has lived in hospitals and breathed a tainted atmosphere so long that his system is poisoned. This radical change of air has developed the disease."

Indeed, the typhoid symptoms progressed so rapidly as to show that the robust look of health had been in appearance only. The injured, weakened brain was the organ which suffered most, and in spite of the physician's best efforts his patient speedily entered into a condition of stupor, relieved only by low, unintelligible mutterings. Jim Wetherby became a tireless watcher, and greatly relieved the grief-stricken parents. Helen earnestly entreated that she might act the part of nurse also, but the doctor firmly forbade her useless exposure to contagion. She drove daily to the house, yet Mrs. Nichol's sad face and words could scarcely dissipate the girl's impression that the whole strange episode was a dream.

At last it was feared that the end was near. One night Dr. Barnes, Mr. and Mrs. Nichol, and Jim Wetherby were watching in the hope of a gleam of intelligence. He was very low, scarcely more than breathing, and they dreaded lest there might be no sign before the glimmer of life faded out utterly.

Suddenly the captain seemed to awake, his glassy eyes kindled, and a noble yet stern expression dignified his visage. In a thick voice he said, "For - " Then, as if all the remaining forces of life asserted themselves, he rose in his bed and exclaimed loudly, "Forward! Company A. Guide right. Ah!" He fell back, now dead in very truth.

"Oh!" cried Jim Wetherby, excitedly, "them was the last words I heard from him just before the shell burst, and he looks now just as he did then."

"Yes," said Dr. Barnes, sadly and gravely, "memory came back to him at the point where he lost it. He has died as we thought at first - a brave soldier leading a charge."

The stern, grand impress of battle remained upon the officer's countenance. Friends and neighbors looked upon his ennobled visage with awe, and preserved in honored remembrance the real man that temporarily had been obscured. Helen's eyes, when taking her farewell look, were not so blinded with tears but that she recognized his restored manhood. Death's touch had been more potent than love's appeal.

In the Wilderness, upon a day fatal to him and so many thousands, Captain Nichol had prophesied of the happy days of peace. They came, and he was not forgotten.

One evening Dr. Barnes was sitting with Martine and Helen at their fireside. They had been talking about Nichol, and Helen remarked thoughtfully, "It was so very strange that he should have regained his memory in the way and at the time he did."

"No," replied the physician, "that part of his experience does not strike me as so very strange. In typhoid cases a lucid interval is apt to precede death. His brain, like his body, was depleted, shrunken slightly by disease. This impoverishment probably removed the cerebral obstruction, and the organ of memory renewed its action at the point where it had been arrested. My theory explains his last ejaculation, 'Ah!' It was his involuntary exclamation as he again heard the shell burst. The reproduction in his mind of this explosion killed him instantly after all. He was too enfeebled to bear the shock. If he had passed from delirium into quiet sleep - ah, well! he is dead, and that is all we can know with certainty."

"Well," said Martine, with a deep breath, "I am glad he had every chance that it was possible for us to give him."

"Yes, Hobart," added his wife, gently, "you did your whole duty, and I do not forget what it cost you."

QUEEN OF SPADES

"Mother," remarked Farmer Banning, discontentedly, "Susie is making a long visit."

"She is coming home next week," said his cheery wife. She had drawn her low chair close to the air-tight stove, for a late March snowstorm was raging without.

"It seems to me that I miss her more and more."

"Well, I'm not jealous."

"Oh, come, wife, you needn't be. The idea! But I'd be jealous if our little girl was sorter weaned away from us by this visit in town."

"Now, see here, father, you beat all the men I ever heard of in scolding about farmers borrowing, and here you are borrowing trouble."

"Well, I hope I won't have to pay soon. But I've been thinking that the old farmhouse may look small and appear lonely after her gay winter. When she is away, it's too big for me, and a suspicion lonely for us both. I've seen that you've missed her more than I have."

"I guess you're right. Well, she's coming home, as I said, and we must make home seem home to her. The

E. P. Roe

child's growing up. Why, she'll be eighteen week after next. You must give her something nice on her birthday."

"I will," said the farmer, his rugged, weather-beaten face softening with memories. "Is our little girl as old as that? Why, only the other day I was carrying her on my shoulder to the barn and tossing her into the haymow. Sure enough, the 10th of April will be her birthday. Well, she shall choose her own present."

On the afternoon of the 5th of April he went down the long bill to the station, and was almost like a lover in his eagerness to see his child. He had come long before the train's schedule time, but was rewarded at last. When Susie appeared, she gave him a kiss before every one, and a glad greeting which might have satisfied the most exacting of lovers. He watched her furtively as they rode at a smart trot up the hill. Farmer Banning kept no old nags for his driving, but strong, well-fed, spirited horses that sometimes drew a light vehicle almost by the reins. "Yes," he thought, "she has grown a little citified. She's paler, and has a certain air or style that don't seem just natural to the hill. Well, thank the Lord! she doesn't seem sorry to go up the hill once more."

"There's the old place, Susie, waiting for you," he said. "It doesn't look so very bleak, does it, after all the fine city houses you've seen?"

"Yes, father, it does. It never appeared so bleak before."

He looked at his home, and in the late gray afternoon, saw it in a measure with her eyes - the long brown, bare slopes, a few gaunt old trees about the house, and the top boughs of the apple-orchard behind a sheltering hill in the rear of the dwelling.

"Father," resumed the girl, "we ought to call our place the Bleak House. I never so realized before how bare and desolate it looks, standing there right in the teeth of the north wind."

His countenance fell, but he had no time for comment. A moment later Susie was in her mother's arms. The farmer lifted the trunk to the horse-block and drove to the barn. "I guess it will be the old story," he muttered. "Home has become 'Bleak House.' I suppose it did look bleak to her eyes, especially at this season. Well, well, some day Susie will go to the city to stay, and then it will be Bleak House sure enough."

"Oh, father," cried his daughter when, after doing his evening work, he entered with the shadow of his thoughts still upon his face - "oh, father, mother says I can choose my birthday present!"

"Yes, Sue; I've passed my word."

"And so I have your bond. My present will make you open your eyes."

"And pocket-book too, I suppose. I'll trust you, however, not to break me. What is it to be?"

"I'll tell you the day before, and not till then."

After supper they drew around the stove. Mrs. Banning got out her knitting, as usual, and prepared for city gossip. The farmer rubbed his hands over the general aspect of comfort, and especially over the regained presence of his child's bright face. "Well, Sue," he remarked, "you'll own that this room IN the house doesn't look very bleak?"

"No, father, I'll own nothing of the kind. Your face and mother's are not bleak, but the room is."

"Well," said the farmer, rather disconsolately, "I fear the old place has been spoiled for you. I was saying to mother before you came home - "

"There now, father, no matter about what you were saying. Let Susie tell us why the room is bleak."

The girl laughed softly, got up, and taking a billet of wood from the box, put it into the air-tight. "The stove has swallowed it just as old Trip did his supper. Shame! you greedy dog," she added, caressing a great Newfoundland that would not leave her a moment. "Why can't you learn to eat your meals like a gentleman?" Then to her father, "Suppose we could sit here and see the flames curling all over and around that stick. Even a camp in the woods is jolly when lighted up by a flickering blaze."

"Oh - h!" said the farmer; "you think an open fire would take away the bleakness?"

"Certainly. The room would be changed instantly, and mother's face would look young and rosy again. The blue-black of this sheet-iron stove makes the room look blue-black."

"Open fires don't give near as much heat," said her father, meditatively. "They take an awful lot of wood;

and wood is getting scarce in these parts."

"I should say so! Why don't you farmers get together, appoint a committee to cut down every tree remaining, then make it a State-prison offence ever to set out another? Why, father, you cut nearly all the trees from your lot a few years ago and sold the wood. Now that the trees are growing again, you are talking of clearing up the land for pasture. Just think of the comfort we could get out of that wood-lot! What crop would pay better? All the upholsterers in the world cannot furnish a room as an open hardwood fire does; and all the produce of the farm could not buy anything else half so nice."

"Say, mother," said her father, after a moment, "I guess I'll get down that old Franklin from the garret to-morrow and see if it can't furnish this room."

The next morning he called rather testily to the hired man, who was starting up the lane with an axe, "Hiram, I've got other work for you. Don't cut a stick in that wood-lot unless I tell you."

The evening of the 9th of April was cool but clear, and the farmer said, genially, "Well, Sue, prospects good for fine weather on your birthday. Glad of it; for I suppose you will want me to go to town with you for your present, whatever it is to be."

"You'll own up a girl can keep a secret now, won't you?"

"He'll have to own more'n that," added his wife; "he must own that an ole woman hasn't lost any sleep from curiosity."

"How much will be left me to own to-morrow night?" said the farmer, dubiously. "I suppose Sue wants a watch studded with diamonds, or a new house, or something else that she darsn't speak of till the last minute, even to her mother."

"Nothing of the kind. I want only all your time tomorrow, and all Hiram's time, after you have fed the stock."

"All our time!

"Yes, the entire day, in which you both are to do just what I wish. You are not going gallivanting to the city, but will have to work hard."

"Well, I'm beat! I don't know what you want any more than I did at first."

"Yes, you do - your time and Hiram's."

"Give it up. It's hardly the season for a picnic. "We might go fishing - "

"We must go to bed, so as to be up early, all hands."

"Oh, hold on, Sue; I do like this wood-fire. If it wouldn't make you vain, I'd tell you how - "

"Pretty, father. Say it out."

"Oh, you know it, do you? Well, how pretty you look in the firelight. Even mother, there, looks ten years younger. Keep your low seat, child, and let me look at you. So you're eighteen? My! my! how the years roll around! It WILL be Bleak House for mother and me, in spite of the wood-fire, when you leave us."

"It won't be Bleak House much longer," she replied with a significant little nod.

The next morning at an early hour the farmer said, "All ready, Sue. Our time is yours till night; so queen it over us." And black Hiram grinned acquiescence, thinking he was to have an easy time.

"Queen it, did you say?" cried Sue, in great spirits. "Well, then, I shall be queen of spades. Get 'em, and come with me. Bring a pickaxe, too." She led the way to a point not far from the dwelling, and resumed: "A hole here, father, a hole there, Hiram, big enough for a small hemlock, and holes all along the northeast side of the house. Then lots more holes, all over the lawn, for oaks, maples, dogwood, and all sorts to pretty trees, especially evergreens.'

"Oh, ho!" cried the farmer; "now I see the hole where the woodchuck went in."

"But you don't see the hole where he's coming out. When that is dug, even the road will be lined with trees. Foolish old father! you thought I'd be carried away with city gewgaws, fine furniture, dresses, and all that sort of thing. You thought I'd be pining for what you couldn't afford, what wouldn't do you a particle of good, nor me either, in the long run. I'm going to make you set out trees enough to double the value of your place and take all the bleakness and bareness from this hillside. To-day is only the beginning. I did get some new notions in the city which made me discontented with my home, but they were not the notions you were worrying about. In the

E. P. Roe

suburbs I saw that the most costly houses were made doubly attractive by trees and shrubbery, and I knew that trees would grow for us as well as for millionaires - My conscience! if there isn't - " and the girl frowned and bit her lips.

"Is that one of the city beaux you were telling us about?" asked her father, sotto voce.

"Yes; but I don't want any beaux around to-day. I didn't think he'd be so persistent." Then, conscious that she was not dressed for company, but for work upon which she had set her heart, she advanced and gave Mr. Minturn a rather cool greeting.

But the persistent beau was equal to the occasion. He had endured Sue's absence as long as he could, then had resolved on a long day's siege, with a grand storming-onset late in the afternoon.

"Please, Miss Banning," he began, "don't look askance at me for coming at this unearthly hour. I claim the sacred rites of hospitality. I'm an invalid. The doctor said I needed country air, or would have prescribed it if given a chance. You said I might come to see you some day, and by playing Paul Pry I found out, you remember, that this was your birthday, and - "

"And this is my father, Mr. Minturn."

Mr. Minturn shook the farmer's hand with a cordiality calculated to awaken suspicions of his designs in a pump, had its handle been thus grasped. "Mr. Banning will forgive me for appearing with the lark," he continued volubly, determining to break the ice. "One can't get the full benefit of a day in the country if he starts in the afternoon."

The farmer was polite, but nothing more. If there was one thing beyond all others with which he could dispense, it was a beau for Sue.

Sue gave her father a significant, disappointed glance, which meant, "I won't get my present to day"; but he turned and said to Hiram, "Dig the hole right there, two feet across, eighteen inches deep." Then he started for the house. While not ready for suitors, his impulse to bestow hospitality was prompt.

The alert Mr. Minturn had observed the girl's glance, and knew that the farmer had gone to prepare his wife for a guest. He determined not to remain unless assured of a welcome. "Come, Miss Banning," he said, "we are at least friends, and should be frank. How much misunderstanding and trouble would often be saved if people would just speak their thought! This is your birthday - YOUR DAY. It should not be marred by any one. It would distress me keenly if I were the one to spoil it. Why not believe me literally and have your way absolutely about this day? I could come another time. Now show that a country girl, at least, can speak her mind."

With an embarrassed little laugh she answered, "I'm half inclined to take you at your word; but it would look so inhospitable."

"Bah for looks! The truth, please. By the way, though, you never looked better than in that trim blue walking-suit."

"Old outgrown working-suit, you mean. How sincere

you are!"

"Indeed I am. Well, I'm de trop; that much is plain. You will let me come another day, won't you?"

"Yes, and I'll be frank too and tell you about THIS day. Father's a busy man, and his spring work is beginning, but as my birthday-present he has given me all his time and all Hiram's yonder. Well, I learned in the city how trees improved a home; and I had planned to spend this long day in setting out trees - planned it ever since my return. So you see - "

"Of course I see and approve," cried Minturn. "I know now why I had such a wild impulse to come out here to-day. Why, certainly. Just fancy me a city tramp looking for work, and not praying I won't find it, either. I'll work for my board. I know how to set out trees. I can prove it, for I planted those thrifty fellows growing about our house in town. Think how much more you'll accomplish, with another man to help - one that you can order around to your heart's content."

"The idea of my putting you to work!"

"A capital idea! and if a man doesn't work when a woman puts him at it he isn't worth the powder - I won't waste time even in original remarks. I'll promise you there will be double the number of trees out by night. Let me take your father's spade and show you how I can dig. Is this the place? If I don't catch up with Hiram, you may send the tramp back to the city." And before she could remonstrate, his coat was off and he at work.

Laughing, yet half in doubt, she watched him. The way

he made the earth fly was surprising. "Oh, come," she said after a few moments, "you have shown your goodwill. A steam-engine could not keep it up at that rate."

"Perhaps not; but I can. Before you engage me, I wish you to know that I am equal to old Adam, and can dig."

"Engage you!" she thought with a little flutter of dismay. "I could manage him with the help of town conventionalities; but how will it be here? I suppose I can keep father and Hiram within earshot, and if he is so bent on - well, call it a lark, since he has referred to that previous bird, perhaps I might as well have a lark too, seeing it's my birthday." Then she spoke. "Mr. Minturn!"

"I'm busy."

"But really - "

"And truly tell me, am I catching up with Hiram?"

"You'll get down so deep that you'll drop through if you're not careful."

"There's nothing like having a man who is steady working for you. Now, most fellows would stop and giggle at such little amusing remarks."

"You are soiling your trousers."

"Yes, you're right. They ARE mine. There; isn't that a regulation hole? 'Two feet across and eighteen deep.'"

"Yah! yah!" cackled Hiram; "eighteen foot deep! Dat ud be a well."

"Of course it would, and truth would lie at its bottom. Can I stay, Miss Banning?"

"Did you ever see the like?" cried the farmer, who had appeared, unnoticed.

"Look here, father," said the now merry girl, "perhaps I was mistaken. This - "

"Tramp - " interjected Minturn.

"Says he's looking for work and knows how to set out trees."

"And will work all day for a dinner," the tramp promptly added.

"If he can dig holes at that rate, Sue," said her father, catching their spirit, "he's worth a dinner. But you're boss to-day; I'm only one of the hands."

"I'm only another," said Minturn, touching his hat.

"Boss, am I? I'll soon find out. Mr. Minturn, come with me and don a pair of overalls. You shan't put me to shame, wearing that spick-and-span suit, neither shall you spoil it. Oh, you're in for it now! You might have escaped, and come another day, when I could have received you in state and driven you out behind father's frisky bays, When you return to town with blistered hands and aching bones, you will at least know better another time."

"I don't know any better this time, and just yearn for those overalls."

"To the house, then, and see mother before you become a wreck."

Farmer Banning looked after him and shook his head. Hiram spoke his employer's thought, "Dar ar gem'lin act like he gwine ter set hisself out on dis farm."

Sue had often said, "I can never be remarkable for anything; but I won't be commonplace." So she did not leave her guest in the parlor while she rushed off for a whispered conference with her mother. The well-bred simplicity of her manner, which often stopped just short of brusqueness, was never more apparent than now. "Mother!" she called from the parlor door.

The old lady gave a few final directions to her maid-of-all-work, and then appeared.

"Mother, this is Mr. Minturn, one of my city friends, of whom I have spoken to you. He is bent on helping me set out trees."

"Yes, Mrs. Banning, so bent that your daughter found that she would have to employ her dog to get me off the place."

Now, it had so happened that in discussing with her mother the young men whom she had met, Sue had said little about Mr. Minturn; but that little was significant to the experienced matron. Words had slipped out now and then which suggested that the girl did more thinking than talking concerning him; and she always referred to him in some light which she chose to regard as ridiculous, but which had not seemed in the least absurd to the attentive listener. When her husband, therefore, said that Mr. Minturn had appeared on the scene, she felt that an era of portentous events had begun. The trees to be set out would change the old place greatly, but a primeval forest shading the door would be as nothing compared with the vicissitude which a favored "beau" might produce. But mothers are more unselfish than fathers, and are their daughters' natural allies unless the suitor is objectionable. Mrs. Banning was inclined to be hospitable on general principles, meantime eager on her own account to see something of this man, about whom she had presentiments. So she said affably, "My daughter can keep her eye on the work which she is so interested in, and yet give you most of her time. - Susan, I will entertain Mr. Minturn while you change your dress."

She glanced at her guest dubiously, receiving for the moment the impression that the course indicated by her mother was the correct one. The resolute admirer knew well what a fiasco the day would be should the conventionalities prevail, and so said promptly: "Mrs. Banning, I appreciate your kind intentions, and I hope some day you may have the chance to carry them out. To-day, as your husband understands, I am a tramp from the city looking for work. I have found it, and have been engaged. - Miss Banning, I shall hold you inflexibly to our agreement - a pair of overalls and dinner."

Sue said a few words of explanation. Her mother laughed, but
urged, "Do go and change your dress."

"I protest!" cried Mr. Minturn. "The walking-suit and overalls go together."

"Walking-suit, indeed!" repeated Sue, disdainfully. "But I shall not change it. I will not soften one feature of the scrape you have persisted in getting yourself into."

"Please don't."

"Mr. Minturn," said the matron, with smiling positiveness, "Susie is boss only out of doors; I am, in the house. There is a fresh-made cup of coffee and some eggs on toast in the dining-room. Having taken such an early start, you ought to have a lunch before being put to work."

"Yes," added Sue, "and the out-door boss says you can't go to work until at least the coffee is sipped."

"She's shrewd, isn't she, Mrs. Banning? She knows she will get twice as much work out of me on the strength of that coffee. Please get the overalls. I will not sip, but swallow the coffee, unless it's scalding, so that no time may be lost. Miss Banning must see all she had set her heart upon accomplished to-day, and a great deal more."

The matron departed on her quest, and as she pulled out the overalls, nodded her head significantly. "Things will be serious sure enough if he accomplishes all he has set his heart on," she muttered. "Well, he doesn't seem afraid to give us a chance to see him. He certainly will look ridiculous in these overalls, but not much more so than Sue in that old dress. I do wish she would change it."

E. P. Roe

The girl had considered this point, but with characteristic decision had thought: "No; he shall see us all on the plainest side of our life. He always seemed a good deal of an exquisite in town, and he lives in a handsome house. If to-day's experience at the old farm disgusts him, so be it. My dress is clean and tidy, if it is outgrown and darned; and mother is always neat, no matter what she wears. I'm going through the day just as I planned; and if he's too fine for us, now is the time to find it out. He may have come just for a lark, and will laugh with his folks to-night over the guy of a girl I appear; but I won't yield even to the putting of a ribbon in my hair."

Mrs. Banning never permitted the serving of cold slops for coffee, and Mr. Minturn had to sip the generous and fragrant beverage slowly. Meanwhile, his thoughts were busy. "Bah! for the old saying, 'Take the goods the gods send,'" he mused. "Go after your goods and take your pick. I knew my head was level in coming out. All is just as genuine as I supposed it would be - simple, honest, homely. The girl isn't homely, though, but she's just as genuine as all the rest, in that old dress which fits her like a glove. No shams and disguises on this field-day of my life. And her mother! A glance at her comfortable amplitude banished my one fear. There's not a sharp angle about her. I was satisfied about Miss Sue, but the term 'mother-in-law' suggests vague terrors to any man until reassured. - Ah, Miss Banning," he said, "this coffee would warm the heart of an anchorite. No wonder you are inspired to fine things after drinking such nectar."

"Yes, mother is famous for her coffee. I know that's fine, and you can praise it; but I'll not permit any ironical remarks concerning myself."

"I wouldn't, if I were you, especially when you are mistress of the situation. Still, I can't help having my opinion of you. Why in the world didn't you choose as your present something stylish from the city?"

"Something, I suppose you mean, in harmony with my very stylish surroundings and present appearance."

"I didn't mean anything of the kind, and fancy you know it. Ah! here are the overalls. Now deeds, not words. I'll leave my coat, watch, cuffs, and all impedimenta with you, Mrs. Banning. Am I not a spectacle to men and gods?" he added, drawing up the garment, which ceased to be nether in that it reached almost to his shoulders.

"Indeed you are," cried Sue, holding her side from laughing. Mrs. Banning also vainly tried to repress her hilarity over the absurd guy into which the nattily-dressed city man had transformed himself.

"Come," he cried, "no frivolity! You shall at least say I kept my word about the trees to-day." And they started at once for the scene of action, Minturn obtaining on the way a shovel from the tool-room.

"To think she's eighteen years old and got a beau!" muttered the farmer, as he and Hiram started two new holes. They were dug and others begun, yet the young people had not returned. "That's the way with young men nowadays - 'big cry, little wool.' I thought I was going to have Sue around with me all day. Might as well get used to it, I suppose. Eighteen! Her mother's wasn't much older when - yes, hang it, there's always a WHEN with these likely girls. I'd just like to start in again on that day when I tossed her into the haymow."

"What are you talking to yourself about, father?"

"Oh! I thought I had seen the last of you to-day."

"Perhaps you will wish you had before night."

"Well, now, Sue! the idea of letting Mr. Minturn rig himself out like that! There's no use of scaring the crows so long before corn-planting." And the farmer's guffaw was quickly joined by Hiram's broad "Yah! yah!"

She frowned a little as she said, "He doesn't look any worse than I do."

"Come, Mr. Banning, Solomon in all his glory could not so take your daughter's eye to-day as a goodly number of trees standing where she wants them. I suggest that you loosen the soil with the pickaxe, then I can throw it out rapidly. Try it."

The farmer did so, not only for Minturn, but for Hiram also. The lightest part of the work thus fell to him. "We'll change about," he said, "when you get tired."

But Minturn did not get weary apparently, and under this new division of the toil the number of holes grew apace.

"Sakes alive, Mr. Minturn!" ejaculated Mr. Banning, "one would think you had been brought up on a farm."

"Or at ditch-digging," added the young man. "No; my profession is to get people into hot water and then make them pay roundly to get out. I'm a lawyer. Times have changed in cities. It's there you'll find young men with muscle, if anywhere. Put your hand here, sir, and you'll know whether Miss Banning made a bad bargain in hiring me for the day."

"Why!" exclaimed the astonished farmer, "you have the muscle of a blacksmith."

"Yes, sir; I could learn that trade in about a month."

"You don't grow muscle like that in a law-office?"

"No, indeed; nothing but bills grow there. A good fashion, if not abused, has come in vogue, and young men develop their bodies as well as brains. I belong to an athletic club in town, and could take to pugilism should everything else fail."

"Is there any prospect of your coming to that?" Sue asked mischievously.

"If we were out walking, and two or three rough fellows gave you impudence - " He nodded significantly.

"What could you do against two or three? They'd close on you."

"A fellow taught to use his hands doesn't let men close on him."

"Yah, yah! reckon not," chuckled Hiram. One of the farm household had evidently been won.

"It seems to me," remarked smiling Sue, "that I saw several young men in town who appeared scarcely equal to carrying their canes."

"Dudes?"

"That's what they are called, I believe."

"They are not men. They are neither fish, flesh, nor fowl, but the beginning of the great downward curve of evolution. Men came up from monkeys, it's said, you know, but science is in despair over the final down-comes of dudes. They may evolute into grasshoppers."

The farmer was shaken with mirth, and Sue could not help seeing that he was having a good time. She, however, felt that no tranquilly exciting day was before her, as she had anticipated. What wouldn't that muscular fellow attempt before night? He possessed a sort of vim and cheerful audacity which made her tremble, "He is too confident," she thought, "and needs a lesson. All this digging is like that of soldiers who soon mean to drop their shovels. I don't propose to be carried by storm just when he gets ready. He can have his lark, and that's all to-day. I want a good deal of time to think before I surrender to him or any one else."

During the remainder of the forenoon these musings prevented the slightest trace of sentimentality from appearing in her face or words. She had to admit mentally that Minturn gave her no occasion for defensive tactics. He attended as strictly to business as did Hiram, and she was allowed to come and go at will. At first she merely ventured to the house, to "help mother," as she said. Then, with growing confidence, she went here and there to select sites for trees; but Minturn dug on no longer "like a steam-engine," yet in an easy, steady, effective way that was a continual surprise to the farmer.

"Well, Sue," said her father at last, "you and mother ought to have an extra dinner; for Mr. Minturn certainly has earned one."

"I promised him only a dinner," she replied; "nothing was said about its being extra."

"Quantity is all I'm thinking of," said Minturn. "I have the sauce which will make it a feast."

"Beckon it's gwine on twelve," said Hiram, cocking his eye at the sun. "Hadn't I better feed de critters?"

"Ah, old man! own up, now; you've got a backache," said Minturn.

"Dere is kin' ob a crik comin' - "

"Drop work, all hands," cried Sue. "Mr. Minturn has a 'crik' also, but he's too proud to own it. How you'll groan for this to-morrow, sir!"

"If you take that view of the case, I may be under the necessity of giving proof positive to the contrary by coming out to-morrow."

"You're not half through yet. The hardest part is to come."

"Oh, I know that," he replied; and he gave her such a humorously appealing glance that she turned quickly toward the house to hide a conscious flush.

The farmer showed him to the spare-room, in which he found his belongings. Left to make his toilet, he muttered, "Ah, better and better! This is not the regulation refrigerator into which guests are put at farmhouses. All needed for solid comfort is here, even to a slight fire in the air-tight. Now, isn't that rosy old lady a jewel of a mother-in-law? She knows that a warm man shouldn't get chilled just as well as if she had studied athletics. Miss Sue, however, is a little chilly. She's on the fence yet. Jupiter! I AM tired. Oh, well, I don't believe I'll have seven years of this kind of thing. You were right, though, old man, if your Rachel was like mine. What's that rustle in the other room? She's dressing for dinner. So must I; and I'm ready for it. If she has romantic ideas about love and lost appetites, I'm a goner."

When he descended to the parlor, his old stylish self again, Sue was there, robed in a gown which he had admired before, revealing the fact to her by approving glances. But now he said, "You don't look half so well as you did before."

"I can't say that of you," she replied.

"A man's looks are of no consequence."

"Few men think so."

"Oh, they try to please such critical eyes as I now am meeting."

"And throw dust in them too sometimes."

"Yes; gold dust, often. I haven't much of that."

"It would be a pity to throw it away if you had."

"No matter how much was thrown, I don't think it

would blind you, Miss Banning."

The dining-room door across the hall opened, and the host and hostess appeared. "Why, father and mother, how fine you look!"

"It would be strange indeed if we did not honor this day," said Mrs. Banning. "I hope you have not so tired yourself, sir, that you cannot enjoy your dinner. I could scarcely believe my eyes as I watched you from the window."

"I am afraid I shall astonish you still more at the table. I am simply ravenous."

"This is your chance," cried Sue. "You are now to be paid in the coin you asked for."

Sue did remark to herself by the time they reached dessert and coffee, "I need have no scruples in refusing a man with such an appetite; he won't pine. He is a lawyer, sure enough. He is just winning father and mother hand over hand."

Indeed, the bosom of good Mrs. Banning must have been environed with steel not to have had throbs of goodwill toward one who showed such hearty appreciation of her capital dinner. But Sue became only the more resolved that she was not going to yield so readily to this muscular suitor who was digging and eating his way straight into the hearts of her ancestors, and she proposed to be unusually elusive and alert during the afternoon. She was a little surprised when he resumed his old tactics.

After drinking a second cup of coffee, he rose, and

said, "As an honest man, I have still a great deal to do after such a dinner."

"Well, it has just done me good to see you," said Mrs. Banning, smiling genially over her old-fashioned coffee-pot. "I feel highly complimented."

"I doubt whether I shall be equal to another such compliment before the next birthday. I hope, Miss Susie, you have observed my efforts to do honor to the occasion?"

"Oh," cried the girl, "I naturally supposed you were trying to get even in your bargain."

"I hope to be about sundown. I'll get into those overalls at once, and I trust you will put on your walking-suit."

"Yes, it will be a walking-suit for a short time. We must walk to the wood-lot for the trees, unless you prefer to ride. - Father, please tell Hiram to get the two-horse wagon ready."

When the old people were left alone, the farmer said, "Well, mother, Sue HAS got a suitor, and if he don't suit her - " And then his wit gave out.

"There, father, I never thought you'd come to that. It's well she has, for you will soon have to be taken care of."

"He's got the muscle to do it. He shall have my law-business, anyway."

"Thank the Lord, it isn't much; but that's not saying he shall have Sue."

"Why, what have you against him?"

"Nothing so far. I was only finding out if you had anything against him."

"Lawyers, indeed! What would become of the men if women turned lawyers. Do you think Sue - "

"Hush!"

They all laughed till the tears came when Minturn again appeared dressed for work; but he nonchalantly lighted a cigar and was entirely at his ease.

Sue was armed with thick gloves and a pair of pruning-nippers. Minturn threw a spade and pickaxe on his shoulder, and Mr. Banning, whom Sue had warned threateningly "never to be far away," tramped at their side as they went up the lane. Apparently there was no need of such precaution, for the young man seemed wholly bent on getting up the trees, most of which she had selected and marked during recent rambles. She helped now vigorously, pulling on the young saplings as they loosened the roots, then trimming them into shape. More than once, however, she detected glances, and his thoughts were more flattering than she imagined. "What vigor she has in that supple, rounded form! Her very touch ought to put life into these trees; I know it would into me. How young she looks in that comical old dress which barely reaches her ankles! Yes, Hal Minturn; and remember, that trim little ankle can put a firm foot down for or against you - so no blundering."

He began to be doubtful whether he would make his grand attack that day, and finally decided against it, unless a very favorable opportunity occurred, until her plan of birthday-work had been carried out and he had fulfilled the obligation into which he had entered in the morning. He labored on manfully, seconding all her wishes, and taking much pains to get the young trees up with an abundance of fibrous roots. At last his assiduity induced her to relent a little, and she smiled sympathetically as she remarked, "I hope you are enjoying yourself. Well, never mind; some other day you will fare better."

"Why should I not enjoy myself?" he asked in well-feigned surprise. "What condition of a good time is absent? Even an April day has forgotten to be moody, and we are having unclouded, genial sunshine. The air is delicious with springtime fragrance. Were ever hemlocks so aromatic as these young fellows? They come out of the ground so readily that one would think them aware of their proud destiny. Of course I'm enjoying myself. Even the robins and sparrows know it, and are singing as if possessed."

"Hadn't you better give up your law-office and turn farmer?"

"This isn't farming. This is embroidery-work."

"Well, if all these trees grow they will embroider the old place, won't they?"

"They'll grow, every mother's son of 'em."

"What makes you so confident?"

"I'm not confident. That's where you are mistaken." And he gave her such a direct, keen look that she suddenly found something to do elsewhere.

"I declare!" she exclaimed mentally, "he seems to read my very thoughts."

At last the wagon was loaded with trees enough to occupy the holes which had been dug, and they started for the vicinity of the farmhouse again. Mr. Banning had no match-making proclivities where Sue was concerned, as may be well understood, and had never been far off. Minturn, however, had appeared so single-minded in his work, so innocent of all designs upon his daughter, that the old man began to think that this day's performance was only a tentative and preliminary skirmish, and that if there were danger it lurked in the unknown future. He was therefore inclined to be less vigilant, reasoning philosophically, "I suppose it's got to come some time or other. It looks as if Sue might go a good deal further than this young man and fare worse. But then she's only eighteen, and he knows it. I guess he's got sense enough not to plant his corn till the sun's higher. He can see with half an eye that my little girl isn't ready to drop, like an over-ripe apple." Thus mixing metaphors and many thoughts, he hurried ahead to open the gate for Hiram.

"I'm in for it now," thought Sue, and she instinctively assumed an indifferent expression and talked volubly of trees.

"Yes, Miss Banning," he said formally, "by the time your hair is tinged with gray the results of this day's labor will be seen far and wide. No passenger in the cars, no traveller in the valley, but will turn his eyes admiringly in this direction."

"I wasn't thinking of travellers," she answered, "but of making an attractive home in which I can grow old contentedly. Some day when you have become a gray-haired and very dignified judge you may come out and dine with us again. You can then smoke your cigar under a tree which you helped to plant."

"Certainly, Miss Banning. With such a prospect, how could you doubt that I was enjoying myself? What suggested the judge? My present appearance?"

The incongruity of the idea with his absurd aspect and a certain degree of nervousness set her off again, and she startled the robins by a laugh as loud and clear as their wild notes.

"I don't care," she cried. "I've had a jolly birthday, and am accomplishing all on which I had set my heart."

"Yes, and a great deal more, Miss Banning," he replied with a formal bow. "In all your scheming you hadn't set your heart on my coming out and - does modesty permit me to say it? - helping a little."

"Now, you HAVE helped wonderfully, and you must not think I don't appreciate it."

"Ah, how richly I am rewarded!"

She looked at him with a laughing and perplexed little frown, but only said, "No irony, sir."

By this time they had joined her father and begun to set out the row of hemlocks. To her surprise, Sue had found herself a little disappointed that he had not availed himself of his one opportunity to be at least "a bit friendly" as she phrased it. It was mortifying to a girl to be expecting "something awkward to meet" and nothing of the kind take place. "After all," she thought, "perhaps he came out just for a lark, or, worse still, is amusing himself at my expense; or he may have come on an exploring expedition and plain old father and mother, and the plain little farmhouse, have satisfied him. Well, the dinner wasn't very plain, but he may have been laughing in his sleeve at our lack of style in serving it. Then this old dress! I probably appear to him a perfect guy." And she began to hate it, and devoted it to the rag-bag the moment she could get it off.

This line of thought, once begun, seemed so rational that she wondered it had not occurred to her before. "The idea of my being so ridiculously on the defensive!" she thought. "No, it wasn't ridiculous either, as far as my action went, for he can never say I ACTED as if I wanted him to speak. My conceit in expecting him to speak the moment he got a chance WAS absurd. He has begun to be very polite and formal. That's always the way with men when they want to back out of anything. He came out to look us over, and me in particular; he made himself into a scarecrow just because I looked like one, and now will go home and laugh it all over with his city friends. Oh, why did he come and spoil my day? Even he said it WAS my day, and he has done a mean thing in spoiling it. Well, he may not carry as much self-complacency back to town as he thinks he will. Such a cold-blooded spirit, too! - to come upon us unawares in order to spy out everything, for fear he might get taken in! You were very attentive and flattering in the city, sir, but now you are disenchanted. Well, so am I."

Under the influence of this train of thought she grew more and more silent. The sun was sinking westward in undimmed splendor, but her face was clouded. The air was sweet, balmy, well adapted to sentiment and the setting out of trees, but she was growing frosty.

"Hiram," she said shortly, "you've got that oak crooked; let me hold it." And thereafter she held the trees for the old colored man as he filled in the earth around them.

Minturn appeared as oblivious as he was keenly observant. At first the change in Sue puzzled and discouraged him; then, as his acute mind sought her motives, a rosy light began to dawn upon him. "I may be wrong," he thought, "but I'll take my chances in acting as if I were right before I go home."

At last Hiram said: "Reckon I'll have to feed de critters again;" and he slouched off.

Sue nipped at the young trees further and further away from the young man who must "play spy before being lover." The spy helped Mr. Banning set out the last tree. Meantime, the complacent farmer had mused: "The little girl's safe for another while, anyhow. Never saw her more offish; but things looked squally about dinner-time. Then, she's only eighteen; time enough years hence." At last he said affably, "I'll go in and hasten supper, for you've earned it if ever a man did, Mr. Minturn. Then I'll drive you down to the evening train." And he hurried away.

Sue's back was toward them, and she did not hear Minturn's step until he was close beside her. "All through," he said; "every tree out. I congratulate you;

for rarely in this vale of tears are plans and hopes crowned with better success."

"Oh, yes," she hastened to reply; "I am more than satisfied. I hope that you are too."

"I have no reason to complain," he said. "You have stood by your morning's bargain, as I have tried to."

"It was your own fault, Mr. Minturn, that it was so one-sided. But I've no doubt you enjoy spicing your city life with a little lark in the country."

"It WAS a one-sided bargain, and I have had the best of it."

"Perhaps you have," she admitted. "I think supper will be ready by the time we are ready for it." And she turned toward the house. Then she added, "You must be weary and anxious to get away."

"You were right; my bones DO ache. And look at my hands. I know you'll say they need washing; but count the blisters."

"I also said, Mr. Minturn, that you would know better next time. So you see I was right then and am right now."

"Are you perfectly sure?"

"I see no reason to think otherwise." In turning, she had faced a young sugar-maple which he had aided her in planting early in the afternoon. Now she snipped at it nervously with her pruning-shears, for he would not budge, and she felt it scarcely polite to leave him.

"Well," he resumed, after an instant, "it has a good look, hasn't it, for a man to fulfil an obligation literally?"

"Certainly, Mr. Minturn," and there was a tremor in her tone; "but you have done a hundred-fold more than I expected, and never were under any obligations."

"Then I am free to begin again?"

"You are as free now as you have been all day to do what you please." And her shears were closing on the main stem of the maple. He caught and stayed her hand. "I don't care!" she cried almost passionately. "Come, let us go in and end this foolish talk."

"But I do care," he replied, taking the shears from her, yet retaining her hand in his strong grasp. "I helped you plant this tree, and whenever you see it, whenever you care for it, when, in time, you sit under its shade or wonder at its autumn hues, I wish you to remember that I told you of my love beside it. Dear little girl, do you think I am such a blind fool that I could spend this long day with you at your home and not feel sorry that I must ever go away? If I could, my very touch should turn the sap of this maple into vinegar. To-day I've only tried to show how I can work for you. I am eager to begin again, and for life."

At first Sue had tried to withdraw her hand, but its tenseness relaxed. As he spoke, she turned her averted face slowly toward him, and the rays of the setting sun flashed a deeper crimson into her cheeks. Her honest eyes looked into his and were satisfied. Then she suddenly gathered the young tree against her heart and kissed the stem she had so nearly severed. "This maple is witness to what you've said," she faltered. "Ah! but it will be a sugar-maple in truth; and if petting will make it live - there, now! behave! The idea! right out on this bare lawn! You must wait till the screening evergreens grow before - Oh, you audacious - I haven't promised anything."

"I promise everything. I'm engaged, and only taking my retaining-fees."

"Mother," cried Farmer Banning at the dining-room window, "just look yonder!"

"And do you mean to say, John Banning, that you didn't expect it?"

"Why, Sue was growing more and more offish."

"Of course! Don't you remember?"

"Oh, this unlucky birthday! As if trees could take Sue's place!"

"Yah!" chuckled Hiram from the barn door, "I knowed dat ar gem'lin was a-diggin' a hole fer hisself on dis farm."

"Mr. Minturn - " Sue began as they came toward the house arm in arm.

"Hal - " he interrupted.

"Well, then, Mr. Hal, you must promise me one thing in dead earnest. I'm the only chick father and mother have. You must be very considerate of them, and let me give them as much of my time as I can. This is all that I stipulate; but this I do."

"Sue," he said in mock solemnity, "the prospects are that you'll be a widow."

"Why do you make such an absurd remark?"

"Because you have struck amidships the commandment with the promise, and your days will be long in the land. You'll outlive everybody."

"This will be no joke for father and mother."

So it would appear. They sat in the parlor as if waiting for the world to come to an end - as indeed it had, one phase of it, to them. Their little girl, in a sense, was theirs no longer.

"Father, mother," said Sue, demurely, "I must break some news to you."

"It's broken already," began Mrs. Banning, putting her handkerchief to her eyes.

Sue's glance renewed her reproaches for the scene on the lawn; but Minturn went promptly forward, and throwing his arm around the matron's plump shoulders, gave his first filial kiss.

"Come, mother," he said, "Sue has thought of you both; and I've given her a big promise that I won't take any more of her away than I can help. And you, sir," wringing the farmer's hand, "will often see a city tramp here who will be glad to work for his dinner. These overalls are my witness."

Then they became conscious of his absurd figure, and the scene ended in laughter that was near akin to tears.

The maple lived, you may rest assured; and Sue's children said there never was such sugar as the sap of that tree yielded.

All the hemlocks, oaks, and dogwood thrived as if conscious that theirs had been no ordinary transplanting; while Minturn's half-jesting prophecy concerning the travellers in the valley was amply fulfilled.

AN UNEXPECTED RESULT

"Jack, she played with me deliberately, heartlessly. I can never forgive her."

"In that case, Will, I congratulate you. Such a girl isn't worth a second thought, and you've made a happy escape."

"No congratulations, if you please. You can talk coolly, because in regard to such matters you are cool, and, I may add, a trifle cold. Ambition is your mistress, and a musty law-book has more attractions for you than any woman living. I'm not so tempered. I am subject to the general law of nature, and a woman's love and sympathy are essential to success in my life and work."

"That's all right; but there are as good fish - "

"Oh, have done with your trite nonsense," interrupted Will Munson, impatiently. "I'd consult you on a point of law in preference to most of the gray-beards, but I was a fool to speak of this affair. And yet as my most intimate friend - "

"Come, Will, I'm not unfeeling;" and John Ackland rose and put his hand on his friend's shoulder. "I admit that the subject is remote from my line of thought and wholly beyond my experience. If the affair is so serious I shall take it to heart."

"Serious! Is it a slight thing to be crippled for life?"

"Oh, come, now," said Ackland, giving his friend a hearty and encouraging thump, "you are sound in mind and limb; what matters a scratch on the heart to a man not twenty-five?"

"Very well; I'll say no more about it. When I need a lawyer I'll come to you. Good-by; I sail for Brazil in the morning."

"Will, sit down and look me in the eyes," said Ackland, decisively. "Will, forgive me. You are in trouble. A man's eyes usually tell me more than all his words, and I don't like the expression of yours. There is yellow fever in Brazil."

"I know it," was the careless reply.

"What excuse have you for going?"

"Business complications have arisen there, and I promptly volunteered to go. My employers were kind enough to hesitate and warn me, and to say that they could send a man less valuable to them, but I soon overcame their objections."

"That is your excuse for going. The reason I see in your eyes. You are reckless, Will."

"I have reason to be."

"I can't agree with you, but I feel for you all the same.

Tell me all about it, for this is sad news to me. I had hoped to join you on the beach in a few days, and to spend August with you and my cousin. I confess I am beginning to feel exceedingly vindictive toward this pretty little monster, and if any harm comes to you I shall be savage enough to scalp her."

"The harm has come already, Jack. I'm hit hard. She showed me a mirage of happiness that has made my present world a desert. I am reckless; I'm desperate. You may think it is weak and unmanly, but you don't know anything about it. Time or the fever may cure me, but now I am bankrupt in all that gives value to life. A woman with an art so consummate that it seemed artless, deliberately evoked the best there was in me, then threw it away as indifferently as a cast-off glove."

"Tell me how it came about."

"How can I tell you? How can I in cold blood recall glances, words, intonations, the pressure of a hand that seemed alive with reciprocal feeling? In addition to her beauty she had the irresistible charm of fascination. I was wary at first, but she angled for me with a skill that would have disarmed any man who did not believe in the inherent falseness of woman. The children in the house idolized her, and I have great faith in a child's intuitions."

"Oh, that was only a part of her guile," said Ackland, frowningly.

"Probably; at any rate she has taken all the color and zest out of my life. I wish some one could pay her back in her own coin. I don't suppose she has a heart; but I wish her vanity might be wounded in a way that would teach her a lesson never to be forgotten."

"It certainly would be a well-deserved retribution," said Ackland, musingly.

"Jack, you are the one, of all the world, to administer the punishment. I don't believe a woman's smiles ever quickened your pulse one beat."

"You are right, Will, it is my cold-bloodedness - to put your thought in plain English - that will prove your best ally."

"I only hope that I am not leading you into danger. You will need an Indian's stoicism."

"Bah! I may fail ignominiously, and find her vanity invulnerable, but I pledge you my word that I will avenge you if it be within the compass of my skill. My cousin, Mrs. Alston, may prove a useful ally. I think you wrote me that the name of this siren was Eva Van Tyne?"

"Yes; I only wish she had the rudiments of a heart, so that she might feel in a faint, far-off way a little of the pain she has inflicted on me. Don't let her make you falter or grow remorseful, Jack. Remember that you have given a pledge to one who may be dead before you can fulfil it."

Ackland said farewell to his friend with the fear that he might never see him again, and a few days later found himself at a New England seaside resort, with a relentless purpose lurking in his dark eyes. Mrs. Alston did unconsciously prove a useful ally, for her wealth and elegance gave her unusual prestige in the house, and in joining her party Ackland achieved immediately all the social recognition he desired.

While strolling with this lady on the piazza he observed the object of his quest, and was at once compelled to make more allowance than he had done hitherto for his friend's discomfiture. Two or three children were leaning over the young girl's chair, and she was amusing them by some clever caricatures. She was not so interested, however, but that she soon noted the new-comer, and bestowed upon him from time to time curious and furtive glances. That these were not returned seemed to occasion her some surprise, for she was not accustomed to be so utterly ignored, even by a stranger. A little later Ackland saw her consulting the hotel register.

"I have at least awakened her curiosity," he thought.

"I've been waiting for you to ask me who that pretty girl is," said Mrs. Alton, laughing; "you do indeed exceed all men in indifference to women."

"I know all about that girl," was the grim reply. "She has played the very deuce with my friend Munson."

"Yes," replied Mrs. Alston, indignantly, "it was the most shameful piece of coquetry I ever saw. She is a puzzle to me. To the children and the old people in the house she is consideration and kindness itself; but she appears to regard men of your years as legitimate game and is perfectly remorseless. So beware! She is dangerous, invulnerable as you imagine yourself to be. She will practice her wiles upon you if you give her half a chance, and her art has much more than her pretty face to enforce it. She is unusually clever."

Ackland's slight shrug was so contemptuous that his cousin was nettled, and she thought, "I wish the girl could disturb his complacent equanimity just a little. It vexes one to see a man so indifferent; it's a slight to woman;" and she determined to give Miss Van Tyne the vantage-ground of an introduction at the first opportunity.

And this occurred before the evening was over. To her surprise Ackland entered into an extended conversation with the enemy. "Well," she thought, "if he begins in this style there will soon be another victim. Miss Van Tyne can talk to as bright a man as he is and hold her own. Meanwhile she will assail him in a hundred covert ways. Out of regard for his friend he should have shown some disapproval of her; but there he sits quietly talking in the publicity of the parlor."

"Mrs. Alston," said a friend at her elbow, "you ought to forewarn your cousin and tell him of Mr. Munson's fate."

"He knows all about Mr. Munson," was her reply. "Indeed, the latter is his most intimate friend. I suppose my cousin is indulging in a little natural curiosity concerning this destroyer of masculine peace, and if ever a man could do so in safety he can."

"Why so?"

"Well, I never knew so unsusceptible a man. With the exception of a few of his relatives, he has never cared for ladies' society."

Mrs. Alston was far astray in supposing that curiosity was Ackland's motive in his rather prolonged conversation with Miss Van Tyne. It was simply part of his tactics, for he proposed to waste no time in skirmishing or in guarded and gradual approaches. He would cross weapons at once, and secure his object by a sharp and aggressive campaign. His object was to obtain immediately some idea of the calibre of the girl's mind, and in this respect he was agreeably surprised, for while giving little evidence of thorough education, she was unusually intelligent and exceedingly quick in her perceptions. He soon learned also that she was gifted with more than woman's customary intuition, that she was watching his face closely for meanings that he might not choose to express in words or else to conceal by his language. While he feared that his task would be far more difficult than he expected, and that he would have to be extremely guarded in order not to reveal his design, he was glad to learn that the foe was worthy of his steel. Meanwhile her ability and self-reliance banished all compunction. He had no scruples in humbling the pride of a woman who was at once so proud, so heartless, and so clever. Nor would the effort be wearisome, for she had proved herself both amusing and interesting. He might enjoy it quite as much as an intricate law case.

Even prejudiced Ackland, as he saw her occasionally on the following day, was compelled to admit that she was more than pretty. Her features were neither regular nor faultless. Her mouth was too large to be perfect, and her nose was not Grecian; but her eyes were peculiarly fine and illumined her face, whose chief charm lay in its power of expression. If she chose, almost all her thoughts and feelings could find their reflex there. The trouble was that she could as readily mask her thought and express what she did not feel. Her eyes were of the darkest blue and her hair seemed light in contrast. It was evident that she had studied grace so thoroughly that her manner and carriage appeared unstudied and natural. She never seemed self-conscious, and yet no one had ever seen her in an ungainly posture or had known her to make an awkward gesture. This grace, however, like a finished style in writing, was tinged so strongly with her own individuality that it appeared original as compared with the fashionable monotony which characterized the manners of so many of her age. She could not have been much more than twenty; and yet, as Mrs. Alston took pains to inform her cousin, she had long been in society, adding, "Its homage is her breath of life, and from all I hear your friend Munson has had many predecessors. Be on your guard."

"Your solicitude in my behalf is quite touching," he replied. "Who is this fair buccaneer that has made so many wrecks and exacts so heavy a revenue from society? Who has the care of her and what are her antecedents?"

"She is an orphan, and possessed, I am told, of considerable property in her own name. A forceless, nerveless maiden aunt is about the only antecedent we see much of. Her guardian has been here once or twice, but practically she is independent."

Miss Van Tyne's efforts to learn something concerning Ackland were apparently quite as casual and indifferent and yet were made with utmost skill. She knew that Mrs. Alston's friend was something of a gossip; and she led her to speak of the subject of her

E. P. Roe

thoughts with an indirect finesse that would have amused the young man exceedingly could he have been an unobserved witness. When she learned that he was Mr. Munson's intimate friend and that he was aware of her treatment of the latter, she was somewhat disconcerted. One so forewarned might not become an easy prey. But the additional fact that he was almost a woman-hater put her upon her mettle at once, and she felt that here was a chance for a conquest such as she had never made before. She now believed that she had discovered the key to his indifference. He was ready enough to amuse himself with her as a clever woman, but knew her too well to bestow upon her even a friendly thought.

"If I can bring him to my feet it will be a triumph indeed," she murmured exultantly; "and at my feet he shall be if he gives me half a chance." Seemingly he gave her every chance that she could desire, and while he scarcely made any effort to seek her society, she noted with secret satisfaction that he often appeared as if accidentally near her, and that he ever made it the easiest and most natural thing in the world for her to join him. His conversation was often as gay and unconventional as she could wish; but she seldom failed to detect in it an uncomfortable element of satire and irony. He always left her dissatisfied with herself and with a depressing consciousness that she had made no impression upon him.

His conquest grew into an absorbing desire; and she unobtrusively brought to bear upon him every art and fascination that she possessed. Her toilets were as exquisite as they were simple. The children were made to idolize her more than ever; but Ackland was candid enough to admit that this was not all guile on her part, for she was evidently in sympathy with the little people, who can rarely be imposed upon by any amount of false interest. Indeed, he saw no reason to doubt that she abounded in good-nature toward all except the natural objects of her ruling passion; but the very skill and deliberateness with which she sought to gratify this passion greatly increased his vindictive feeling. He saw how naturally and completely his friend had been deceived and how exquisite must have been the hopes and anticipations so falsely raised. Therefore he smiled more grimly at the close of each succeeding day, and was more than ever bent upon the accomplishment of his purpose.

At length Miss Van Tyne changed her tactics and grew quite oblivious to Ackland's presence in the house; but she found him apparently too indifferent to observe the fact. She then permitted one of her several admirers to become devoted; Ackland did not offer the protest of even a glance. He stood, as it were, just where she had left him, ready for an occasional chat, stroll, or excursion, if the affair came about naturally and without much effort on his part. She found that she could neither induce him to seek her nor annoy him by an indifference which she meant should be more marked than his own.

Some little time after there came a windy day when the surf was so heavy that there were but few bathers. Ackland was a good swimmer, and took his plunge as usual. He was leaving the water when Miss Van Tyne ran down the beach and was about to dart through the breakers in her wonted fearless style.

"Be careful," he said to her; "the undertow is strong, and the man who has charge of the bathing is ill and not here. The tide is changing - in fact, running out already, I believe." But she would not even look at him, much less answer. As there were other gentlemen present, he started for his bath-house, but had proceeded but a little way up the beach before a cry brought him to the water's edge instantly.

"Something is wrong with Miss Van Tyne," cried half a dozen voices. "She ventured out recklessly, and it seems as if she couldn't get back."

At that moment her form rose on the crest of a wave, and above the thunder of the surf came her faint cry, "Help!"

The other bathers stood irresolute, for she was dangerously far out, and the tide had evidently turned. Ackland, on the contrary, dashed through the breakers and then, in his efforts for speed, dived through the waves nearest to the shore. When he reached the place where he expected to find her he saw nothing for a moment or two but great crested billows that every moment were increasing in height under the rising wind. For a moment he feared that she had perished, and the thought that the beautiful creature had met her death so suddenly and awfully made him almost sick and faint. An instant later, however, a wave threw her up from the trough of the sea into full vision somewhat on his right, and a few strong strokes brought him to her side.

"Oh, save me!" she gasped.

"Don't cling to me," he said sternly. "Do as I bid you. Strike out for the shore if you are able; if not, lie on your back and float."

She did the latter, for now that aid had reached her she apparently recovered from her panic and was perfectly tractable. He placed his left hand under her and struck out quietly, aware that the least excitement causing exhaustion on his part might cost both of them their lives.

As they approached the shore a rope was thrown to them, and Ackland, who felt his strength giving way, seized it - desperately. He passed his arm around his companion with a grasp that almost made her breathless, and they were dragged half suffocated through the water until strong hands on either side rushed them through the breakers.

Miss Van Tyne for a moment or two stood dazed and panting, then disengaged herself from the rather warm support of the devoted admirer whom she had tried to play against Ackland, and tried to walk, but after a few uncertain steps fell senseless on the sand, thus for the moment drawing to herself the attention of the increasing throng. Ackland, glad to escape notice, was staggering off to his bath-house when several ladies, more mindful of his part in the affair than the men had been, overtook him with a fire of questions and plaudits.

"Please leave me alone," he said almost savagely, without looking around.

"What a bear he is! Any one else would have been a little complacent over such an exploit," they chorused, as they followed the unconscious girl, who was now being carried to the hotel.

Ackland locked the door of his little apartment and

sank panting on the bench. "Maledictions on her!" he muttered. "At one time there was a better chance of her being fatal to me than to Munson with his yellow-fever tragedy in prospect. Her recklessness to-day was perfectly insane. If she tries it again she may drown for all that I care, or at least ought to care." His anger appeared to act like a tonic, and he was soon ready to return to the house. A dozen sprang forward to congratulate him, but they found such impatience and annoyance at all reference to the affair that with many surmises the topic was dropped.

"You are a queer fellow," remarked his privileged cousin, as he took her out to dinner. "Why don't you let people speak naturally about the matter, or rather, why don't you pose as the hero of the occasion?"

"Because the whole affair was most unnatural, and I am deeply incensed. In a case of necessity I am ready to risk my life, although it has unusual attractions for me; but I'm no melodramatic hero looking for adventures. What necessity was there in this case? It is the old story of Munson over again in another guise. The act was that of an inconsiderate, heartless woman who follows her impulses and inclinations, no matter what may be the consequences." After a moment he added less indignantly, "I must give her credit for one thing, angry as I am - she behaved well in the water, otherwise she would have drowned me."

"She is not a fool. Most women would have drowned you."

"She is indeed not a fool; therefore she's the more to blame. If she is ever so reckless again, may I be asleep in my room. Of course one can't stand by and see a woman drown, no matter who or what she is."

"Jack, what made her so reckless?" Mrs. Alston asked, with a sudden intelligence lighting up her face.

"Hang it all! How should I know? What made her torture Munson? She follows her impulses, and they are not always conducive to any one's well-being, not even her own."

"Mark my words, she has never shown this kind of recklessness before."

"Oh, yes, she has. She was running her horse to death the other hot morning and nearly trampled on a child;" and he told of an unexpected encounter while he was taking a rather extended ramble.

"Well," exclaimed Mrs. Alston, smiling significantly, "I think I understand her symptoms better than you do. If you are as cold-blooded as you seem, I may have to interfere."

"Oh, bah!" he answered impatiently. "Pardon me, but I should despise myself forever should I become sentimental, knowing what I do."

"Jack, had you no compunctions when fearing that such a beautiful girl might perish? We are going to have an awful night. Hear the wind whistle and moan, and the sky is already black with clouds. The roar of the surface grows louder every hour. Think of that lovely form being out in those black angry waves, darted at and preyed upon by horrible slimy monsters. Oh, it fairly makes my flesh creep!"

"And mine too," he said with a strong gesture of disgust; "especially when I remember that I should have kept her company, for of course I could not return without her. I confess that when at first I could not find her I was fairly sick at the thought of her fate. But remember how uncalled for it all was - quite as much so as that poor Will Munson is on his way to die with the yellow fever, like enough."

"Jack," said his cousin, affectionately, laying her hand on his arm, "blessings on your courage to-day! If what might have happened so easily had occurred, I could never have looked upon the sea again without a shudder. I should have been tormented by a horrible memory all my life. It was brave and noble - "

"Oh, hush!" he said angrily. "I won't hear another word about it even from you. I'm not brave and noble. I went because I was compelled to go; I hated to go. I hate the girl, and have more reason now than ever. If we had both drowned, no doubt there would have been less trouble in the world. There would have been one lawyer the less, and a coquette extinguished. Now we shall both prey on society in our different ways indefinitely."

"Jack, you are in an awful mood to-day."

"I am; never was in a worse."

"Having so narrowly escaped death, you ought to be subdued and grateful."

"On the contrary, I'm inclined to profanity. Excuse me; don't wish any dessert. I'll try a walk and a cigar. You will now be glad to be rid of me on any terms."

"Stay, Jack. See, Miss Van Tyne has so far recovered as to come down. She looked unutterable things at you as she entered."

"Of course she did. Very few of her thoughts concerning me or other young men would sound well if uttered. Tell your friends to let this topic alone, or I shall be rude to them," and without a glance toward the girl he had rescued he left the dining-room.

"Well, well," murmured Mrs. Alston, "I never saw Jack in such a mood before. It is quite as unaccountable as Miss Tyne's recklessness. I wonder what is the matter with HIM."

Ackland was speedily driven back from his walk by the rain, which fact he did not regret, for he found himself exhausted and depressed. Seeking a retired piazza in order to be alone, he sat down with his hat drawn over his eyes and smoked furiously. Before very long, however, he was startled out of a painful revery by a timid voice saying:

"Mr. Ackland, won't you permit me to thank you?"

He rose. Miss Van Tyne stood before him with outstretched hand. He did not notice it, but bowing coldly, said:

"Please consider that you have thanked me and let the subject drop."

"Do not be so harsh with me," she pleaded. "I cannot help it if you are. Mr. Ackland, you saved my life."

"Possibly."

"And possibly you think that it is scarcely worth saving."

"Possibly your own conscience suggested that thought to you."

"You are heartless," she burst out indignantly. He began to laugh. "That's a droll charge for you to make," he said.

She looked at him steadfastly for a moment, and then murmured: "You are thinking of your friend, Mr. Munson."

"That would be quite natural. How many more can you think of?"

"You are indeed unrelenting," she faltered, tears coming into her eyes; "but I cannot forget that but for you *I* should now be out there" - and she indicated the sea by a gesture, then covered her face with her hands, and shuddered.

"Do not feel under obligations. I should have been compelled to do as much for any human being. You seem to forget that I stood an even chance of being out there with you, and that there was no more need of the risk than there was that my best friend's life should be blight - "

"You - you out there?" she cried, springing toward him and pointing to the sea.

"Certainly. You cannot suppose that having once found you, I could come ashore without you. As it was, my strength was rapidly giving way, and were it not for the rope - "

"Oh, forgive me," she cried passionately, seizing his hand in spite of him. "It never entered my mind that you could drown. I somehow felt that nothing could harm you. I was reckless - I didn't know what I was doing - I don't understand myself any more. Please - please forgive me, or I shall not sleep to-night."

"Certainly," he said lightly, "if you will not refer to our little episode again."

"Please don't speak in that way," she sighed, turning away.

"I have complied with your request."

"I suppose I must be content," she resumed sadly. Then turning her head slowly toward him she added hesitatingly: "Will you forgive me for - for treating your friend - "

"No," he replied, with such stern emphasis that she shrank from him and trembled.

"You are indeed heartless," she faltered, as she turned to leave him.

"Miss Van Tyne," he said indignantly, "twice you have charged me with being heartless. Your voice and manner indicate that I would be unnatural and unworthy of respect were I what you charge. In the name of all that's rational what does this word 'heartless' mean to you? Where was your heart when you sent my friend away so wretched and humbled that he is virtually seeking the death from which you are so glad to escape?"

"I did not love him," she protested faintly.

He laughed bitterly, and continued, "Love! That's a word which I believe has no meaning for you at all, but it had for him. You are a remarkably clever woman, Miss Van Tyne. You have brains in abundance. See, I do you justice. What is more, you are beautiful and can be so fascinating that a man who believed in you might easily worship you. You made him believe in you. You tried to beguile me into a condition that with my nature would be ruin indeed. You never had the baby plea of a silly, shallow woman. I took pains to find that out the first evening we met. In your art of beguiling an honest, trusting man you were as perfect as you were remorseless, and you understood exactly what you were doing."

For a time she seemed overwhelmed by his lava-like torrent of words, and stood with bowed head and shrinking, trembling form; but when he ceased she turned to him and said bitterly and emphatically:

"I did NOT understand what I was doing, nor would my brain have taught me were I all intellect like yourself. I half wish you had left me to drown," and with a slight, despairing gesture she turned away and did not look back.

Ackland's face lighted up with a sudden flash of intelligence and deep feeling. He started to recall her, hesitated, and watched her earnestly until she disappeared; then looking out on the scowling ocean, he took off his hat and exclaimed in a deep, low tone:

"By all that's divine, can this be? Is it possible that through the suffering of her own awakening heart she is learning to know the pain she has given to others? Should this be true, the affair is taking an entirely new aspect, and Munson will be avenged as neither of us ever dreamed would be possible."

He resumed his old position and thought long and deeply, then rejoined his cousin, who was somewhat surprised to find that his bitter mood had given place to his former composure.

"How is this, Jack?" she asked. "As the storm grows wilder without, you become more serene."

"Only trying to make amends for my former bearishness," he said carelessly, but with a little rising color.

"I don't understand you at all," she continued discontentedly. "I saw you sulking in that out-of-the-way corner, and I saw Miss Van Tyne approach you hesitatingly and timidly, with the purpose, no doubt, of thanking you. Of course I did not stay to watch, but a little later I met Miss Van Tyne, and she looked white and rigid. She has not left her room since."

"You take a great interest in Miss Van Tyne. It is well you are not in my place."

"I half wish I was and had your chances. You are more pitiless than the waves from which you saved her."

"I can't help being just what I am," he said coldly. "Good-night." And he too disappeared for the rest of the evening.

The rain continued to fall in blinding torrents, and the building fairly trembled under the violence of the wind. The guests drew together in the lighted rooms, and sought by varied amusements to pass the time until the fierceness of the storm abated, few caring to retire while the uproar of the elements was so great.

At last as the storm passed away, and the late-rising moon threw a sickly gleam on the tumultuous waters, Eva looked from her window with sleepless eyes, thinking sadly and bitterly of the past and future. Suddenly a dark figure appeared on the beach in the track of the moonlight. She snatched an opera-glass, but could not recognize the solitary form. The thought would come, however, that it was Ackland; and if it were, what were his thoughts and what place had she in them? Why was he watching so near the spot that might have been their burial-place?

"At least he shall not think that I can stolidly sleep after what has occurred," she thought, and she turned up her light, opened her window, and sat down by it again. Whoever the unseasonable rambler might be, he appeared to recognize the gleam from her window, for he walked hastily down the beach and disappeared. After a time she darkened her room again and waited in vain for his return. "If it were he, he shuns even the slightest recognition," she thought despairingly; and the early dawn was not far distant when she fell into an unquiet sleep.

For the next few days Miss Van Tyne was a puzzle to all except Mrs. Alston. She was quite unlike the girl she had formerly been, and she made no effort to disguise the fact. In the place of her old exuberance of life and spirits, there was lassitude and great depression. The rich color ebbed steadily from her face, and dark lines under her eyes betokened sleepless nights. She saw the many curious glances in her direction, but apparently did not care what was thought or surmised. Were it not that her manner to Ackland was so misleading, the tendency to couple their names together would have been far more general. She neither sought nor shunned his society; in fact, she treated him as she did the other gentlemen of her acquaintance. She took him at his word. He had said he would forgive her on condition that she would not speak of what he was pleased to term that "little episode," and she never referred to it.

Her aunt was as much at fault as the others, and one day querulously complained to Mrs. Alston that she was growing anxious about Eva. "At first I thought she was disappointed over the indifference of that icy cousin of yours; but she does not appear to care a straw for him. When I mention his name she speaks of him in a natural, grateful way, then her thoughts appear to wander off to some matter that is troubling her. I can't find out whether she is ill or whether she has heard some bad news of which she will not speak. She never gave me or any one that I know of much of her confidence."

Mrs. Alston listened but made no comments. She was sure she was right in regard to Miss Van Tyne's trouble, but her cousin mystified her. Ackland had become perfectly inscrutable. As far as she could judge by any word or act of his he had simply lost his interest in Miss Van Tyne, and that was all that could be said; and yet a fine instinct tormented Mrs. Alston with the doubt that this was not true, and that the young girl was the subject of a sedulously concealed scrutiny.

Was he watching for his friend or for his own sake, or was he, in a spirit of retaliation, enjoying the suffering of one who had made others suffer? His reserve was so great that she could not pierce it, and his caution baffled even her vigilance. But she waited patiently, assured that the little drama must soon pass into a more significant phase.

And she was right. Miss Van Tyne could not maintain the line of action she had resolved upon. She had thought, "I won't try to appear happy when I am not. I won't adopt the conventional mask of gayety when the heart is wounded. How often I have seen through it and smiled at the transparent farce - farce it seemed then, but I now fear it was often tragedy. At any rate there was neither dignity nor deception in it. I have done with being false, and so shall simply act myself and be a true woman. Though my heart break a thousand times, not even by a glance shall I show that it is breaking for him. If he or others surmise the truth, they may; let them. It is a part of my penance; and I will show the higher, stronger pride of one who makes no vain, useless pretence to happy indifference, but who can maintain a self-control so perfect that even Mrs. Alston shall not see one unmaidenly advance or overture."

She succeeded for a time, as we have seen, but she overrated her will and underrated her heart, that with deepening intensity craved the love denied her. With increasing frequency she said to herself, "I must go away. My only course is to hide my weakness and never see him again. He is inflexible, yet his very obduracy increases my love a hundred-fold."

At last after a lonely walk on the beach she concluded,

"My guardian must take me home on Monday next. He comes to-night to spend Sunday with us, and I will make preparations to go at once."

Although her resolution did not fail her, she walked forward more and more slowly, her dejection and weariness becoming almost overpowering. As she was turning a sharp angle of rocks that jutted well down to the water she came face to face with Ackland and Mrs. Alston. She was off her guard; and her thoughts of him had been so absorbing that she felt he must be conscious of them. She flushed painfully and hurried by with slight recognition and downcast face, but she had scarcely passed them when, acting under a sudden impulse, she stopped and said in a low tone:

"Mr. Ackland - "

He turned expectantly toward her. For a moment she found it difficult to speak, then ignoring the presence of Mrs. Alston, resolutely began:

"Mr. Ackland, I must refer once more to a topic which you have in a sense forbidden. I feel partially absolved, however, for I do not think you have forgiven me anything. At any rate I must ask your pardon once more for having so needlessly and foolishly imperilled your life. I say these words now because I may not have another opportunity; we leave on Monday." With this she raised her eyes to his with an appeal for a little kindness which Mrs. Alston was confident could not be resisted. Indeed, she was sure that she saw a slight nervous tremor in Ackland's hands, as if he found it hard to control himself. Then he appeared to grow rigid. Lifting his hat, he said gravely and unresponsively:

E. P. Roe

"Miss Van Tyne, you now surely have made ample amends. Please forget the whole affair."

She turned from him at once, but not so quickly but that both he and his cousin saw the bitter tears that would come. A moment later she was hidden by the angle of the rock. As long as she was visible Ackland watched her without moving, then he slowly turned to his cousin, his face as inscrutable as ever. She walked at his side for a few moments in ill-concealed impatience, then stopped and said decisively:

"I'll go no further with you to-day. I am losing all respect for you."

Without speaking, he turned to accompany her back to the house. His reticence and coldness appeared to annoy her beyond endurance, for she soon stopped and sat down on a ledge of the rocks that jutted down the beach where they had met Miss Van Tyne.

"John, you are the most unnatural man I ever saw in my life," she began angrily.

"What reason have you for so flattering an opinion," he asked coolly.

"You have been giving reason for it every day since you came here," she resumed hotly. "I always heard it said that you had no heart; but I defended you and declared that your course toward your mother even when a boy showed that you had, and that you would prove it some day. But I now believe that you are unnaturally cold, heartless, and unfeeling. I had no objection to your wounding Miss Van Tyne's vanity and encouraged you when that alone bid fair to suffer.

But when she proved she had a heart and that you had awakened it, she deserved at least kindness and consideration on your part. If you could not return her affection, you should have gone away at once; but I believe that you have stayed for the sole and cruel purpose of gloating over her suffering."

"She has not suffered more than my friend, or than I would if - "

"You indeed! The idea of your suffering from any such cause! I half believe you came here with the deliberate purpose of avenging your friend, and that you are keeping for his inspection a diary in which the poor girl's humiliation to-day will form the hateful climax."

They did not dream that the one most interested was near. Miss Van Tyne had felt too faint and sorely wounded to go further without rest. Believing that the rocks would hide her from those whose eyes she would most wish to shun, she had thrown herself down beyond the angle and was shedding the bitterest tears that she had ever known. Suddenly she heard Mrs. Alston's words but a short distance away, and was so overcome by their import that she hesitated what to do. She would not meet them again for the world, but felt so weak that she doubted whether she could drag herself away without being discovered, especially as the beach trended off to the left so sharply a little further on that they might discover her. While she was looking vainly for some way of escape she heard Ackland's words and Mrs. Alston's surmise in reply that he had come with the purpose of revenge. She was so stung by their apparent truth that she resolved to clamber up through an opening of the rocks if the thing were possible. Panting and exhausted she gained the summit, and then hastened to an adjacent grove, as some wounded, timid creature would run to the nearest cover. Ackland had heard sounds and had stepped around the point of the rocks just in time to see her disappearing above the bank. Returning to Mrs. Alston, he said impatiently:

"In view of your opinions my society can have no attractions for you. Shall I accompany you to the hotel?"

"No," was the angry reply. "I'm in no mood to speak to you again to-day."

He merely bowed and turned as if to pursue his walk. The moment she was hidden, however, he also climbed the rocks in time to see Miss Van Tyne entering the grove. With swift and silent tread he followed her, but could not at once discover her hiding-place. At last passionate sobs made it evident that she was concealed behind a great oak a little on his left. Approaching cautiously, he heard her moan:

"Oh, this is worse than death! He makes me feel as if even God had no mercy for me. But I will expiate my wrong; I will, at the bitterest sacrifice which a woman can make."

She sprang up to meet Ackland standing with folded arms before her. She started violently and leaned against the tree for support. But the weakness was momentary, for she wiped the tears from her eyes, and then turned to him so quietly that only her extreme pallor proved that she realized the import of her words.

"Mr. Ackland," she asked, "have you Mr. Munson's address?"

It was his turn now to start, but he merely answered: "Yes."

"Do - do you think he still cares for me?"

"Undoubtedly."

"Since then you are so near a friend, will you write to him that I will try" - she turned away and would not look at him as, after a moment's hesitation, she concluded her sentence - "I will try to make him as happy as I can."

"Do you regret your course?" he asked with a slight tremor in his voice.

"I regret that I misled - that I wronged him beyond all words. I am willing to make all the amends in my power."

"Do you love him?"

She now turned wholly away and shook her head.

"And yet you would marry him?"

"Yes, if he wished it, knowing all the truth."

"Can you believe he would wish it?" he asked indignantly. "Can you believe that any man - "

"Then avenge him to your cruel soul's content," she exclaimed passionately. "Tell him that I have no heart to give to him or to any one. Through no effort or fault of mine I overheard Mrs. Alston's words and yours. I know your design against me. Assuage your friend's grief by assuring him of your entire success, of which you are already so well aware. Tell him how you triumphed over an untaught, thoughtless girl who was impelled merely by the love of power and excitement, as you are governed by ambition and a remorseless will. I did not know - I did not understand how cruel I was, although now that I do know I shall never forgive myself. But if you had the heart of a man you might have seen that you were subjecting me to torture. I did not ask or expect that you should care for me; but I had a right to hope for a little kindness, a little manly and delicate consideration, a little healing sympathy for the almost mortal wound that you have made. But I now see that you have stood by and watched like a grand inquisitor. Tell your friend that you have transformed the thoughtless girl into a suffering woman. I cannot go to Brazil. I cannot face dangers that might bring rest. I must keep my place in society - keep it too under a hundred observant and curious eyes. You have seen it all of late in this house; I was too wretched to care. It was a part of my punishment, and I accepted it. I would not be false again even in trying to conceal a secret which it is like death to a woman to reveal. I only craved one word of kindness from you. Had I received it, I would have gone away in silence and suffered in silence. But your course and what I have heard have made me reckless and despairing. You do not leave me even the poor consolation of self-sacrifice. You are my stony-hearted fate. I wish you had left me to drown. Tell your friend that I am more wretched than he ever can be, because I am a woman. Will he be satisfied?"

"He ought to be," was the low, husky reply.

"Are you proud of your triumph?"

"No, I am heartily ashamed of it; but I have kept a pledge that will probably cost me far more than it has you."

"A pledge?"

"Yes, my pledge to make you suffer as far as possible as he suffered."

She put her hand to her side as if she had received a wound, and after a moment said wearily and coldly:

"Well, tell him that you succeeded, and be content;" and she turned to leave him.

"Stay," he cried impetuously. "It is now your turn. Take your revenge."

"My revenge?" she repeated in unfeigned astonishment.

"Yes, your revenge. I have loved you from the moment I hoped you had a woman's heart, yes, and before - when I feared I might not be able to save your life. I know it now, though the very thought of it enraged me then. I have watched and waited more to be sure that you had a woman's heart than for aught else, though a false sense of honor kept me true to my pledge. After I met you on the beach I determined at once to break my odious bond and place myself at your mercy. You may refuse me in view of my course - you probably will; but every one in that house there shall know that you refused me, and your triumph shall be more complete than mine."

She looked into his face with an expression of amazement and doubt; but instead of coldness, there was now a devotion and pleading that she had never seen before.

She was too confused and astounded, however, to comprehend his words immediately, nor could the impression of his hostility pass away readily.

"You are mocking me," she faltered, scarcely knowing what she said.

"I cannot blame you that you think me capable of mocking the noble candor which has cost you so dear, as I can now understand. I cannot ask you to believe that I appreciate your heroic impulse of self-sacrifice - your purpose to atone for wrong by inflicting irreparable wrong on yourself. It is natural that you should think of me only as an instrument of revenge with no more feeling than some keen-edged weapon would have. This also is the inevitable penalty of my course. When I speak of my love I cannot complain if you smile in bitter incredulity. But I have at least proved that I have a resolute will and that I keep my word; and I again assure you that it shall be known this very night that you have refused me, that I offered you my hand, that you already had my heart, where your image is enshrined with that of my mother, and that I entreated you to be my wife. My cousin alone guessed my miserable triumph; all shall know of yours."

As he spoke with impassioned earnestness, the confusion passed from her mind. She felt the truth of his words; she knew that her ambitious dream had been fulfilled, and that she had achieved the conquest of a man upon whom all others had smiled in vain. But how immeasurably different were her emotions from those which she had once anticipated! Not her beauty, not her consummate skill in fascination had wrought this miracle, but her woman's heart, awakened at last; and it thrilled with such unspeakable joy that she turned away to hide its reflex in her face. He was misled by the act into believing that she could not forgive him, and yet was perplexed when she murmured with a return of her old piquant humor:

"You are mistaken, Mr. Ackland; it shall never be known that I refused you."

"How can you prevent it?"

"If your words are sincere, you will submit to such terms as I choose to make."

"I am sincere, and my actions shall prove it; but I shall permit no mistaken self-sacrifice on your part, nor any attempt to shield me from the punishment I well deserve,"

She suddenly turned upon him a radiant face in which he read his happiness, and faltered:

"Jack, I do believe you, although the change seems wrought by some heavenly magic. But it will take a long time to pay you up. I hope to be your dear torment for a lifetime."

He caught her in such a strong, impetuous embrace that she gasped:

E. P. Roe

"I thought you were - cold to our sex."

"It's not your sex that I am clasping, but you - YOU, my Eve. Like the first man, I have won my bride under the green trees and beneath the open sky."

"Yes, Jack; and I give you my whole heart as truly as did the first woman when there was but one man in all the world. That is MY REVENGE."

This is what Will Munson wrote some weeks later:

"Well, Jack, I've had the yellow fever, and it was the most fortunate event of my life. I was staying with a charming family, and they would not permit my removal to a hospital. One of my bravest and most devoted nurses has consented to become my wife. I hope you punished that little wretch Eva Van Tyne as she deserved."

"Confound your fickle soul!" muttered Ackland. "I punished her as she did not deserve; and I risked more than life in doing so. If her heart had not been as good as gold and as kind as Heaven she never would have looked at me again."

Ackland is quite as indifferent to the sex as ever, but Eva has never complained that he was cold to her.

A CHRISTMAS-EVE SUIT

The Christmas holidays had come, and with them a welcome vacation for Hedley Marstern. Although as yet a briefless young lawyer, he had a case in hand which absorbed many of his thoughts - the conflicting claims of two young women in his native village on the Hudson. It must not be imagined that the young women were pressing their claims except as they did so unconsciously, by virtue of their sex and various charms. Nevertheless, Marstern was not the first lawyer who had clients over whom midnight oil was burned, they remaining unaware of the fact.

If not yet a constitutional attorney, he was at least constitutionally one. Falling helplessly in love with one girl simplifies matters. There are no distracting pros and cons - nothing required but a concentration of faculties to win the enslaver, and so achieve mastery. Marstern did not appear amenable to the subtle influences which blind the eyes and dethrone reason, inspiring in its place an overwhelming impulse to capture a fortuitous girl because (to a heated imagination) she surpasses all her sex. Indeed, he was level-headed enough to believe that he would never capture any such girl; but he hoped to secure one who promised to make as good a wife as he would try to be a husband, and with a fair amount of self-esteem, he was conscious of imperfections. Therefore, instead of

E. P. Roe

fancying that any of his fair acquaintances were angels, he had deliberately and, as some may think, in a very cold-blooded fashion, endeavored to discover what they actually were. He had observed that a good deal of prose followed the poetry of wooing and the lunacy of the honeymoon; and he thought it might be well to criticise a little before marriage as well as after it.

There were a number of charming girls in the social circle of his native town; and he had, during later years, made himself quite impartially agreeable to them. Indeed, without much effort on his part he had become what is known as a general favorite. He had been too diligent a student to become a society man, but was ready enough in vacation periods to make the most of every country frolic, and even on great occasions to rush up from the city and return at some unearthly hour in the morning when his partners in the dance were not half through their dreams. While on these occasions he had shared in the prevailing hilarity, he nevertheless had the presentiment that some one of the laughing, light-footed girls would one day pour his coffee and send him to his office in either a good or a bad mood to grapple with the problems awaiting him there. He had in a measure decided that when he married it should be to a girl whom he had played with in childhood and whom he knew a good deal about, and not to a chance acquaintance of the world at large. So, beneath all his diversified gallantries he had maintained a quiet little policy of observation, until his thoughts had gradually gathered around two of his young associates who, unconsciously to themselves, as we have said, put in stronger and stronger claims every time he saw them. They asserted these claims in the only way in which he would have recognized them - by being more charming, agreeable, and, as he fancied, by being better than the others. He had not made them aware, even by manner, of the distinction accorded to them; and as yet he was merely a friend.

But the time had come, he believed, for definite action. While he weighed and considered, some prompter fellows might take the case out of his hands entirely; therefore he welcomed this vacation and the opportunities it afforded.

The festivities began with what is termed in the country a "large party"; and Carrie Mitchell and Lottie Waldo were both there, resplendent in new gowns made for the occasion. Marstern thought them both charming. They danced equally well and talked nonsense with much the same ease and vivacity. He could not decide which was the prettier, nor did the eyes and attentions of others afford him any aid. They were general favorites, as well as himself, although it was evident that to some they might become more, should they give encouragement. But they were apparently in the heyday of their girlhood, and thus far had preferred miscellaneous admiration to individual devotion. By the time the evening was over Marstern felt that if life consisted of large parties he might as well settle the question by the toss of a copper.

It must not be supposed that he was such a conceited prig as to imagine that such a fortuitous proceeding, or his best efforts afterward, could settle the question as it related to the girls. It would only decide his own procedure. He was like an old marauding baron, in honest doubt from which town he can carry off the richest booty - that is, in case he can capture any one of them. His overtures for capitulation might be met with the "slings and arrows of outrageous fortune" and he be sent limping off the field. Nevertheless, no man regrets that he must take the initiative, and he would be less than a man who would fear to do so. When it came to this point in the affair, Marstern shrugged his shoulders and thought, "I must take my chances like the rest." But he wished to be sure that he had attained this point, and not lay siege to one girl only to wish afterward it had been the other.

His course that evening proved that he not only had a legal cast of mind but also a judicial one. He invited both Miss Mitchell and Miss Waldo to take a sleigh-ride with him the following evening, fancying that when sandwiched between them in the cutter he could impartially note his impressions. His unsuspecting clients laughingly accepted, utterly unaware of the momentous character of the trial scene before them.

As Marstern smoked a cigar before retiring that night, he admitted to himself that it was rather a remarkable court that was about to be held. He was the only advocate for the claims of each, and finally he proposed to take a seat on the bench and judge between them. Indeed, before he slept he decided to take that august position at once, and maintain a judicial impartiality while noting his impressions.

Christmas Eve happened to be a cold, clear, star-lit night; and when Marstern drove to Miss Waldo's door, he asked himself, "Could a fellow ask for anything daintier and finer" than the red-lipped, dark-eyed girl revealed by the hall-lamp as she tripped lightly out, her anxious mamma following her with words of unheeded caution about not taking cold, and coming home early. He had not traversed the mile which intervened between the residences of the two girls before he almost wished he could continue the drive under the present auspices, and that, as in the old times, he could take toll at every bridge, and encircle his companion with his arm as they bounced over the "thank-'ee mams." The frosty air appeared to give keenness and piquancy to Miss Lottie's wit, and the chime of the bells was not merrier or more musical than her voice. But when a little later he saw blue-eyed Carrie Mitchell in her furs and hood silhouetted in the window, his old dilemma became as perplexing as ever. Nevertheless, it was the most delightful uncertainty that he had ever experienced; and he had a presentiment that he had better make the most of it, since it could not last much longer. Meanwhile, he was hedged about with blessings clearly not in disguise, and he gave utterance to this truth as they drove away.

"Surely there never was so lucky a fellow. Here I am kept warm and happy by the two finest girls in town."

"Yes," said Lottie; "and it's a shame you can't sit on both sides of us."

"I assure you I wish it were possible. It would double my pleasure."

"I'm very well content," remarked Carrie, quietly, "as long as I can keep on the right side of people - "

"Well, you are not on the right side to-night," interrupted Lottie.

"Good gracious!" thought Marstern, "she's next to my heart. I wonder if that will give her unfair advantage;" but Carrie explained:

"Of course I was speaking metaphorically."

"In that aspect of the case it would be a shame to me if any side I have is not right toward those who have so honored me," he hastened to say.

"Oh, Carrie has all the advantage - she is next to your heart."

"Would you like to exchange places?" was the query flashed back by Carrie.

"Oh, no, I'm quite as content as you are."

"Why, then, since I am more than content - exultant, indeed - it appears that we all start from excellent premises to reach a happy conclusion of our Christmas Eve," cried Marstern.

"Now you are talking shop, Mr. Lawyer - Premises and Conclusions, indeed!" said Lottie; "since you are such a happy sandwich, you must be a tongue sandwich, and be very entertaining."

He did his best, the two girls seconding his efforts so genially that he found himself, after driving five miles, psychologically just where he was physically - between them, as near to one in his thoughts and preferences as to the other.

"Let us take the river road home," suggested Lottie.

"As long as you agree," he answered, "you both are sovereign potentates. If you should express conflicting wishes, I should have to stop here in the road till one abdicated in favor of the other, or we all froze."

"But you, sitting so snugly between us, would not freeze," said Lottie. "If we were obstinate we should have to assume our pleasantest expressions, and then you could eventually take us home as bits of sculpture. In fact, I'm getting cold already."

"Are you also, Miss Carrie?"

"Oh, I'll thaw out before summer. Don't mind me."

"Well, then, mind me," resumed Lottie. "See how white and smooth the river looks. Why can't we drive home on the ice? It will save miles - I mean it looks so inviting."

"Oh, dear!" cried Carrie, "I feel like protesting now. The longest way round may be both the shortest and safest way home."

"You ladies shall decide. This morning I drove over the route we would take to-night, and I should not fear to take a ton of coal over it."

"A comparison suggesting warmth and a grate-fire. I vote for the river," said Lottie, promptly.

"Oh, well, Mr. Marstern, if you've been over the ice so recently - I only wish to feel reasonably safe."

"I declare!" thought Marstern, "Lottie is the braver and more brilliant girl; and the fact that she is not inclined to forego the comfort of the home-fire for the pleasure of my company, reveals the difficulty of, and therefore incentive to, the suit I may decide to enter upon before New Year's."

Meanwhile, his heart on Carrie's side began to grow warm and alert, as if recognizing an affinity to some object not far off. Granting that she had not been so brilliant as Lottie, she had been eminently companionable in a more quiet way. If there had not been such bursts of enthusiasm at the beginning of the drive, her enjoyment appeared to have more staying powers. He liked her none the less that her eyes were often turned toward the stars or the dark silhouettes of the leafless trees against the snow. She did not keep saying, "Ah, how lovely! What a fine bit that is!" but he had only to follow her eyes to see something worth looking at.

"A proof that Miss Carrie also is not so preoccupied with the pleasure of my company that she has no thoughts for other things," cogitated Marstern. "It's rather in her favor that she prefers Nature to a grate fire. They're about even yet."

Meanwhile the horse was speeding along on the white, hard expanse of the river, skirting the west shore. They now had only about a mile to drive before striking land again; and the scene was so beautiful with the great dim outlines of the mountains before them that both the girls suggested that they should go leisurely for a time.

"We shouldn't hastily and carelessly pass such a picture as that, any more than one would if a fine copy of it were hung in a gallery," said Carrie. "The stars are so brilliant along the brow of that highland yonder that they form a dia - oh, oh! what IS the matter?" and she clung to Marstern's arm.

The horse was breaking through the ice.

"Whoa!" said Marstern, firmly. Even as he spoke, Lottie was out of the sleigh and running back on the ice, crying and wringing her hands.

"We shall be drowned," she almost screamed hysterically.

"Mr. Marstern, what SHALL we do? Can't we turn around and go back the way we came?"

"Miss Carrie, will you do what I ask? Will you believe me when I say that I do not think you are in any danger?"

"Yes, I'll do my best," she replied, catching her breath. She grew calm rapidly as he tried to reassure Lottie, telling her that water from the rising of the tide had overflowed the main ice and that thin ice had formed over it, also that the river at the most was only two or three feet deep at that point. But all was of no avail; Lottie stood out upon the ice in a panic, declaring that he never should have brought them into such danger, and that he must turn around at once and go back as they came.

"But, Miss Waldo, the tide is rising, and we may find wet places returning. Besides, it would bring us home very late. Now, Miss Carrie and I will drive slowly across this place and then return for you. After we have been across it twice you surely won't fear."

"I won't be left alone; suppose you two should break through and disappear, what would become of ME?"

"You would be better off than we," he replied, laughing.

"I think it's horrid of you to laugh. Oh, I'm so cold and frightened! I feel as if the ice were giving way under my feet."

"Why, Miss Lottie, we just drove over that spot where you stand. Here, Miss Carrie shall stay with you while I drive back and forth alone."

"Then if you were drowned we'd both be left alone to freeze to death."

"I pledge you my word you shall be by that grate-fire within less than an hour if you will trust me five minutes."

"Oh, well, if you will risk your life and ours too; but Carrie must stay with me."

"Will YOU trust me, Miss Carrie, and help me out of this scrape?"

Carrie was recovering from her panic, and replied, "I have given you my promise."

He was out of the sleigh instantly, and the thin ice broke with him also. "I must carry you a short distance," he said. "I cannot allow you to get your feet wet. Put one arm around my neck, so; now please obey as you promised."

She did so without a word, and he bore her beyond the water, inwardly exulting and blessing that thin ice. His decision was coming with the passing seconds; indeed, it had come. Returning to the sleigh he drove slowly forward, his horse making a terrible crunching and splashing, Lottie meanwhile keeping up a staccato accompaniment of little shrieks.

"Ah, my charming creature," he thought, "with you it was only, 'What will become of ME?' I might not have found out until it was too late the relative importance of 'me' in the universe had we not struck this bad crossing; and one comes to plenty of bad places to cross in a lifetime."

The area of thin ice was not very narrow, and he was becoming but a dim and shadowy outline to the girls. Lottie was now screaming for his return. Having crossed the overflowed space and absolutely assured himself that there was no danger, he returned more rapidly and found Carrie trying to calm her companion.

"Oh," sobbed Lottie, "my feet are wet and almost frozen. The ice underneath may have borne you, but it won't bear all three of us. Oh, dear, I wish I hadn't - I wish I was home; and I feel as if I'd never get there."

"Miss Lottie, I assure you that the ice will hold a ton, but I'll tell you what I'll do. I shall put you in the sleigh, and Miss Carrie will drive you over. You two together do not weigh much more than I do. I'll walk just behind you with my hands on the back of the sleigh, and if I see the slightest danger I'll lift you out of the sleigh first and carry you to safety."

This proposition promised so well that she hesitated, and he lifted her in instantly before she could change her mind, then helped Carrie in with a quiet pressure of the hand, as much as to say, "I shall depend on you."

"But, Mr. Marstern, you'll get your feet wet," protested Carrie.

E. P. Roe

"That doesn't matter," he replied good-naturedly. "I shall be no worse off than Miss Lottie, and I'm determined to convince her of safety. Now go straight ahead as I direct."

Once the horse stumbled, and Lottie thought he was going down head first. "Oh, lift me out, quick, quick!" she cried.

"Yes, indeed I will, Miss Lottie, as soon as we are opposite that grate fire of yours."

They were soon safely over, and within a half-hour reached Lottie's home. It was evident she was a little ashamed of her behavior, and she made some effort to retrieve herself. Bat she was cold and miserable, vexed with herself and still more vexed with Marstern. That a latent sense of justice forbade the latter feeling only irritated her the more. Individuals as well as communities must have scapegoats; and it is not an unusual impulse on the part of some to blame and dislike those before whom they have humiliated themselves.

She gave her companions a rather formal invitation to come in and get warm before proceeding further; but Marstern said very politely that he thought it was too late, unless Miss Carrie was cold. Carrie protested that she was not so cold but that she could easily wait till she reached her own fireside.

"Well, good-night, then," and the door was shut a trifle emphatically.

"Mr. Marstern," said Carrie, sympathetically, "your feet must be very cold and wet after splashing through all that ice-water."

"They are," he replied; "but I don't mind it. Well, if I had tried for years I could not have found such a test of character as we had to-night."

"What do you mean?"

"Oh, well, you two girls did not behave exactly alike. I liked the way you behaved. You helped me out of a confounded scrape."

"Would you have tried for years to find a test?" she asked, concealing the keenness of her query under a laugh.

"I should have been well rewarded if I had, by such a fine contrast," he replied.

Carrie's faculties had not so congealed but that his words set her thinking. She had entertained at times the impression that she and Lottie were his favorites. Had he taken them out that night together in the hope of contrasts, of finding tests that would help his halting decision? He had ventured where the intuitions of a girl like Carrie Mitchell were almost equal to second-sight; and she was alert for what would come next.

He accepted her invitation to come in and warm his feet at the glowing fire in the grate, which Carrie's father had made before retiring. Mrs. Mitchell, feeling that her daughter was with an old friend and playmate, did not think the presence of a chaperon essential, and left the young people alone. Carrie bustled about, brought cake, and made hot lemonade, while Marstern stretched his feet to the grate with a luxurious sense of comfort and complacency, thinking how homelike it all was and how paradisiacal life would become if such a charming little Hebe presided over his home. His lemonade became nectar offered by such hands.

She saw the different expression in his eyes. It was now homage, decided preference for one and not mere gallantry to two. Outwardly she was demurely oblivious and maintained simply her wonted friendliness. Marstern, however, was thawing in more senses than one, and he was possessed by a strong impulse to begin an open siege at once.

"I haven't had a single suit of any kind yet, Carrie," he said, dropping the prefix of "Miss," which had gradually been adopted as they had grown up.

"Oh, well, that was the position of all the great lawyers once," she replied, laughing. Marstern's father was wealthy, and all knew that he could afford to be briefless for a time.

"I may never be great; but I shall work as hard as any of them," he continued. "To tell you the honest truth, however, this would be the happiest Christmas Eve of my life if I had a downright suit on my hands. Why can't I be frank with you and say I'd like to begin the chief suit of my life now and here - a suit for this little hand? I'd plead for it as no lawyer ever pleaded before. I settled that much down on the ice."

"And if I hadn't happened to behave on the ice in a manner agreeable to your lordship, you would have pleaded with the other girl?" she remarked, withdrawing her hand and looking him directly in the eyes.

"What makes you think so?" he asked somewhat confusedly.

"You do."

He sprang up and paced the room a few moments, then confronted her with the words, "You shall have the whole truth. Any woman that I would ask to be my wife is entitled to that," and he told her just what the attitude of his mind had been from the first.

She laughed outright, then gave him her hand as she said, "Your honesty insures that we can be very good friends; but I don't wish to hear anything more about suits which are close of kin to lawsuits."

He looked very dejected, feeling that he had blundered fatally in his precipitation.

"Come now, Hedley, be sensible," she resumed, half laughing, half serious. "As you say, we can be frank with each other. Why, only the other day we were boy and girl together coasting downhill on the same sled. You are applying your legal jargon to a deep experience, to something sacred - the result, to my mind, of a divine instinct. Neither you nor I have ever felt for each other this instinctive preference, this subtle gravitation of the heart. Don't you see? Your head has been concerned about me, and only your head. By a kindred process you would select one bale of merchandise in preference to another. Good gracious! I've faults enough. You'll meet some other girl that will stand some other test far better than I. I want a little of what you call silly romance in my courtship. See; I can talk about this suit as coolly and fluently as you can. We'd make a nice pair of lovers, about as frigid as the ice-water you waded through so good-naturedly;" and the girl's laugh rang out merrily, awakening echoes in the old house. Mr. and Mrs. Mitchell might rest securely when their daughter could laugh like that. It was the mirth of a genuine American girl whose self-protection was better than the care of a thousand duennas.

He looked at her with honest admiration in his eyes, then rose quietly and said, "That's fine, Carrie. Your head's worth two of mine, and you'd make the better lawyer. You see through a case from top to bottom. You were right - I wasn't in love with you; I don't know whether I'm in love with you now, and you haven't an infinitesimal spark for me. Nevertheless, I begin my suit here and now, and I shall never withdraw it till you are engaged to another fellow. So there!"

Carrie looked rather blank at this result of her reductio ad absurdum process; and he did not help her by adding, "A fellow isn't always in love. There must be a beginning; and when I arrive at this beginning under the guidance of reason, judgment, and observation, I don't see as I'm any more absurd than the fellow who tumbles helplessly in love, he doesn't know why. What becomes of all these people who have divine gravitations? You and I both know of some who had satanic repulsions afterward. They used their eyes and critical faculties after marriage instead of before. The romance exhaled like a morning mist; and the facts came out distinctly. They learned what kind of man and woman they actually were, and two idealized creatures were sent to limbo. Because I don't blunder upon the woman I wish to marry, but pick her out, that's no reason I can't and won't love her. Your analysis and judgment were correct only up to date. You have now to meet a suit honestly, openly announced. This may be bad policy on my part; yet I have so much faith in you and respect for you that I don't believe you will let my precipitation create a prejudice. Give me a fair hearing; that's all I ask."

"Well, well, I'll promise not to frown, even though some finer paragon should throw me completely in the shade."

"You don't believe in my yet," he resumed, after a moment of thought. "I felt that I had blundered awfully a while ago; but I doubt it. A girl of your perceptions would soon have seen it all. I've not lost anything by being frank from the start. Be just to me, however. It wasn't policy that led me to speak, but this homelike scene, and you appearing like the good genius of a home."

He pulled out his watch, and gave a low whistle as he held it toward her. Then his manner suddenly became grave and gentle. "Carrie," he said, "I wish you, not a merry Christmas, but a happy one, and many of them. It seems to me it would be a great privilege for a man to make a woman like you happy."

"Is this the beginning of the suit?" she asked with a laugh that was a little forced.

"I don't know. Perhaps it is; but I spoke just as I felt. Good-night."

She would not admit of a trace of sentiment on her part. "Good-night," she said. "Merry Christmas! Go home and hang up your stocking."

"Bless me!" she thought, as she went slowly up the stairs, "I thought I was going to be through with him for good and all, except as a friend; but if he goes on this way - "

The next morning a basket of superb roses was left at her home. There was no card, and mamma queried and surmised; but the girl knew. They were not displeasing to her, and somehow, before the day was over, they found their way to her room; but she shook her head decidedly as she said, "He must be careful not to send me other gifts, for I will return them instantly. Flowers, in moderation, never commit a girl."

But then came another gift - a book with pencillings here and there, not against sentimental passages, but words that made her think. It was his manner in society, however, that at once annoyed, perplexed, and pleased her. On the first occasion they met in company with others, he made it clear to every one that he was her suitor; yet he was not a burr which she could not shake off. He rather seconded all her efforts to have a good time with any and every one she chose. Nor did he, wallflower fashion, mope in the meanwhile and look unutterable things. He added to the pleasure of a score of others, and even conciliated Lottie, yet at the same time surrounded the girl of his choice with an atmosphere of unobtrusive devotion. She was congratulated on her conquest - rather maliciously so by Lottie. Her air of courteous indifference was well maintained; yet she was a woman, and could not help being flattered. Certain generous traits in her nature were touched also by a homage which yielded everything and exacted nothing.

The holidays soon passed, and he returned to his work.

She learned incidentally that he toiled faithfully, instead of mooning around. At every coigne of vantage she found him, or some token of his ceaseless effort. She was compelled to think of him, and to think well of him. Though mamma and papa judiciously said little, it was evident that they liked the style of lover into which he was developing.

Once during the summer she said: "I don't think it's right to let you go on in this way any longer."

"Are my attentions so very annoying?"

"No, indeed. A girl never had a more agreeable or useful friend."

"Are you engaged to some other fellow?"

"Of course not. You know better."

"There is no 'of course not' about it. I couldn't and wouldn't lay a straw in the way. You are not bound, but I."

"You bound?"

"Certainly. You remember what I said."

"Then I must accept the first man that asks me - "

"I ask you."

"No; some one else, so as to unloose your conscience and give you a happy deliverance,"

"You would leave me still bound and hopeless in that

E. P. Roe

case. I love you now, Carrie Mitchell."

"Oh, dear! you are incorrigible. It's just a lawyer's persistence in winning a suit."

"You can still swear on the dictionary that you don't love me at all?"

"I might - on the dictionary. There, I won't talk about such things any more," and she resolutely changed the subject.

But she couldn't swear, even on the dictionary. She didn't know where she stood or how it would all end; but with increasing frequency the words, "I love you now," haunted her waking and dreaming hours.

The holidays were near again, and then came a letter from Marstern, asking her to take another sleigh-ride with him on Christmas Eve. His concluding words were: "There is no other woman in the world that I want on the other side of me." She kissed these words, then looked around in a startled, shamefaced manner, blushing even in the solitude of her room.

Christmas Eve came, but with it a wild storm of wind and sleet. She was surprised at the depth of her disappointment. Would he even come to call through such a tempest?

He did come, and come early; and she said demurely: "I did not expect you on such a night as this."

He looked at her for a moment, half humorously, half seriously, and her eyes drooped before his. "You will know better what to expect next time," was his comment.

"When is next time?"

"Any and every time which gives me a chance to ses you. Who should know that better than you?"

"Are you never going to give up?" she asked with averted face.

"Not till you become engaged."

"Hush! They are all in the parlor."

"Well, they ought to know as much, by this time, also."

She thought it was astonishing how he made himself at home in the family circle. In half an hour there was scarcely any restraint left because a visitor was present. Yet, as if impelled by some mysterious influence, one after another slipped out; and Carrie saw with strange little thrills of dismay that she would soon be alone with that indomitable lawyer. She signalled to her mother, but the old lady's eyes were glued to her knitting.

At last they were alone, and she expected a prompt and powerful appeal from the plaintiff; but Marstern drew his chair to the opposite side of the hearth and chatted so easily, naturally, and kindly that her trepidation passed utterly. It began to grow late, and a heavier gust than usual shook the house. It appeared to waken him to the dire necessity of breasting the gale, and he rose and said:

E. P. Roe

"I feel as if I could sit here forever, Carrie. It's just the impression I had a year ago to-night. You, sitting there by the fire, gave then, and give now to this place the irresistible charm of home. I think I had then the decided beginning of the divine gravitation - wasn't that what you called it? - which has been growing so strong ever since. You thought then that the ice-water I waded was in my veins. Do you think so now? If you do I shall have to take another year to prove the contrary. Neither am I convinced of the absurdity of my course, as you put it then. I studied you coolly and deliberately before I began to love you, and reason and judgment have had no chance to jeer at my love."

"But, Hedley," she began with a slight tremor in her tones, "you are idealizing me as certainly as the blindest. I've plenty of faults."

"I haven't denied that; so have I plenty of faults. What right have I to demand a perfection I can't offer? I have known people to marry who imagined each other perfect, and then come to court for a separation on the ground of incompatibility of temperament. They learned the meaning of that long word too late, and were scarcely longer about it than the word itself. Now, I'm satisfied that I could cordially agree with you on some points and lovingly disagree with you on others. Chief of all it's your instinct to make a home. You appear better at your own fireside than when in full dress at a reception. You - "

"See here, Hedley, you've got to give up this suit at last. I'm engaged," and she looked away as if she could not meet his eyes.

"Engaged?" he said slowly, looking at her with startled eyes.

"Well, about the same as engaged. My heart has certainly gone from me beyond recall." He drew a long breath. "I was foolish enough to begin to hope," he faltered.

"You must dismiss hope to-night, then," she said, her face still averted.

He was silent and she slowly turned toward him. He had sunk into a chair and buried his face in his hands, the picture of dejected defeat.

There was a sudden flash of mirth through tear-gemmed eyes, a glance at the clock, then noiseless steps, and she was on her knees beside him, her arm about his neck, her blushing face near his wondering eyes as she breathed:

"Happy Christmas, Hedley! How do you like your first gift; and what room is there now for hope?"

E. P. Roe

THREE THANKSGIVING KISSES

It was the day before Thanksgiving. The brief cloudy November afternoon was fast merging into early twilight. The trees, now gaunt and bare, creaked and groaned in the passing gale, clashing their icy branches together with sounds sadly unlike the slumberous rustle of their foliage in June. And that same foliage was now flying before the wind, swept hither and thither, like exiles driven by disaster from the moorings of home, at times finding a brief abiding-place, and then carried forward to parts unknown by circumstances beyond control. The street leading into the village was almost deserted; and the few who came and went hastened on with fluttering garments, head bent down, and a shivering sense of discomfort. The fields were bare and brown; and the landscape on the uplands rising in the distance would have been utterly sombre had not green fields of grain, like childlike faith in wintry age, relieved the gloomy outlook and prophesied of the sunshine and golden harvest of a new year and life.

But bleak November found no admittance in Mrs. Alford's cosey parlor. Though, as usual, it was kept as the room for state occasions, it was not a stately room. It was furnished with elegance and good taste; but what was better, the genial home atmosphere from the rest of the house had invaded it, and one did not feel, on entering it from the free-and-easy sitting-room, as if passing from a sunny climate to the icebergs of the Pole. Therefore I am sure my reader will follow me gladly out of the biting, bolsterous wind into the homelike apartment, and as we stand in fancy before the glowing grate, we will make the acquaintance of the May-day creature who is its sole occupant.

Elsie Alford, just turning seventeen, appeared younger than her years warranted. Some girls carry the child far into their teens, and Head the mirthful innocence of infancy with the richer, fuller life of budding womanhood. This was true of Elsie. Hers was not the forced exotic bloom of fashionable life; but rather one of the native blossoms of her New England home, having all the delicacy and at the same time hardiness of the windflower. She was also as shy and easily agitated, and yet, like the flower she resembled, well rooted among the rocks of principle and truth. She was the youngest and the pet of the household, and yet the "petting" was not of that kind that develops selfishness and wilfulness, but rather a genial sunlight of love falling upon her as a focus from the entire family. They always spoke of her as "little Sis," or the "child." And a child it seemed she would ever be, with her kittenish ways, quick impulses, and swiftly alternating moods. As she developed into womanly proportions, her grave, businesslike father began to have misgivings. After one of her wild sallies at the table, where she kept every one on the qui vive by her unrestrained chatter, Mr. Alford said:

"Elsie, will you ever learn to be a woman?"

Looking mischievously at him through her curls, she replied, "Yes; I might if I became as old as

Mrs. Methuselah."

They finally concluded to leave Elsie's cure to care and trouble - two certain elements of earthly life; and yet her experience of either would be slight indeed, could their love shield her.

But it would not be exactly care or trouble that would sober Elsie into a thoughtful woman, as our story will show.

Some of the November wind seemed in her curling hair upon this fateful day; but her fresh young April face was a pleasant contrast to the scene presented from the window, to which she kept flitting with increasing frequency. It certainly was not the dismal and darkening landscape that so intensely interested her. The light of a great and coming pleasure was in her face, and her manner was one of restless, eager expectancy. Little wonder. Her pet brother, the one next older than herself, a promising young theologue, was coming home to spend Thanksgiving. It was time he appeared. The shriek of the locomotive had announced the arrival of the train; and her ardent little spirit could scarcely endure the moments intervening before she would almost concentrate herself into a rapturous kiss and embrace of welcome, for the favorite brother had been absent several long months.

Her mother called her away for a few moments, for the good old lady was busy indeed, knowing well that merely full hearts would not answer for a New England Thanksgiving. But the moment Elsie was free she darted back to the window, just in time to catch a glimpse, as she supposed, of her brother's well-remembered dark-gray overcoat, as he was ascending the front steps.

A tall, grave-looking young man, an utter stranger to the place and family, had his hand upon the doorbell; but before he could ring it, the door flew open, and a lovely young creature precipitated herself on his neck, like a missile fired from heavenly battlements, and a kiss was pressed upon his lips that he afterward admitted to have felt even to the "toes of his boots."

But his startled manner caused her to lift her face from under his side-whiskers; and though the dusk was deepening, she could see that her arms were around an utter stranger. She recoiled from him with a bound, and trembling like a windflower indeed, her large blue eyes dilating at the intruder with a dismay beyond words. How the awkward scene would have ended it were hard to tell had not the hearty voice of one coming up the path called out:

"Hi, there, you witch! who is that you are kissing, and then standing off to see the effect?"

There was no mistake this time; so, impelled by love, shame, and fear of "that horrid man," she fled, half sobbing, to his arms.

"No, he isn't a 'horrid man,' either," whispered her brother, laughing. "He is a classmate of mine. Why, Stanhope, how are you? I did not know that you and my sister were so well acquainted," he added, half banteringly and half curiously, for as yet he did not fully understand the scene.

The hall-lamp, shining through the open door, had revealed the features of the young man (whom we

E. P. Roe

must now call Mr. Stanhope), so that his classmate had recognized him. His first impulse had been to slip away in the darkness, and so escape from his awkward predicament; but George Alford's prompt address prevented this and brought him to bay. He was painfully embarrassed, but managed to stammer: "I was taken for you, I think. I never had the pleasure - honor of meeting your sister."

"Oh, ho! I see now. My wild little sister kissed before she looked. Well, that was your good-fortune. I could keep two Thanksgiving days on the strength of such a kiss as that," cried the light-hearted student, shaking the diffident, shrinking Mr. Stanhope warmly by the hand. "You will hardly need a formal introduction now. But, bless me, where is she? Has the November wind blown her away?"

"I think your sist - the lady passed around to the side entrance. I fear I have annoyed her sadly."

"Nonsense! A good joke - something to tease the little witch about. But come in. I'm forgetting the sacred rites."

And before the bewildered Mr. Stanhope could help himself, he was half dragged into the lighted hall, and the door shut between him and escape.

In the meantime, Elsie, like a whirlwind, had burst into the kitchen, where Mrs. Alford was superintending some savory dishes.

"Oh, mother, George has come and has a horrid man with him, who nearly devoured me."

And, with this rather feminine mode of stating the case, she darted into the dusky, fire-lighted parlor, from whence, unseen, she could reconnoitre the hall. Mr. Stanhope was just saying:

"Please let me go. I have stood between you and your welcome long enough. I shall only be an intruder; and besides, as an utter stranger, I have no right to stay." To all of which Elsie devoutly whispered to herself, "Amen."

But Mrs. Alford now appeared, and after a warm, motherly greeting to her son, turned in genial courtesy to welcome his friend, as she supposed.

George was so happy that he wished every one else to be the same. The comical episode attending Mr. Stanhope's unexpected appearance just hit his frolicsome mood, and promised to be a source of endless merriment if he could only keep his classmate over the coming holiday. Moreover, he long had wished to become better acquainted with this young man, whose manner at the seminary had deeply interested him. So he said:

"Mother, this is Mr. Stanhope, a classmate of mine. I wish you would help me persuade him to stay."

"Why, certainly, I supposed you expected to stay with us, of course," said Mrs. Alford, heartily.

Mr. Stanhope looked ready to sink through the floor, his face crimson with vexation.

"I do assure you, madam," he urged, "it is all a mistake. I am not an invited guest. I was merely calling on a little matter of business, when - " and there he stopped. George exploded into a hearty, uncontrollable laugh; while Elsie, in the darkness, shook her little fist at the stranger, who hastened to add, "Please let me bid you good-evening, I have not the slightest claim on your hospitality."

"Where are you staying?" asked Mrs. Alford, a little mystified. "We would like you to spend at least part of the time with us."

"I do not expect to be here very long. I have a room at the hotel."

"Now, look here, Stanhope," cried George, barring all egress by planting his back against the door, "do you take me, a half-fledged theologue, for a heathen? Do you suppose that I could be such a churl as to let a classmate stay at our dingy, forlorn little tavern and eat hash on Thanksgiving Day? I could never look you in the face at recitation again. Have some consideration for my peace of mind, and I am sure you will find our home quite as endurable as anything Mr. Starks can provide."

"Oh! as to that, from even the slight glimpse that I have had, this seems more like a home than anything I have known for many years; but I cannot feel it right that I, an unexpected stranger - "

"Come, come! No more of that! You know what is written about 'entertaining strangers;' so that is your strongest claim. Moreover, that text works both ways sometimes, and the stranger angel finds himself among angels. My old mother here, if she does weigh well on toward two hundred, is more like one than anything I have yet seen, and Elsie, if not an angel, is at least part witch and part fairy. But you need not fear ghostly entertainment from mother's larder. As you are a Christian, and not a Pagan, no more of this reluctance. Indeed, nolens volens, I shall not permit you to go out into this November storm to-night;" and Elsie, to her dismay, saw the new-comer led up to the "spare room" with a sort of hospitable violence.

With flaming cheeks and eyes half full of indignant tears, she now made onslaught on her mother, who had returned to the kitchen, where she was making preparations for a supper that might almost answer for the dinner the next day.

"Mother, mother," she exclaimed, "how could you keep that disagreeable stranger! He will spoil our Thanksgiving."

"Why, child, what is the matter?" said Mrs. Alford, raising her eyes in surprise to her daughter's face, that looked like a red moon through the mist of savory vapors rising from the ample cooking-stove. "I don't understand you. Why should not your brother's classmate add to the pleasure of our Thanksgiving?"

"Well, perhaps if we had expected him, if he had come in some other way, and we knew more about him - "

"Bless you, child, what a formalist you have become. You stand on a fine point of etiquette, as if it were the broad foundation of hospitality; while only last week you wanted a ragged tramp, who had every appearance of being a thief, to stay all night. Your brother thinks it a special providence that his friend should have turned up so unexpectedly."

"Oh, dear!" sighed Elsie. "If that is what the doctrine of special providence means, I shall need a new confession of faith." Then, a sudden thought occurring to her, she vanished, while her mother smiled, saying:

"What a queer child she is, to be sure!"

A moment later Elsie gave a sharp knock at the spare room door, and in a second was in the further end of the dark hall. George put his head out.

"Come here," she whispered. "Are you sure it's you?" she added, holding him off at arm's-length.

His response was such a tempest of kisses and embraces that in her nervous state she was quite panic-stricken.

"George," she gasped, "have mercy on me!"

"I only wished to show you how he felt, so you would have some sympathy for him."

"If you don't stop," said the almost desperate girl, "I will shut myself up and not appear till he is gone. I will any way, if you don't make me a solemn promise."

"Leave out the 'solemn.'"

"No, I won't. Upon your word and honor, promise never to tell what has happened - my mistake, I mean."

"Oh, Elsie, it's too good to keep," laughed George.

"Now, George, if you tell," sobbed Elsie, "you'll spoil my holiday, your visit, and everything."

"If you feel that way, you foolish child, of course I won't tell. Indeed, I suppose I should not, for Stanhope seems half frightened out of his wits also."

"Serves him right, though I doubt whether he has many to lose," said Elsie, spitefully.

"Well, I will do my best to keep in," said George, soothingly, and stroking her curls. "But you will let it all out; you see. The idea of your keeping anything with your April face!"

Elsie acted upon the hint, and went to her room in order to remove all traces of agitation before the supper-bell should summon her to meet the dreaded stranger.

In the meantime, Mr. Alford and James, the second son, had come up from the village, where they had a thriving business. They greeted George's friend so cordially that it went some way toward putting the diffident youth at his ease; but he dreaded meeting Elsie again quite as much as she dreaded meeting him.

"Who is this Mr. Stanhope?" his parents asked, as they drew George aside for a little private talk after his long absence.

"Well, he is a classmate with whom I have long wished to get better acquainted; but he is so shy and retiring that I have made little progress. He came from another seminary, and entered our class in this the middle year. No one seems to know much about him; and indeed he has shunned all intimacies and devotes himself wholly to his books. The recitation-room is the one place where he appears well - for there he speaks out, as if

E. P. Roe

forgetting himself, or rather, losing himself in some truth under contemplation. Sometimes he will ask a question that wakes up both class and professor; but at other times it seems difficult to pierce the shell of his reserve or diffidence. And yet, from little things I have seen, I know that he has a good warm heart; and the working of his mind in the recitation-room fascinates me. Further than this I know little about him, but have just learned, from his explanation as to his unexpected appearance at our door, that he is very poor, and purposed to spend his holiday vacation as agent for a new magazine that is offering liberal premiums. I think his poverty is one of the reasons why he has so shrunk from companionship with the other students. He thinks he ought to go out and continue his efforts tonight."

"This stormy night!" ejaculated kind Mrs. Alford. "It would be barbarous."

"Certainly it would, mother. We must not let him. But you must all be considerate, for he seems excessively diffident and sensitive; and besides - but no matter."

"No fear but that we will soon make him at home. And it's a pleasure to entertain people who are not surfeited with attention. I don't understand Elsie, however, for she seems to have formed a violent prejudice against him. From the nature of her announcement of his presence I gathered that he was a rather forward young man."

There was a twinkle in George's eye; but he merely said:

"Elsie is full of moods and tenses; but her kind little heart is always the same, and that will bring her around all right."

They were soon after marshalled to the supper-room.
Elsie slipped in among the others, but was so stately
and demure, and with her curls brushed down so
straight that you would scarcely have known her. Her
father caught his pet around the waist, and was about
to introduce her, when George hastened to say with the
solemnity of an undertaker that Elsie and Mr. Stanhope
had met before.

Elsie repented the promise she had wrung from her
brother, for any amount of badinage would be better
than this depressing formality. She took her seat, not
daring to look at the obnoxious guest; and the family
noticed with surprise that they had never seen the little
maiden so quenched and abashed before. But George
good-naturedly tried to make the conversation general,
so as to give them time to recover themselves.

Elsie soon ventured to steal shy looks at Mr. Stanhope,
and with her usual quickness discovered that he was
more in terror of her than she of him, and she exulted
in the fact.

"I'll punish him well, if I get a chance," she thought
with a certain phase of the feminine sense of justice.
But the sadness of his face quite disarmed her when
her mother, in well-meant kindness, asked:

"Where is your home located, Mr. Stanhope?"

"In the seminary," he answered in rather a low tone.

"You don't mean to say that you have no better
one than a forlorn cell in Dogma Hall?" exclaimed

George, earnestly.

Mr. Stanhope crimsoned, and then grew pale, but tried to say lightly, "An orphan of my size and years is not a very moving object of sympathy; but one might well find it difficult not to break the Tenth Commandment while seeing how you are surrounded."

Elsie was vexed at her disposition to relent toward him; she so hardened her face, however, that James rallied her:

"Why, Puss, what is the matter? Yours is the most unpromising Thanksgiving phiz I have seen today. 'Count your marcies.'"

Elsie blushed so violently, and Mr. Stanhope looked so distressed that James finished his supper in puzzled silence, thinking, however, "What has come over the little witch? For a wonder, she seems to have met a man that she is afraid of: but the joke is, he seems even more afraid of her."

In the social parlor some of the stiffness wore off; but Elsie and Mr. Stanhope kept on opposite sides of the room and had very little to say to each other. Motherly Mrs. Alford drew the young man out sufficiently, however, to become deeply interested in him.

By the next morning time for thought had led him to feel that he must trespass on their hospitality no longer. Moreover, he plainly recognized that his presence was an oppression and restraint upon Elsie; and he was very sorry that he had stayed at all. But when he made known his purpose the family would not listen to it.

"I should feel dreadfully hurt if you left us now," said Mrs. Alford, so decidedly that he was in a dilemma, and stole a timid look toward Elsie, who at once guessed his motive in going away. Her kind heart got the better of her; and her face relented in a sudden reassuring smile. Then she turned hastily away. Only George saw and understood the little side scene and the reason Mr. Stanhope was induced to remain. Then Elsie, in her quickly varying moods, was vexed at herself, and became more cold and distant than ever. "He will regard me as only a pert, forward miss, but I will teach him better," she thought; and she astonished the family more and more by a stateliness utterly unlike herself. Mr. Stanhope sincerely regretted that he had not broken away, in spite of the others; but in order not to seem vacillating he resolved to stay till the following morning, even though he departed burdened with the thought that he had spoiled the day for one of the family. Things had now gone so far that leaving might only lead to explanations and more general annoyances, for George had intimated that the little mistake of the previous evening should remain a secret.

And yet he sincerely wished she would relent toward him, for she could not make her sweet little face repellent. The kiss she had given him still seemed to tingle in his very soul, while her last smile was like a ray of warmest sunshine. But her face, never designed to be severe, was averted.

After having heard the affairs of the nation discussed in a sound, scriptural manner, they all sat down to a dinner such as had never blessed poor Mr. Stanhope's vision before. A married son and daughter returned after church, and half a dozen grandchildren enlivened the gathering. There was need of them, for Elsie, usually in a state of wild effervescence upon such occasions, was now demure and comparatively silent. The children, with whom she was accustomed to romp like one of them, were perplexed indeed; and only the intense excitement of a Thanksgiving dinner diverted their minds from Aunt Elsie, so sadly changed. She was conscious that all were noting her absent manner, and this embarrassed and vexed her more; and yet she seemed under a miserable paralysis that she could neither explain nor escape.

"If we had only laughed it off at first," she groaned to herself; "but now the whole thing grows more absurd and disagreeable every moment."

"Why, Elsie," said her father, banteringly, "you doubted the other day whether Mrs. Methuselah's age would ever sober you; and yet I think that good old lady would have looked more genial on Thanksgiving Day. What is the matter?"

"I was thinking of the sermon," she said.

Amid the comic elevation of eyebrows, George said slyly:

"Tell us the text."

Overwhelmed with confusion, she darted a reproachful glance at him and muttered:

"I did not say anything about the text."

"Well, tell us about the sermon then," laughed James.

"No," said Elsie, sharply. "I'll quote you a text: 'Eat, drink, and be merry,' and let me alone."

They saw that for some reason she could not bear teasing, and that such badinage troubled Mr. Stanhope also. George came gallantly to the rescue, and the dinner-party grew so merry that Elsie thawed perceptibly and Stanhope was beguiled into several witty speeches. At each one Elsie opened her eyes in wider and growing appreciation. At last, when they rose from their coffee, she come to the surprising conclusion -

"Why, he is not stupid and bad-looking after all."

George was bent on breaking the ice between them, and so proposed that the younger members of the family party should go up a swollen stream and see the fall. But Elsie flanked herself with a sister-in-law on one side and a niece on the other, while Stanhope was so diffident that nothing but downright encouragement would bring him to her side. So George was almost in despair. Elsie's eyes had been conveying favorable impressions to her reluctant mind throughout the walk. She sincerely regretted that such an absurd barrier had grown up between her and Stanhope, but could not for the life of her, especially before others, do anything to break the awkward spell.

At last they were on their return, and were all grouped together on a little bluff, watching the water pour foamingly through a narrow gorge.

"Oh, see," cried Elsie, suddenly pointing to the opposite bank, "what beautiful moss that is over there! It is just the kind I have been wanting. Oh, dear! there isn't a bridge within half a mile."

Stanhope glanced around a moment, and then said gallantly, "I will get you the moss, Miss Alford." They saw that in some inconceivable way he intended crossing where they stood. The gorge was much too wide for the most vigorous leap, so Elsie exclaimed eagerly:

"Oh, please don't take any risk! What is a little moss?"

"I say, Stanhope," remonstrated George, seriously, "it would be no laughing matter if you should fall in there."

But Stanhope only smiled, threw off his overcoat, and buttoned his undercoat closely around him. George groaned to himself, "This will be worse than the kissing scrape," and was about to lay a restraining grasp upon his friend. But he slipped away, and lightly went up hand-over-hand a tall, slender sapling on the edge of the bank, the whole party gathering round in breathless expectation. Having reached its slender, swaying top, he threw himself out on the land side. The tree bent at once to the ground with his weight, but without snapping, showing that it was tough and fibrous. Holding firmly to the top, he gave a strong spring, which, with the spring of the bent sapling, sent him well over the gorge on the firm ground beyond.

There was a round of applause from the little group he had just left, in which Elsie joined heartily. Her eyes were glowing with admiration, for when was not power and daring captivating to a woman? Then, in sudden alarm and forgetfulness of her former coolness, she exclaimed:

"But how will you get back?"

"This is my bridge," he replied, smiling brightly across to her, and holding on to the slender young tree. "You perceive that I was brought up in the country."

So saying, he tied the sapling down to a root with a handkerchief, and then proceeded to fill another with moss.

As George saw Elsie's face while she watched Stanhope gather the coveted trifle, he chuckled to himself -

"The ice is broken between them now."

But Stanhope had insecurely fastened the sapling down. The strain upon the knot was too severe, and suddenly the young tree flew up and stood erect but quivering, with his handkerchief fluttering in its top as a symbol of defeat. There was an exclamation of dismay and Elsie again asked with real anxiety in her tone:

"How will you get back now?"

Stanhope shrugged his shoulders.

"I confess I am defeated, for there is no like sapling on this side; but I have the moss, and can join you at the bridge below, if nothing better offers."

"George," said Elsie, indignantly, "don't go away and leave Mr. Stanhope's handkerchief in that tree."

"Bless you, child," cried George, mischievously, and

leading the way down the path, "I can't climb anymore than a pumpkin. You will have to go back with him after it, or let it wave as a memento of his gallantry on your behalf."

"If I can only manage to throw them together without any embarrassing third parties present, the ridiculous restraint they are under will soon vanish," he thought; and so he hastened his steps. The rest trooped after him, while Stanhope made his way with difficulty on the opposite bank, where there was no path. His progress therefore was slow; and Elsie saw that if she did not linger he would be left behind. Common politeness forbade this, and so she soon found herself alone, carrying his overcoat on one bank, and he keeping pace with her on the other. She comforted herself at first with the thought that with the brawling, deafening stream between them, there would be no chance for embarrassing conversation. But soon her sympathies became aroused, as she saw him toilsomely making his way over the rocks and through the tangled thickets: and as she could not speak to him, she smiled her encouragement so often that she felt it would be impossible to go back to her old reserve.

Stanhope now came to a little opening in the brush. The cleared ground sloped evenly down to the stream, and its curent was divided by a large rock. He hailed the opportunity here offered with delight, for he was very anxious to speak to her before they should join the others. So he startled Elsie by walking out into the clearing, away from the stream.

"Well, I declare; that's cool, to go and leave me alone without a word," she thought.

But she was almost terror-stricken to see him turn and dart to the torrent like an arrow. With a long flying leap, he landed on the rock in the midst of the stream, and then, without a second's hesitation, with the impetus already acquired, sprang for the solid ground where she stood, struck it, wavered, and would have fallen backward into the water had not she, quick as thought, stepped forward and given him her hand.

"You have saved me from a ducking, if not worse," he said, giving the little rescuing hand a warm pressure.

"Oh!" exclaimed she, panting, "please don't do any more dreadful things. I shall be careful how I make any wishes in your hearing again."

"I am sorry to hear you say that," he replied. And then there was an awkward silence.

Elsie could think of nothing better than to refer to the handkerchief they had left behind.

"Will you wait for me till I run and get it?" he asked.

"I will go back with you, if you will permit me," she said timidly.

"Indeed, I could not ask so much of you as that."

"And yet you could about the same as risk your neck to gratify a whim of mine," she said more gratefully than she intended.

"Please do not think," he replied earnestly, "that I have been practicing cheap heroics. As I said, I was a country boy, and in my early home thought nothing of doing such things." But even the brief reference to that vanished home caused him to sigh deeply, and Elsie gave him a wistful look of sympathy.

For a few moments they walked on in silence. Then Mr. Stanhope turned, and with some hesitation said:

"Miss Alford, I did very wrong to stay after - after last evening. But my better judgment was borne down by invitations so cordial that I hardly knew how to resist them. At the same time I now realize that I should have done so. Indeed, I would go away at once, would not such a course only make matters worse. And yet, after receiving so much kindness from your family, more than has blessed me for many long years - for since my dear mother died I have been quite alone in the world - I feel I cannot go away without some assurance or proof that you will forgive me for being such a kill-joy in your holiday."

Elsie's vexation with herself now knew no bounds. She stopped in the path, determining that she would clear up matters, cost what it might.

"Mr. Stanhope," she said, "will you grant a request that will contain such assurance, or rather, will show you that I am heartily ashamed of my foolish course? Will you not spend next Thanksgiving with us, and give me a chance to retrieve myself from first to last?"

His face brightened wonderfully as he replied, "I will only be too glad to do so, if you truly wish it."

"I do wish it," she said earnestly. "What must you think of me?" (His eyes then expressed much admiration; but hers were fixed on the ground and half filled with tears of vexation.) Then, with a pretty humility that was exquisite in its simplicity and artlessness, she added:

"You have noticed at home that they call me 'child' - and indeed, I am little more than one - and now see that I have behaved like a very silly and naughty one toward you. I have trampled on every principle of hospitality, kindness, and good-breeding. I have no patience with myself, and I wish another chance to show that I can do better. I - "

"Oh, Miss Alford, please do not judge yourself so harshly and unjustly," interrupted Stanhope.

"Oh, dear!" sighed Elsie, "I'm so sorry for what happened last night. We all might have had such a good time."

"Well, then," said Stanhope, demurely, "I suppose I ought to be also."

"And do you mean to say that you are not?" she asked, turning suddenly upon him.

"Oh, well, certainly, for your sake," he said with rising color.

"But not for your own?" she asked with almost the naivete of a child.

He turned away with a perplexed laugh and replied: "Really, Miss Alford, you are worse than the Catechism."

She looked at him with a half-amused, half-surprised

expression, the thought occurring to her for the first time that it might not have been so disagreeable to him after all; and somehow this thought was quite a relief to her. But she said: "I thought you would regard me as a hoyden of the worst species."

"Because you kissed your brother? I have never for a moment forgotten that it was only your misfortune that I was not he."

"I should have remembered that it was not your fault. But here is your handkerchief, flying like a flag of truce; so let bygones be bygones. My terms are that you come again another year, and give me a chance to entertain my brother's friend as a sister ought."

"I am only too glad to submit to them," he eagerly replied, and then added, so ardently as to deepen the roses already in her cheeks, "If such are your punishments, Miss Alford, how delicious must be your favors!"

By common consent the subject was dropped; and with tongues released from awkward restraint, they chatted freely together, till in the early twilight they reached her home. The moment they entered George exultingly saw that the skies were serene.

But Elsie would never be the frolicsome child of the past again. As she surprised the family at dinner, so now at supper they could scarcely believe that the elegant, graceful young lady was the witch of yesterday. She had resolved with all her soul to try to win some place in Mr. Stanhope's respect before he departed, and never did a little maiden succeed better.

In the evening they had music; and Mr. Stanhope pleased them all with his fine tenor, while Elsie delighted him by her clear, birdlike voice. So the hours fled away.

"You think better of the 'horrid man,' little Sis," said George, as he kissed her good-night.

"I was the horrid one," said Elsie, penitently. "I can never forgive myself my absurd conduct. But he has promised to come again next Thanksgiving, and give me a chance to do better; so don't you fail to bring him."

George gave a long, low whistle, and then said: "Oh! ah! Seems to me you are coming on, for an innocent. Are we to get mixed up again in the twilight?"

"Nonsense!" said Elsie, with a peony face, and she slammed her door upon him.

The next morning the young man took his leave, and Elsie's last words were:

"Mr. Stanhope, remember your promise."

And he did remember more than that, for this brief visit had enshrined a sweet, girlish face within his heart of hearts, and he no longer felt lonely and orphaned. He and George became the closest friends, and messages from the New England home came to him with increasing frequency, which he returned with prodigal interest. It also transpired that he occasionally wrote for the papers, and Elsie insisted that these should be sent to her; while he of course wrote much better with the certainty that she would be his critic.

Thus, though separated, they daily became better acquainted, and during the year George found it not very difficult to induce his friend to make several visits.

But it was with joy that seemed almost too rich for earthly experience that he found himself walking up the village street with George the ensuing Thanksgiving Eve. Elsie was at the door; and he pretended to be disconsolate that his reception was not the same as on the previous year. Indeed she had to endure not a little chaffing, for her mistake was a family joke now.

It was a peerless Thanksgiving eve and day - one of the sun-lighted heights of human happiness.

After dinner they all again took a walk up the brawling stream, and Stanhope and Elsie became separated from the rest, though not so innocently as on the former occasion.

"See!" cried Elsie, pointing to the well-remembered sapling, which she had often visited. "There fluttered our flag of truce last year."

Stanhope seized her hand and said eagerly: "And here I again break the truce, and renew the theme we dropped at this place. Oh, Elsie, I have felt that kiss in the depths of my heart every hour since; and in that it led to my knowing and loving you, it has made every day from that time one of thanksgiving. If you could return my love, as I have dared to hope, it would be a happiness beyond words. If I could venture to take one more kiss, as a token that it is returned, I could keep Thanksgiving forever."

Her hand trembled in his, but was not withdrawn. Her blushing face was turned away toward the brawling stream; but she saw not its foam, she heard not its hoarse murmurs. A sweeter music was in her ears. She seemed under a delicious spell, but soon became conscious that a pair of dark eyes were looking down eagerly, anxiously for her answer. Shyly raising hers, that now were like dewy violets, she said, with a little of her old witchery:

"I suppose you will have to kiss me this Thanksgiving, to make things even."

Stanhope needed no broader hint.

"I owe you a heavy grudge," said Mr. Alford, in the evening. "A year ago you robbed me of my child, for little, kittenish Elsie became a thoughtful woman from the day you were here; and now you are going to take away the daughter of my old age."

"Yes, indeed, husband. Now you know how my father felt," said Mrs. Alford, at the same time wiping something from the corner of her eye.

"Bless me, are you here?" said the old gentleman, wheeling round to his wife. "Mr. Stanhope, I have nothing more to say."

"I declare," exulted George, "that 'horrid man' will devour Elsie yet."

"Haw! haw! haw!" laughed big-voiced, big-hearted James. "The idea of our little witch of an Elsie being a minister's wife!"

* * * * * * *

It is again Thanksgiving Eve. The trees are gaunt, the fields bare and brown, with dead leaves whirling across them; but a sweeter than June sunshine seems filling the cosey parlor where Elsie, a radiant bride, is receiving her husband's first kiss almost on the moment that she with her lips so unexpectedly kindled the sacred fire, three years before.

SUSIE ROLLIFFE'S CHRISTMAS

Picnicking in December would be a dreary experience even if one could command all the appliances of comfort which outdoor life permitted. This would be especially true in the latitude of Boston and on the bleak hills overlooking that city and its environing waters. Dreary business indeed Ezekiel Watkins regarded it as he shivered over the smoky camp-fire which he maintained with difficulty. The sun was sinking into the southwest so early in the day that he remarked irritably: "Durned if it was worth while for it to rise at all."

Ezekiel Watkins, or Zeke, as he was generally known among his comrades, had ceased to be a resident on that rocky hillside from pleasure. His heart was in a Connecticut valley in more senses than one; and there was not a more homesick soldier in the army. It will be readily guessed that the events of our story occurred more than a century ago. The shots fired at Bunker Hill had echoed in every nook and corner of the New England colonies, and the heart of Zeke Watkins, among thousands of others, had been fired with military ardor. With companions in like frame of mind he had trudged to Boston, breathing slaughter and extermination against the red-coated instruments of English tyranny. To Zeke the expedition had many of the elements of an extended bear-hunt, much exalted.

E. P. Roe

There was a spice of danger and a rich promise of novelty and excitement. The march to the lines about Boston had been a continuous ovation; grandsires came out from the wayside dwellings and blessed the rustic soldiers; they were dined profusely by the housewives, and if not wined, there had been slight stint in New England rum and cider; the apple-cheeked daughters of the land gave them the meed of heroes in advance, and abated somewhat of their ruddy hues at the thought of the dangers to be incurred. Zeke was visibly dilated by all this attention, incense, and military glory; and he stepped forth from each village and hamlet as if the world were scarcely large enough for the prowess of himself and companions. Even on parade he was as stiff as his long-barrelled flintlock, looking as if England could hope for no quarter at his hands; yet he permitted no admiring glances from bright eyes to escape him. He had not traversed half the distance between his native hamlet and Boston before he was abundantly satisfied that pretty Susie Rolliffe had made no mistake in honoring him among the recruits by marks of especial favor. He wore in his squirrel-skin cap the bit of blue ribbon she had given him, and with the mien of a Homeric hero had intimated darkly that it might be crimson before she saw it again. She had clasped her hands, stifled a little sob, and looked at him admiringly. He needed no stronger assurance than her eyes conveyed at that moment. She had been shy and rather unapproachable before, sought by others than himself, yet very chary of her smiles and favors to all. Her ancestors had fought the Indians, and had bequeathed to the demure little maiden much of their own indomitable spirit. She had never worn her heart on her sleeve, and was shy of her rustic admirers chiefly because none of them had realized her ideals of manhood created by fireside stories of the past.

Zeke's chief competitor for Susie's favor had been Zebulon Jarvis; and while he had received little encouragement, he laid his unostentatious devotion at her feet unstintedly, and she knew it. Indeed, she was much inclined to laugh at him, for he was singularly bashful, and a frown from her overwhelmed him. Unsophisticated Susie reasoned that any one who could be so afraid of HER could not be much of a man. She had never heard of his doing anything bold and spirited. It might be said, indeed, that the attempt to wring a livelihood for his widowed mother and for his younger brothers and sisters from the stumpy, rocky farm required courage of the highest order; but it was not of a kind that appealed to the fancy of a romantic young girl. Nothing finer or grander had Zebulon attempted before the recruiting officer came to Opinquake, and when he came, poor Zeb appeared to hang back so timorously that he lost what little place he had in Susie's thoughts. She was ignorant of the struggle taking place in his loyal heart. More intense even than his love for her was the patriotic fire which smouldered in his breast; yet when other young men were giving in their names and drilling on the village green, he was absent. To the war appeals of those who sought him, he replied briefly. "Can't leave till fall."

"But the fighting will be over long before that," it was urged.

"So much the better for others, then, if not for me."

Zeke Watkins made it his business that Susie should hear this reply in the abbreviated form of, "So much the better, then."

She had smiled scornfully, and it must be added, a little bitterly. In his devotion Zeb had been so helpless, so diffidently unable to take his own part and make advances that she, from odd little spasms of sympathy, had taken his part for him, and laughingly repeated to herself in solitude all the fine speeches which she perceived he would be glad to make. But, as has been intimated, it seemed to her droll indeed that such a great stalwart fellow should appear panic-stricken in her diminutive presence. In brief, he had been timidity embodied under her demurely mischievous blue eyes; and now that the recruiting officer had come and marched away with his squad without him, she felt incensed that such a chicken-hearted fellow had dared to lift his eyes to her.

"It would go hard with the Widow Jarvis and all those children if Zeb 'listed," Susie's mother had ventured in half-hearted defence, for did she not look upon him as a promising suitor.

"The people of Opinquake wouldn't let the widow or the children starve," replied Susie, indignantly. "If I was a big fellow like him, my country would not call me twice. Think how grandfather left grandma and all the children!"

"Well, I guess Zeb thinks he has his hands full wrastling with that stony farm."

"He needn't come to see me any more, or steal glances at me 'tween meetings on Sunday," said the girl, decisively. "He cuts a sorry figure beside Zeke Watkins, who was the first to give in his name, and who began to march like a soldier even before he left us."

"Yes," said Mrs. Rolliffe; "Zeke was very forward. If he holds out as he began - Well, well, Zeke allus was a little forward, and able to speak for himself. You are young yet, Susan, and may learn before you reach my years that the race isn't allus to the swift. Don't be in haste to promise yourself to any of the young men."

"Little danger of my promising myself to a man who is afraid even of me! I want a husband like grandfather. He wasn't afraid to face anything, and he honored his wife by acting as if she wasn't afraid either."

Zeb gave Susie no chance to bestow the rebuffs she had premeditated. He had been down to witness the departure of the Opinquake quota, and had seen Susie's farewell to Zeke Watkins. How much it had meant he was not sure - enough to leave no hope or chance for him, he had believed; but he had already fought his first battle, and it had been a harder one than Zeke Watkins or any of his comrades would ever engage in. He had returned and worked on the stony farm until dark. From dawn until dark he continued to work every secular day till September.

His bronzed face grew as stern as it was thin; and since he would no longer look at her, Susie Rolliffe began to steal an occasional and wondering glance at him "'tween meetings."

No one understood the young man or knew his plans except his patient, sad-eyed mother, and she learned more by her intuitions than from his spoken words. She idolized him, and he loved and revered her: but the terrible Puritan restraint paralyzed manifestations of affection. She was not taken by surprise when one evening he said quietly, "Mother, I guess I'll start in a day or two."

She could not repress a sort of gasping sob however, but after a few moments was able to say steadily, "I supposed you were preparing to leave us."

"Yes, mother, I've been a-preparing. I've done my best to gather in everything that would help keep you and the children and the stock through the winter. The corn is all shocked, and the older children can help you husk it, and gather in the pumpkins, the beans, and the rest. As soon as I finish digging the potatoes I think I'll feel better to be in the lines around Boston. I'd have liked to have gone at first, but in order to fight as I ought I'd want to remember there was plenty to keep you and the children."

"I'm afraid, Zebulon, you've been fighting as well as working so hard all summer long. For my sake and the children's, you've been letting Susan Rolliffe think meanly of you."

"I can't help what she thinks, mother; I've tried not to act meanly."

"Perhaps the God of the widow and the fatherless will shield and bless you, my son. Be that as it may," she added with a heavy sigh, "conscience and His will must guide in everything. If He says go forth to battle, what am I that I should stay you?" Although she did not dream of the truth, the Widow Jarvis was a disciplined soldier herself. To her, faith meant unquestioning submission and obedience; she had been taught to revere a jealous and an exacting God rather than a loving one. The heroism with which she pursued her toilsome, narrow, shadowed pathway was as sublime as it was unrecognized on her part. After she had retired she wept sorely, not only because her eldest child was going to danger, and perhaps death, but also for the reason that her heart clung to him so weakly and selfishly, as she believed. With a tenderness of which she was half-ashamed she filled his wallet with provisions which would add to his comfort, then, both to his surprise and her own, kissed him good-by. He left her and the younger brood with an aching heart of which there was little outward sign, and with no loftier ambition than to do his duty; she followed him with deep, wistful eyes till he, and next the long barrel of his rifle, disappeared in an angle of the road, and then her interrupted work was resumed.

Susie Rolliffe was returning from an errand to a neighbor's when she heard the sound of long rapid steps.

A hasty glance revealed Zeb in something like pursuit. Her heart fluttered slightly, for he had looked so stern and sad of late that she had felt a little sorry for him in spite of herself. But since he could "wrastle" with nothing more formidable than a stony farm, she did not wish to have anything to say to him, or meet the embarrassment of explaining a tacit estrangement. She was glad, therefore, that her gate was so near, and passed in as if she had not recognized him. She heard his steps become slower and pause at the gate, and then almost in shame in being guilty of too marked discourtesy, she turned to speak, but hesitated in surprise, for now she recognized his equipment as a soldier.

"Why, Mr. Jarvis, where are you going?" she exclaimed.

A dull red flamed through the bronze of his thin cheeks as he replied awkwardly, "I thought I'd take a turn in the lines around Boston."

"Oh, yes," she replied, mischievously, "take a turn in the lines. Then we may expect you back by corn-husking?"

He was deeply wounded, and in his embarrassment could think of no other reply than the familiar words, "'Let not him that girdeth on his harness boast himself as he that putteth it off.'"

"I can't help hoping, Mr. Jarvis, that neither you nor others will put it off too soon - not, at least, while King George claims to be our master. When we're free I can stand any amount of boasting."

"You'll never hear boasting from me, Miss Susie;" and then an awkward silence fell between them.

Shyly and swiftly she raised her eyes. He looked so humble, deprecatory, and unsoldier-like that she could not repress a laugh. "I'm not a British cannon," she began, "that you should be so fearful."

His manhood was now too deeply wounded for further endurance even from her, for he suddenly straightened himself, and throwing his rifle over his shoulder, said sternly, "I'm not a coward. I never hung back from fear, but to keep mother from charity, so I could fight or die as God wills. You may laugh at the man who never gave you anything but love, if you will, but you shall never laugh at my deeds. Call that boasting or not as you please," and he turned on his heel to depart.

His words and manner almost took away the girl's breath, so unexpected were they, and unlike her idea of the man. In that brief moment a fearless soldier had flashed himself upon her consciousness, revealing a spirit that would flinch at nothing - that had not even quailed at the necessity of forfeiting her esteem, that his mother might not want. Humiliated and conscience-stricken that she had done him so much injustice, she rushed forward, crying, "Stop, Zebulon; please do not go away angry with me! I do not forget that we have been old friends and playmates. I'm willing to own that I've been wrong about you, and that's a good deal for a girl to do. I only wish I were a man, and I'd go with you."

Her kindness restored him to his awkward self again, and he stammered, "I wish you were - no, I don't - I merely stopped, thinking you might have a message; but I'd rather not take any to Zeke Watkins - will, though, if you wish. It cut me all up to have you think I was afraid," and then he became speechless.

"But you acted as if you were afraid of me, and that seemed so ridiculous."

He looked at her a moment so earnestly with his dark, deep-set eyes that hers dropped. "Miss Susie," he said slowly, and speaking with difficulty, "I AM afraid of you, next to God. I don't suppose I've any right to talk to you so, and I will say good-by. I was reckless when I spoke before. Perhaps - you'll go and see mother. My going is hard on her."

His eyes lingered on her a moment longer, as if he were taking his last look, then he turned slowly away.

"Good-by, Zeb," she called softly. "I didn't - I don't understand. Yes, I will go to see your mother."

Susie also watched him as he strode away. He thought he could continue on steadfastly without looking back, but when the road turned he also turned, fairly tugged right about by his loyal heart. She stood where he had left her, and promptly waved her hand. He doffed his cap, and remained a moment in an attitude that appeared to her reverential, then passed out of view.

The moments lapsed, and still she stood in the gateway, looking down the vacant road as if dazed. Was it in truth awkward, bashful Zeb Jarvis who had just left her? He seemed a new and distinct being in contrast to the youth whom she had smiled at and in a measure scoffed at. The little Puritan maiden was not a reasoner, but a creature of impressions and swift intuitions. Zeb had not set his teeth, faced his hard duty, and toiled that long summer in vain. He had developed a manhood and a force which in one brief moment had enabled him to compel her recognition.

"He will face anything," she murmured. "He's afraid of only God and me; what a strange thing to say - afraid of me next to God! Sounds kind of wicked. What can he mean? Zeke Watkins wasn't a bit afraid of me. As mother said, he was a little forward, and I was fool enough to take him at his own valuation. Afraid of me! How he stood with his cap off. Do men ever love so? Is there a kind of reverence in some men's love? How absurd that a great strong, brave man, ready to face cannons, can bow down to such a little - "Her fragmentary exclamations ended in a peal of laughter, but tears dimmed her blue eyes.

Susie did visit Mrs. Jarvis, and although the reticent woman said little about her son, what she did say meant volumes to the girl who now had the right clew in interpreting his action and character. She too was reticent. New England girls rarely gushed in those days, so no one knew she was beginning to understand. Her eyes, experienced in country work, were quick, and her mind active. "It looks as if a giant had been wrestling with this stony farm," she muttered.

Zeb received no ovations on his lonely tramp to the lines, and the vision of Susie Rolliffe waving her hand from the gateway would have blinded him to all the bright and admiring eyes in the world. He was hospitably entertained, however, when there was occasion; but the advent of men bound for the army had become an old story. Having at last inquired his way to the position occupied by the Connecticut troops, he was assigned to duty in the same company with Zeke Watkins, who gave him but a cool reception, and sought to overawe him by veteran-like airs. At first poor Zeb was awkward enough in his unaccustomed duties, and no laugh was so scornful as that of his rival. Young Jarvis, however, had not been many days in camp before he guessed that Zeke's star was not in the ascendant. There was but little fighting required, but much digging of intrenchments, drill, and monotonous picket duty. Zeke did not take kindly to such tasks, and shirked them when possible. He was becoming known as the champion grumbler in the mess, and no one escaped his criticism, not even "Old Put" - as General Putnam, who commanded the Connecticut quota, was called. Jarvis, on the other hand, performed his military duties as he had worked the farm, and rapidly acquired the bearing of a soldier. Indomitable Putnam gave his men little rest, and was ever seeking to draw his lines

E. P. Roe

nearer to Boston and the enemy's ships. He virtually fought with pick and shovel, and his working parties were often exposed to fire while engaged in fortifying the positions successively occupied. The Opinquake boys regarded themselves as well seasoned to such rude compliments, and were not a little curious to see how Zeb would handle a shovel with cannon-balls whizzing uncomfortably near. The opportunity soon came. Old Put himself could not have been more coolly oblivious than the raw recruit. At last a ball smashed his shovel to smithereens; he quietly procured another and went on with his work. Then his former neighbors gave him a cheer, while his captain clapped him on the shoulder and said, "Promote you to be a veteran on the spot!"

The days had grown shorter, colder, and drearier, and the discomforts of camp-life harder to endure. There were few tents even for the officers, and the men were compelled to improvise such shelter as circumstances permitted. Huts of stone, wood, and brush, and barricades against the wind, lined the hillside, and the region already was denuded of almost everything that would burn. Therefore, when December came, Zeke Watkins found that even a fire was a luxury not to be had without trouble. He had become thoroughly disgusted with a soldier's life, and the military glory which had at first so dazzled him now wore the aspect of the wintry sky. He had recently sought and attained the only promotion for which his captain now deemed him fitted - that of cook for about a dozen of his comrades; and the close of the December day found him preparing the meagre supper which the limited rations permitted. By virtue of his office, Zeke was one of the best-fed men in the army, for if there were any choice morsels he could usually manage to secure them; still, he was not happy. King George and Congress were both pursuing policies inconsistent with his comfort, and he sighed more and more frequently for the wide kitchen-hearth of his home, which was within easy visiting distance of the Rolliffe farmhouse. His term of enlistment expired soon, and he was already counting the days. He was not alone in his discontent, for there was much homesickness and disaffection among the Connecticut troops. Many had already departed, unwilling to stay an hour after the expiration of their terms; and not a few had anticipated the periods which legally released them from duty. The organization of the army was so loose that neither appeals nor threats had much influence, and Washington, in deep solicitude, saw his troops melting away.

It was dark by the time the heavy tramp of the working party was heard returning from the fortifications. The great mess-pot, partly filled with pork and beans, was bubbling over the fire; Zeke, shifting his position from time to time to avoid the smoke which the wind, as if it had a spite against him, blew in his face, was sourly contemplating his charge and his lot, bent on grumbling to the others with even greater gusto than he had complained to himself. His comrades carefully put away their intrenching tools, for they were held responsible for them, and then gathered about the fire, clamoring for supper.

"Zeke, you lazy loon," cried Nat Atkinson, "how many pipes have you smoked to-day? If you'd smoke less and forage and dun the commissary more, we'd have a little fresh meat once in a hundred years."

"Yes, just about once in a hundred years!" snarled Zeke.

"YOU find something to keep fat on, anyhow. We'll broil you some cold night. Trot out your beans if there's nothing else."

"Growl away," retorted Zeke. "'Twon't be long before I'll be eating chickens and pumpkin-pie in Opinquake, instead of cooking beans and rusty pork for a lot of hungry wolves."

"You'd be the hungriest wolf of the lot if you'd 'a' been picking and shovelling frozen ground all day."

"I didn't 'list to be a ditch-digger!" said Zeke. "I thought I was going to be a soldier."

"And you turned out a cook!" quietly remarked Zeb Jarvis.

"Well, my hero of the smashed shovel, what do you expect to be - Old Put's successor? You know, fellows, it's settled that you're to dig your way into Boston, tunnel under the water when you come to it. Of course Put will die of old age before you get half there. Zeb'll be the chap of all others to command a division of shovellers. I see you with a pickaxe strapped on your side instead of a sword."

"Lucky I'm not in command now," replied Zeb, "or you'd shovel dirt under fire to the last hour of your enlistment. I'd give grumblers like you something to grumble about. See here, fellows, I'm sick of this seditious talk in our mess. The Connecticut men are getting to be the talk of the army. You heard a squad of New Hampshire boys jeer at us to-day, and ask, 'When are ye going home to mother?' You ask, Zeke Watkins, what I expect to be. I expect to be a soldier, and obey orders as long as Old Put and General Washington want a man. All I ask is to be home summers long enough to keep mother and the children off the town. Now what do you expect to be after you give up your cook's ladle?"

"None o' your business."

"He's going home to court Susie Rolliffe," cried Nat Atkinson. "They'll be married in the spring, and go into the chicken business. That'd just suit Zeke."

"It would not suit Susie Rolliffe," said Zeb, hotly. "A braver, better girl doesn't breathe in the colonies, and the man that says a slurring word against her's got to fight me."

"What! Has she given Zeke the mitten for your sake, Zeb?" piped little Hiram Woodbridge.

"She hasn't given me anything, and I've got no claim; but she is the kind of girl that every fellow from Opinquake should stand up for. We all know that there is nothing chicken-hearted about her."

"Eight, by George - George W., I mean, and not the king," responded Hiram Woodbridge. "Here's to her health, Zeb, and your success! I believe she'd rather marry a soldier than a cook."

"Thank you," said Zeb. "You stand as good a chance as I do; but don't let's bandy her name about in camp any more'n we would our mother's. The thing for us to do now is to show that the men from Connecticut have as much backbone as any other fellows in the army, North or South. Zeke may laugh at Old Put's digging, but you'll soon find that he'll pick his way to a point where he can give the Britishers a dig under the fifth rib. We've got the best general in the army. Washington, with all his Southern style, believes in him and relies on him. Whether their time's up or not, it's a burning shame that so many of his troops are sneaking off home."

"It's all very well for you to talk, Zeb Jarvis," growled Zeke. "You haven't been here very long yet; and you stayed at home when others started out to fight. Now that you've found that digging and not fighting is the order of the day, you're just suited. It's the line of soldiering you are cut out for. When fighting men and not ditch-diggers are wanted, you'll find me -"

"All right, Watkins," said the voice of Captain Dean from without the circle of light. "According to your own story you are just the kind of man needed to-night - no ditch-digging on hand, but dangerous service. I detail you, for you've had rest compared with the other men. I ask for volunteers from those who've been at work all day."

Zeb Jarvis was on his feet instantly, and old Ezra Stokes also began to rise with difficulty. "No, Stokes," resumed the officer, "you can't go. I know you've suffered with the rheumatism all day, and have worked well in spite of it. For to-night's work I want young fellows with good legs and your spirit. How is it you're here anyhow Stokes? Your time's up."

"We ain't into Boston yet," was the quiet reply.

"So you want to stay?"

"Yes, sir."

"Then you shall cook for the men till you're better. I won't keep so good a soldier, though, at such work any longer than I can help. Your good example and that of the gallant Watkins has brought out the whole squad. I think I'll put Jarvis in command, though; Zeke might be rash, and attempt the capture of Boston before morning;" and the facetious captain, who had once been a neighbor, concluded, "Jarvis, see that every man's piece is primed and ready for use. Be at my hut in fifteen minutes." Then he passed on to the other camp-fires.

In a few minutes Ezra Stokes was alone by the fire, almost roasting his lame leg, and grumbling from pain and the necessity of enforced inaction. He was a taciturn, middle-age man, and had been the only bachelor of mature years in Opinquake. Although he rarely said much, he had been a great listener, and no one had been better versed in neighborhood affairs. In brief, he had been the village cobbler, and had not only taken the measure of Susie Rolliffe's little foot, but also of her spirit. Like herself he had been misled at first by the forwardness of Zeke Watkins and the apparent backwardness of Jarvis. Actual service had changed his views very decidedly. When Zeb appeared he had watched the course of this bashful suitor with interest which had rapidly ripened into warm but undemonstrative goodwill. The young fellow had taken pains to relieve the older man, had carried his tools for him, and more than once with his strong hands had almost rubbed the rheumatism out of the indomitable cobbler's leg. He had received but slight thanks, and had acted as if he didn't care for any. Stokes was not a man to return favors in words; be brooded over his gratitude as if it were a grudge. "I'll get even with that young Jarvis yet," he muttered, as he nursed his leg over the fire. "I know he worships the ground that little Rolliffe girl treads on, though she don't tread on much at a time. She never trod on me nuther, though I've had her foot in my hand more'n once. She looked at the man that made her shoes as if she would like to make him happier. When a little tot, she used to say I could come and live with her when I got too old to take care of myself. Lame as I be, I'd walk to Opinquake to give her a hint in her choosin'. Guess Hi Woodbridge is right, and she wouldn't be long in making up her mind betwixt a soger and a cook - a mighty poor one at that. Somehow or nuther I must let her know before Zeke Watkins sneaks home and parades around as a soldier 'bove ditch-digging. I've taken his measure.

"He'll be putting on veteran airs, telling big stories of what he's going to do when soldiers are wanted, and drilling such fools as believe in him. Young gals are often taken by such strutters, and think that men like Jarvis, who darsn't speak for themselves, are of no account. But I'll put a spoke in Zeke's wheel, if I have to get the captain to write."

It thus may be gathered that the cobbler had much to say to himself when alone, though so taciturn to others.

The clouds along the eastern horizon were stained with red before the reconnoitring party returned. Stokes had managed, by hobbling about, to keep up the fire and to fill the mess-kettle with the inevitable pork and beans. The hungry, weary men therefore gave their new cook a cheer when they saw the good fire and provision awaiting them. A moment later, however, Jarvis observed how lame Stokes had become; he took the cobbler by the shoulder and sat him down in the warmest nook, saying, "I'll be assistant cook until you are better. As Zeke says, I'm a wolf sure enough; but as soon's the beast's hunger is satisfied, I'll rub that leg of yours till you'll want to dance a jig;" and with the ladle wrung from Stokes's reluctant hand, he began stirring the seething contents of the kettle.

Then little Hi Woodbridge piped in his shrill voice, "Another cheer for our assistant cook and ditch-digger! I say, Zeke, wouldn't you like to tell Erza that Zeb has showed himself fit for something more than digging? You expressed your opinion very plain last night, and may have a different one now."

Zeke growld something inaudible, and stalked to his hut in order to put away his equipments.

"I'm cook-in-chief yet," Stokes declared; "and not a bean will any one of you get till you report all that happened."

"Well," piped Hi, "you may stick a feather in your old cap, Ezra, for our Opinquake lad captured a British officer last night, and Old Put is pumping him this blessed minute."

"Well, well, that is news. It must have been Zeke who did that neat job," exclaimed Stokes, ironically; "he's been a-pining for the soldier business."

"No, no; Zeke's above such night scrimmages. He wants to swim the bay and walk right into Boston in broad daylight, so everybody can see him. Come, Zeb, tell how it happened. It was so confounded dark, no one can tell but you."

"There isn't much to tell that you fellows don't know," was Zeb's laconic answer. "We had sneaked down on the neck so close to the enemy's lines -"

"Yes, yes, Zeb Jarvis," interrupted Stokes, "that's the kind of sneaking you're up to - close to the enemy's lines. Go on."

"Well, I crawled up so close that I saw a Britisher going the round of the sentinels, and I pounced on him and brought him out on the run, that's all."

"Oho! you both ran away, then? That wasn't good soldiering either, was it, Zeke?" commented Stokes, in his dry way.

"It's pretty good soldiering to stand fire within an inch of your nose," resumed Hi, who had become a loyal friend and adherent of his tall comrade. "Zeb was so close on the Britisher when he fired his pistol that we saw the faces of both in the flash; and a lot of bullets sung after us, I can sell you, as we dusted out of those diggin's."

"Compliments of General Putnam to Sergeant Zebulon Jarvis,' said an orderly, riding out of the dim twilight of the morning. "The general requests your presence at headquarters."

"Sergeant! promoted! Another cheer for Zeb!" and the Opinquake boys gave it with hearty goodwill.

"Jerusalem, fellows! I'd like to have a chance at those beans before I go!" but Zeb promptly tramped off with the orderly.

When he returned he was subjected to a fire of questions by the two or three men still awake, but all they could get out of him was that he had been given a good breakfast. From Captain Dean, who was with the general at the time of the examination, it leaked out that Zeb was in the line of promotion to a rank higher than that of sergeant.

The next few days passed uneventfully; and Zeke was compelled to resume the pick and shovel again. Stokes did his best to fulfil his duties, but it had become evident to all that the exposure of camp would soon disable him utterly. Jarvis and Captain Dean persuaded him to go home for the winter, and the little squad raised a sum which enabled him to make the journey in a stage. Zeke, sullen toward his jeering comrades, but immensely elated in secret, had shaken the dust - snow and slush rather - of camp-life from his feet the day before. He had the grace to wait till the time of his enlistment expired, and that was more than could be said of many.

It spoke well for the little Opinquake quota that only two others besides Zeke availed themselves of their liberty. Poor Stokes was almost forced away, consoled by the hope of returning in the spring. Zeb was sore-hearted on the day of Zeke's departure. His heart was in the Connecticut Valley also. No message had come to him from Susie Rolliffe. Those were not the days of swift and frequent communication. Even Mrs. Jarvis had written but seldom, and her missives were brief. Mother-love glowed through the few quaint and scriptural phrases like heat in anthracite coals. All that poor Zeb could learn from them was that Susie Rolliffe had kept her word and had been to the farm more than once; but the girl had been as reticent as the mother.

Zeke was now on his way home to prosecute his suit in person, and Zeb well knew how forward and plausible he could be. There was no deed of daring that he would not promise to perform after spring opened, and Zeb reasoned gloomily that a present lover, impassioned and importunate, would stand a better chance than an absent one who had never been able to speak for himself.

When it was settled that Stokes should return to Opinquake, Zeb determined that he would not give up the prize to Zeke without one decisive effort; and as he was rubbing the cobbler's leg, he stammered, "I say Ezra, will you do me a turn? 'Twon't be so much, what I ask, except that I'll like you to keep mum about it, and you're a good hand at keeping mum."

"I know what yer driving at, Zeb. Write yer letter and I'll deliver it with my own hands."

"Well, now, I'm satisfied, I can stay on and fight it out with a clear mind. When Zeke marched away last summer, I thought it was all up with me; and I can tell you that any fighting that's to do about Boston will be fun compared with the fighting I did while hoeing corn and mowing grass. But I don't believe that Susie Rolliffe is promised to Zeke Watkins, or any one else yet, and I'm going to give her a chance to refuse me plump."

"That's the way to do it, Zeb," said the bachelor cobbler, with an emphasis that would indicate much successful experience. "Asking a girl plump is like standing up in a fair fight. It gives the girl a chance to bowl you over, if that's her mind, so there can't be any mistake about it; and it seems to me the women-folks ought to have all the chances that in any way belong to them. They have got few enough anyhow."

"And you think it'll end in my being bowled over?"

"How should I know, or you either, unless you make a square trial? You're such a strapping, fighting feller that nothing but a cannon-ball or a woman ever will knock you off your pins."

"See here, Ezra Stokes, the girl of my heart may refuse me just as plump as I offer myself; and if that's her mind she has a right to do it. But I don't want either you or her to think I won't stand on my feet. I won't even fight any more recklessly than my duty requires. I have a mother to take care of, even if I never have a wife."

"I'll put in a few pegs right along to keep in mind what you say; and I'll give you a fair show by seeing to it that the girl gets your letter before Zeke can steal a march on you."

"That's all I ask," said Zeb, with compressed lips. "She shall choose between us. It's hard enough to write, but it will be a sight easier than facing her. Not a word of this to another soul, Ezra; but I'm not going to use you like a mail-carrier, but a friend. After all, there are few in Opinquake, I suppose, but know I'd give my eyes for her, so there isn't much use of my putting on secret airs."

"I'm not a talker, and you might have sent your letter by a worse messenger'n me," was the laconic reply.

Zeb had never written a love-letter, and was at a loss

how to begin or end it. But time pressed, and he had to say what was uppermost in his mind. It ran as follows:

"I don't know how to write so as to give my words weight. I cannot come home; I will not come as long as mother and the children can get on without me. And men are needed here; men are needed. The general fairly pleads with the soldiers to stay. Stokes would stay if he could. We're almost driving him home. I know you will be kind to him, and remember he has few to care for him. I cannot speak for myself in person very soon, if ever. Perhaps I could not if I stood before you. You laugh at me; but if you knew how I love you and remember you, how I honor and almost worship you in my heart, you might understand me better. Why is it strange I should be afraid of you? Only God has more power over me than you. Will you be my wife? I will do anything to win you that YOU can ask. Others will plead with you in person. Will you let this letter plead for the absent?"

Zeb went to the captain's quarters and got some wax with which to seal this appeal, then saw Stokes depart with the feeling that his destiny was now at stake.

Meanwhile Zeke Watkins, with a squad of homeward-bound soldiers, was trudging toward Opinquake. They soon began to look into one another's faces in something like dismay. But little provision was in their wallets when they had started, for there was little to draw upon, and that furnished grudgingly, as may well be supposed. Zeke had not cared. He remembered the continuous feasting that had attended his journey to camp, and supposed that he would only have to present himself to the roadside farmhouses in order to enjoy the fat of the land. This hospitality he proposed to repay abundantly by camp reminiscences in which it would not be difficult to insinuate that the hero of the scene was present.

In contrast to these rose-hued expectations, doors were slammed in their faces, and they were treated little better than tramps. "I suppose the people near Boston have been called on too often and imposed on, too," Zeke reasoned rather ruefully. "When we once get over the Connecticut border we'll begin to find ourselves at home;" and spurred by hunger and cold, as well as hope, they pushed on desperately, subsisting on such coarse provisions as they could obtain, sleeping in barns when it stormed, and not infrequently by a fire in the woods. At last they passed the Connecticut border, and led by Zeke they urged their way to a large farmhouse, at which, but a few months before, the table had groaned under rustic dainties, and feather-beds had luxuriously received the weary recruits bound to the front. They approached the opulent farm in the dreary dark of the evening, and pursued by a biting east wind laden with snow. Not only the weather, but the very dogs seemed to have a spite against them; and the family had to rush out to call them off.

"Weary soldiers ask for shelter," began Zeke.

"Of course you're bound for the lines," said the matronly housewife. "Come in."

Zeke thought they would better enter at once before explaining; and truly the large kitchen, with a great fire blazing on the hearth, seemed like heaven. The door leading into the family sitting-room was open, and there was another fire, with the red-cheeked girls and the white-haired grandsire before it, their eyes turned expectantly toward the new-comers. Instead of hearty welcome, there was a questioning look on every face, even on that of the kitchen-maid. Zeke's four companions had a sort of hang-dog look - for they had been cowed by the treatment received along the road; but he tried to bear himself confidently, and began with an insinuating smile, "Perhaps I should hardly expect you to remember me. I passed this way last summer -"

"Passed this way last summer?" repeated the matron, her face growing stern. "We who cannot fight are ready and glad to share all we have with those who fight for us. Since you carry arms we might very justly think you are hastening forward to use them."

"These are our own arms; we furnished them ourselves," Zeke hastened to say.

"Oh, indeed," replied the matron, coldly; "I supposed that not only the weapons, but the ones who carry them, belonged to the country. I hope you are not deserting from the army."

"I assure you we are not. Our terms of enlistment have expired."

"And your country's need was over at the same moment? Are you hastening home at this season to plow and sow and reap?"

"Well, madam, after being away so long we felt like having a little comfort and seeing the folks. We stayed a long as we agreed. When spring opens, or before, if need be -"

"Pardon me, sir; the need is now. The country is not to be saved by men who make bargains like day-laborers, and who quit when the hour is up, but by soldiers who give themselves to their country as they would to their wives and sweethearts. My husband and sons are in the army you have deserted. General Washington has written to our governor asking whether an example should not be made of the men who have deserted the cause of their country at this critical time when the enemy are receiving re-enforcements. We are told that Connecticut men have brought disgrace on our colony and have imperilled the whole army. You feel like taking comfort and seeing the folks. The folks do not feel like seeing you. My husband and the brave men in the lines are in all the more danger because of your desertion, for a soldier's time never expires when the enemy is growing stronger and threatening every home in the land. If all followed your example, the British would soon be upon your heels, taking from us our honor and our all. We are not ignorant of the critical condition of our army; and I can tell you, sir, that if many more of our men come home, the women will take their places."

Zeke's companions succumbed to the stern arraignment, and after a brief whispered consultation one spoke for the rest. "Madam," he said, "you put it in a way that we hadn't realized before. We'll right-about-face and march back in the morning, for we feel that we'd rather face all the British in Boston than any more Connecticut women."

"Then, sirs, you shall have supper and shelter and welcome," was the prompt reply.

Zeke assumed an air of importance as he said: "There

are reasons why I must be at home for a time, but I not only expect to return, but also to take many back with me."

"I trust your deeds may prove as large as your words," was the chilly reply; and then he was made to feel that he was barely tolerated. Some hints from his old associates added to the disfavor which the family took but little pains to conceal. There was a large vein of selfish calculation in Zeke's nature, and he was not to be swept away by any impulses. He believed he could have a prolonged visit home, yet manage so admirably that when he returned he would be followed by a squad of recruits, and chief of all he would be the triumphant suitor of Susie Rolliffe. Her manner in parting had satisfied him that he had made go deep an impression that it would be folly not to follow it up. He trudged the remainder of the journey alone, and secured tolerable treatment by assuring the people that he was returning for recruits for the army. He reached home in the afternoon of Christmas; and although the day was almost completely ignored in the Puritan household, yet Mrs. Watkins forgot country, Popery, and all, in her mother love, and Zeke supped on the finest turkey of the flock. Old Mr. Watkins, it is true, looked rather grim, but the reception had been reassuring in the main; and Zeke had resolved on a line of tactics which would make him, as he believed, the military hero of the town. After he had satisfied an appetite which had been growing ever since he left camp, he started to call on Susie in all the bravery of his best attire, filled with sanguine expectations inspired by memories of the past and recent potations of cider.

Meanwhile Susie had received a guest earlier in the day. The stage had stopped at the gate where she had stood in the September sunshine and waved her bewildered farewell to Zeb. There was no bewilderment or surprise now at her strange and unwonted sensations. She had learned why she had stood looking after him dazed and spellbound. Under the magic of her own light irony she had seen her drooping rustic lover transformed into the ideal man who could face anything except her unkindness. She had guessed the deep secret of his timidity. It was a kind of fear of which she had not dreamed, and which touched her innermost soul.

When the stage stopped at the gate, and she saw the driver helping out Ezra Stokes, a swift presentiment made her sure that she would hear from one soldier who was more to her than all the generals. She was soon down the walk, the wind sporting in her light-gold hair, supporting the cobbler on the other side.

"Ah, Miss Susie!" he said, "I am about worn out, sole and upper. It breaks my heart, when men are so sorely needed, to be thrown aside like an old shoe."

The girl soothed and comforted him, ensconced him by the fireside, banishing the chill from his heart, while Mrs. Rolliffe warmed his blood by a strong, hot drink. Then the mother hastened away to get dinner, while Susie sat down near, nervously twisting and untwisting her fingers, with questions on her lips which she dared not utter, but which brought blushes to her cheeks. Stokes looked at her and sighed over his lost youth, yet smiled as he thought: "Guess I'll get even with that Zeb Jarvis to-day." Then he asked, "Isn't there any one you would like to hear about in camp?"

She blushed deeper still, and named every one who

had gone from Opinquake except Zeb. At last she said a little ironically: "I suppose Ezekiel Watkins is almost thinking about being a general about this time?"

"Hasn't he been here telling you what he is thinking about?"

"Been here! Do you mean to say he has come home?"

"He surely started for home. All the generals and a yoke of oxen couldn't 'a' kept him in camp, he was so homesick - lovesick too, I guess. Powerful compliment to you, Miss Susie," added the politic cobbler, feeling his way, "that you could draw a man straight from his duty like one of these 'ere stump-extractors."

"No compliment to me at all!" cried the girl, indignantly. "He little understands me who seeks my favor by coming home at a time like this. The Connecticut women are up in arms at the way our men are coming home. No offence to you, Mr. Stokes. You're sick, and should come; but I'd like to go myself to show some of the strong young fellows what we think of them."

"Coming home was worse than rheumatism to me, and I'm going back soon's I kin walk without a cane. Wouldn't 'a' come as 'tis, if that Zeb Jarvis hadn't jes' packed me off. By Jocks! I thought you and he was acquainted, but you don't seem to ask arter him."

"I felt sure he would try - I heard he was doing his duty," she replied with averted face.

"Zeke Watkins says he's no soldier at all - nothing but a dirt-digger."

For a moment, as the cobbler had hoped, Susie forgot her blushes and secret in her indignation. "Zeke Watkins indeed!" she exclaimed. "He'd better not tell ME any such story. I don't believe there's a braver, truer man in the - Well," she added in sudden confusion, "he hasn't run away and left others to dig their way into Boston, if that's the best way of getting there."

"Ah, I'm going to get even with him yet," chuckled Stokes to himself. "Digging is only the first step, Miss Susie. When Old Put gets good and ready, you'll hear the thunder of the guns a'most in Opinquake."

"Well, Mr. Stokes," stammered Susie, resolving desperately on a short cut to the knowledge she craved, "you've seen Mr. Jarvis a-soldiering. What do you think about it?"

"Well, now, that Zeb Jarvis is the sneakin'ist fellow -"

"What?" cried the girl, her face aflame.

"Wait till I get in a few more pegs," continued Stokes, coolly. "The other night he sneaked right into the enemy's lines and carried off a British officer as a hawk takes a chicken. The Britisher fired his pistol right under Zeb's nose; but, law! he didn't mind that any more'n a 'sketer-bite. I call that soldiering, don't you? Anyhow, Old Put thought it was, and sent for him 'fore daylight, and made a sergeant of him. If I had as good a chance of gettin' rid of the rheumatiz as he has of bein' captain in six months, I'd thank the Lord."

Susie sat up very straight, and tried to look severely judicial; but her lip was quivering and her whole plump little form trembling with excitement and emotion. Suddenly she dropped her face in her hands and cried in a gust of tears and laughter: "He's just like grandfather; he'd face anything!"

"Anything in the 'tarnal uinverse, I guess, 'cept you, Miss Susie. I seed a cannon-ball smash a shovel in his hands, and he got another, and went on with his work cool as a cucumber. Then I seed him writin' a letter to you, and his hand trembled -"

"A letter to me!" cried the girl, springing up.

"Yes; 'ere it is. I was kind of pegging around till I got to that; and you know -"

But Susie was reading, her hands trembling so she could scarcely hold the paper. "It's about you," she faltered, making one more desperate effort at self-preservation. "He says you'd stay if you could; that they almost drove you home. And he asks that I be kind to you, because there are not many to care for you - and - and -"

"Oh, Lord! never can get even with that Zeb Jarvis," groaned Ezra. "But you needn't tell me that's all the letter's about."

Her eyes were full of tears, yet not so full but that she eaw the plain, closing words in all their significance. Swiftly the letter went to her lips, then was thrust into her bosom, and she seized the cobbler's hand, exclaiming: "Yes, I will! I will! You shall stay with us, and be one of us!" and in her excitement she put her left hand caressingly on his shoulder.

"SUSAN!" exclaimed Mr. Rolliffe, who entered at that moment, and looked aghast at the scene.

"Yes, I WILL!" exclaimed Susie, too wrought up now for restraint.

"Will what?" gasped the mother.

"Be Zebulon Jarvis's wife. He's asked me plump and square like a soldier; and I'll answer as grandma did, and like grandma I'll face anything for his sake."

"WELL, this IS suddent!" exclaimed Mrs. Rolliffe, dropping into a chair. "Susan, do you think it is becoming and seemly for a young woman -"

"Oh, mother dear, there's no use of your trying to make a prim Puritan maiden of me. Zeb doesn't fight like a deacon, and I can't love like one. Ha! ha! ha! to think that great soldier is afraid of little me, and nothing else! It's too funny and heavenly -"

"Susan, I am dumfounded at your behavior!"

At this moment Mr. Rolliffe came in from the wood-lot, and he was dazed by the wonderful news also. In his eagerness to get even with Zeb, the cobbler enlarged and expatiated till he was hoarse. When he saw that the parents were almost as proud as the daughter over their prospective son-in-law, he relapsed into his old taciturnity, declaring he had talked enough for a month.

Susie, the only child, who apparently had inherited all the fire and spirit of her fighting ancestors, darted out, and soon returned with her rosebud of a face enveloped in a great calyx of a woollen hood.

"Where are you going?" exclaimed her parents.

"You've had the news. I guess Mother Jarvis has the next right." And she was off over the hills with almost the lightness and swiftness of a snowbird.

In due time Zeke appeared, and smiled encouragingly on Mrs. Rolliffe, who sat knitting by the kitchen fire. The matron did not rise, and gave him but a cool salutation. He discussed the coldness of the weather awkwardly for a few moments, and then ventured: "Is Miss Susan at home?"

"No, sir," replied Mrs. Rolliffe; "she's gone to make a visit to her mother-in-law that is to be, the Widow Jarvis. Ezra Stokes is sittin' in the next room, sent home sick. Perhaps you'd like to talk over camp-life with him."

Not even the cider now sustained Zeke. He looked as if a cannon-ball had wrecked all his hopes and plans instead of a shovel. "Good-evening, Mrs. Rolliffe," he stammered; "I guess I'll - I'll - go home."

Poor Mrs. Jarvis had a spiritual conflict that day which she never forgot. Susie's face had flashed at the window near which she had sat spinning, and sighing perhaps that Nature had not provided feathers or fur for a brood like hers; then the girl's arms were about her neck, the news was stammered out - for the letter could never be shown to any one - in a way that tore primness to tatters. The widow tried to act as if it were a dispensation of Providence which should be received in solemn gratitude; but before she knew it she was laughing and crying, kissing her sweet-faced daughter, or telling how good and brave Zeb had been when his heart was almost breaking.

Compunction had already seized upon the widow. "Susan," she began, "I fear we are not mortifyin' the flesh as we ought -"

"No mortifying just yet, if you please," cried Susie. "The most important thing of all is yet to be done. Zeb hasn't heard the news; just think of it! You must write and tell him that I'll help you spin the children's clothes and work the farm; that we'll face everything in Opinquake as long as Old Put needs men. Where is the ink-horn? I'll sharpen a pen for you and one for me, and SUCH news as he'll get! Wish I could tell him, though, and see the great fellow tremble once more. Afraid of me! Ha! ha! ha! that's the funniest thing - Why, Mother Jarvis, this is Christmas Day!"

"So it is," said the widow, in an awed tone. "Susie, my heart misgives me that all this should have happened on a day of which Popery has made so much."

"No, no," cried the girl. "Thank God it IS Christmas! and hereafter I shall keep Christmas as long as love is love and God is good."

JEFF'S TREASURE

CHAPTER I

ITS DISCOVERY

Jeff, the hero of my tale, was as truly a part of the Southern Confederacy as the greater Jeff at Richmond. Indeed, were it not for the humbler Jeff and the class he represented, the other Jeff would never have attained his eminence.

Jeff's prospects were as dark as himself. He owned nothing, not even himself, yet his dream of riches is the motive of my tale. Begarded as a chattel, for whom a bill of sale would have been made as readily as for a bullock, he proved himself a man and brother by a prompt exhibition of traits too common to human nature when chance and some heroism on his part gave into his hands the semblance of a fortune.

Jeff was a native Virginian and belonged to an F.F.V. in a certain practical, legal sense which thus far had not greatly disturbed his equanimity. His solid physique and full shining face showed that slavery had brought no horrors into his experience. He had indulged, it is true, in vague yearnings for freedom, but these had been checked by hearing that liberty meant "working for Yankees" - appalling news to an indolent soul. He was house-servant and man-of-all-work in a family whose means had always been limited, and whose men were in the Confederate army. His "missus" evinced a sort of weary content when he had been scolded or threatened into the completion of his tasks by nightfall. He then gave her and her daughters some compensation for their trials with him by producing his fiddle and making the warm summer evening resonant with a kind of music which the negro only can evoke. Jeff was an artist, and had a complacent consciousness of the fact. He was a living instance of the truth that artists are born, not made. No knowledge of this gifted class had ever suggested kinship; he did not even know what the word meant, but when his cheek rested lovingly against his violin he felt that he was made of different clay from other "niggahs." During the day he indulged in moods by the divine right and impulse of genius, imitating his gifted brothers unconsciously. In waiting on the table, washing dishes, and hoeing the garden, he was as great a laggard as Pegasus would have been if compelled to the labors of a cart-horse; but when night came, and uncongenial toil was over, his soul expanded. His corrugated brow unwrinkled itself; his great black fingers flew back and forth over the strings as if driven by electricity; and electric in effect were the sounds produced by his swiftly-glancing bow.

While the spirit of music so filled his heart that he could play to the moon and silent stars, an audience inspired him with tenfold power, especially if the floor was cleared or a smooth sward selected for a dance. Rarely did he play long before all who could trip a measure were on their feet, while even the super-annuated nodded and kept time, sighing that they were old. His services naturally came into great demand, and he was catholic in granting them - his mistress in good-natured tolerance acceding to requests which promised many forgetful hours at a time when the land was shadowed by war. So it happened that Jeff was often at the more pretending residences of the neighborhood, sometimes fiddling in the detached kitchen of a Southern mansion to the shuffle of heavy feet, again in the lighted parlor, especially when Confederate troops were quartered near. It was then that his strains took on their most inspiring and elevated character. He gave wings to the dark-eyed Southern girls; their feet scarcely touched the floor as they whirled with their cavaliers in gray, or threaded the mazes of the cotillon then and there in vogue.

Nor did he disdain an invitation to a crossroads tavern, frequented by poor whites and enlisted men, or when the nights were warm, to a moonlit sward, on which he would invite his audience to a reel which left all breathless. While there was a rollicking element in the strains of his fiddle which a deacon could not resist, he, with the intuition of genius, adapted himself to the class before him. In the parlor, he called off the figures of a quadrille with a "by-yer-leave-sah" air, selecting, as a rule, the highest class of music that had blessed his ears, for he was ear-taught only. He would hold a half-washed dish suspended minutes at a time while listening to one "ob de young missys at de pianny. Dat's de way I'se pick up my most scrumptious pieces. Dey cyant play nuffin in de daytime dat I cyant 'prove on in de ebenin';" and his vanity did not lead him much astray. But when with those of his own color, or with the humbler classes, he gave them the musical vernacular of the region - rude traditional quicksteps and songs, strung together with such variations of his own as made him the envy and despair of all other fiddlers in the vicinity. Indeed, he could rarely get away from a great house without a sample of his powers in this direction, and then blending with the rhythmical cadence of feet, the rustle of garments, would be evoked ripples of mirth and bursts of laughter that were echoed back from the dim pine-groves without. Finally, when with his great foot beating time on the floor and every muscle of his body in motion, he ended with an original arrangement of "Dixie," the eyes of the gentlest maiden would flash as she joined the chorus of the men in gray, who were scarcely less excited for the moment than they would have been in a headlong cavalry charge.

These were moments of glory for Jeff. In fact, on all similar occasions he had a consciousness of his power; he made the slave forget his bondage, the poor whites their poverty, maidens the absence of their fathers, brothers, and lovers, and the soldier the chances against his return.

At last there came a summer day when other music than that of Jeff's fiddle resounded through that region. Two armies met and grappled through the long sultry hours. Every moment death wounds were given and received, for thick as insects in woods, grove, and thicket, bullets whizzed on their fatal mission; while from every eminence the demoniacal shells shrieked in exultation over the havoc they wrought.

Jeff's home was on the edge of the battlefield, and as he trembled in the darkest corner of the cellar, he thought, "Dis yer beats all de thunder-gusts I eber heered crack, run togedder in one big hurricane."

With the night came silence, except as it was broken by the groans and cries of wounded men; and later the contending forces departed, having accorded to the fallen such poor burial as was given them when life was cheap and death the chief harvester in Virginia.

For a day or two Jeff's conscience was active, and the memory of the resolutions inspired by the din of war gave to his thin visage a preternatural seriousness. Dishes were washed in such brief time and so thoroughly, and such havoc made in the garden-weeds that the world might make a note of Jeff's idea of reform (to its advantage). In the evening his fiddle wailed out psalm-tunes to the entire exclusion of its former carnal strains.

It must be admitted, however, that Jeff's grace was like the early dew. On the third evening, "Ole Dan Tucker" slipped in among the hymns, and these were played in a time scarcely befitting their character. Then came a bit of news that awakened a wholly different train of thought and desire. A colored boy, more venturous than himself, was said to have picked up some "Linkum" money on the battlefield. This information shed on the wild wooded tract where the war trumpet had raged the most fiercely a light more golden than that of the moon then at its full; and Jeff resolved that with the coming night he also would explore a region which, nevertheless, had nameless terrors for him.

"Ef dere's spooks anywhere dey's dereaway," he muttered over his hoe; "but den, ki! dey woan 'fere wid dis yer niggah. What hab I'se got ter do wid de wah and de fighten an de jabbin'? De spooks cyant lay nufnn ter me eben ef ole marse an' de res' am a-fighten ter keep dere slabes, as folks say."

Having thus satisfied himself that the manes of the dead thousands could have no controversy with him, Jeff mustered sufficient resolution to visit the field that night. He took no one into his confidence, fearing if he discovered treasures of any kind he could not be left in undisturbed possession. During the day the rudiments of imagination which made him a musician had been conjuring up the possible results of his expedition.

"De ting fer dis cullud pusson ter do is ter p'ramberlate ter de Linkum lines. Ki! I doan wan' what drap outen OUR sogers' pockets. I kin git Virginny leaf widouten runnin' 'mong de spooks arter it. De place fer a big fine is whar de brush is tick and de Linkum men crawl away so dey woan be tromp on. Who knows but I kin fine a place whar a ginral hide hisself? Ob cose if he hab a lot of gole he'd stick it in de bush or kiver it right smart, so dat oders moutn't get it foh he could helf hisself."

Jeff thought he had reasoned himself into such a valorous state that he could walk across the deserted battlefield with nonchalance; but as he entered on a deeply shadowed dirt-road long since disused to any extent, he found strange creeping sensations running up and down his back. The moonlight filtered through the leaves with fantastic effects. A young silver poplar looked ghastly in the distance; and now and then a tree out off by a shot looked almost human in its mutilation.

He had not gone very far before he saw what appeared to be the body of a man lying across the road. With a sudden chill of blood he stopped and stared at the object. Gradually it resolved itself into a low mound in the dim light. Approaching cautiously, he discovered

E. P. Roe

with a dull sense of horror that a soldier had been buried where he had fallen, but covered so slightly that the tumulus scarcely more than outlined his form.

"Ob cose I knowed I d hab ter see dese tings foh I started. What Isuch a fool fer? De Feds nor de Yanks am' a-gwine ter bodder me if I am' steppin' on 'em or ober 'em." And he went scrupulously on the other side of the road.

By and by, however, he came to a part of the wood-lane where men had fallen by the score, and bodies had been covered in twos, threes, and dozens. His head felt as if his very wool were straightening itself out, as he wound here and there and zigzagged in all directions lest he should step on or over a grave. A breeze stirred the forest as if all the thousands buried in its shades had heaved a long deep sigh. With chattering teeth Jeff stopped to listen, then, reassured, continued to pick his tortuous way. Suddenly there was an ominous rustling in a thicket just behind. He broke into a headlong flight across and over everything, when the startled grunt of a hog revealed the prosaic nature of this spook. Scarcely any other sound could have been more reassuring. The animal suggested bacon and hominy and hoe-cake, everything except the ghostly. He berated himself angrily:

"Ki! you niggah! dat ar hog got mo' co'age dan you. He know he hab nuffin mo' ter do wid de spooks dan you hab. De run ain' far, and when I gits ober dat de spooks on de side dis way cyant cross arter me;" and he hastened toward the spot where he supposed the Federals had been massed the most heavily, crossing an open field and splashing through a shallow place in the river, that their ghost-ships might be reminded of running water.

On the further slope were the same sad evidences of poor mortality, graves here and there and often all too shallow, broken muskets, bullet perforated canteens and torn knapsacks - the debris of a pitched battle. Many trees and shrubs were so lacerated that their foliage hung limp and wilting, while boughs with shrivelled leaves strewed the ground. Nature's wounds indicated that men had fought here and been mutilated as ruthlessly.

For a time nothing of value rewarded Jeff's search, and he began to succumb to the grewsome associations of the place. At last he resolved to examine one more thicket that bordered an old rail-fence, and then make a long detour rather than go back by the graveyard road over which he had come. Pushing the bushes aside, he peered among their shadows for some moments, and then uttered an exclamation of surprise and terror as he bounded backward. There was no mistake this time; he had seen the figure of a man with a ray of moonlight filtering through the leaves on a ghastly bullet-hole in his temple. He sat with his back against the fence, and had not moved after receiving the shock. At his feet, dropped evidently from his nerveless hand, lay a metal box. All had flashed almost instantaneously on Jeff's vision.

For some moments he was in doubt whether to take to his heels homeward or reconnoitre again. The soldier sat in such a lifelike attitude that while Jeff knew the man must be dead, taking the box seemed like robbing the living. Yes, worse than that, for, to the superstitious negro, the dead soldier appeared to be watching his treasure.

E. P. Roe

Jeff's cupidity slowly mastered his fears. Cautiously approaching the figure, he again pushed aside the screening boughs, and with chattering teeth and trembling limbs, looked upon the silent guardian of the treasure, half expecting the dead man to raise his head, and warn him off with a threatening gesture. Since the figure remained motionless, Jeff made a headlong plunge, clutched the box, then ran half a mile without thinking to look back.

Not for his life would he cross the battlefield again; so it was late when by wide circuit he approached the dwelling of his mistress. His panic had gradually subsided, and as he noted familiar objects, he felt that he was beyond the proper range of the unjust spirits of the dead.

The soldier he had left sitting against the fence troubled him, it is true; and he was not quite sure that he was through with one so palpably robbed. That he had not been followed appeared certain; that the question of future ownership of the treasure could be settled was a matter of superstitious belief. There was only one way - he must hide the box in a secret nook, and if it remained undisturbed for a reasonable length of time, he might hope for its undisturbed enjoyment. Accordingly he stole into a dense copse and buried his booty at the foot of a persimmon-tree, then gained his humble quarter and slept so late and soundly that he had to be dragged almost without the door the next morning before he shook off his lethargy.

CHAPTER II

ITS INFLUENCE

With the exception of aptitude which enabled Jeff to catch and fix a tune in his mind with a fair degree of correctness, his mental processes were slow. Moreover, whether he should ever have any trouble with "spooks" or not, one thing was true of him, as of many others in all stations of life, he was haunted by the ghost of a conscience. This uneasy spirit suggested to him with annoying iteration that his proceedings the night before had been of very unusual and doubtful character. When at last fully awake, he sought to appease the accusing voice by unwonted diligence in all his tasks, until the fat cook, a devout Baptist, took more than one occasion to say, "You'se in a promisin' frame, Jeff. Ef I'se ony shoah dat yer hole out long anuff ter get 'mersed, I'd hab hopes on yer, but, law! yer'll be a-fiddlin' de debil's tunes 'fo' de week is out. I'se afeared dat dere must be an awful prov'dence, like a battle or harricane, onst a week, ter keep yer ser'ous;" and the old woman sniffed down at him with ill-concealed disdain from her superior spiritual height.

Jeff was as serious as could have been wished all that day, for there was much on his mind. Perplexing questions tinged with supernatural terrors tormented him. Passing over those having a moral point, the most urgent one was, "S'pose dat ar soger miss him box an come arter it ternight. Ki! If I go ter see, I mont run right on ter de spook. I'se a-gwine ter gib 'im his chance, an' den take mine." So that evening Jeff fortified himself and increased the cook's hope by a succession of psalm-tunes in which there was no lapse toward the "debil's" music.

Next morning, after a long sleep, Jeff's nerves were stronger, and he began to take a high hand with conscience.

"Dat ar soger has hab his chance," he reasoned. "Ef he want de box he mus' 'a' com arter it las' night. I'se done bin fa'r wid him, an' now ter-night, ef dat ar box ain' 'sturbed, I'se a-gwine ter see de 'scription an' heft on it. Toder night I was so 'fuscated dat I couldn't know nuffin straight."

When all were sleeping, he stole to the persimmon-tree and was elated to find his treasure where he had slightly buried it. The little box seemed heavy, and was wholly unlike anything he ever seen before.

"Ob cose it's got money in it," Jeff reasoned. "Nuffin else 'ud be done up to tight and strong. I'se woan open it jes' yet, feared de missus or de colored boys 'spec' someting. Ki! I isn't a-gwine ter be tied up, an' hab dat box whip out in me. I'll tink how I kin hide an' spen' de money kine of slowcution like." With this he restored the prize to its shallow excavation and covered it with leaves that no trace of fresh earth might be visible.

Jeff's deportment now began to evince a new evolution in mental and moral process. The influence of riches was quite as marked upon him as upon so many of his white brothers and sisters, proving their essential kinship. To-day he began to sniff disdainfully at his menial tasks; and in the evening "Ole Dan Tucker" resounded from his fiddle with a rollicking abandon over which the cook groaned in despair, "Dat ar niggah's 'ligion drop off ob 'im like a yaller pig from de bush. 'Ligion dat's skeert inter us hain't no 'count anyhow."

During the next few days it was evident that Jeff was falling from grace rapidly. Never had he been so slow and careless in his tasks. More than once the thought crossed his mind that he had better take his box and "cut stick" for Washington, where he believed that wealth and his fiddle would give him prominence over his race. For prudential and other reasons he was in no haste to open the box, preferring rather to gloat over it and to think how he could spend the money to the greatest advantage. He had been paying his court to a girl as black as himself on a neighboring plantation; but he now regarded that affair as preposterous.

"She ain' good nuff fer me no mo'," he reasoned. "I'se a-gwine ter shine up ter dat yeller Suky dat's been a-holdin' her head so high ober ter Marse Perkins's. I'se invited ter play ober dar ter-night, an' I'll make dat gal open her eye. Ki! she tinks no culled gemmen in dese parts fit ter hole a cannle when she braid her long straight ha'r, but when she see de ribbin I kin git her ter tie dat ha'r up wid, an' de earrings I kin put in her ears, she larf on toder side ob her face. 'Fo' I go I'se a-gwine ter buy dat ar gole ring ob Sam Milkins down at de tavern. S'pose it does take all I'se been sabin' up, I'se needn't sabe any mo'. Dat ar box got nuff in it ter keep me like a lawd de rest ob my life. I'd open it ter-night if I wasn't goin' ter Marse Perkins's."

Jeff carried out his high-handed measures and appeared that evening at "Marse Perkins's" with a ring of portentous size squeezed on the little finger of his left hand. It had something of the color of gold, and that is the best that can be said of it; but it had left its purchaser penniless. This fact sat lightly on Jeff's mind, however, as he remembered the box at the foot of the persimmon-tree; and he stalked into the detached kitchen, where a dusky assemblage were to indulge in a shuffle, with the air of one who intends that his superiority shall be recognized at once.

"Law sakes, Jeff!" said Mandy, his hitherto ebon flame, "yer comes in like a turkey gobbler. Doesn't yer know me?"

"Sartin I know yer, Mandy. You'se a good gal in you'se way, but, law! you'se had yer spell. A culled gemmen kin change his min' when he sees dat de 'finity's done gone."

"Look here, Jeff Wobbles, does yer mean ter give me de sack?"

"I mean ter gib yer good-ebenin', Miss Mandy Munson. Yer kyant 'spec' a gemmen to be degaged in de music an' a gal at de same time," replied Jeff, with oppressive gravity.

"Mister Johnsing, I'se tank yer fo' yer arm," said Mandy to a man near, with responsive dignity. "Yer wait on me here, an' yer kin wait on me home. I'se 'shamed on mysef dat I took up wid a lout dat kin do nuffin but fiddle; but I was kine ob sorry fer him, he sich a fool."

"Go 'long," remarked Jeff, smiling mysteriously. 'Ef yer knowed, yer 'ud be wringin' yer han's wuss dan yer did at de las' 'tracted meetin'. Ah, Miss Suky, dat you?" and Jeff for the first time doffed his hat.

"Wat's in de win', Jeff, dat yer so scrumptious an' bumptious like dis ebenin'?" Suky asked a trifle scornfully.

"Wen de 'freshments parse 'roun', I'se 'steem it a oblergation ter me ef yer'll let me bring yer de cake an' cider. I'se sumpin fer yer. Gemmen an' ladies, took yer places," he added in a stentorian voice; "I ax yer' sideration fer bein' late, cose I had 'portant business; now,

"Bow dar, scrape dar; Doan hang about de doah. Shine up ter de pretty gals. An,' lead 'em on de floah" -

his fiddle seconding his exhortation with such inciting strains that soon there was not a foot but was keeping time.

Suky observed that the musician had eyes for her only, and that toward all others he maintained his depressing superiority. In vain did Mandy lavish tokens of favor on "Mister Johnsing." Jeff did not lose his sudden and unexpected indifference; while the great ring glistening on his finger added to the mystery. There were many whispered surmises; but gradually the conjecture that he had "foun' a heap ob Linkum money" was regarded as the best explanation of the marked change in his bearing.

Curiosity soon became more potent than Jeff's fiddle, and the "'freshments" were hurried up. So far from resenting this, Jeff put his violin under his arm and stalked across the improvised ball-room to Miss Suky, oblivious of the fact that she had a suitor on either side.

"Gemmen," he remarked with condescension, "dis lady am degaged ter me durin' de 'freshments period,'" and he held out his arm in such a way that the massive ring glittered almost under Suky's nose. The magnet drew. His arm was taken in spite of the protests of the enamored swains.

"Permit me de suggestion," continued Jeff, "dat ter a lady ob yer 'finement, dis place am not fit ter breve in. Wha's mo', I doan 'cline ter hab dese yer common niggahs a-whisperin' an' a-pintin' an' a-'jecturin' about us. Lemme yet yer a seat under de lite ob de risin' moon. De dusk'll obscuate yer loveliness so I'se dar' tell all de news."

Suky, mystified and expectant, but complacent over another conquest, made no objections to these whispered "suggestions," and was led to a seat under the shadow of a tree. A chorus of not very flattering remarks broke out, ceasing as suddenly when Jeff returned for a portion of the cake and cider.

"Mister Wobbles, yer's prettin' on high de airs ter-night," Suky remarked, with an interrogation point in her voice.

"Here's ter de health ob Mrs. Wobbles," he answered, lifting the cider to his lips.

"I'se no 'jections ter dat. Who is she ter be?" replied Suky, very innocently.

"It's not my 'tention ter go furder and far' wuss. Dis am a case wha de presen' company am not 'cepted."

"No, not axcepted jes' yet, Mr. Wobbles, if yer'se 'dressin' yer remarks ter me. Yer is goin' on jes' a little too far."

"P'raps a little far; but yer'll soon catch up wid me. Yer'se a lady dat got a min' ob her own, I hope?"

"It's mine yet, anyhow."

"An' yer kin keep as mum as a possum w'en de cawn is in de milk?"

"Dat 'pends."

"Obcose it does. But I'll trus' yer; yer ain' de one ter bite yer own nose off. Does yer see dat ar ring, Suky? Law! how pretty dat look on yer degaged finger!"

"'Tain' dar yet."

"Lemme put it dar. Ki! wouldn't dey look an' gape an' pint in dar yonder w'en yer come a-sailin' in wid dat ring on?"

"Yes; dey tink me a big fool ter be captivated by a ring - brass, too, like anuff."

"No, Suky, it's gole - yallow gole, di 'plexion ob yer own fair han'. But, law! dis ain' nuffin ter what I'se 'll git yer. Yer'se shall hab rings an' dresses an' jules till yer 'stinguish de oder gals like de sun put out de stars."

"What yer foun', Jeff Wobbles?"

"I'se foun' what'll make yer a lady if yer hab sense. I'se gib yer de compliment ob s'lecting yer ter shar' my fine if yer'll lemme put dis ring on yer degaged finger."

"Yer doan say nuffin 'bout lub in dis yer 'rangement," Suky simpered, sidling up to him.

"Oh, dat kind ob sent'ment 'll do fer common niggahs," Jeff explained with dignity. "I'se hurd my missus talk 'bout 'liances 'twixt people of quality. Ki! Suky, I'se in a'sition now ter make a 'liance wid yer. Yer ain' like dat low gal, Mandy. What Mister Johnsing ebber hab ter gib her but a lickin' some day? I'se done wid dat common class; I may fiddle fur 'em now an' den, jes' ter see dem sport deysefs, while I'se lookin' on kin' ob s'periur like, yer know. But den, dey ain' our kin' ob folks. Yer'se got qulities dat'll shine like de risin' moon dar." Then in a whisper he added, "De Linkum sogers is off dar ter the east'erd. One night's trabel an' dey'd sen' us on ter Washin'on. Onst yer git dar, an' hab all de jules an' dresses dat I gib yer, dar's not a culled gemmen dereaway but 'ud bow down ter yer."

Here was a dazzling vista that Suky could not resist. Her ideas of freedom, like those of Jeff, were not very exalted. At that period, slave property in the vicinity of the Union lines was fast melting away; and scarcely a night elapsed but some one was missing, the more adventurous and intelligent escaping first, and others following as opportunity and motive pointed the way. The region under consideration had not yet been occupied by the Federals, and there was still no slight risk involved in flight. Suky did not realize the magnitude of the project. She was not the first of her sex to be persuaded by a cavalier and promised gold to take a leap into the dark.

As a result of Jeff's representations the "'liance" was made there and then, secrecy promised, and an escape to Washington agreed upon as soon as circumstances permitted - Suky's mind, I regret to say, dwelling more on "gemmen bowing down" to her than on the devotion of the allied suitor.

No lady of rank in Timbuctoo could have sailed into the kitchen ball-room with greater state than Suky now after the compact had been made, Jeff supporting her on his arm with the conscious air of one who has taken the prize from all competitors. With the assurance of a potentate he ensconced himself in the orchestra corner and called the dancers to their feet.

But the spirit of mutiny was present. Eager eyes noted that the ring on his bow-hand was gone. Then it was seen glistening on Suky's hand as she ostentatiously fanned herself. The clamor broke out, "Mister Johnsing," incited by Mandy and the two swains between whom Suky had been sandwiched, leading the revolt against Jeff's arrogance and success.

There were many, however, who had no personal wrongs to right, and who did not relish being made a cat's-paw by the disaffected. These were bent on the natural progression and conclusion of the dance. In consequence of the wordy uproar the master of the premises appeared and cleared them all out, sending his own servants to their quarters.

Jeff nearly came to grief that night, for a party of the malcontents followed him on his homeward walk. Suspecting their purpose, he dodged behind some shrubbery, heard their threats to break his head and smash his fiddle, and then went back to a tryst with Suky.

That sagacious damsel had been meditating on the proposed alliance. Even in her rather sophisticated mind she had regarded a semblance of love as essential; but since Jeff had put everything on such superior grounds, she felt that she should prove herself fit for new and exalted conditions of life by seeing to it that he made good all his remarkable promises. She remembered that he had not yet opened the box of money, and became a little sceptical as to its contents. Somebody might have watched Jeff, and have carried it off.

True, she had the ring, but that was not the price of her hand. Nothing less than had been promised would answer now; and when she stole out to meet Jeff she told him so. Under the witching moonlight he began to manifest tendencies to sentiment and tenderness. Her response was prompt: "Go 'long! what dese common niggah ways got ter do wid a 'liance? Yer show me de gole in dat box - dat's de bargain. Den de 'liance hole me fas', an' I'll help yer spen' de money in Washin'on. We'll hab a weddin' scrumptious as white folks. But, law sakes! Jeff Wobbles, 't ain' no kin' ob 'liance till I see dat gole an' hab some ob it too!"

Jeff had to succumb like many a higher-born suitor before him, with the added chagrin of remembering that he had first suggested the purely businesslike aspect of his motive.

"Berry well; meet me here ter-morrer night when I whistle like a whip-o'-will. But yer ain' so smart as yer tink yer are, Suky. Yer'se made it cl'ar ter me dat I'se got ter keep de han'lin' ob dat gole or you'll be a-carryin' dis 'liance business too far! If I gib yer gole, I expec' yer ter shine up an be 'greeable-like ter me ebbery way yer know how. Dat's only fa'r, doggoned ef it ain'!" and Jeff spoke in a very aggrieved tone.

Wily Suky chucked him under the chin, saying: "Show me de color ob de gole an' de 'liance come out all right." Then she retired, believing that negotiations had proceeded far enough for the present.

Jeff went home feeling that he had been forewarned and forearmed. Since her heart responded to a golden key only, he would keep that key and use it judiciously.

During the early hours of the following night Jeff was very wary and soon discovered that he was watched. He coolly slipped the collar from a savage dog, and soon there was a stampede from a neighboring grove. An hour after, when all had become quiet again, he took the dog and, armed with an axe, started out, fully resolved on breaking the treasure-box which he had been hoarding.

The late moon had risen, giving to Jeff a gnome-like aspect as he dug at the root of the persimmon-tree. The mysterious box soon gleamed with a pale light in his hand, like the leaden casket that contained Portia's radiant face. Surely, when he struck the "open sesame" blow, that beauty which captivates young and old alike would dazzle his eyes. With heart now devoid of all compunction, and exultant in anticipation, he struck the box, shaving off the end he held furthest from him. An "ancient fish-like smell" filled the air; Jeff sank on the ground and stared at sardines and rancid oil dropping instead of golden dollars from his treasure-box. They scarcely touched the ground before the dog snapped them all up.

The bewildered negro knew not what to think. Had fish been the original contents of the box, or had the soldier's spook transformed the gold into this horrid mess? One thing, however, was clear - he had lost, not only Suky, but prestige. The yellow girl would scorn him, and tell of his preposterous promises. Mandy had been offended beyond hope, and he would become the laughing-stock and byword of all the colored boys for miles around.

"Dar's nuffin lef fer me but ter put out fer freedom," he soliloquized; "ki! I'se a-gwine ter git eben wid dat yallar gal yet. I'll cut stick ter-morrer night and she'll tink I 'sconded alone, totin' de box wid me, and dat she was too sharp in dat 'liance business."

So it turned out; Jeff and his fiddle vanished, leaving nothing to sustain Suky under the gibes of her associates except the ring, which she eventually learned was as brazen as her own ambition.

Jefi wandered into the service of a Union officer whose patience he tried even more than that of his tolerant Southern mistress; but when by the camp-fire he brought out his violin, all his shortcomings were condoned.

CAUGHT ON THE EBB-TIDE

The August morning was bright and fair, but Herbert Scofield's brow was clouded. He had wandered off to a remote part of the grounds of a summer hotel on the Hudson, and seated in the shade of a tree, had lapsed into such deep thought that his cigar had gone out and the birds were becoming bold in the vicinity of his motionless figure.

It was his vacation time and he had come to the country ostensibly for rest. As the result, he found himself in the worst state of unrest that he had ever known. Minnie Madison, a young lady he had long admired, was the magnet that had drawn him hither. Her arrival had preceded his by several weeks; and she had smiled a little consciously when in looking at the hotel register late one afternoon his bold chirography met her eye.

"There are so many other places to which he might have gone," she murmured.

Her smile, however, was a doubtful one, not expressive of gladness and entire satisfaction. In mirthful, saucy fashion her thoughts ran on: "The time has come when he might have a respite from business. Does he still mean business by coming here? I'm not sure that I do, although the popular idea seems to be that a girl should

E. P. Roe

have no vacation in the daily effort to find a husband. I continually disappoint the good people by insisting that the husband must find me. I have a presentiment that Mr. Scofield is looking for me; but there are some kinds of property which cannot be picked up and carried off, nolens volens, when found."

Scofield had been animated by no such clearly defined purpose as he was credited with when he sought the summer resort graced by Miss Madison. His action seemed to him tentative, his motive ill-defined even in his own consciousness, yet it had been strong enough to prevent any hesitancy. He knew he was weary from a long year's work. He purposed to rest and take life very leisurely, and he had mentally congratulated himself that he was doing a wise thing in securing proximity to Miss Madison. She had evoked his admiration in New York, excited more than a passing interest, but he felt that he did not know her very well. In the unconventional life now in prospect he could see her daily and permit his interest to be dissipated or deepened, as the case might be, while he remained, in the strictest sense of the world, uncommitted. It was a very prudent scheme and not a bad one. He reasoned justly: "This selecting a wife is no bagatelle. A man wishes to know something more about a woman than he can learn in a drawing-room or at a theatre party."

But now he was in trouble. He had been unable to maintain this judicial aspect. He had been made to understand at the outset that Miss Madison did not regard herself as a proper subject for deliberate investigation, and that she was not inclined to aid in his researches. So far from meeting him with engaging frankness and revealing her innermost soul for his inspection, he found her as elusive as only a woman of tact can be when so minded, even at a place where people meet daily. It was plain to him from the first that he was not the only man who favored her with admiring glances; and he soon discovered that young Merriweather and his friend Hackley had passed beyond the neutral ground of non-committal. He set himself the task of learning how far these suitors had progressed in her good graces; he would not be guilty of the folly of giving chase to a prize already virtually captured. This too had proved a failure. Clearly, would he know what Mr. Merriweather and Mr. Hackley were to Miss Madison he must acquire the power of mind reading. Each certainly appeared to be a very good friend of hers - a much better friend than he could claim to be, for in his case she maintained a certain unapproachableness which perplexed and nettled him.

After a week of rest, observation, and rather futile effort to secure a reasonable share of Miss Madison's society and attention, he became assured that he was making no progress whatever so far as she was concerned, but very decided progress in a condition of mind and heart anything but agreeable should the affair continue so one-sided. He had hoped to see her daily, and was not disappointed. He had intended to permit his mind to receive such impressions as he should choose; and now his mind asked no permission whatever, but without volition occupied itself with her image perpetually. He was not sure whether she satisfied his preconceived ideals of what a wife should be or not, for she maintained such a firm reticence in regard to herself that he could put his finger on no affinities. She left no doubt as to her intelligence, but beyond that she would not reveal herself to him. He was almost satisfied that she discouraged him utterly and that it would be wiser to depart before his feelings

E. P. Roe

became more deeply involved. At any rate he had better do this or else make love in dead earnest. Which course should he adopt?

There came a day which brought him to a decision.

A party had been made up for an excursion into the Highlands, Miss Madison being one of the number. She was a good pedestrian and rarely missed a chance for a ramble among the hills. Scofield's two rivals occasionally got astray with her in the perplexing wood-roads, but he never succeeded in securing such good-fortune. On this occasion, as they approached a woodchopper's cottage (or rather, hovel), there were sounds of acute distress within - the piercing cries of a child evidently in great pain. There was a moment of hesitancy in the party, and then Miss Madison's graceful indifference vanished utterly. As she ran hastily to the cabin, Scofield felt that now probably was a chance for more than mere observation, and he kept beside her. An ugly cur sought to bar entrance; but his vigorous kick sent it howling away. She gave him a quick pleased look as they entered. A slatternly woman was trying to soothe a little boy, who at all her attempts only writhed and shrieked the more. "I dunno what ails the young one," she said. "I found him a moment ago yellin' at the foot of a tree. Suthin's the matter with his leg."

"Yes," cried Miss Madison, delicately feeling of the member - an operation which, even under her gentle touch, caused increased outcry, "it is evidently broken. Let me take him on my lap;" and Scofield saw that her face had softened into the tenderest pity.

"I will bring a surgeon at the earliest possible

moment," exclaimed Scofield, turning to go.

Again she gave him an approving glance which warmed his heart. "The ice is broken between us now," he thought, as he broke through the group gathering at the open door.

Never before had he made such time down a mountain, for he had a certain kind of consciousness that he was not only going after the doctor, but also after the girl. Securing a stout horse and wagon at the hotel, he drove furiously for the surgeon, explained the urgency, and then, with the rural healer at his side, almost killed the horse in returning.

He found his two rivals at the cabin door, the rest of the party having gone on. Miss Madison came out quickly. An evanescent smile flitted across her face as she saw his kindled eyes and the reeking horse, which stood trembling and with bowed head. His ardor was a little dampened when she went directly to the poor beast and said, "This horse is a rather severe indictment against you, Mr. Scofield. There was need of haste, but - " and she paused significantly.

"Yes," added the doctor, springing out, "I never saw such driving! It's lucky our necks are not broken"

"You are all right, Doctor, and ready for your work," Scofield remarked brusquely. "As for the horse, I'll soon bring him around;" and he rapidly began to unhitch the over-driven animal.

"What are you going to do?" Miss Madison asked curiously.

"Rub him into as good shape as when he started."

She turned away to hide a smile as she thought, "He has waked up at last."

The boy was rendered unconscious, and his leg speedily put in the way of restoration. "He will do very well now if my directions are carried out strictly," the physician was saying when Scofield entered.

Mr. Merriweather and Mr. Hackley stood rather helplessly in the background and were evidently giving more thought to the fair nurse than to the patient. The mother was alternating between lamentations and invocations of good on the "young leddy's" head. Finding that he would come in for a share of the latter, Scofield retreated again. Miss Madison walked quietly out, and looking critically at the horse, remarked, "You have kept your word very well, Mr. Scofield. The poor creature does look much improved." She evidently intended to continue her walk with the two men in waiting, for she said demurely with an air of dismissal, "You will have the happy consciousness of having done a good deed this morning."

"Yes," replied Scofield, in significant undertone; "you, of all others, Miss Madison, know how inordinately happy I shall be in riding back to the village with the doctor."

She raised her eyebrows in a little well-feigned surprise at his words, then turned away.

During the remainder of the day he was unable to see her alone for a moment, or to obtain any further reason to believe that the ice was in reality broken between them. But his course was no longer noncommittal, even to the most careless observer. The other guests of the house smiled; and Mr. Merriweather and Mr. Hackley looked askance at one who threw their assiduous attentions quite into the shade. Miss Madison maintained her composure, was oblivious as far as possible, and sometimes when she could not appear blind, looked a little surprised and even offended.

He had determined to cast prudence and circumlocution to the winds. On the morning following the episode in the mountains he was waiting to meet her when she came down to breakfast. "I've seen that boy, Miss Madison, and he's doing well."

"What! so early? You are a very kind-hearted man, Mr. Scofield."

"About as they average. That you are kind-hearted I know - at least to every one except me - for I saw your expression as you examined the little fellow's injury yesterday. You thought only of the child - "

"I hope you did also, Mr. Scofield," she replied with an exasperating look of surprise.

"You know well I did not," he answered bluntly. "I thought it would be well worth while to have my leg broken if you would look at me in the same way."

"Truly, Mr. Scofield, I fear you are not as kind-hearted as I supposed you to be;" and then she turned to greet Mr. Merriweather.

"Won't you let me drive you up to see the boy?"

interposed Scofield, boldly.

"I'm sorry, but I promised to go up with the doctor this morning."

And so affairs went on. He thought at times her color quickened a little when he approached suddenly; he fancied that he occasionally surprised a half-wistful, half-mirthful glance, but was not sure. He knew that she was as well aware of his intentions and wishes as if he had proclaimed them through a speaking-trumpet. His only assured ground of comfort was that neither Mr. Merriweather nor Mr. Hackley had yet won the coveted prize, though they evidently were receiving far greater opportunities to push their suit than he had been favored with.

At last his vacation was virtually at an end. But two more days would elapse before he must be at his desk again in the city. And now we will go back to the time when we found him that early morning brooding over his prospects, remote from observation. What should he do - propose by letter? "No," he said after much cogitation. "I can see that little affected look of surprise with which she would read my plain declaration of what she knows so well. Shall I force a private interview with her? The very word 'force,' which I have unconsciously used, teaches me the folly of this course. She doesn't care a rap for me, and I should have recognized the truth long ago. I'll go back to the hotel and act toward her precisely as she has acted toward me. I can then at least take back to town a little shred of dignity."

He appeared not to see her when she came down to breakfast. After the meal was over he sat on the piazza engrossed in the morning paper. An excursion party for the mountains was forming. He merely bowed politely as she passed him to join it, but he ground his teeth as he saw Merriweather and Hackley escorting her away. When they were out of sight he tossed the paper aside and went down to the river, purposing to row the fever out of his blood. He was already satisfied how difficult his tactics would be should he continue to see her, and he determined to be absent all day, to so tire himself out that exhaustion would bring early sleep on his return.

Weary and leaden-spirited enough he was, as late in the afternoon he made his way back, but firm in sudden resolve to depart on an early train in the morning and never voluntarily to see the obdurate lady of his affections again.

Just as the sun was about sinking he approached a small wooded island about half a mile from the boat-house, and was surprised to notice a rowboat high and dry upon the beach. "Some one has forgotten that the tide is going out," he thought, as he passed; but it was no affair of his.

A voice called faintly, "Mr. Scofield!"

He started at the familiar tones, and looked again. Surely that was Miss Madison standing by the prow of the stranded skiff! He knew well indeed it was she; and he put his boat about with an energy not in keeping with his former languid strokes. Then, recollecting himself, he became pale with the self-control he purposed to maintain, "She is in a scrape," he thought; "and calls upon me as she would upon any one else to get her out of it."

E. P. Roe

Weariness and discouragement inclined him to be somewhat reckless and brusque in his words and manner. Under the compulsion of circumstances she who would never graciously accord him opportunities must now be alone with him; but as a gentleman, he could not take advantage of her helplessness, to plead his cause, and he felt a sort of rage that he should be mocked with an apparent chance which was in fact no chance at all.

His boat stranded several yards from the shore. Throwing down his oars, he rose and faced her. Was it the last rays of the setting sun which made her face so rosy, or was it embarrassment?

"I'm in a dilemma, Mr. Scofield," Miss Madison began hesitatingly.

"And you would rather be in your boat," he added.

"That would not help me any, seeing where my boat is. I have done such a stupid thing! I stole away here to finish a book, and - well - I didn't notice that the tide was running out. I'm sure I don't know what I'm going to do."

Scofield put his shoulder to an oar and tried to push his craft to what deserved the name of shore, but could make little headway. He was glad to learn by the effort, however, that the black mud was not unfathomable in depth. Hastily reversing his action, he began pushing his boat back in the water.

"Surely, Mr. Scofield, you do not intend to leave me," began Miss Madison.

"Surely not," he replied; "but then, since you are so averse to my company, I must make sure that my boat does not become as fast as yours on this ebb-tide, otherwise we should both have to wait till the flood."

"Oh, beg pardon! I now understand. But how can you reach me?"

"Wade," he replied coolly, proceeding to take off his shoes and stockings.

"What! through that horrid black mud?"

"I couldn't leap that distance, Miss Madison."

"It's too bad! I'm so provoked with myself! The mud may be very deep, or there may be a quicksand or something."

"In which case I should merely disappear a little earlier;" and he sprang overboard up to his knees, dragged the boat till it was sufficiently fast in the ooze to be stationary, then he waded ashore.

"Well," she said with a little deprecatory laugh, "it's a comfort not to be alone on a desert island."

"Indeed! Can I be welcome under any circumstances?"

"Truly, Mr. Scofield, you know that you were never more welcome. It's very kind of you."

"Any man would be glad to come to your aid. It is merely your misfortune that I happen to be the one."

"I'm not sure that I regard it as a very great misfortune.

You proved in the case of that little boy that you can act very energetically."

"And get lectured for my intemperate zeal. Well, Miss Madison, I cannot make a very pleasing spectacle with blackamoor legs, and it's time I put my superfluous energy to some use. Suppose you get in your boat, and I'll try to push it off"

She complied with a troubled look in her face. He pushed till the veins knotted on his forehead. At this she sprang out, exclaiming, "You'll burst a blood-vessel."

"That's only a phase of a ruptured heart, and you are used to such phenomena."

"It's too bad for you to talk in that way," she cried.

"It certainly is. I will now attend strictly to business."

"I don't see what you can do."

"Carry you out to my boat - that is all I can do."

"Oh, Mr. Scofield!"

"Can you suggest anything else?"

She looked dubiously at the intervening black mud, and was silent.

"I could go up to the hotel and bring Mr. Merriweather and Mr. Hackley."

She turned away to hide her tears.

"Or I could go after a brawny boatman; but delay is serious, for the tide is running out fast and the stretch of mud growing wider. Can you not imagine me Mike or Tim, or some fellow of that sort."

"No, I can't."

"Then perhaps you wish me to go for Mike or Tim?"

"But the tide is running out so fast, you said."

"Yes, and it will soon be dark."

"Oh, dear!" and there was distress in her tones.

He now said kindly, "Miss Madison, I wish that like Sir Walter Raleigh I had a mantle large enough for you to walk over. You can at least imagine that I am a gentleman, that you may soon be at the hotel, and no one ever be any the wiser that you had to choose between me and the deep - ah, well - mud."

"There is no reason for such an allusion, Mr. Scofield."

"Well, then, that you had no other choice."

"That's better. But how in the world can you manage it?"

"You will have to put your arm around my neck."

"Oh!"

"You would put your arm around a post, wouldn't you?" he asked with more than his old brusqueness.

"Yes-s; but - "

"But the tide is going out. My own boat will soon be fast. Dinner will grow cold at the hotel, and you are only the longer in dispensing with me. You must consider the other dire alternatives."

"Ob, I forgot that you were in danger of losing a warm dinner."

"You know I have lost too much to think of that or much else. But there is no need of satire, Miss Madison. I will do whatever you wish. That truly is carte blanche enough even for this occasion."

"I didn't mean to be satirical. I - I - Well, have your own way."

"Not if you prefer some other way."

"You have shown that practically there isn't any other way. I'm sorry that my misfortune, or fault rather, should also be your misfortune. You don't know how heavy - "

"I soon will, and you must endure it all with such grace as you can. Put your arm round my neck, so - oh, that will never do! Well, you'll hold tight enough when I'm floundering in the mud."

Without further ado he picked her up, and started rapidly for his boat. Stepping on a smooth stone he nearly fell, and her arm did tighten decidedly.

"If you try to go so fast," she said, "you will fall."

"I was only seeking to shorten your ordeal, but for obvious reasons must go slowly;" and he began feeling his way.

"Mr. Scofield, am I not very heavy?" she asked softly.

"Not as heavy as my heart, and you know it."

"I'm sure I - "

"No, you are not to blame. Moths have scorched their wings before now, and will always continue to do so."

Her head rested slightly against his shoulder; her breath fanned his cheek; her eyes, soft and lustrous, sought his. But he looked away gloomy and defiant, and she felt his grasp tighten vise-like around her. "I shall not affect any concealment of the feelings which she has recognized so often, nor shall I ask any favors," he thought. "There," he said, as he placed her in his boat, "you are safe enough now. Now go aft while I push off."

When she was seated he exerted himself almost as greatly as before, and the boat gradually slid into the water. He sprang in and took the oars.

"Aren't you going to put on your shoes and stockings?"

"Certainly, when I put you ashore."

"Won't that be a pretty certain way of revealing the plight in which you found me?"

"Pardon my stupidity; I was preoccupied with the thought of relieving you from the society which you have hitherto avoided so successfully;" and bending over his shoes he tied them almost savagely.

There was a wonderful degree of mirth and tenderness in her eyes as she watched him. They had floated by a little point; and as he raised his head he saw a form which he recognized as Mr. Merriweather rowing toward them. "There comes one of your shadows," he said mockingly. "Be careful how you exchange boats when he comes along-side. I will give you no help in such a case."

She looked hastily over her shoulder at the approaching oarsman. "I think it will be safer to remain in your boat," she said.

"Oh, it will be entirely safe," he replied bitterly.

"Mr. Merriweather must have seen you carrying me."

"That's another thing which I can't help."

"Mr. Scofield," she began softly.

He arrested his oars, and turned wondering eyes to hers. They were sparkling with mirth as she continued, "Are you satisfied that a certain young woman whom you once watched very narrowly is entirely to your mind?"

He caught her mirthful glance and misunderstood her. With dignity he answered, "I'm not the first man who blundered to his cost, though probably it would have made no difference. You must do me the justice, however, to admit that I did not maintain the role of observer very long - that I wooed you so openly that every one was aware of my suit. Is it not a trifle cruel to taunt me after I had made such ample amends?"

"I was thinking of Mr. Merriweather - "

"Undoubtedly"

"Since he has seen me with my arm around your neck - you know I couldn't help it - perhaps he might row the other way if - if - well, if he saw you - what shall I say - sitting over here - by me - or - Somehow I don't feel very hungry, and I wouldn't mind spending another hour - "

Scofield nearly upset the boat in his precipitous effort to gain a seat beside her - and Mr. Merriweather did row another way.

CHRISTMAS EVE IN WAR TIMES

It was the beginning of a battle. The skirmish line of the Union advance was sweeping rapidly over a rough mountainous region in the South, and in his place on the extreme left of this line was Private Anson Marlow. Tall trees rising from underbrush, rocks, bowlders, gulches worn by spring torrents, were the characteristics of the field, which was in wild contrast with the parade-grounds on which the combatants had first learned the tactics of war. The majority, however, of those now in the ranks had since been drilled too often under like circumstances, and with lead and iron shotted guns, not to know their duty, and the lines of battle were as regular as the broken country allowed. So far as many obstacles permitted, Marlow kept his proper distance from the others on the line and fired coolly when he caught glimpses of the retreating Confederate skirmishers. They were retiring with ominous readiness toward a wooded height which the enemy occupied with a force of unknown strength. That strength was soon manifested in temporary disaster to the Union forces, which were driven back with heavy loss.

Neither the battle nor its fortunes are the objects of our present concern, but rather the fate of Private Marlow. The tide of battle drifted away and left the soldier desperately wounded in a narrow ravine, through which babbled a small stream. Excepting the voices of his wife and children no music had ever sounded so sweetly in his ears. With great difficulty he crawled to a little bubbling pool formed by a tiny cascade and encircling stones, and partially slaked his intolerable thirst.

He believed he was dying - bleeding to death. The very thought blunted his faculties for a time; and he was conscious of little beyond a dull wonder. Could it be possible that the tragedy of his death was enacting in that peaceful, secluded nook? Could Nature be so indifferent or so unconscious if it were true that he was soon to lie there DEAD? He saw the speckled trout lying motionless at the bottom of the pool, the gray squirrels sporting in the boughs over his head. The sunlight shimmered and glinted through the leaves, flecking with light his prostrate form. He dipped his hand in the blood that had welled from his side, and it fell in rubies from his fingers. Could that be his blood - his life-blood; and would it soon all ooze away? Could it be that death was coming through all the brightness of that summer afternoon?

From a shadowed tree further up the glen, a wood-thrush suddenly began its almost unrivalled song. The familiar melody, heard so often from his cottage-porch in the June twilight, awoke him to the bitter truth. His wife had then sat beside him, while his little ones played here and there among the trees and shrubbery. They would hear the same song to-day; he would never hear it again. That counted for little; but the thought of their sitting behind the vines and listening to their favorite bird, spring after spring and summer after summer, and he ever absent, overwhelmed him.

E. P. Roe

"Oh, Gertrude, my wife, my wife! Oh, my children!" he groaned.

His breast heaved with a great sigh; the blood welled afresh from his wound; what seemed a mortal weakness crept over him; and he thought he died.

* * * * * * *

"Say, Eb, is he done gone?"

"'Clar to grashus if I know. 'Pears mighty like it." These words were spoken by two stout negroes, who had stolen to the battlefield as the sounds of conflict died away.

"I'm doggoned if I tink dat he's dead. He's only swoonded," asserted the man addressed as Eb. "'Twon't do to lebe 'im here to die, Zack."

"Sartin not; we'd hab bad luck all our days."

"I reckon ole man Pearson will keep him; and his wife's a po'ful nuss."

"Pearson orter; he's a Unioner."

"S'pose we try him; 'tain't so bery fur off."

* * * * * * *

On the morning of the 24th of December, Mrs. Anson Marlow sat in the living-room of her cottage, that stood well out in the suburbs of a Northern town. Her eyes were hollow and full of trouble that seemed almost beyond tears, and the bare room, that had been stripped of nearly every appliance and suggestion of comfort, but too plainly indicated one of the causes. Want was stamped on her thin face, that once had been so full and pretty; poverty in its bitter extremity was unmistakably shown by the uncarpeted floor, the meagre fire, and scanty furniture. It was a period of depression; work had been scarce, and much of the time she had been too ill and feeble to do more than care for her children. Away back in August her resources had been running low; but she had daily expected the long arrears of pay which her husband would receive as soon as the exigencies of the campaign permitted. Instead of these funds, so greatly needed, came the tidings of a Union defeat, with her husband's name down among the missing. Beyond that brief mention, so horrible in its vagueness, she had never heard a word from the one who not only sustained her home, but also her heart. Was he languishing in a Southern prison, or, mortally wounded, had he lingered out some terrible hours on that wild battlefield, a brief description of which had been so dwelt upon by her morbid fancy that it had become like one of the scenes in Dante's "Inferno"? For a long time she could not and would not believe that such an overwhelming disaster had befallen her and her children, although she knew that similar losses had come to thousands of others. Events that the world regards as not only possible but probable are often so terrible in their personal consequences that we shrink from even the bare thought of their occurrence.

If Mrs. Marlow had been told from the first that her husband was dead, the shock resulting would not have been so injurious as the suspense that robbed her of rest for days, weeks, and months. She haunted the post-office, and if a stranger was seen coming up the

E. P. Roe

street toward her cottage she watched feverishly for his turning in at her gate with the tidings of her husband's safety. Night after night she Jay awake, hoping, praying that she might hear his step returning on a furlough to which wounds or sickness had entitled him. The natural and inevitable result was illness and nervous prostration.

Practical neighbors had told her that her course was all wrong; that she should be resigned and even cheerful for her children's sake; that she needed to sleep well and live well, in order that she might have strength to provide for them. She would make pathetic attempts to follow this sound and thrifty advice, but suddenly when at her work or in her troubled sleep, that awful word "missing" would pierce her heart like an arrow, and she would moan, and at times in the depths of her anguish cry out, "Oh, where is he? Shall I ever see him again?"

But the unrelenting demands of life are made as surely upon the breaking as upon the happy heart. She and her children must have food, clothing, and shelter. Her illness and feebleness at last taught her that she must not yield to her grief, except so far as she was unable to suppress it; that for the sake of those now seemingly dependent upon her, she must rally every shattered nerve and every relaxed muscle. With a heroism far beyond that of her husband and his comrades in the field, she sought to fight the wolf from the door, or at least to keep him at bay. Although the struggle seemed a hopeless one, she patiently did her best from day to day, eking out her scanty earnings by the sale or pawning of such of her household goods as she could best spare. She felt that she would do anything rather than reveal her poverty or accept charity. Some help was more or less kindly offered, but beyond such aid as one neighbor may receive of another, she had said gently but firmly, "Not yet."

The Marlows were comparative strangers in the city where they had resided. Her husband had been a teacher in one of its public schools, and his salary small. Patriotism had been his motive for entering the army, and while it had cost him a mighty struggle to leave his family, he felt that he had no more reason to hold back than thousands of others. He believed that he could still provide for those dependent upon him, and if he fell, those for whom he died would not permit his widow and children to suffer. But the first popular enthusiasm for the war had largely died out; the city was full of widows and orphans; there was depression of spirit, stagnation in business, and a very general disposition on the part of those who had means, to take care of themselves, and provide for darker days that might be in the immediate future. Sensitive, retiring Mrs. Marlow was not the one to push her claims or reveal her need. Moreover, she could never give up the hope that tidings from her husband might at any time bring relief and safety.

But the crisis had come at last; and on this dreary December day she was face to face with absolute want. The wolf, with his gaunt eyes, was crouched beside her cold hearth. A pittance owed to her for work had not been paid. The little food left in the house had furnished the children an unsatisfying breakfast; she had eaten nothing. On the table beside her lay a note from the agent of the estate of which her home was a part, bidding her call that morning. She knew why - the rent was two months in arrears. It seemed like death to leave the house in which her husband had placed her,

E. P. Roe

and wherein she had spent her happiest days. It stood well away from the crowded town. The little yard and garden, with their trees, vines, and shrubbery, some of which her husband had planted, were all dear from association. In the rear there was a grove and open fields, which, though not belonging to the cottage, were not forbidden to the children; and they formed a wonderland of delight in spring, summer, and fall. Must she take her active, restless boy Jamie, the image of his father, into a crowded tenement? Must golden-haired Susie, with her dower of beauty, be imprisoned in one close room, or else be exposed to the evil of corrupt association just beyond the threshold?

Moreover, her retired home had become a refuge. Here she could hide her sorrow and poverty. Here she could touch what he had touched, and sit during the long winter evenings in his favorite corner by the fire. Around her, within and without, were the little appliances for her comfort which his hands had made, flow could she leave all this and live? Deep in her heart also the hope would linger that he would come again and seek her where he had left her.

"O God!" she cried suddenly. "Thou wouldst not, couldst not permit him to die without one farewell word," and she buried her face in her hands and rocked back and forth, while hard, dry sobs shook her slight, famine-pinched form.

The children stopped their play and came and leaned upon her lap.

"Don't cry, mother," said Jamie, a little boy of ten. "I'll soon be big enough to work for you; and I'll get rich, and you shall have the biggest house in town. I'll take care of you if papa don't come back."

Little Sue knew not what to say, but the impulse of her love was her best guide. She threw her arms around her mother's neck with such an impetuous and childlike outburst of affection that the poor woman's bitter and despairing thoughts were banished for a time. The deepest chord of her nature, mother love, was touched; and for her children's sake she rose up once more and faced the hard problems of her life. Putting on her bonnet and thin shawl (she had parted with much that she now so sorely needed), she went out into the cold December wind. The sky was clouded like her hopes, and the light, even in the morning hours, was dim and leaden-hued.

She first called on Mr. Jackson, the agent from whom she rented her home, and besought him to give her a little more time.

"I will beg for work from door to door," she said. "Surely in this Christian city there must be those who will give me work; and that is all I ask."

The sleek, comfortable man, in his well-appointed office, was touched slightly, and said in a voice that was not so gruff as he at first had intended it should be:

"Well, I will wait a week or two longer. If then you cannot pay something on what is already due, my duty to my employers will compel me to take the usual course. You have told me all along that your husband would surely return, and I have hated to say a word to discourage you; but I fear you will have to bring yourself to face the truth and act accordingly, as so many others have done. I know it's very hard for you,

E. P. Roe

but I am held responsible by my employer, and at my intercession he has been lenient, as you must admit. You could get a room or two in town for half what you must pay where you are. Good-morning."

She went out again into the street, which the shrouded sky made sombre in spite of preparations seen on every side for the chief festival of the year. The fear was growing strong that like Him in whose memory the day was honored, she and her little ones might soon not know where to lay their heads. She succeeded in getting the small sum owed to her and payment also for some sewing just finished. More work she could not readily obtain, for every one was busy and preoccupied by the coming day of gladness.

"Call again," some said kindly or carelessly, according to their nature. "After the holidays are over we will try to have or make some work for you."

"But I need - I must have work now," she ventured to say whenever she had the chance.

In response to this appeal there were a few offers of charity, small indeed, but from which she drew back with an instinct so strong that it could not be overcome. On every side she heard the same story. The times were very hard; requests for work and aid had been so frequent that purses and patience were exhausted. Moreover, people had spent their Christmas money on their households and friends, and were already beginning to feel poor.

At last she obtained a little work, and having made a few purchases of that which was absolutely essential, she was about to drag her weary feet homeward when the thought occurred to her that the children would want to hang up their stockings at night; and she murmured: "It may be the last chance I shall ever have to put a Christmas gift in them. Oh, that I were stronger! Oh, that I could take my sorrow more as others seem to take theirs! But I cannot, I cannot! My burden is greater than I can bear. The cold of this awful day is chilling my very heart, and my grief, as hope dies, is crushing my soul. Oh, he must be dead, he must be dead! That is what they all think. God help my little ones! Oh, what will become of them if I sink, as I fear I shall! If it were not for them I feel as if I would fall and die here in the street. Well, be our fate what it may, they shall owe to me one more gleam of happiness;" and she went into a confectioner's shop and bought a few ornamented cakes. These were the only gifts she could afford, and they must be in the form of food.

Before she reached home the snow was whirling in the frosty air, and the shadows of the brief winter day deepening fast. With a smile far more pathetic than tears she greeted the children, who were cold, hungry, and frightened at her long absence; and they, children-like, saw only the smile, and not the grief it masked. They saw also the basket which she had placed on the table, and were quick to note that it seemed a little fuller than of late.

"Jamie," she said, "run to the store down the street for some coal and kindlings that I bought, and then we will have a good fire and a nice supper;" and the boy, at such a prospect, eagerly obeyed.

She was glad to have him gone, that she might hide her weakness. She sank into a chair, so white and faint that even little Susie left off peering into the basket, and came to her with a troubled face.

"It's nothing, dearie," the poor creature said. "Mamma's only a little tired. See," she added, tottering to the table, "I have brought you a great piece of gingerbread."

The hungry child grasped it, and was oblivious and happy.

By the time Jamie returned with his first basket of kindling and coal, the mother had so far rallied from her exhaustion as to meet him smilingly again and help him replenish the dying fire.

"Now you shall rest and have your gingerbread before going for your second load," she said cheerily; and the boy took what was ambrosia to him, and danced around the room in joyous reaction from the depression of the long weary day, during which, lonely and hungry, he had wondered why his mother did not return.

"So little could make them happy, and yet I cannot seem to obtain even that little," she sighed. "I fear - indeed, I fear - I cannot be with them another Christmas; therefore they shall remember that I tried to make them happy once more, and the recollection may survive the long sad days before them, and become a part of my memory."

The room was now growing dark, and she lighted the lamp. Then she cowered shiveringly over the reviving fire, feeling as if she could never be warm again.

The street-lamps were lighted early on that clouded, stormy evening, and they were a signal to Mr. Jackson, the agent, to leave his office. He remembered that he had ordered a holiday dinner, and now found himself in a mood to enjoy it. He had scarcely left his door before a man, coming up the street with great strides and head bent down to the snow-laden blast, brushed roughly against him. The stranger's cap was drawn over his eyes, and the raised collar of his blue army overcoat nearly concealed his face. The man hurriedly begged pardon, and was hastening on when Mr. Jackson's exclamation of surprise caused him to stop and look at the person he had jostled.

"Why, Mr. Marlow," the agent began, "I'm glad to see you. It's a pleasure I feared I should never have again."

"My wife," the man almost gasped, "she's still in the house I rented of you?"

"Oh, certainly," was the hasty reply. "It'll be all right' now."

"What do you mean? Has it not been all right?"

"Well, you see," said Mr. Jackson, apologetically, "we have been very lenient to your wife, but the rent has not been paid for over two months, and - "

"And you were about to turn her and her children out-of-doors in midwinter," broke in the soldier, wrathfully. "That is the way you sleek, comfortable stay-at-home people care for those fighting your battles. After you concluded that I was dead, and that the rent might not be forthcoming, you decided to put my wife into the street. Open your office, sir, and you

E. P. Roe

shall have your rent."

"Now, Mr. Marlow, there's no cause for pitching into me in this way. You know that I am but an agent, and - "

"Tell your rich employer, then, what I have said, and ask him what he would be worth to-day were there not men like myself, who are willing to risk everything and suffer everything for the Union. But I've no time to bandy words. Have you seen my wife lately?"

"Yes," was the hesitating reply; "she was here to-day, and I - "

"How is she? What did you say to her?"

"Well, she doesn't look very strong. I felt sorry for her, and gave her more time, taking the responsibility myself - "

"How much time?"

"I said two weeks, but no doubt I could have had the time extended."

"I have MY doubts. Will you and your employer please accept my humble gratitude that you had the grace not to turn her out-of-doors during the holiday season? It might have caused remark; but that consideration and some others that I might name are not to be weighed against a few dollars and cents. I shall now remove the strain upon your patriotism at once, and will not only pay arrears, but also for two months in advance."

"Oh, there's no need of that to-day."

"Yes, there is. My wife shall feel to-night that she has a home. She evidently has not received the letter I wrote as soon as I reached our lines, or you would not have been talking to her about two weeks more of shelter."

The agent reopened his office and saw a roll of bills extracted from Marlow's pocket that left no doubt of the soldier's ability to provide for his family. He gave his receipt in silence, feeling that words would not mend matters, and then trudged off to his dinner with a nagging appetite.

As Marlow strode away he came to a sudden resolution - he would look upon his wife and children before they saw him; he would feast his eyes while they were unconscious of the love that was beaming upon them. The darkness and storm favored his project, and in brief time he saw the light in his window. Unlatching the gate softly, and with his steps muffled by the snow that already carpeted the frozen ground, he reached the window, the blinds of which were but partially closed. His children frolicking about the room were the first objects that caught his eye, and he almost laughed aloud in his joy. Then, by turning another blind slightly, he saw his wife shivering over the fire.

"Great God!" he muttered, "how she has suffered!" and be was about to rush in and take her into his arms. On the threshold he restrained himself, paused, and said, "No, not jet; I'll break the news of my return in my own way. The shock of my sudden appearance might be too great for her;" and he went back to the window. The wife's eyes were following her children with such

E. P. Roe

a wistful tenderness that the boy, catching her gaze, stopped his sport, came to her side, and began to speak. They were but a few feet away, and Marlow caught every word.

"Mamma," the child said, "you didn't eat any breakfast, and I don't believe you have eaten anything to-day. You are always giving everything to us. Now I declare I won't eat another bit unless you take half of my cake;" and he broke off a piece and laid it in her lap.

"Oh, Jamie," cried the poor woman, "you looked so like your father when you spoke that I could almost see him;" and she caught him in her arms and covered him with kisses.

"I'll soon be big enough to take care of you. I'm going to grow up just like papa and do everything for you," the boy said proudly as she released him.

Little Susie also came and placed what was left of her cake in her mother's lap, saying:

"I'll work for you, too, mamma; and to-morrow I'll sell the doll Santa Claus gave me last Christmas, and then we'll all have plenty to eat."

Anson Marlow was sobbing outside the window as only a man weeps; and his tears in the bitter cold became drops of ice before they reached the ground.

"My darlings!" the mother cried. "Oh, God spare me to you and provide some way for us! Your love should make me rich though I lack all else. There, I won't cry any more, and you shall have as happy a Christmas as I can give you. Perhaps He who knew what it was to be homeless and shelterless will provide for our need; so we'll try to trust Him and keep His birthday. And now, Jamie, go and bring the rest of the coal, and then we will make the dear home that papa gave us cheery and warm once more. If he were only with us we wouldn't mind hunger or cold, would we? Oh, my husband!" she broke out afresh, "if you could only come back, even though crippled and helpless, I feel that I could live and grow strong from simple gladness."

"Don't you think, mamma," Jamie asked, "that God will let papa come down from heaven and spend Christmas with us? He might be here like the angels, and we not see him."

"I'm afraid not," the sad woman replied, shaking her head and speaking more to herself than to the child. "I don't see how he could go back to heaven and be happy if he knew all. No, we must be patient and try to do our best, so that we can go to him. Go now, Jamie, before it gets too late. I'll get supper, and then we'll sing a Christmas hymn; and you and Susie shall hang up your stockings, just as you did last Christmas, when dear papa was with us. We'll try to do everything he would wish, and then by and by we shall see him again."

As the boy started on his errand his father stepped back out of the light of the window, then followed the child with a great yearning in his heart. He would make sure the boy was safe at home again before he carried out his plan. From a distance he saw the little fellow receive the coal and start slowly homeward with the burden, and he followed to a point where the light of the street-lamps ceased, then joined the child, and said in a gruff voice, "Here, little man, I'm going your way.

E. P. Roe

Let me carry your basket;" and he took it and strode on so fast that the boy had to run to keep pace with him. Jamie shuffled along through the snow as well as he could, but his little legs were so short in comparison with those of the kindly stranger that he found himself gradually falling behind. So he put on an extra burst of speed and managed to lay hold of the long blue skirt of the army overcoat.

"Please, sir, don't go quite so fast," he panted.

The stranger slackened his pace, and in a constrained tone of voice, asked:

"How far are you going, little man?"

"Only to our house - mamma's. She's Mrs. Marlow, you know."

"Yes, I know - that is, I reckon I do. How much further is it?"

"Oh, not much; we're most half-way now. I say, you're a soldier, aren't you?"

"Yes, my boy," said Marlow, with a lump in his throat. "Why?"

"Well, you see, my papa is a soldier, too, and I thought you might know him. We haven't heard from him for a good while, and - " choking a bit - "mamma's afraid he is hurt, or taken prisoner or something." He could not bring himself to say "killed."

Jamie let go the overcoat to draw his sleeve across his eyes, and the big man once more strode on faster than ever, and Jamie began to fear lest the dusky form might disappear in the snow and darkness with both basket and coal; but the apparent stranger so far forgot his part that he put down the basket at Mrs. Marlow's gate, and then passed on so quickly that the panting boy had not time to thank him. Indeed, Anson Marlow knew that if he lingered but a moment he would have the child in his arms.

"Why, Jamie," exclaimed his mother, "how could you get back so soon with that heavy basket? It was too heavy for you, but you will have to be mamma's little man mow."

"A big man caught up with me and carried it. I don't care if he did have a gruff voice, I'm sure he was a good kind man. He knew where we lived too, for he put the basket down at our gate before I could say a word, I was so out of breath, and then he was out of sight in a minute." Some instinct kept him from saying anything about the army overcoat.

"It's some neighbor that lives further up the street, I suppose, and saw you getting the coal at the store," Mrs. Marlow said, "Yes, Jamie, it was a good, kind act to help a little boy, and I think he'll have a happier Christmas for doing it."

"Do you really think he'll have a happier Christmas, mamma?"

"Yes, I truly think so. We are so made that we cannot do a kind act without feeling the better for it."

"Well, I think he was a queer sort of a man if he was kind. I never knew any one to walk so fast. I spoke to him once, but he did not answer. Perhaps the wind roared so he couldn't hear me."

"No doubt he was hurrying home to his wife and children," she said with a deep sigh.

When his boy disappeared within the door of the cottage, Marlow turned and walked rapidly toward the city, first going to the grocery at which he had been in the habit of purchasing his supplies. The merchant stared for a moment, then stepped forward and greeted his customer warmly.

"Well," he said, after his first exclamations of surprise were over, "the snow has made you almost as white as a ghost; but I'm glad you're not one. We scarce ever thought to see you again."

"Has my wife an open account here now?" was the brief response.

"Yes, and it might have been much larger. I've told her so too. She stopped taking credit some time ago, and when she's had a dollar or two to spare she's paid it on the old score. She bought so little that I said to her once that she need not go elsewhere to buy; that I'd sell to her as cheap as any one: that I believed you'd come back all right, and if you didn't she could pay me when she could. What do you think she did? Why, she burst out crying, and said, 'God bless you, sir, for saying my husband will come back! So many have discouraged me.' I declare to you her feeling was so right down genuine that I had to mop my own eyes. But she wouldn't take any more credit, and she bought so little that I've been troubled. I'd have sent her something, but your wife somehow ain't one of them kind that you can give things to, and - "

Marlow interrupted the good-hearted, garrulous shop-man by saying significantly, "Come with me to your back-office"; for the soldier feared that some one might enter who would recognize him and carry the tidings to his home prematurely.

"Mr. Wilkins," he said rapidly, "I wanted to find out if you too had thriftily shut down on a soldier's wife. You shall not regret your kindness."

"Hang it all!" broke in Wilkins, with compunction, "I haven't been very kind. I ought to have gone and seen your wife and found out how things were; and I meant to, but I've been so confoundedly busy - "

"No matter now; I've not a moment to spare. You must help me to break the news of my return in my own way. I mean they shall have such a Christmas in the little cottage as was never known in this town. You could send a load right over there, couldn't you?"

"Certainly, certainly," said Wilkins, under the impulse of both business thrift and goodwill; and a list of tea, coffee, sugar, flour, bread, cakes, apples, etc., was dashed off rapidly; and Marlow had the satisfaction of seeing the errand-boy, the two clerks, and the proprietor himself busily working to fill the order in the shortest possible space of time.

He next went to a restaurant, a little further down the street, where he had taken his meals for a short time before he brought his family to town, and was greeted with almost equal surprise and warmth. Marlow cut short all words by his almost feverish haste. A huge turkey had just been roasted for the needs of the coming holiday, and this with a cold ham and a pot of coffee was ordered to be sent in a covered tray within a quarter of an hour. Then a toy-shop was visited, and such a doll purchased! for tears came into Marlow's eyes whenever he thought of his child's offer to sell her dolly for her mother's sake.

After selecting a sled for Jamie, and directing that they should be sent at once, he could restrain his impatience no longer, and almost tore back to his station at the cottage window. His wife was placing the meagre little supper on the table, and how poor and scanty it was!

"Is that the best the dear soul can do on Christmas Eve?" he groaned. "Why, there's scarcely enough for little Sue. Thank God, my darling, I will sit down with you to a rather different supper before long!"

He bowed his head reverently with his wife as she asked God's blessing, and wondered at her faith. Then he looked and listened again with a heart-hunger which had been growing for months.

"Do you really think Santa Claus will fill our stockings to-night?" Sue asked.

"I think he'll have something for you," she replied. "There are so many poor little boys and girls in the city that he may not be able to bring very much to you."

"Who is Santa Claus, anyway?" questioned Jamie.

Tears came into the wife's eyes as she thought of the one who had always remembered them so kindly as far as his modest means permitted.

She hesitated in her reply; and before she could decide upon an answer there was a knock at the door. Jamie ran to open it, and started back as a man entered with cap, eyebrows, beard, and shaggy coat all white with the falling snow. He placed two great baskets of provisions on the floor, and said they were for Mrs. Anson Marlow.

"There is some mistake," Mrs. Marlow began; but the children, after staring a moment, shouted, "Santa Claus! Santa Claus!"

The grocer's man took the unexpected cue instantly, and said, "No mistake, ma'am. They are from Santa Claus;" and before another word could be spoken he was gone. The face of the grocer's man was not very familiar to Mrs. Marlow, and the snow had disguised him completely. The children had no misgivings and pounced upon the baskets and with, exclamations of delight drew out such articles as they could lift.

"I can't understand it," said the mother, bewildered and almost frightened.

"Why, mamma, it's as plain as day," cried Jamie. "Didn't he look just like the pictures of Santa Claus - white beard and white eyebrows? Oh, mamma, mamma, here is a great paper of red-cheeked apples!" and he and Susie tugged at it until they dragged it over the side of the basket, when the bottom of the bag came out, and the fruit flecked the floor with red and gold. Oh, the bliss of picking up those apples; of comparing one with another; of running to the mother and asking which was the biggest and which the reddest and most beautifully streaked!

"There must have been some mistake," the poor woman kept murmuring as she examined the baskets and found how liberal and varied was the supply, "for who could or would have been so kind?"

"Why, mommie," said little Sue, reproachfully, "Santa Claus brought 'em. Haven't you always told us that Santa Claus liked to make us happy?"

The long-exiled father felt that he could restrain himself but a few moments longer, and he was glad to see that the rest of his purchases were at the door. With a look so intent, and yearning concentration of thought so intense that it was strange that they could not feel his presence, he bent his eyes once more upon a scene that would imprint itself upon his memory forever.

But while he stood there, another scene came before his mental vision. Oddly enough his thought went back to that far-off Southern brookside, where he had lain with his hands in the cool water. He leaned against the window-casing, with the Northern snow whirling about his head; but he breathed the balmy breath of a Southern forest, the wood-thrush sang in the trees overhead, and he could - so it seemed to him - actually feel the water-worn pebbles under his palms as he watched the life-blood ebbing from his side. Then there was a dim consciousness of rough but kindly arms bearing him through the underbrush, and more distinctly the memory of weary weeks of convalescence in a mountaineer's cabin. All these scenes of peril, before he finally reached the Union lines, passed before him as he stood in a species of trance beside the window of his home.

The half-grown boys sent from the restaurant and

toy-shop could not be mistaken for Santa Claus even by the credulous fancy of the children, and Mrs. Marlow stepped forward eagerly and said:

"I am sure there is some mistake. You are certainly leaving these articles at the wrong house." The faces of the children began to grow anxious and troubled also, for even their faith could not accept such marvellous good-fortune. Jamie looked at the sled with a kind of awe, and saw at a glance that it was handsomer than any in the street "Mr. Lansing, a wealthy man, lives a little further on," Mrs. Marlow began to urge; "and these things must be meant - "

"Isn't your name Mrs. Anson Marlow?" asked the boy from the restaurant.

"Yes."

"Then I must do as I've been told;" and he opened his tray and placed the turkey, the ham, and the coffee on the table.

"If he's right, I'm right too," said he of the toy-shop. "Them was my directions;" and they were both about to depart when the woman sprang forward and gasped: "Stay!"

She clasped her hands and trembled violently.

"Who sent these things?" she faltered.

"Our bosses, mum," replied the boy from the restaurant, hesitatingly.

She sprang toward him, seized his arm, and looked

imploringly into his face. "Who ordered them sent?" she asked in a low, passionate voice.

The young fellow began to smile, and stammered awkwardly, "I don't think I'm to tell."

She released his arm and glanced around with a look of intense expectation.

"Oh, oh!" she gasped with quick short sobs, "can it be - " Then she sprang to the door, opened it, and looked out into the black, stormy night. What seemed a shadow rushed toward her; she felt herself falling, but strong arms caught and bore her, half fainting, to a lounge within the room.

Many have died from sorrow, but few from joy. With her husband's arms around her Mrs. Marlow's weakness soon passed. In response to his deep, earnest tones of soothing and entreaty, she speedily opened her eyes and gave him a smile so full of content and unutterable joy that all anxiety in her behalf began to pass from his mind.

"Yes," she said softly, "I can live now. It seems as if a new and stronger life were coming back with every breath."

The young fellows who had been the bearers of the gifts were so touched that they drew their rough sleeves across their eyes as they hastened away, closing the door on the happiest family in the city.

A BRAVE LITTLE QUAKERESS

A TRADITION OF THE REVOLUTION

Not very far from the Highlands of the Hudson, but at a considerable distance from the river, there stood, one hundred years ago, a farmhouse that evidently had been built as much for strength and defence as for comfort. The dwelling was one story and a half in height, and was constructed of hewn logs, fitted closely together, and made impervious to the weather by old-fashioned mortar, which seems to defy the action of time. Two entrances facing each other led to the main or living room, and they were so large that a horse could pass through them, dragging in immense back-logs. These, having been detached from a chain when in the proper position, were rolled into the huge fireplace that yawned like a sooty cavern at the farther end of the apartment. A modern housekeeper, who finds wood too dear an article for even the air-tight stove, would be appalled by this fireplace. Stalwart Mr. Reynolds, the master of the house, could easily walk under its stony arch without removing his broad-brimmed Quaker hat. From the left side, and at a convenient height from the hearth, a massive crane swung in and out; while high above the centre of the fire was an iron hook, or trammel, from which by chains were suspended the capacious iron pots used in those days for culinary or for stock-feeding purposes.

This trammel, which hitherto had suggested only good cheer, was destined to have in coming years a terrible significance to the household.

When the blaze was moderate, or the bed of live coals not too ample, the children could sit on either side of the fireplace and watch the stars through its wide flue; and this was a favorite amusement of Phebe Reynolds, the eldest daughter of the house.

A door opened from the living-room into the other apartments, furnished in the old massive style that outlasts many generations. All the windows were protected by stout oaken shutters which, when closed, almost transformed the dwelling into a fortress, giving security against any ordinary attack. There were no loopholes in the walls through which the muzzle of the deadly rifle could be thrust and fired from within. This feature, so common in the primitive abodes of the country, was not in accordance with John Reynolds's Quaker principles. While indisposed to fight, it was evident that the good man intended to interpose between himself and his enemies all the passive resistance that his stout little domicile could offer.

And he knew that he had enemies of the bitterest and most unscrupulous character. He was a stanch Whig, loyal to the American cause, and, above all, resolute and active in the maintenance of law and order in those lawless times. He thus had made himself obnoxious to his Tory neighbors, and an object of hate and fear to a gang of marauders, who, under the pretence of acting with the British forces, plundered the country far and near. Claudius Smith, the Robin Hood of the Highlands and the terror of the pastoral low country, had formerly been their leader; and the sympathy shown by Mr. Reynolds with all the efforts to bring him to justice which finally resulted in his capture and execution, and awakened among his former associates an intense desire for revenge. This fact, well known to the farmer, kept him constantly on his guard, and filled his wife and daughter Phebe with deep apprehension.

At the time of our story, Phebe was only twelve years of age, but was mature beyond her years. There were several younger children, and she had become almost womanly in aiding her mother in their care. Her stout, plump little body had been developed rather than enfeebled by early toil, and a pair of resolute and often mirthful blue eyes bespoke a spirit not easily daunted. She was a native growth of the period, vitalized by pure air and out-of-door pursuits, and she abounded in the shrewd intelligence and demure refinement of her sect to a degree that led some of their neighbors to speak of her as "a little old woman." When alone with the children, however, or in the woods and fields, she would doff her Quaker primness, and romp, climb trees, and frolic with the wildest.

But of late, the troublous times and her father's peril had brought unwonted thoughtfulness into her blue eyes, and more than Quaker gravity to the fresh young face, which, in spite of exposure to sun and wind, maintained much of its inherited fairness of complexion. Of her own accord she was becoming a vigilant sentinel, for a rumor had reached Mr. Reynolds that sooner or later he would have a visit from the dreaded mountain gang of hard riders. Two roads leading to the hills converged on the main highway not far from his dwelling; and from an adjacent knoll Phebe often watched this place, while her father, with a lad in his employ, completed their

E. P. Roe

work about the barn. When the shadows deepened, all was made as secure as possible without and within, and the sturdy farmer, after committing himself and his household to the Divine protection, slept as only brave men sleep who are clear in conscience and accustomed to danger.

His faith was undoubtedly rewarded; but Providence in the execution of its will loves to use vigilant human eyes and ready, loving hands. The guardian angel destined to protect the good man was his blooming daughter Phebe, who had never thought of herself as an angel, and indeed rarely thought of herself at all, as is usually the case with those who do most to sweeten and brighten the world. She was a natural, wholesome, human child, with all a child's unconsciousness of self. She knew she could not protect her father like a great stalwart son, but she could watch and warn him of danger, and as the sequel proved, she could do far more.

The farmer's habits were well known, and the ruffians of the mountains were aware that after he had shut himself in he was much like Noah in his ark. If they attempted to burn him out, the flames would bring down upon them a score of neighbors not hampered by Quaker principles. Therefore they resolved upon a sudden onslaught before he had finished the evening labors of the farm. This was what the farmer feared; and Phebe, like a vigilant outpost, was now never absent from her place of observation until called in.

One spring evening she saw two mounted men descending one of the roads which led from the mountains. Instead of jogging quietly out on the highway, as ordinary travellers would have done, they disappeared among the trees. Soon afterward she caught a glimpse of two other horsemen on the second mountain road. One of these soon came into full view, and looked up and down as if to see that all was clear. Apparently satisfied, he gave a low whistle, when three men joined him. Phebe waited to see no more, but sped toward the house, her flaxen curls flying from her flushed and excited face.

"They are coming, father! Thee must be quick!" she cried.

But a moment or two elapsed before all were within the dwelling, the doors banged and barred, the heavy shutters closed, and the home-fortress made secure. Phebe's warning had come none too soon, for they had scarcely time to take breath before the tramp of galloping horses and the oaths of their baffled foes were heard without. The marauders did not dare make much noise, for fear that some passing neighbor might give the alarm. Tying their horses behind the house, where they would be hidden from the road, they tried various expedients to gain an entrance, but the logs and heavy planks baffled them. At last one of the number suggested that they should ascend the roof and climb down the wide flue of the chimney. This plan was easy of execution, and for a few moments the stout farmer thought that his hour had come. With a heroism far beyond that of the man who strikes down his assailant, he prepared to suffer all things rather than take life with his own hands.

But his wife proved equal to this emergency. She had been making over a bed, and a large basket of feathers was within reach. There were live coals on the hearth, but they did not give out enough heat to prevent the

E. P. Roe

ruffians from descending. Two of them were already in the chimney, and were threatening horrible vengeance if the least resistance was offered. Upon the coals on the hearth the housewife instantly emptied her basket of feathers; and a great volume of pungent, stifling smoke poured up the chimney. The threats of the men, who by means of ropes were cautiously descending, were transformed into choking, half-suffocated sounds, and it was soon evident that the intruders were scrambling out as fast as possible. A hurried consultation on the roof ensued, and then, as if something had alarmed them, they galloped off. With the exception of the cries of the peepers, or hylas, in an adjacent swamp, the night soon grew quiet around the closed and darkened dwelling. Farmer Reynolds bowed in thanksgiving over their escape, and then after watching a few hours, slept as did thousands of others in those times of anxiety.

But Phebe did not sleep. She grew old by moments that night as do other girls by months and years; as never before she understood that her father's life was in peril. How much that life meant to her and the little brood of which she was the eldest! How much it meant to her dear mother, who was soon again to give birth to a little one that would need a father's protection and support! As the young girl lay in her little attic room, with dilated eyes and ears intent on the slightest sound, she was ready for any heroic self-sacrifice, without once dreaming that she was heroic.

The news of the night-attack spread fast, and there was a period of increased vigilance which compelled the outlaws to lie close in their mountain fastnesses. But Phebe knew that her father's enemies were still at large with their hate only stimulated because baffled for a time. Therefore she did not in the least relax her watchfulness; and she besought their nearest neighbors to come to their assistance should any alarm be given.

When the spring and early summer passed without further trouble, they all began to breathe more freely, but one July night John Reynolds was betrayed by his patriotic impulses. He was awakened by a loud knocking at his door. Full of misgiving, he rose and hastily dressed himself: Phebe, who had slipped on her clothes at the first alarm, joined him and said earnestly:

"Don't thee open the door, father, to anybody, at this time of night;" and his wife, now lying ill and helpless on a bed in the adjoining room, added her entreaty to that of her daughter. In answer, however, to Mr. Reynolds's inquiries a voice from without, speaking quietly and seemingly with authority, asserted that they were a squad from Washington's forces in search of deserters, and that no harm would ensue unless he denied their lawful request. Conscious of innocence, and aware that detachments were often abroad on such authorized quests, Mr. Reynolds unbarred his door. The moment he opened it he saw his terrible error; not soldiers, but the members of the mountain gang, were crouched like wild beasts ready to spring upon him.

"Fly, father!" cried Phebe. "They won't hurt us;" but before the bewildered man could think what to do, the door flew open from the pressure of half a dozen wild-looking desperadoes, and he was powerless in their grasp. They evidently designed murder, but not a quick and merciful "taking off"; they first heaped upon their victim the vilest epithets, seeking in their thirst for revenge to inflict all the terrors of death in anticipation. The good man, however, now face to face with his fate, grew calm and resigned. Exasperated by his courage, they began to cut and torture him with their swords and knives. Phebe rushed forward to interpose her little form between her father and the ruffians, and was dashed, half stunned, into a corner of the room. Even for the sake of his sick wife, the brave farmer could not refrain from uttering groans of anguish which brought the poor woman with faltering steps into his presence. After one glance at the awful scene she sank, half fainting, on a settee near the door.

When the desire for plunder got the better of their fiendish cruelty, one of the gang threw a noosed rope over Mr. Reynolds's head, and then they hanged him to the trammel or iron hook in the great chimney.

"You can't smoke us out this time," they shouted. "You've now got to settle with the avengers of Claudius Smith; and you and some others will find us ugly customers to settle with."

They then rushed off to rob the house, for the farmer was reputed to have not a little money in his strong box. The moment they were gone Phebe seized a knife and cut her father down. Terror and excitement gave her almost supernatural strength, and with the aid of the boy in her father's service she got the poor man on a bed which he had occupied during his wife's illness. Her reviving mother was beginning to direct her movements when the ruffians again entered; and furious with rage, they again seized and hanged her father, while one, more brutal than the others, whipped the poor child with a heavy rope until he thought she was disabled. The girl at first cowered and shivered under the blows, and then sank as if lifeless on the floor. But the moment she was left to herself she darted forward and once more cut her father down. The robbers then flew upon the prostrate man and cut and stabbed him until they supposed he was dead. Toward his family they meditated a more terrible and devilish cruelty. After sacking the house and taking all the plunder they could carry, they relieved the horror-stricken wife and crying, shrieking children of their presence. Their further action, however, soon inspired Phebe with a new and more awful fear, for she found that they had fastened the doors on the outside and were building a fire against one of them.

For a moment an overpowering despair at the prospect of their fate almost paralyzed her. She believed her father was dead. The boy who had aided her at first was now dazed and helpless from terror. If aught could be done in this supreme moment of peril she saw that it must be done by her hands. The smoke from the kindling fire without was already curling in through the crevices around the door. There was not a moment, not a second to be lost. The ruffians' voices were growing fainter and she heard the sounds of their horses' feet. Would they go away in time for her to extinguish the fire? She ran to her attic room and cautiously opened the shutter. Yes, they were mounting; and in the faint light of the late-rising moon she saw that they were taking her father's horses. A moment later, as if fearing that the blaze might cause immediate pursuit, they dashed off toward the mountains.

The clatter of their horses' hoofs had not died away before the intrepid girl had opened the shutter of a window nearest the ground, and springing lightly out with a pail in her hand she rushed to the trough near the barn, which she knew was full of water. Back and

E. P. Roe

forth she flew between the fire and the convenient reservoir with all the water that her bruised arms and back permitted her to carry. Fortunately the night was a little damp, and the stout thick door had kindled slowly. To her intense joy she soon gained the mastery of the flames, and at last extinguished them.

She did not dare to open the door for fear that the robbers might return, but clambering in at the window, made all secure as had been customary, for now it was her impulse to do just as her father would have done.

She found her mother on her knees beside her father, who would indeed have been a ghastly and awful object to all but the eyes of love.

"Oh, Phebe, I hope - I almost believe thy father lives!" cried the woman. "Is it my throbbing palm, or does his heart still beat?"

"I'm sure it beats, mother!" cried the girl, putting her little hand on the gashed and mangled body.

"Oh, then there's hope! Here, Abner," to the boy, "isn't there any man in thee? Help Phebe get him on the bed, and then we must stop this awful bleeding. Oh, that I were well and strong! Phebe, thee must now take my place. Thee may save thy father's life. I can tell thee what to do if thee has the courage."

Phebe had the courage and with deft hands did her mother's bidding. She stanched the many gaping wounds; she gave spirits at first drop by drop, until at last the man breathed and was conscious. Even before the dawn began to brighten over the dreaded Highlands which their ruthless enemies were already climbing,

Phebe was flying, bare-headed, across the fields to their nearest neighbor. The good people heard of the outrage with horror and indignation. A half-grown lad sprang on the bare back of a young horse and galloped across the country for a surgeon. A few moments later the farmer, equipped for chase and battle, dashed away at headlong pace to alarm the neighborhood. The news sped from house to house and hamlet to hamlet like fire in prairie grass. The sun had scarcely risen before a dozen bronzed and stern-browed men were riding into John Reynolds's farm-yard under the lead of young Hal June - the best shot that the wars had left in the region. The surgeon had already arrived, and before he ceased from his labors he had dressed thirty wounds.

The story told by Phebe had been as brief as it was terrible - for she was eager to return to her father and sick mother. She had not dreamed of herself as the heroine of the affair, and had not given any such impression, although more than one had remarked that she was "a plucky little chick to give the alarm before it was light." But when the proud mother faintly and tearfully related the particulars of the tragedy, and told how Phebe had saved her father's life and probably her mother's - for, "I was too sick to climb out of a window," she said; when she told how the child after a merciless whipping had again cut her father down from the trammel-hook, had extinguished the fire, and had been nursing her father back to life, while all the time in almost agony herself from the cruel blows that had been rained upon her - Phebe was dazed and bewildered at the storm of applause that greeted her. And when the surgeon, in order to intensify the general desire for vengeance, showed the great welts and scars on her arms and neck, gray-bearded fathers who had known her from infancy took her into their arms and blessed and kissed her. For once in his life young Hal June wished he was a gray-beard, but his course was much more to the mind of Phebe than any number of caresses would have been. Springing on his great black horse, and with his dark eyes burning with a fire that only blood could quench, he shouted:

"Come, neighbors, it's time for deeds. That brave little woman ought to make a man of every mother's son of us;" and he dashed away so furiously that Phebe thought with a strange little tremor at her heart that he might in his speed face the robbers all alone. The stout yeomen clattered after him; the sound of their pursuit soon died away; and Phebe returned to woman's work of nursing, watching, and praying.

The bandits of the hills, not expecting such prompt retaliation, were overtaken, and then followed a headlong race over the rough mountain roads - guilty wretches flying for life, and stern men almost reckless in the burning desire to avenge a terrible wrong. Although the horses of the marauders were tired, their riders were so well acquainted with the fastnesses of the wilderness that they led the pursuers through exceedingly difficult and dangerous paths. At last, June ever in the van, caught sight of a man's form, and almost instantly his rifle awoke a hundred echoes among the hills. When they reached the place, stains of blood marked the ground, proving that at least a wound had been given. Just beyond, the gang evidently had dispersed, each one for himself, leaving behind everything that impeded their progress. The region was almost impenetrable in its wildness except by those who knew all its rugged paths. The body of the man whom June had wounded, however, was found, clothed in a suit of Quaker drab stolen from Mr.

Reynolds. The rest of the band with few exceptions met with fates that accorded with their deeds.

Phebe had the happiness of nursing her father back to health, and although maimed and disfigured, he lived to a ripe old age. If the bud is the promise of the flower, Phebe must have developed a womanhood that was regal in its worth; at the same time I believe that she always remained a modest, demure little Quakeress, and never thought of her virtues except when reminded of them in plain English.

NOTE - In the preceding narrative I have followed almost literally a family tradition of events which actually occurred.

E. P. Roe